PRAISE FOR JOSEPH

"Flynn is an excellent storyteller." — *Booklist*

"Flynn propels his plot with potent but flexible force."
— *Publishers Weekly*

Digger
"A mystery cloaked as cleverly as (and perhaps better than)
any John Grisham work." — *Denver Post*

"Surefooted, suspenseful and in its breathless final moments
unexpectedly heartbreaking." — *Booklist*

The Next President
"*The Next President* bears favorable comparison to such
classics as *The Best Man*, *Advise and Consent* and
The Manchurian Candidate."
— *Booklist*

"A thriller fast enough to read in one sitting."
— *Rocky Mountain News*

The President's Henchman (A Jim McGill Novel)
"Marvelously entertaining." — *ForeWord Magazine*

ALSO BY JOSEPH FLYNN

Part 1:
The Last Ballot Cast
by

Joseph Flynn

Stray Dog Press, Inc.
Springfield, IL
2012

Published by Stray Dog Press, Inc.
Springfield, IL 62704, U.S.A.

Originally published as an eBook, July, 2012
First Stray Dog Press, Inc. Printing, September, 2012
Copyright © kandrom, inc., 2012
All rights reserved

Visit the author's web site: *www.josephflynn.com*

Flynn, Joseph
    Part 1: The Last Ballot Cast / Joseph Flynn
    392 p.
    ISBN 978-0-9837975-7-9
    eBook ISBN 978-0-9837975-5-5

Printed in the United States of America

PUBLISHER'S NOTE
This is a work of fiction. Names, characters, places, and incidents are
either the product of the author's imagination or are used fictitiously; any
resemblance to actual persons, living or dead, events, or locales is entirely
coincidental.

Book design by Aha! Designs

DEDICATION

Part 1 of *The Last Ballot Cast* is dedicated to all the readers who were kind enough to write to me and tell me how much they like my books, especially those of you who took the time to post reviews online or otherwise spread the good word.

Thank you.

ACKNOWLEDGEMENTS

My thanks to Jim Sullivan, instructor for Natural Spirit International, who shared with me some of his encyclopedic knowledge of the martial arts. And to Susan C. McIntyre, nurse practitioner, my senior go-to person on medical matters. If I got anything wrong in either of these areas, it's either a matter of literary license or I just messed up.

The Last Ballot Cast
Part 1

AUTHOR'S NOTE

This is a work of fiction. Some of it overlaps current realities, political and otherwise, but is in no way intended to mirror the real world. How could it? This novel, like the other Jim McGill books, feature a female U.S. president and her husband who's a private investigator. Some readers have told me they wish these characters were real but they aren't.

This book brings several story lines from previous McGill books to a conclusion, as well as telling the story of an imagined presidential campaign. That's a lot of ground to cover and took 900 pages to do so. In order to make the novel a more accessible buying and reading experience, I divided it into two approximately equal parts.

Read this one first.

CAST OF CHARACTERS

James J. (Jim) McGill, 2nd husband of President Patricia Darden Grant, *aka* The President's Henchman

Patricia Darden Grant, President of the United States, former Congresswoman, wife of Jim McGill, widow of Andrew Hudson Grant

Margaret "Sweetie" Sweeney, Jim McGill's investigative partner, former police partner

Putnam Shady, lobbyist, landlord and lover of Margaret Sweeney

Galia Mindel, Chief of Staff to President Grant

Stephen Norwood, Galia Mindel's Chief of Staff

Edwina Byington, the president's personal secretary

Mather Wyman, Vice President, Kira's Fahey Yates' uncle

Celsus Crogher, Secret Service Agent in charge of White House Security Detail

Elspeth Kendry, Secret Service Special Agent

Donald "Deke" Ky, McGill's Secret Service bodyguard

Leo Levy, McGill's armed driver, ex NASCAR

Carolyn [McGill] Enquist, first wife of Jim McGill

Lars Enquist, Carolyn's [McGill] second husband

Abbie McGill, oldest child of Jim McGill and his first wife Carolyn

Kenny McGill, middle child, only son of Jim McGill and his first wife Carolyn

Caitie McGill, youngest child of Jim McGill and his first wife Carolyn

Andrew Hudson Grant, President Grant's 1st husband [murdered]

Captain Welborn Yates, Air Force Office of Special Investigations

Kira Fahey Yates, wife of Welborn Yates

Artemus Nicolaides, White House physician

Clare Tracy, Jim McGill's college sweetheart

Dikran "Dikki" Missirian, McGill's business landlord

Sir Robert Reed, Welborn Yates' British father

Carina Linberg, USAF colonel, retired

CAST OF CHARACTERS
(continued)

Liesl Eberhardt, Kenny's first girlfriend
Chana Lochlan, television reporter; source of leaks from
  WorldWide News
Admiral David Dexter, Chairman of the Join Chiefs
Byron DeWitt, FBI Deputy Director
Daryl Cheveyo, CIA officer, Todd's agency contact
Michael Jaworsky, Attorney General
Linda Otani, Deputy Attorney General
Rev. Burke Godfrey, Pastor of Salvation's Path Church, husband of Erna
Erna Godfrey, anti-abortion activist, incarcerated murderer;
  wife of Rev. Burke Godfrey
Benton Williams, lawyer for Rev. Godfrey
Sir Edbert Bickford, CEO of global media empire WorldWide News
Hugh Collier, nephew of Sir Bickford, works for WorldWide News
Ellie Booker, producer for WorldWide News
Damon Todd, deranged psychotherapist, *aka Dan Templeton*
Arn Crosby, "retired" member of CIA
Olin Anderson, "retired" member of CIA
Linley Boland, auto thief [aka Jackie Richmond]
Alice Tompkins, [aka Mary] owner of Mango Mary's bar in Key West
Tom T. Wright, billionaire and Super Pac contributor
Reynard Dix, Chairman of the Republican National Committee
Henry Melchior, Chairman of the Democratic National Committee

Elected Officials and Staff

Charles Talbert, Senator from Indiana, Republican [retiring]
Sheryl Kimbrough, professor at Indiana University,
  Republican elector from Indiana
Cassidy Kimbrough, daughter of Sheryl Kimbrough
Howard Hurlbert, Senator from Mississippi, Republican,
  co-sponsor of SOMA
Merilee Parker, press secretary for Sen. Howard Hurlbert;
  one of Galia Mindel's spies
Bobby Beckley, Sen Hurlbert's campaign manager and chief of staff
Derek Geiger, deceased Republican Speaker of the House
Roger Michaelson, Senator from Oregon, Democrat

CAST OF CHARACTERS
(continued)

Bob Merriman, former Chief of Staff to Senator Michaelson; running for Senate

John Wexford, Senator from Michigan, Democrat, Senate Majority Leader

Richard Bergen, Senator from Illinois, Democrat, assistant to Senator Wexford

Marlene Berman, Representative from New York, Democrat, House minority leader

Diego Paz, Representative from California, Democrat, assistant to Marlene Berman

Peter Profitt, Representative from North Carolina, Republican, House Majority Leader

Darrin Neff, Senator from South Carolina, [Republican]

Jim McKee, Senator from North Carolina, [Republican]

Beau Brunelle, Senator from Louisiana, [Republican]

Dan Crockett, Senator from Tennessee, [Republican]

Jean Morrissey, Governor of Minnesota, [Democrat]

Frank Morrissey, Governor Morrissey's brother and lawyer

Eugene Rinaldo, Governor of New York [Democrat]

Edward Mulcahy, Governor of Illinois [Democrat]

Lara Chavez, Governor of California [Democrat]

John Patrick Granby, Secretary of State from New Hampshire

Paul Brandstetter, Secretary of State from Iowa

Charles Delmain, Secretary of State from South Carolina

Alberto Calendri, Chief Justice of the U.S. Supreme Court

Titus Hawkins, Associate Justice of the U.S. Supreme Court

1

Saturday, August 20, 2011
George Washington University Hospital

James J. McGill stood outside the operating room — he couldn't go inside without breaking the sterile field — where his wife Patti, the President of the United States, lay anesthetized.

Artemus Nicolaides, the White House physician, had told him he had to decide quickly whether to allow the procedure to harvest the president's bone marrow cells to continue.

McGill's son, Kenny, was suffering from acute myelogenous leukemia. He'd already received the chemotherapy and radiation treatments needed to destroy all the diseased bone marrow cells in his body. Now, Kenny had to have the infusion of healthy cells from Patti that would keep him alive — and he had to have it fast.

Patti was the only donor available with compatible cells.

But Nick had just told McGill there was a problem with the president.

"It's called mitral valve prolapse," Nick said. "The president had no history of this condition, had been completely asymptomatic until her heart began to beat irregularly as she entered the second stage of anesthesia. We were fortunate that —"

"Nick, just get to it," McGill ordered. "Tell me what the risks are for Patti and Kenny."

The physician nodded. "For the president, the risk is that a reflux of blood from the left ventricle could enter the atrium and possibly cause a stroke. The stroke might be either disabling or fatal."

McGill felt his own heart turn to stone.

"But without the infusion from Patti —"

"Kenny will surely die," Nick said with a mournful look.

"What are the chances Patti will suffer a stroke?"

"We can't say precisely."

That left McGill with no real choice. There was only one way that the lives of both the people he loved might be saved.

He told Nick, "Tell the doctors to harvest the cells for Kenny."

"You're sure?" He didn't remind McGill it was the president's life he was risking.

"I am. Do it. Don't let anyone decide otherwise."

The grim expression on McGill's face made clear that anyone refusing to follow his wishes would be placing his own life in jeopardy.

Looking through a window in one of the doors to the OR, the White House physician tapped an intercom button on the wall twice, producing two buzzes.

Someone inside the OR must have looked questioningly at Nick.

As if to say: *You're sure about that?*

Nick nodded.

McGill put his face next to Nick's to make sure the message was received.

But everybody in the operating room already had their eyes back on Patti.

Except for the capped-and-gowned Secret Service agents standing guard.

Maybe they had been the ones to second-guess McGill's decision.

Too damn bad. It was his choice alone to make.

Having done so, McGill was now too numb to either hope or pray.

All he could do was wait.

Northern Virginia

The place, appropriate to its purposes, had many names. Officially, it was referred to as a military reservation known as the Armed Forces Experimental Training Activity (AFETA). In a more colloquial fashion, it was called Camp Peary. Its nickname was simply The Farm.

As foreign intelligence agencies and fans of popular culture all knew, the nine-thousand acre, enclosed woodland was the developmental facility for "career trainees," some of whom would graduate to become CIA spies. Less well known was the cluster of rehabilitated buildings on the site that dated back to Colonial times. This hub was surrounded by its own security features and housed a number of "inpatients," former agents who had suffered "cognitive impairment." That was, as a result of stress, post-traumatic or simply job related, they'd suffered mental breakdowns. They could no longer be trusted not to reveal the secrets they'd sworn to take to their graves with them.

The facilities for these damaged agents were known collectively as The Funny Farm.

Of the inpatients, there was only one who had never been on the Company payroll. He had been a wannabe, a psychiatrist who had aspired to work for the CIA. The man had developed a technique for resisting interrogations called crafted personalities. It had aroused genuine interest from the people at the top of the national security food chain. Before the shrink could be brought into the fold, though, he had gone off the deep end and had tried to kill the president's husband, James J. McGill.

The wannabe's name was Dr. Damon Todd.

He currently presented himself as a ten-year-old boy, Danny Templeton.

Most of the staff at The Funny Farm called him Twitch.

The docs and the interrogators at The Funny Farm had been trying for almost three years to coax or coerce Dr. Todd into abandoning his assumed persona as ten-year-old Danny without a hint of success. The irony was that the longer Todd resisted their efforts the more they wanted to succeed. If Todd would only come forward and share his secret with the agency, it would give the United States a huge advantage in the field of human intelligence gathering.

A spy who couldn't be made to reveal secrets would be a wish come true.

From what the agency had learned first hand from working on Todd, he had found the holy grail, a way to make operatives interrogation resistant, if not for a lifetime at least long enough to render time-sensitive intelligence obsolete.

The bastard had been truly cunning in conceiving his cover identity. Danny Templeton, to around-the-clock observation, believed he was a young boy from Eau Claire, Wisconsin. He thought he lived on a family farm with his mother, Lorraine, known as Lori, his father, Chester, known as Chet, his older brother, Michael, known as Chill, and younger brother, Charles, known as Chucky. He was a student in the fifth grade at Lakeshore Elementary School. He went to church at Grace Lutheran. He was a member of Cub Scout den 175.

The cover identity was so detailed and so consistently repeated in dozens of interrogations that the agency sent a team to Eau Claire to check Todd's story for accuracy. Damn, if he didn't have things exactly right. There was a farm family named Templeton there. The school, church and Cub Scout den were real, too. The only thing missing was any documentary evidence that Danny Templeton had ever existed. Reading the investigators' report produced a great sense of respect for Todd's craftsmanship.

Until one deep thinker suggested that maybe Danny Templeton had been part of a sleeper cell, and Damon Todd had been his cover identity. Maybe the Russians had left the Templetons in place and one or both of the other sons or even Mom and Dad would be activated for some nefarious purpose in the future.

Speculative paranoia was one of the primary mindsets at the CIA.

Another team was sent to Wisconsin to investigate the farm family, going back at least as far as either Mom or Dad had been alive.

Meanwhile, the interrogation teams continued to deal with a subject who presented himself as a young boy. His emotional vulnerability, senses of terror and despair were spot on. Techniques such as sleep deprivation, minimal calorie diets and enforced exercise were met with cries for "Mom," tears and pathetic pleadings to stop.

Danny Templeton wound up screwing with his interrogators' sense of self-worth.

The more strategies they tried to open him up, the less they thought of themselves as decent human beings. In desperation, a plan was hatched to use drugs. Nothing exotic or extreme. Simple sedative-hypnotics. Sleeping pills. The thought was if Todd got a long period of deep sleep, his consciousness might reboot to its root personality.

The sleeping pill trial would not last so long as to form a state of dependency. As such drugs were contraindicated for young children, there was a debate whether they should be given to Todd at all, and if they were whether the usual strength should be mitigated. The conclusion was that Todd, whatever his real identity, was a physically mature adult and for the purposes of the drug trial he would be given full doses for four consecutive nights.

That idea was cut short by half when on the third morning Todd woke up still presenting as Danny Templeton and showing repetitive twitches and tics. The medical staff was at a loss to understand that as the drugs they'd used had never produced tardive dyskenisia before. Even so, Danny now moaned through the day as his body jerked uncontrollably at irregular intervals.

Twitch was born.

In frustration, the team assigned to break Damon Todd called in Daryl Cheveyo, the shrink who had been the agency's initial contact with Todd and who had been in on his capture after Todd had attempted to kill James J. McGill.

Cheveyo read the reports detailing Todd's time at The Funny Farm and watched hours of surreptitiously shot video of the subject.

His conclusion was, "You've been up in his face the whole time he's been here. Give him some room. Feed him a normal diet. Let him wake up and go to sleep when he wants. Allow him to interact with other patients and, without crowding him, see if he strikes up any conversations."

"See if we can find a jailhouse snitch?" the chief interrogator asked.

Cheveyo said, "Or maybe after the years of constant pressure letting him relax will feel so good he'll even start talking with you. But whatever you do, do not let the SOB get away."

The warning received a chorus of laughter.

"I'm telling you," Cheveyo said. "He's not the kid he's pretending to be. He's smart and dangerous."

Everybody conceded that point, but Cheveyo was assured *nobody* ever got away from The Funny Farm. Famous last words.

GWU Hospital

McGill sat alone in the lounge down the hall from the room where Kenny had stayed while waiting for his transplant. He didn't know whether Kenny would be returned to the same room or even if … *Dear God,* he thought, *please don't let my son die. Don't let Patti die.*

He tried desperately to find some handhold of faith to grasp, but —

"Boss."

McGill looked up. He saw Deke Ky, his personal Secret Service bodyguard, and Leo Levy, his driver, standing at the entrance to the lounge. Both men had been given the day off; the plan had been for McGill to use the president's protection detail at the wedding of Welborn Yates and Kira Fahey. Deke and Leo must have heard that Congressman Zachary Garner and Speaker Derek Geiger had died at Vice President Wyman's home and had sought him out.

Were there for him now. Ready to do anything they could.

"Company coming," Deke said.

"Family and friends," Leo elaborated.

The two men stepped aside as McGill's daughters, Abbie and Caitie, ran to embrace him as he got to his feet. They were both crying, but McGill hadn't been able to discern the emotion that lay behind the tears in their eyes. He saw his ex-wife Carolyn and her husband Lars approach.

He didn't have to ask. Carolyn wore a brave smile.

"Kenny's infusion was successful," she said.

"And Patti?" McGill asked.

Artemus Nicolaides stepped forward. "The president continues to be monitored closely, but her heartbeat has returned to a normal rhythm and she has suffered no adverse consequences."

McGill might have collapsed if his daughters hadn't been holding him up.

That was when he noticed that SAC Crogher was present and he remembered that another life had hung in the balance. In his preoccupation with his wife and son, he had forgotten that. He felt ashamed.

Special Agent August Latz had taken a bullet that Speaker Geiger had intended for McGill.

"Celsus?" he asked. "Special Agent Latz?"

The SAC showed the president's henchman the first genuine smile he'd ever seen from the man. He gave McGill a thumbs-up. "He's going to make it. Probably won't look too pretty, but he'll live."

Dr. Divya Sahir Jones, Kenny's chief oncologist, moved to the head of the line with two other doctors. She looked at McGill and all the others present. Her expression was guarded.

She said, "So far, so good. But for Kenny — and the president and Special Agent Latz — this is still Day Zero. They will all face many challenges. My colleagues and I will tell —"

Crogher interrupted Dr. Jones.

He said, "Kenny McGill's condition is a matter for his family to discuss. The president's prognosis is for Mr. McGill's ears only. Special Agent Latz is *my* concern."

Caitie McGill wasn't about to have Crogher tell her who could hear what.

"Patti is my stepmother," she said. "*My* concern. Just like Kenny."

McGill kissed the top of his daughter's head.

"SAC Crogher is right, sweetheart. We have to do things a certain way." He looked Caitie in the eye. "We're not the only ones interested in Patti. People all over the country and around the world want to know how the president is doing and will make decisions based on what they learn. Not all of those people have our country's best interests at heart."

Crogher nodded. He was glad Holmes understood the situation.

McGill looked at the White House physician.

"We'll say the president is resting comfortably and will resume her office ..."

He gestured to Nick to complete the sentence.

Nick had a moment of quiet consultation with one of the doctors who had accompanied Dr. Jones. What he heard was, "There's no telling." What he said was, "The moment she gives the word."

Tough to argue with that, McGill thought.

Nick was playing along with Crogher; specifics were for him alone.

But Caitie seemed to be satisfied, and no one else pressed for details.

"We'll work it out so everybody's happy," McGill told his family.

Dr. Jones asked to have the room for Kenny's immediate family. They needed to understand he wasn't out of the woods yet. Him or the president. Both of them were going to need a lot of help.

The White House

Chief of Staff Galia Mindel sat alone in her office a few steps down the hall from the Oval Office. She had spent the past two hours ignoring her work to dust off memories of prayers she had learned as a girl. Her parents had been members of Reform Judaism, the branch of the faith that believed Jewish traditions should be modernized and made compatible with participation in contemporary culture. That wasn't to say that prayer was something to be practiced only on the high holidays or occasions of personal note. The most important part of daily prayer was the opportunity to look within yourself, to understand your place in the world and your relationship with God.

Galia hadn't prayed since she lost her dear husband, Nathan.

Oh, how she'd prayed when Nate fell ill. Before that, she hadn't had time. After Nate had died, she saw no point, and she'd filled her life with raising her sons and doing her work. She'd gotten busy again. Too busy even to think of taking the time to pray.

Now, with the president in unexpected jeopardy, she strained to find the sincere faith that prayer would be anything more than a temporary distraction from fear. Still, she remembered the words she had learned as a child, and if there was any chance they might mean something more than whispering into the wind she would be a fool not to seize the opportunity.

Galia bowed her head and closed her eyes.

Please God, she thought, bring healing to Patricia Darden Grant. And to Kenny McGill.

May the One who was the source of blessing for our ancestors ...

The verses of the prayer unfolded in Galia's mind and she stepped out of the moment and into a sense of peace. Unlike the vision Erna Godfrey had spoken of, she didn't see the face of God nor did she see Nate, as Erna had spoken of seeing Andy Grant. But she felt the presence of a grand design. The awareness that life had meaning beyond the moment brought a feeling of warmth and security to Galia. Doing the right things for the right reasons mattered.

Further insight disappeared into the sound of her desk phone ringing.

She lifted the receiver and with a clear mind said, "Yes."

Her deputy chief of staff, Stephen Norwood, was calling from the hospital.

"The president's condition has stabilized and she should be regaining consciousness soon."

Galia sighed in relief — and then a question occurred to her.

"You had no trouble getting information from the medical staff?"

When Stephen had called Galia to tell her of the episode of mitral valve prolapse the president had suffered and of James J. McGill's decision to continue with the bone marrow transplant, she had assumed the information had been passed along as a matter of national interest. Now, she wasn't so sure.

Stephen said, "Mr. McGill gave written permission for you to be notified of any significant medical development."

Galia smiled. She'd done a favor for McGill, had given him a bucket of political dirt on late Speaker Derek Geiger, and here he was starting to repay her already. If the two of them weren't careful they might wind up becoming friends.

"It took only a bit of persuasion," her deputy added, "for the hospital staff to accept me as your surrogate."

"Good work, Stephen. Were the doctors able to forecast how soon the president will be able to resume her office?"

"They were vague on that. I couldn't pin them down and didn't think it was the right time to push the matter."

"You were right about that. So what's your gut feeling?" Galia asked.

"My gut? Acting President Wyman is going to have more than fifteen minutes of fame."

The White House Situation Room

Acting President Mather Wyman sat at the head of the table,

only now realizing the gravity of the situation before him. His time as chief executive was going to be far more than ceremonial. Looking at the faces around him, he saw the national security adviser, the director of national intelligence, the chairman of the joint chiefs of staff and the attorney general. Each of the grandees had brought support staff, of course. There were, however, no representatives from the Congressional leadership; whatever course was to be taken would be for him alone to decide.

He'd be the decider, as Patricia Grant's predecessor had styled himself.

Wyman had long thought that label had been a clumsy attempt to say decision maker, the product of a man whose facility with language had been anything but facile. Now, confronting the matter of what to do about the paramilitary resistance to the arrest of Reverend Burke Godfrey, he felt that the decider was apt shorthand for the mantle that had fallen upon his shoulders.

Wyman turned to the attorney general and asked, "Michael, as I understand the law, I am permitted to use the armed forces in the situation we face in Virginia only if the resources of the state under the direction of the governor are incapable of maintaining public order. Is that right?"

The attorney general said, "Yes, sir. If domestic violence occurs to the extent the state authorities can't maintain public order, the use of federal resources, including the military, becomes your prerogative. Congress is to be informed immediately, if you choose to do so, and it must be kept current every fourteenth day thereafter."

The acting president nodded. "Does someone have the governor of the Commonwealth of Virginia on the phone for me?"

An aide handed a phone receiver to Wyman.

No one mentioned the fact, but the call was being recorded, for far more than reasons of quality assurance. The governor of Virginia was about to lose deniability for anything he said.

"Bob? This is Acting President Mather Wyman. I'd like to know if you want to — and you're able to — handle the situation at the Salvation's Path compound." Wyman listened to the response and his jaw tightened. "No, Bob. In my opinion, waiting them out is not an option. I've been informed that those people have enough food, water and, presumably, ammunition to last more than a year."

Maybe right through the presidential election, and wouldn't that make for a lively campaign? Galia Mindel had passed along the information about how well supplied Reverend Godfrey's forces were. She'd gleaned that knowledge from Erna Godfrey.

Wyman continued, "The longer we wait, the more we embolden other ... misguided individuals, allowing them to think they can raise their own armies and defy legitimate warrants for arrest. I won't allow the seeds of anarchy to be sown in this country."

Wyman listened once more to his counterpart in Virginia.

"No, not even a week ... Yes, I remember what happened in Waco. Do you remember what happened in Richmond earlier today? The people inside the barricades at Salvation's Path shot at an FBI helicopter. It was only by the grace of God that neither anyone on the aircraft nor any innocent bystanders in the neighborhood nearby were hit. Do you want to give these ... misguided individuals the chance to discharge their firearms again? Will you take responsibility for any deaths or injuries that might ensue? I'm sorry, do I think what?"

The acting president listened closely to the governor.

"I'll ask the people I have here with me. They'll be better able to assess." Wyman spoke to the people around the table. "The governor would like to know if its possible the trucks blocking the entrances to the Salvation's Path grounds might have fertilizer bombs or other explosives in them."

The chairman of the joint chiefs, Admiral David Dexter, said, "That would be in keeping with the delusion they are an actual military unit."

"Did you hear that, Bob?" Wyman asked.

The acting president started nodding. The governor had seen the light.

"Yes, thank you, Bob. I'll take it from here. I'd like you to put your consent in writing and ... you've already done that? Good.

Send it right along, will you? Yes, Bob, we'll all pray for a swift and peaceful resolution. Goodbye."

The aide took the phone from Wyman.

He told the others, "The governor of Virginia has ceded responsibility to the federal government. His written declaration is being transmitted to the White House as I speak."

Wyman turned to David Dexter.

"Admiral, I want more than shock and awe. I want those people at Salvation's Path to think the very wrath of God is crashing down upon them. I want it soon. If at all possible, I want it done with no one suffering more than blurred vision, ringing ears and pounding headaches. Can you manage that?"

"Yes, sir, Mr. President." Dexter thought about the mission he'd just accepted. "We might have to temporarily relocate some of the nearby civilian population and we'll be breaking quite a bit of glass. Is that acceptable, sir?"

"It is," Wyman said. "Don't let me keep you."

The chairman rose and saluted.

"Oh, one more thing, Admiral. Before you draw up your plans, talk with Galia Mindel, see if she might have any more intelligence to share with you."

"Yes, sir."

Mather Wyman knew that, by reputation, the White House chief of staff liked to keep a secret or two tucked up her sleeve. That wouldn't do in this case. It was only after the acting president left the Situation Room that he wondered if Patricia Darden Grant would have chosen the same course of action. He quickly dismissed the question. He couldn't be someone else.

He could only do his best.

Sunday, August 21, 2011
Salvation's Path Church — Richmond, Virginia

Shortly after midnight, Ellie Booker made her move to get a gun. She had decided not to try to filch one from somebody else.

She was going to either charm or con a firearm from the guy wearing fatigues in the basement of the administration building where Reverend Burke Godfrey kept his armory. There was no other word for it. Crate upon crate of assault rifles and other weapons lined the walls behind a chain-link enclosure.

The guy behind the counter up front had sergeant's stripes on his sleeves and was holding what looked to Ellie like a LAW, a light antitank weapon. Sarge moved his gaze from a manual on the counter in front of him to the weapon in his hands and back again.

Nothing like on-the-job training, Ellie thought.

She produced top-shelf programming for WorldWide News, the crown jewel of the global media empire owned by Sir Edbert Bickford. Ellie had gone to the Salvation's Path campus to interview Reverend Godfrey about his plans to deal with the accusation made by his incarcerated wife, Erna, that he had been a coconspirator in the murder of Andrew Hudson Grant, President Patricia Darden Grant's first husband.

A victim of bad timing, Ellie had arrived at Salvation's Path shortly before the FBI had come to take Reverend Godfrey into custody. The reverend had declined arrest by blocking access to the church grounds with old garbage-hauling trucks parked across roadways and with men carrying automatic weapons. When a government helicopter had flown over the grounds for a look-see, some moron had fired a burst at it. Soon after that, the government had trucked in prefab slabs of concrete and built a wall to enclose the property.

Presto. Instant federal penitentiary.

Ellie had tried to persuade her immediate boss, Hugh Collier, Sir Edbert's nephew, to call the feds and get her the hell out of there. Both Hugh and Sir Edbert had resisted, pointing out that Ellie, the sole reporter inside the walls, had a unique opportunity to tell the story of what would happen at Salvation's Path. Then the government had jammed all communications between the church and the outside world before Ellie could curse her bosses and tell them she was no damn war correspondent.

Sarge looked up from his studies and noticed Ellie.

Glanced curiously at the leather courier bag on her shoulder.

The name tag on Sarge's shirt said Hobart.

Ellie came straight to the point. "I'd like a gun and some ammunition, please."

The sergeant put on a pair of wire-rim glasses to bring Ellie into focus. Great, she thought, a nearsighted guy learning his away around a weapon he'd never fired before. The SEALs were going to have a tough time getting past him.

"Are you a member of the militia, Sister?" Hobart asked.

"The militia?" Ellie asked.

"The soldiers of Salvation's Path."

The sergeant turned to show her the flag patch on the right shoulder of his uniform. The red and white stripes and the blue rectangle in the upper left corner were identical to an American flag, but the stars weren't laid out in nine parallel rows. Instead, they formed a cross. No separation of church and state here.

"No, Sergeant. I'm a member of the press," Ellie said.

To his credit, Hobart didn't point the LAW at her, but his eyes narrowed.

Ellie quickly explained, "Reverend Godfrey invited me here to interview him. I'm with WorldWide News."

Now, the sergeant smiled. He put his weapon down and extended a hand to Ellie.

"Well, why didn't you say so? I don't watch anything but WorldWide."

A fan, Ellie thought. That might help. She shook his hand.

"So you'll give me a gun?"

Hobart's happy expression fell back to neutral.

"Are you thinking of signing up? I might have a set of cammies that'd fit you."

No, Ellie thought, she was *not* going to put on a uniform. She was counting on her civilian clothing to afford her some measure of protection when the feds stormed the place.

"I can't do that, Sergeant. I'm an observer. I have to stay honest and forthright."

Hobart's head bobbed. "That's the WorldWide slogan, all right, and I wouldn't have my news any other way. But if you don't want to join up, why do you want a gun?"

Ellie told him, "The same reason anyone wants a gun: If I get into a bad spot, I want the other guy to say, 'Oh, shit.'"

The sergeant smiled as though she'd given the verbatim answer to a catechism question.

"Yeah, that'd be great, wouldn't it?" he said. "I gave my wife a LadySmith for our last anniversary. A sweet little .38 revolver. Just the right size for her hand."

Domestic bliss, Ellie thought.

But now she knew she wouldn't walk away unarmed.

So she decided to interview Sergeant Hobart and find out just what kind of a guy he was, thinking he could go toe to toe with law enforcement. No, now it would be the military. She would bet on that. The sergeant was not an uneducated man; he had a pharmacy degree. He told her there were two doctors and an oral surgeon at Salvation's Path to bind up the troops' wounds.

Ellie wanted to ask if there was anyone versed in mortuary science on hand.

Some questions, though, you just had to leave unspoken.

If the other medical guys fell in the line of duty, Hobart continued, he'd read up on being a combat medic. He said he had two children and he was standing with the reverend in part because he wanted to retake the country for them. He showed no sign of lunacy while making his declaration, no hint of doubt that he was doing the right thing.

Ellie took careful notes. Robert Hobart didn't know it yet but she was going to make him famous. She got him to show her just what kinds of firepower the soldiers of Salvation's Path had available to them. Besides the assault rifles, they had not one but a half-dozen LAWs ... and then there was an empty crate with Cyrillic markings on it that made Ellie very uneasy.

She knew from having produced a special on America's love

affair with weaponry that anyone with enough money could buy almost any kind of gun imaginable. You could buy a .50 caliber sniper rifle that could kill someone more than a mile away. But there was one piece of ordnance no civilian was supposed to have, ever.

"That's not what I think it is, is it?" Ellie asked.

"I don't know. What do you think it is?"

"A shipping container for Russian surface-to-air missile launchers." Getting their hands on SAMs was every terrorist's wet dream. "SA-7 or SA-9."

Hobart looked around as if someone might be eavesdropping.

A sly smile appeared on his face and Ellie saw another side of the man.

In a whisper, he told her, "SA-9. You sure know your business."

"I know something else," Ellie said. "Our military jets have countermeasures against these things. You fire one at, say, an F-15, you're almost certain to miss. But if there's a commercial jet anywhere nearby, you'll kill lots innocent people."

Hobart's smile disappeared.

"You sure about that?"

Ellie told the guy who'd been studying a LAW manual minutes earlier she was sure.

"Please pass the word to anyone who has one of these things," she said.

"I sure will. Right away. We don't want to shoot Grandma out of the sky."

"No, we don't."

Grateful for the warning, the sergeant told Ellie to look around at what else they had on hand and be sure to let him know if there was anything else he needed to warn people about. He went into a cubicle in a corner of the room and made a phone call.

Must have been some kind of internal hard-wired system the feds hadn't been able to jam, Ellie thought. More likely, though, the government had been smart enough to let it be as they eavesdropped. She'd heard rumors the NSA had found a way to turn people's house phones into listening devices; no need to plant bugs. Was the reverend's high command savvy enough to consider the possibility snoopers were at work and maybe they should speak to each other in tongues? She didn't think so.

Ellie found a stash of Beretta 92s, the standard sidearm of the U.S. Army. She helped herself to one and continued shopping. She added three clips of ammunition and four sets of Maxcuff plastic restraints to her cart and did an express check-out, no credit card necessary. She put everything into her courier's bag.

Hobart was still on the phone as Ellie waved goodbye to him.

"You're good with the other stuff," she said.

Like she was talking about so many kids' toys.

He nodded and smiled at her. Gave her a thumbs-up.

Now, taking a deep breath, she'd have to pretend she had a pair of big brass balls. The only way to get out of this mess legally, professionally and in one piece, she'd decided, was to get the drop on Reverend Burke Godfrey and have him tied up with a ribbon and a bow when the government hard boys came to collect him. She was sure the feds would make at least one more phone call to Godfrey to urge him to give up and avoid bloodshed.

She intended to pick up his phone when it rang.

Tell the feds Godfrey was ready for pick up.

Hope to hell she didn't have to kill anyone to make that happen.

Mango Mary's, Key West, Florida

For the first time in his life, Linley Boland exchanged cash for a car.

The transaction took place at 4:30 a.m., a half-hour after Mango Mary's bar had closed, two minutes after the cleaning crew had left and thirty seconds after Mary had locked the front door.

Boland put ten grand on the bar and Mary gave him the keys to her four-year-old Jeep Wrangler Soft Top.

"You want a last drink, Jackie?" Mary asked.

Boland had introduced himself as Jackie Richmond, a kid he'd known growing up. Jackie had been into street racing. He'd had talent as a driver, but he got his ticket punched when a guy who'd lost his girlfriend to Jackie showed up at a race and threw a steam iron at Jackie's car. The damn thing caught Jackie bang on his head just as he shifted into high gear. That might have been enough to kill him, but jumping a curb and hitting a brick wall surely did.

Several of Jackie's friend ran down the guy who threw the iron. Boland went to Jackie's wrecked car. One look was enough to tell him Jackie was dead, and would have no further use for the contents of his wallet. Boland didn't take any money or credit cards. Didn't take the picture of the girl whose wayward heart had caused all the trouble. All he took were Jackie's driver's license and his Social Security card.

There was a fair resemblance between Boland and Jackie and with the Social Security card as backup, he'd never had a bit of trouble getting a new license in Jackie's name. When Boland had gone over to the guys beating the iron-tosser and told them Jackie was dead, that was it for the punk. Boland slipped away without trying to get a lick in.

What with two guys getting killed and six more getting charged with murder, the cops didn't sweat the fact that Jackie had been driving without a license.

Thing was, Jackie Richmond was the identity of last resort for Boland. He'd never used it before. A guy got killed by a flying steam iron, you had to think maybe anyone with his name was going to be unlucky.

Only now, Linley Boland figured nobody's luck could be worse than his. He almost got caught trying to steal the tricked-out Chevy the president's henchman used. He did get caught trying to steal a Porsche in Baltimore, and just barely made bail. Then he tried to nail a hot Mercedes in Naples, should have been a gimme, and wound up killing the geezer at the wheel and his old witch of a wife, and had to leave the car behind.

Having someone throw an iron at him would probably mean things were looking up.

He told Mary, "I'll have whatever your drinking."

"Who says I'm drinking anything?"

"If that's the case, I'm good, too."

He'd had a Land Shark Lager when he'd entered the bar at midnight. After that, he'd switched to ginger ale. Didn't remember how many of them he'd had. Bet Mary could tell him, though. She'd started sizing him up the minute he'd stepped into the place.

Decided he looked like someone who might have the money and the disposition for the deal she had in mind. She'd said she needed a loan of ten grand before the sun came up, which wasn't far off now. She didn't tell him why she needed the money and he didn't ask.

She told him he could hold her ride as collateral. She'd repay him within a week.

Boland asked to see the title. It would have been very foolish for a car thief to get busted driving a hot car he was holding as surety for a loan. To his expert eye, the title looked legit.

His only condition for the loan was that Mary give him a lead on where he might rent a quiet room in a private home for an indefinite time. She'd looked at him, trying to decide if he might be a crazy who got hard hurting people.

Or maybe he was just trying to *avoid* someone like that.

She'd told him she might know a place.

Mary took a bottle off the back bar. Chivas Regal, twelve years old. Poured two shots.

"How about you let me drop you off and I use the Jeep to run my errand?" she asked.

"Sure, as long as you make sure I get tucked in somewhere first."

She took out another key and said, "My place. Spare room's toward the back."

They touched glasses and drank.

"I'm not going to regret this, am I, Jackie?" she asked.

"Not at all. I'm clean, quiet and keep my hands to myself. In fact, if I'm staying with you, you might as well keep your car key. I could use some exercise, and this town looks like a good place for walking."

"I've got a bicycle you could use," Mary told him.

"Never learned to ride one," Jackie said.

GWU Hospital — Washington, D.C.

Kenny McGill opened his eyes. Slowly. Like somebody else was turning a crank to move his lids. The world that lay before him was a blur. The quality of light he perceived, though, looked familiar. Fluorescent. Neither a heavenly glow nor a hellish glare. That was good, he thought.

He extended the fingers of his right hand.

Felt the polished cotton of a bed sheet.

He flared his nostrils and knew from the first sniff he was still in the hospital.

Alive.

He'd come through the transplant and now he had … Patti's bone marrow cells inside him. They hadn't told him who his donor would be. He just felt it. And there was no other reason he could think of that Patti's face had just popped up in his mind. She was smiling at him.

He tried to say, "Thank you," but his throat was too dry to speak.

So he just let the words form in his mind. Patti would know he was grateful.

The light before his eyes dimmed and for a second Kenny feared that he was losing consciousness, maybe even that he was dying. Then he felt a hand take his. It was a rubbery feeling hand, but it was still completely reassuring.

He tried to speak again and this time was able to croak, "Mom?"

"Yes, honey, it's me."

Kenny felt the corners of his mouth rise. That seemed like someone else was doing the work, too. He didn't care, as long as

Mom could see his smile, knew he was happy she was there. He wanted to look at her.

After a couple tries, he said, "Can't see right."

One shadow stepped back and another moved forward.

Now, Kenny was sure someone else was gently holding his eyelids open, first one eye, then the other. He felt drops of something wet land on his eyes. Then he was able to blink and his vision cleared. He saw a woman wearing a surgical mask. He got the impression she was smiling at him. She stepped back and his mother moved forward. She, too, was wearing a mask and a cap over her hair. But he'd know Mom's eyes anywhere.

She had a cup in her hand with a bent straw sticking out of it.

"Would you like a sip of water, honey?" she asked.

More than anything in the world, Kenny thought. Mom understood without his saying a word. She leaned forward and put the straw between his lips. She was wearing transparent gloves. Explained the rubbery hand he'd felt. The water was delicious, made his throat feel so much better.

He wanted to drink a gallon of it, but Mom moved the straw out of his mouth after a few sips, and he knew he'd had enough. The drops had cleared his vision to the point where he could see Mom and the nurse were the only people in the room.

"Where's Dad? Abbie and Caitie?"

"I'll get your father in just a minute. The girls are sleeping. It's still quite early."

At the moment, Kenny hadn't reacquired a sense of time. Early? For what?

He thought to ask one more question.

"How's Patti?"

One room over from Kenny, James J. McGill sat in a chair at the side of the bed on which Patti lay sleeping. Her immune system was sufficiently functional that he didn't need to wear surgical garb to protect against infection. He had, however, showered and shaved at the hospital during the night and at his request, Blessing, the head butler at the White House, had brought him a clean set of his DePaul University sweat clothes and a new pair of sneakers.

In the room with him were Artemus Nicolaides, the White House physician, and two female Secret Service special agents. More of their colleagues were stationed in and around the building. Elspeth Kendry, McGill's personal threat assessment coordinator, stepped into the room. She crouched beside his chair and whispered good news into his ear.

"Clare Tracy came through her donation without a hitch. The little girl who received her bone marrow cells seems to be doing well, too."

McGill smiled. Almost thirty years had passed without his seeing Clare, but when his old college sweetheart had heard Kenny needed a donor, she'd volunteered without hesitation. Had been a perfect match, too. But when it was determined that Patti was also a match for Kenny, Clare had graciously stepped aside, and made a donation to another child.

Before McGill could ask for an update on his son, Elspeth told him, "Kenny has awakened. He's speaking with Mrs. Enquist." Carolyn. McGill's ex. Kenny's mother.

A tremor of relief passed through McGill.

He clenched a fist in support of his son.

There might be setbacks, but Kenny was going to make it.

"You want to gown up and see him?" Elspeth asked him.

The medical team was allowing only one family visitor in the room at a time, until Kenny's immune system was firmly reestablished.

"Not yet," he said. "Let Carolyn have as much time as she needs. She or Kenny will let me know when it's my turn."

McGill turned to look at Patti's heart monitor.

It showed a steady, normal rhythm.

"The president is looking strong, sir," Elspeth said.

McGill nodded. He'd half-convinced himself that Patti's recovery depended on his force of will to keep things running down the right track. Might be a lifelong frame of mind for him.

"If you don't need me for anything else, sir, I have to meet with SAC Crogher at the White House. Special Agent Ky will be able to reach me, if you find something for me to do."

Elspeth had just straightened up when McGill beckoned her back to his side.

He told her, "I honestly try not to jerk Celsus around too much. In a perverse way, I've come to respect the man. That being said, if the powers that be decide a human sacrifice is required for what happened at Vice President Wyman's house, I won't let it be you. You tell SAC Crogher, or the director, if either of them tries to reassign you, that I said you're golden. You're staying right where you are." After a pause, McGill added, "Tell Celsus I said he's golden, too."

Special Agent Kendry stood again and saluted McGill.

He went back to watching his wife's heart monitor.

Made sure the damn thing didn't get any funny ideas.

Tried to guess what Patti would say about his decision to continue with the transplant.

Dumbarton Oaks

The late Nathan Mindel's financial standing had been nowhere near that of billionaire Andrew Hudson Grant, but he'd been a successful tax attorney and had left Galia, Aaron and Joshua comfortably situated. Except for a total of four years when her sons were infants and toddlers, Galia had always worked, too. So when Patricia Darden Grant moved to Pennsylvania Avenue, Galia found a very nice house in Dumbarton Oaks and paid cash.

The only household help was a cleaning lady who came in every other Sunday morning — when the chief of staff wasn't traveling with the president — and Galia kept a discreet, electronic eye on Mrs. Nesbitt every minute she was in the house. A firm referred by the Secret Service had provided the security system for her residence. Galia had introduced herself to the Metropolitan Police Department's chief of police, explained her particular security concerns and made a generous annual donation to the chief's choice of charities, each of them worthy and completely legitimate.

In short, Galia had done everything she could to keep political enemies, the media and overreaching burglars at bay.

At seven a.m. as most of official Washington continued to lie abed, she opened her front door and watched as her deputy, Stephen Norwood, pulled up in his personal Cadillac Escalade. Stephen hopped out of his seat and hurried to open the front and rear passenger doors. Galia kept an eye out for photographers lurking in the middle distance but spotted none.

All three of the arriving guests did their parts to add to the covert air of the meeting by wearing hats and sunglasses. Galia briefly shook hands with the two men as she greeted them, and bussed the woman on the cheek. None of the arrivals lingered on her doorstep, and Galia tarried only for a moment to speak with Stephen.

"The latest on the president?" Galia asked.

"She'd just awakened and was speaking to Mr. McGill as I left the hospital."

"Kenny McGill?"

"Also awake. His mother's in with him."

Galia smiled. Thought her prayers couldn't have hurt. "I'll call twenty minutes before I need you to return. Then you can go home and get some sleep."

"Not that I need it," Norwood said with a tired grin.

"Of course not. We'd have to be *human* for that."

Galia stepped inside and closed the door.

The phone rang, earning itself a dirty look, but she answered just in case …

The president hadn't called; it was Admiral David Dexter, chairman of the joint chiefs. He told her what he needed, asked if she might help. Galia hesitated for half a breath before complying. She informed Dexter that Erna Godfrey had told her Reverend Godfrey had dug a system of tunnels under the grounds of Salvation's Path. She gave him the details and the name of the firm that had done the excavation. Dexter replied with a simple thank you, ma'am, but Galia heard the excitement in his voice.

A military adventure was in the offing. Acting President Wyman was about to act.

Galia felt uneasy. If Wyman made a mess of things ... especially as an election year loomed ... or if he scored a victory ... well, that had implications, too.

The only certain outcome of the call of which she might approve was that the nation's top military officer now owed her a favor.

She put other possibilities out of her mind as she joined her guests.

The governors of New York, Illinois and California.

GWU Hospital

The president opened her eyes and saw the hospital room ceiling. She turned her head to the right and there was McGill, sitting and staring at her. His eyes looked about to overflow. He smiled and waggled his fingers at her.

"You were supposed to give me a kiss," Patti said. "To wake me up."

"I gave you six."

"Oh. That's right, you're a henchman not Prince Charming."

"I am, and you're the president not Snow White."

"I auditioned but I didn't get the part ... please tell me Kenny's okay."

McGill, still smiling, stepped over to the bed and took his wife's hand.

"He's in the next room. Celsus wanted all his eggs in one corner. Kenny's awake and talking with Carolyn."

Patti closed her eyes momentarily and when she opened them they were as misty as McGill's.

"We did well, Kenny and me?"

"You both did great," McGill said. He lowered the safety railing and sat on the bed next to his wife. Then he remembered there was an audience in the room. Nick and the two Secret Service special agents had their eyes on the First Couple. "Please give us a few minutes."

Patti nodded her assent. The big boss was awake now. She was the one who gave the marching orders. Nick opened the door for the two female agents. He said, "I'll let your medical team know you're awake, Madam President. How much time shall I tell them you need?"

"Jim will let you know," she said.

Nick bowed his head and left.

The agents would wait just outside the door; that was acceptable.

"You have some terrible secret to share with me, Mr. McGill."

"I do. I had a tough call to make, and you should hear about it from me now."

Patti didn't like the sound of that, but she kept a frown off her face.

"If it's not me and it's not Kenny, who is it?"

"It was *almost* you," McGill said, and he explained.

"Mitral valve prolapse? I never suspected, and apparently neither did any of my doctors. What did Nick say?"

McGill told her, "No personal history, and you'd been completely asymptomatic."

"And he couldn't know the extent of the risk for continuing with the procedure?"

"No. But Kenny was a hundred percent certainty."

Patti blinked and tears rolled down her cheeks. She squeezed McGill's hand.

"In your place, I'd have done the same thing," she said.

"You're not ... just a little out of sorts."

"You've already told me you'd die for me."

McGill reminded her, "But you're more important than I am, to just about everyone."

Patti smiled. "There's a whole political party willing to argue with that. Not to mention several people named McGill. But this is the sort of question best left to minds better than those of politicians and private detectives."

McGill leaned forward and kissed Patti, loving her more than ever.

She basked in the moment, too, and then asked, "How is Clare?"

"Elspeth Kendry told me she's fine, and the little girl she helped is doing well, too."

"That's wonderful. So as far as we know, all's well."

McGill replayed Dr. Jones' words. "Kenny's not out of the woods yet, and you have to take it easy for a while. No rushing back to save the world."

Patti thought about that and nodded.

"We'll watch the leaves turn color at Camp David, all of us. We'll let Mather Wyman take care of the rest of the world. He's a good man."

Dumbarton Oaks

Galia provided refreshments to her guests in the solarium of her home. Governor Eugene Rinaldo of New York and Governor Edward Mulcahy of Illinois went with Sumatran Sunset coffee, Governor Lara Chavez of California chose a cup of mint medley herbal tea. The three governors had come to Washington for a conference of their *Democratic* peers. They were planning how best to defend the statehouses their party held and how best to attack the Republican governors they considered the most vulnerable.

Receiving an invitation to visit privately with the chief of staff to a president who had just left the GOP had proved irresistible. Unspoken, though, were two questions all the guests had occupying their minds: What scheme had Galia cooked up and why just the three of them?

Galia had chosen a bottle of White House Ice Tea, the unsweetened version, as her beverage. Prior to the arrival of James J.

McGill, the president's kitchen had served ice tea only by the glass or the pitcher. McGill had opined it was a shame the wonderful drink couldn't be bottled, and only a year later, the blink of an eye by government standards, it was bottled.

The label was a tasteful rendering of the Executive Mansion with the simple description Ice Tea beneath the illustration and in fine print below that — there was always fine print in any government document — one of two words: sweetened or unsweetened.

The ingredients of the ice tea were classified top secret by presidential order.

In the spirit of McGill's suggestion, the libation was available to all staffers and visitors to the White House. At one Cabinet meeting, the secretary of the treasury suggested the government produce the ice tea commercially to help reduce the budget deficit. Everyone had laughed, but Galia had seen in several pairs of eyes the recognition that the idea had merit. The more astute recognized it would not only make money, it would also show that the federal government was able to do something extremely well.

Lara Chavez asked Galia, "How are the president and Mr. McGill's son doing?"

"It's early days for Kenny yet, but the infusion was successful, and I've heard he was talking with his mother this morning."

The three governors, parents all, nodded and smiled.

Galia continued, "The president was awake and talking with her husband the last I heard."

She wasn't about to let the cat out of the bag about Patti's episode of mitral valve prolapse. The timing, wording and delivery of that message was the president's prerogative, and hers alone. Unless Jim McGill blabbed. No, he wouldn't do that. Unless Patricia Darden Grant chose him to make the announcement.

"The president has set a wonderful example to the country," Gene Rinaldo said.

"Amen," Ed Mulcahy added.

"I'll relay your kind words to her," Galia said.

"When you tell her how we reacted to whatever proposal you

have for us?" Mulcahy asked.

Galia nodded. She knew Ed Mulcahy from when she headed Patti Grant's first campaign for Congress. Mulcahy had been the U.S. attorney for the Northern District of Illinois. He had indicted, tried and convicted a large number of municipal and state office-holders. It was during his time as prosecutor that a reader of the *Chicago Tribune* had suggested that the state motto be changed to: Will the defendant please rise?

Having done his best to scourge the moneylenders from the temple of government, Mulcahy had decided to see what he could do to end corruption from within. He'd won the race for governor in a landslide, and he was the linchpin for the idea Galia would propose that morning.

She said, "In my eyes, with the exception of Patricia Darden Grant, the nominating process the two major parties have used to produce candidates for the presidency the past fifty years has been a mixed bag at best. Bill Clinton, bless him, produced budget surpluses, but it can be argued he didn't go after Osama bin Laden soon enough or relentlessly enough. Ronald Reagan sat down with Mikhail Gorbachev and managed the dissolution of the Soviet Union, but he didn't redirect our military to anticipate and adapt to new and different threats."

"You're excluding your boss because she made history by becoming the first female president?" Lara Chavez asked.

"That's certainly a consideration. I also have personal and professional biases. Trying to be objective, I'd say the Grant administration has advanced some very important ideas: lobbying reform, redistribution of global defense responsibilities among our allies, the reindustrialization of our country, the most favored enterprise doctrine. In terms of turning policies into laws, we've faced problems."

"Mostly from the obstinacy of the president's own ... the president's former party," Gene Rinaldo said.

"That and the efforts of some Democrats who sympathize with the obstructionists," Galia replied.

Her guests had to accept that point; their party wasn't without sin.

"My point is," Galia said, "Reagan and Clinton were the best their parties produced for over half a century. Just imagine how much worse a mess our country would be in if some of the, let's say, less qualified candidates had finagled their way into the Oval Office."

Rinaldo and Chavez smiled ruefully. Mulcahy came right out and laughed.

"What you're not saying, Galia," he told her, "is that each of us certainly consider that lesser candidates have won and left us in our current mess."

"You're right, Ed, I'm not saying that, and I won't."

"But you do have an idea, Galia, how we might find better candidates on both sides," Rinaldo suggested.

Lara Chavez smiled slyly and said, "Oh, I know. No more little states holding the first primary elections, the way we do now. From this point forward, we start with the most populous states."

Mulcahy shook his head. "That's not quite the idea here. If population numbers were what mattered most, we'd have Governor Hendry of Texas and Governor Thomason of Florida in the room with us. But then they're both Republicans."

Galia said, "Consider them to be here in spirit. If we come to an agreement, they'll follow along close behind us."

Mulcahy persisted. "Come on, Galia. Time to spill the beans."

Galia nodded. It was time; she pitched her idea.

"What I'm thinking is, letting small states with sparse populations go first in the primary election process allows marginal candidates with extreme ideas to advance their causes in the national spotlight. The candidates themselves don't stand a chance of being elected, but their pernicious ideas are advanced in presidential debates."

Rinaldo said, "So you're proposing we help you stifle the free expression of ideas?"

Galia smiled. She always liked having to sell her own ideas to a tough crowd.

"What I'm saying, Gene, is just because you can sing in the shower doesn't mean you're ready to, or have a right to, go onstage at Carnegie Hall."

Eugene Rinaldo liked the allusion of New York being the standard for the big time.

Galia knew he would. She continued in the same vein, turning to Mulcahy.

"You can tell a joke that cracks up your poker buddies? That doesn't mean you're ready for the main stage at Second City."

Lara Chavez anticipated what was coming next. She said, "You do summer stock in Ottumwa, you're not ready for your close-up in Hollywood."

Galia nodded. "Exactly. Candidates who have to start out in populous, ethnically and politically diverse states, will have to offer platforms that are broadly appealing. Workable. Doable when they get to Washington and have to make compromises. Progress will be slow and steady. Demonization of the man or woman on the other side of the aisle will be risky."

Mulcahy grinned and said, "All that sounds great, Galia. Normally, I'd ask at this point 'Who do we have to kill?' But I know the answer: Iowa, New Hampshire and South Carolina. Question is, will they — or our two major parties — sit still for it while we execute them?"

Galia said, "If I can get the three of you to go along with me, they won't have any choice."

She told them her plan in detail. The governors discussed the idea privately for an hour.

Then they all toasted their commitment to each other with White House Ice Tea.

The Funny Farm

Danny Templeton woke up with his hand on a boner. It took him a second to realize the erection belonged to him. He couldn't remember the last time his cock had been hard but, boy oh boy, it sure felt good. Just giving it a light stroke made him tingle all over. If he kept going —

He didn't. He looked around. There were three other beds in the new room where they had put him. There was a man in each bed. All of them seemed to be asleep. None of them was moving, not more than the occasional dream twitch or two he remembered seeing in his dog, Beau, back home.

Thinking of his Golden Retriever was almost enough to make him cry. He wanted so badly to return home. He didn't understand why these people were keeping him at this strange place. He didn't know why they kept asking him questions when he didn't know the answers to any of them. Sometimes they kept him up way past his bedtime. Sometimes they gave him so little to eat his stomach hurt. They were mean to him all the time and he didn't know why.

He cried himself to sleep just about every night.

Then, yesterday, something happened. They stopped being mean to him, didn't take him into that awful room where they asked all their crazy questions. They asked him what he'd like to eat more than anything else. He didn't get his hopes too high, but he told them: a double cheeseburger, a big basket of fries and a chocolate milkshake with whipped cream and a cherry on top.

Wasn't more than twenty minutes later he got exactly what he'd wanted.

Along with the food, they brought him three graphic novels. Immortals, Watchmen and ... one of those Japanese comic books with naked women. The words were all written in those little boxy lines instead of regular letters, but the pictures were all there in bright colors, and they showed everything.

Danny almost forgot about his cheeseburger. But his stomach rumbled and reminded him how hungry he was. He put the Japanese book under the other two and finished his meal. He wanted to look at the pictures of the women some more, but he got the feeling it would be dangerous to do that. At least right out in the open where he was eating.

When he finished the last sip of his milkshake, two of the men who usually took him to the questioning room came and got him. His food started to turn sour in his stomach as he thought about having to answer questions he'd answered a million times before. That or tell them he didn't know what they were talking about.

This time, though, they hadn't taken him to the questioning room. They took him outside. He couldn't remember the last time he'd been out of the building where they kept him. The air was warm and wet just like at home in the summer. The sun on his face almost made him swoon, and having just eaten he wanted nothing more than to fall on the grass and go to sleep.

They wouldn't let him do that, though. They marched him into a house that looked like it had been built a real long time ago but had been kept up real nice. He didn't know why but he got the feeling somebody rich owned it or had at one time. The two men walked him into the house, showed him a room with a big TV and lots of books, even some more of those dirty Japanese comic books. He was told the people who lived in the house had to agree what to watch on the TV. If there were any arguments about that, the TV would stay off. Books could be read in that room or taken to the bedroom.

It was a big bedroom, up on the second floor, but there were four beds in it. Three of the beds had men lying on them, even though it was the middle of the day. Danny was told the remaining bed was his. He was shown where the bathroom was; all four of them in the room had to use it.

Two of the men he had to share the room with looked real scary to Danny. They needed to shave and comb their hair and maybe not let their eyes look so crazy. The other man was younger than the two scary ones. He was sleeping, so quietly he looked like he might be dead.

Danny didn't want to be in the room with the men.

He asked, "Can't I be in with some other kids?"

The two guys who walked him everywhere only smiled at him and closed him into the room with the others. Danny got into the bed he'd been told was his and crawled under the covers even though the room was warm.

One of the scary men, the one with a scar running down his forehead, grinned at Danny and asked him, "What're you in for, kid?"

Danny rolled over and faced the wall.

He heard two of the men laugh at him.

The other guy was probably still asleep — or dead.

Danny must have fallen asleep, too, because the next thing he knew he woke up with a boner in his hand. At first, he thought he must have been dreaming of the pictures he saw in the manga comic book. Then an image popped into his head of a real woman — who was as bare naked as any of the girls in the drawings. Only her effect on him was far more powerful. He almost moaned in ecstasy.

Almost, but something told him to turn his mouth into the pillow and stifle the sound. Still, he had to do something to relieve himself. It wasn't hard to figure out what. He'd have to be careful, though. His big brother, Chill, had told him not to jerk off in bed without having something to catch his squirt.

Making sure to be quiet so he didn't wake the others, Danny slipped out of bed and into the bathroom. There was no lock on the bathroom door but he felt safer in there than in the bedroom. If he was quick about it, no one would catch him.

Would they?

He listened closely for sounds from the other room, heard the steady rasp of two guys — the scary ones, he thought — snoring. Nothing from that third guy. What about all those other guys, though, the ones who walked him around. The ones who asked him questions. The ones who watched him all the time. He listened some more and didn't hear anyone moving around.

Maybe they'd forgotten about him. Maybe they just didn't care about him any more.

Well, he didn't care about them either.

It was the time to take his boner for a ride.

He put a hand against the wall over the toilet and closed his eyes. There she was, the woman who got him so worked up. She was standing now, too. Showing herself to him front and back, anything he wanted to see. It surprised him a little but what he wanted to look at most was her face. God, she was beautiful.

And when she smiled at him —

Oh, Christ! He'd forgotten the toilet paper. His free hand shot out and grabbed the whole roll right off the holder. The plastic spindle went flying and ricochetted around the room sounding, to his ears, like a church bell clanging.

Not that he could stop then. The pleasure went on and on. Made him dizzy.

Then a voice, the guy with the scar, called out to him.

"Hey, kid! You wanna hurry up in there? You're not the only one who wants to jack off."

The intrusion would have scared the hell out of Danny Templeton, but he was gone.

Dr. Damon Todd was back. Smiling. Grateful to his dream girl, Chana Lochlan.

Fucking CIA had tried everything they could think of to bring him out of hiding.

Never occurred to them all they needed to do was give him a hand job.

Salvation's Path Administration Building

Ellie Booker decided to run the risk of having Reverend Burke Godfrey send for her rather than go to him. She'd have the element of surprise that way, but maybe the feds would make their call demanding the surrender of Godfrey and all his people while she waited. The Rev might tell them to fuck off. Then there would be no stopping a government onslaught, and she'd have lost the chance to show she was on the good guys' side.

Would lose the opportunity to grab Godfrey and surrender him to the feds.

Her hunch, though, was the call would come later in the day. Special ops units liked to get things rolling in the dead of night when the bad guys could barely keep their eyes open. Of course, Godfrey might have his ragtag militia amped up on meth and ready to shoot at anything that moved, but Ellie didn't see that. Drugs wouldn't fit with the Rev's holier-than-thou world view. Of course, it probably hadn't taken anything more than *zeal* to get that clown to fire a burst at the FBI helicopter.

So, really, she couldn't be sure what Godfrey's people might do. Still, she had to trust her instincts. Ellie, now armed and dangerous, went back to her car and dictated a narrative of the siege at Salvation's Path up to that moment. Having fulfilled her professional responsibility, she cracked the windows of her car an inch to keep the temperature bearable, reclined the driver's seat and went to sleep.

She dreamed of Hugh Collier and Sir Edbert Bickford cursing her as she told them to go fuck themselves. She no longer worked for WorldWide News. She was keeping the publication, broadcast and movie rights to her account of the takedown at Salvation's Path. Hugh and Sir Edbert threatened to sue her. She laughed at them. She'd lived through the firefight at the church compound, shooting video and taking notes as the battle raged around her.

If she could survive that, two jerks like Hugh and Sir Edbert couldn't scare her.

What woke her with a jolt was a hand rapping on her car window. She raised her head to see, what was his name? Art … Dunston. Yeah. Reverend Burke's public information officer. The lunatic who had raised the idea that the defenders of Salvation's Path might emulate the ancient Israelis who had defended the fortress at Masada. Those madmen had spoiled the fun of the attacking Roman legions by committing mass suicide.

It was all Ellie could do not to reach for the Beretta in her courier's bag.

"You want something?" she asked.

If the guy said anything about Kool-Aid, she was going for

her gun.

But Dunston only smiled at her.

"Reverend Godfrey would like to do an interview with you, Ms. Booker, the two of you on camera. I'll handle the camera. If you need a few minutes to brush your hair and put on a little makeup, that would be fine."

"How come you're not doing the interview? You're on-air talent."

Dunston had told her he'd worked as an anchor at network affiliates in Georgia and South Carolina.

"I could do it," he agreed, "but I was small market talent. You're WorldWide News."

Despite her dream, Ellie was going to hang on to that perception as long as it had any possible value to her.

"Okay," she said. She looked at the sky and saw the sun was going down. The clock on the dashboard said it was 7:15. "You think maybe you could get me ginger ale or something?"

She unlocked the door and Dunston opened it for her.

"Whatever you like, Ms. Booker. I'm here to please."

Yeah, right up to the moment it was time for everyone to take that last jump. She slung her bag over her shoulder and wondered if she'd have to kill Dunston to make her plan work.

The Oval Office

Until that moment — 8:00 p.m. — Mather Wyman had chosen not to sit behind Patricia Grant's desk in the Oval Office. It was all well and good, and certainly necessary, that he fulfill the responsibilities with which he'd been entrusted, but the last thing he wanted was to seem too eager about filling the president's ... well, no, not her shoes. They'd be far too small for him. But her role.

He was waiting to take a call from Patti Grant and had thought to do it at Edwina Byington's desk. The president's secretary had told him the only proper place for him to take or make any call was at the president's desk — which for the time being was his desk. He was no mere functionary dotting i's and crossing t's; he, too, had sworn an oath to support and defend the Constitution. The country was depending on him now, and the American people had to be reassured that he was up to the job.

Wyman was fewer than ten years younger than Edwina, but hearing her speak he imagined his mother would have said the same to him, gently lecturing him about the proper way to do things and his obligations to others. He'd long thought his mother had been the only person in his family who knew he was gay. She'd never said so directly; that would have been anything but her style. He suspected she wouldn't have criticized him had he revealed himself to her and the world.

He just hadn't had the courage to take the chance of doing anything that might make her think less of him. His fear, he came to think, had caused him to fail to give his mother sufficient credit. Letting her go to her grave without being honest with her was a great regret.

His comfort was that could she see him now she would think well of him.

As he sat behind the president's desk, he felt he belonged there.

In Patricia Grant's absence, he could think of no one better to be in his position.

He had called George Washington University Hospital an hour earlier. Jim McGill had taken the call. He said the president would be happy to speak with him, but she wouldn't be available for a little while. Where might she call him back? To his credit, he hadn't said Edwina's desk; he'd said the Oval Office.

He was pleased that McGill hadn't been affronted.

The phone rang and Wyman picked up.

Edwina told him, "Mr. Acting-President, Madam President is on the line."

He heard laughter in the background.

"Madam President, is that you?" he asked.

"It is, Mather. Are you happy now, Edwina?"

"I am, Madam President. Thank you for obliging me."

The president's secretary clicked off.

"What was that all about?" Wyman asked.

"Edwina thought a phone introduction between the two of us would make a good line for volume one of her memoirs," Patti said.

Wyman chuckled. "I'd better be careful what I say around her."

"She'll treat both of us kindly, I'm sure. How are you, Mather?"

"Coping well, I think. How are you, Madam President?"

"I just had a medical once over. I'm afraid the company of watchful physicians is going to be a regular thing for the near future. After that, I was allowed to take a warm bath which left me feeling wonderful."

Wyman was happy to hear that, but didn't think it proper for him to comment on any woman's bath, much less that of the president.

He said, "Would I be remiss to give you a briefing on the situation at Salvation's Path, and to ask your opinion on one point of what I have in mind for Reverend Godfrey? I wouldn't want to spoil your feeling of well-being."

There was a beat of silence.

Then Patti said, "Mather, if I didn't trust you completely, I wouldn't have asked you to join me on the ticket. Whatever you decide, short of a presidential pardon, you have my complete support. If you want to let me know what you intend, especially now that you've made me curious, I'll be happy to listen. If you'd like my advice, I'll be happy to give it."

Wyman said, "I wasn't sure of the proper etiquette for this situation."

Patti told him, "Make the boss look good usually works."

"I'll make a note of that."

They both laughed. Wyman told Patti of the plan the military had devised.

"Galia told Admiral Dexter about the tunnels?" Patti asked.

"Yes."

"Has anyone considered that Burke Godfrey might already have used them to make an escape?" Patti asked.

"We have. FBI agents are watching the exits. Nobody has left that we can tell. That leads to the only point left for me to consider. Should I make a call to Godfrey, give him a last chance to surrender?"

Patti said, "That would be one way to determine if he's still around. If you're told he won't talk to you, that would be a good sign that he's already on the run. But an implied ultimatum — this is your last chance — would let the people inside the wall know the battle was about to begin."

"That's what Admiral Dexter has told me. He thinks talking to Godfrey would increase the chances that his people would take casualties."

Patti was momentarily silent again.

Then she said, "Not if … he's planning to use special forces, I assume."

"Yes, Madam President."

"What I would do then, Mather, is have Admiral Dexter move his people as close to church grounds as possible, either in the tunnels or if possible onto the property itself. If Godfrey refuses your offer or doesn't take your call, have the assault team strike immediately. My guess is an amateur militia won't be up to dealing with special ops people that quickly. You'll need to get the military's opinion of that idea, but it seems to me to preserve most, if not all, of the element of surprise while giving us the high ground of offering Godfrey one last chance."

Mather Wyman was humbled. Patricia Grant had come up with that idea off the top of her head. From her hospital room. He might be capable of doing the job he'd been handed, but he didn't have the mastery of the boss.

"An excellent idea, Madam President," Wyman said. "I'll call Admiral Dexter."

"Thank you for calling, Mather. You've made me feel I'm still useful. I hope, I think, all will go well. I'd like to hear from you again, whatever happens. If I'm not available, please tell Jim. He'll make sure I hear."

"Yes, Madam President. Be well. We all look forward to welcoming you back."

"Thank you, Mather, and remember, a win will look good for both of us."

Founding Farmers Restaurant — Washington, D.C.

Elspeth Kendry got to the restaurant at 8:30 p.m., as requested. The shrink from Georgetown University, who used to work for the CIA and had called to request the meeting, was waiting for her when she arrived. He'd told her his name was Daryl Cheveyo and had said he would be the best looking Hopi-Navajo guy in the joint. It helped that he wore a button on his lapel that said: *Native American before you were.*

Elspeth extended her hand to him and said, "You've got me there. I was born overseas."

"No reason to be ashamed," Cheveyo told her. "Immigration's been quite the fad the past four or five centuries."

A hostess showed them to a table for two in a corner, twenty feet from the next closest diner. The restaurant closed at ten on Sunday and the evening rush had come and gone. Elspeth got the feeling that Cheveyo had motivated the staff to maintain their zone of privacy.

He'd also been considerate enough to pick a place just blocks from the White House.

They browsed their menus and ordered salads: Late Harvest for her, 17 Vegetables for him.

"That is a cool button," Elspeth told him, smiling.

"An acquaintance, Marlene Flower Moon, gave it to me. She works for the BIA. Went to some big three-day law enforcement conference here in town. What I heard was, some starchy, arrived-on-the-Mayflower types were lording it over their lesser colleagues. Marlene showed up the next day wearing a button like this one. Got some dirty looks from the Mayflower crowd, but they suddenly got a lot more modest about their origins."

"Good for her."

"Yeah, well, she can be quite a handful herself, but I like the button, too."

Their meals and drinks came. Elspeth allowed a three-forkful grace period before asking, "What can I do for you, Dr. Cheveyo?"

"You've already done a lot just by not being Celsus Crogher. Did he tell you that he almost broke my neck?"

Crogher hadn't. But that certainly explained why he had sent her to talk with Cheveyo. Elspeth listened closely to the shrink's story. It was always helpful to know your superior had a homicidal streak in him.

She said, "I've read the file on Damon Todd as part of getting up to speed on my new job, but I didn't see anything about you and SAC Crogher."

Cheveyo laughed. "You want to publish a bestseller? Compile all the things that get left out of government reports."

"If somebody tried that, I believe the current Supreme Court would find that prior restraint didn't violate the First Amendment after all," Elspeth told him.

"No doubt. Freedom of the press? Who needs it? Anyway, the reason I'm talking with you is I made a promise to James J. McGill to let him know if anything changed regarding Dr. Todd's status."

"Has it?" Elspeth asked.

She knew from doing her homework that Todd had tried to kill the president's husband after McGill went to work for Chana Lochlan. She was his first client as a private investigator and he had brought an end to a really creepy relationship between Dr. Todd and Ms. Lochlan.

Taking umbrage, Todd had tried to kill McGill.

Things hadn't worked out for Todd and a court remanded him to the custody of the CIA.

"I can't say for certain that it has," Cheveyo told her, "but that's the feeling I have."

"Based on what?"

"Sad to say, my former colleagues have been unable to penetrate the cover personality Todd constructed for himself — after three years of trying. Things have gotten so bad they called on me for advice, and you know how government agencies hate to admit they can't handle anything in house."

"Too true," Elspeth said. "So what did you tell them?"

"I suggested they ease off. See if the release of pressure might open him up."

"They went along with that?"

Cheveyo nodded. "Then I did one more thing. Todd is a mature man posing as a young boy. I thought maybe I should slip him something that might provoke a reaction in both his root and assumed personae."

"What did you give him?" Elspeth asked.

"Japanese porn."

She smiled sardonically. "A strategy based on advanced academic study."

"That and the guy is a jerk-off." Cheveyo smiled, too. "I thought popping his weasel for the first time in years might cause other things to break loose. With that in mind, I warned my former colleagues that Todd is still quite dangerous. I didn't like the way they seemed to dismiss my assessment. So I called the Secret Service."

"Dr. Todd is still in custody, right?"

"As far as I know."

"Do you think it's possible he might escape?"

"That's beyond my area of expertise. But I will say the man is resourceful."

Elspeth paused to consider the situation.

"I should contact the CIA. Soon."

Cheveyo said, "Very soon. You know how long it takes to get bureaucracies to talk to each other."

"I do," Elspeth said.

GWU Hospital

Between Kenny's taking naps, getting his vital signs checked hourly and having Abbie and Caitie edge him out for one-on-

one visits, McGill didn't get to see his son until that night. When McGill saw Kenny beam at him as he entered his hospital room, he knew the wait had been well worth it. From the look on Kenny's face, his *joie de vivre* was making a comeback.

As if to confirm that point, Kenny asked, "You bring me a cheeseburger, Dad?"

"Deke's getting it," McGill said, not missing a beat. "I told him to hold the fries."

He had Kenny going for a moment. Then his son laughed.

McGill had never heard a more pleasing sound.

He leaned over the bed and put his masked lips to Kenny's forehead.

The younger McGill asked, "How's Patti doing?"

His father chose to be honest. "There was a scary moment or two, but she's coming back strong."

"What happened?" Kenny asked, his face clouding.

"An unexpected reaction to the anesthesia, but she'll be fine. In fact, the two of you are going to spend some time together at Camp David. Get your A-games back."

"I'm getting out of the hospital?" Kenny's mood brightened at the idea.

"Not just yet. But as soon as Dr. Jones says it's okay, Camp David is the next stop."

Kenny considered the implications of what he'd been told.

"Will Mom be there, too?" he asked.

"She'll be a regular visitor. You'll have to put up with your sisters, too, on some weekends. I'll be in and out regularly. Mostly, though, for company, you'll have to make do with the president of the United States."

"Patti's great," he said with a smile. "I can feel her inside me."

McGill's eyes moistened. "I'll be sure to tell her. She'll love hearing that."

"What about school?" Kenny asked. "I don't want to fall behind."

That from a formerly indifferent student, McGill thought. His son really was a new ... not a man yet. But he was getting there.

He told Kenny, "Mom and I talked about that. Your first job is to get better, rebuild your strength. Once Dr. Jones says it's okay, you can crack the books. We thought what we might do is get your curriculum from school back home and have a tutor take you through the material at Camp David."

"That sounds good. Maybe I could Skype with my teachers at school, too. Make sure I'm on the right page."

McGill nodded. "I think we could work out something like that."

"Maybe I could even Skype with a few classmates. You know, after my hair grows back."

Liesl Eberhardt, McGill thought. Kenny was still a sly dog, and he was glad to see it.

"Yeah, why not?" he told his son.

Smiling, Kenny said, "Hey, Dad. Did you and Sweetie get that case of yours worked out?"

"We did," McGill said, glad now his face was masked. "Got the bad guy."

Kenny bobbed his head, as if he had expected nothing less.

McGill didn't tell him Zack Garner had died. He didn't need to hear that anytime soon.

He gave his son another cloth-covered kiss and told him to sleep well.

Returning to Patti's room, he learned that Mather Wyman was about to launch an attack on Reverend Burke Godfrey's redoubt. More good news.

Dumbarton Oaks

Galia Mindel said goodbye to Stephen Norwood at her front door.

"Go home," she said. "Give your wife a little time to be with you. Sleep in."

"Tomorrow is Monday, Galia, a working day. The start of the week."

Galia replied, "I won't arrive at the White House until noon tomorrow. If I see or even hear that you got in earlier, you're fired."

"Don't want to lose my job," Norwood said.

"Don't lose your wife either."

Her deputy saluted and departed in his Escalade.

Galia watched her automatic gates close and lock behind him. Then she went inside.

The air conditioning was on to keep the heat and humidity of the late August night at bay. The chill was almost too much … but just right when she thought of having a cup of hot cocoa before going to bed. Consuming all those calories right before going to sleep was something she wouldn't ordinarily allow herself. She had her weight down to within two pounds of her goal. Most of her clothes were now oversized. Things had almost gotten to the point where …

She stopped in front of her check-your-look-before-you-go-out-the-door mirror.

Turned to her right and left, looked over one shoulder and then the other.

Aside from the fatigue on her face, she liked everything she saw. She wasn't almost to the point; she was there. For the first time since college, she was vain about her physical appearance. She had worked so hard to get there. McGill taunting her with a box of donuts not long after the president's inauguration had only spurred her on, as had her one night out with Sir Robert Reed.

Give her a good night's sleep — which she intended to get — and she'd look damn good.

Too good to worry about one cup of hot cocoa setting her back. She went to the kitchen, whipped it up, sipped it to the last drop and washed out the cup and pan.

She showered, brushed her teeth and slipped into bed.

Galia felt the rare satisfaction of someone who had made a positive difference for her country. Gene Rinaldo, Ed Mulcahy and Lara Chavez had all gotten back to Stephen Norwood that evening. They'd been in touch with the party leaders of their respective legislatures in New York, Illinois and California. Not only had the leaders approved of the idea Galia had brought to the governors, they were sure they had the votes to pass the legislation — on a bipartisan basis.

In short order, three out of the five most populous states in the nation would have laws pegging the timing of their presidential primaries to "one minute after whatsoever time New Hampshire shall begin its presidential primary voting."

That wording would provide New Hampshire with a symbolic bow to its first-in-the-nation status. Not that it would quell the outrage sure to erupt in the Granite State, but that was too damn bad. The current nominating system had produced a preponderance of mediocrities and failures. The country needed to do better, and Patricia Darden Grant had said she wanted to change things even at the cost of her own presidency.

Only this was Galia's idea not the president's.

So what? If Galia got fired, she'd write a book.

Give speeches for money.

Greet shoppers at Bergdorf Goodman.

Oh, the two major parties would cry foul right along with New Hampshire, and threaten to penalize New York, Illinois and California. The counter to that threat was child's play. The legislation would effectively say, "Fine, you take away our convention delegates, your candidates don't get lines on the ballots in our states. See if you can sell a forty-seven-state president as legitimate."

The party bosses would run in circles like their heinies were on fire.

They'd threaten to sue, take the matter to the Supreme Court.

Thing was, no political party's candidates had a constitutional right to be placed on a ballot.

If the high court did choose to review the matter, Galia had thought of that, too. Five of the justices were from: New York, Illinois and California. There were seventy-million-plus people in those three states, most of whom would think getting first crack at deciding who should be president was a great idea. No doubt they'd make homecoming miserable for any justice who chose to vote against them.

It was possible the whole plan could blow up, but once the idea had been exposed to the light and heat of public debate, things would never be allowed to remain the same crappy way they were now.

Galia fell asleep with a smile on her face ... and just the slightest fear in her heart that any job she found outside the White House wouldn't be half as much fun.

The Funny Farm

Dr. Damon Todd and the other three men in the new room where he'd been quartered made their breakout attempt shortly before midnight. They didn't wait until the wee hours of the morning because at The Funny Farm that was when the security people were on their toes. The idea was to leave early and catch the guards looking the other way.

Todd hadn't conceived the plan or even offered a suggestion. He was simply a last-minute beneficiary of an effort that had been a year in the making. Todd was normally suspicious of anything resembling good luck, but this was an opportunity not to be overlooked. He'd joined the effort wholeheartedly.

Which had saved his life — for the moment.

That morning, shortly after emerging from the bathroom and lying down on his bed, Todd got the uneasy feeling he'd been had. The frigging CIA hadn't been able to put a smudge on his Danny Templeton persona for ... he wasn't sure how long it had been. Subjectively, he'd been held captive and interrogated for a very long time; he felt sure his frustrated tormentors must have thought it an equally protracted period.

After all their time and effort, they had suddenly decided to do what, take a breather? Give up? Bullshit. His enduring resistance would only make them more determined to find out his secrets. What he had to offer them was priceless.

But not without a price tag. They should have offered him a billion.

If only the bastards hadn't been so shortsighted. If only they had —

Seen reason from the first. Who had been his first contact with the Agency? Daryl Cheveyo.

Who had been with McGill when the Agency threw a net over him? Cheveyo,

That Indian bastard had to have a hand in his new circumstances. Todd needed less than a minute to figure out Cheveyo's contribution. Someone had provided him with three graphic novels. Two bang-bang action stories ... and one porn mag. Illustrated not photographed, a form known to appeal to both younger and older onanists.

Jerk-offs, if you wanted to be frank about it.

Was that what Cheveyo thought of him? Of course, it was.

Damon Todd had been just an Agency wannabe. A crank who had maybe come up with something brilliant. But not someone you'd ever want to work with. Not long term.

Bastard.

Todd wanted to get his hands on Cheveyo right that moment. Choke him out. Do to him just what he did to that cretin who had tried to mug him on the Georgetown campus. He extended his hands in mimicked memory and began to squeeze.

"Look at that, would you? They put the Boston Strangler in with us."

Todd's mind turned outward and he saw the guy with the scar on his forehead.

Ugly SOB.

"Somebody stick your face under a paper-cutter?" he asked the shithead.

Danny Templeton never would have said that. If the room was monitored with a camera, the interrogators would see the difference and come for him on the run. As it was, the creep he'd insulted made a move on him, but the other guy yanked him back.

All it took was one tug. The insulted party didn't fight it.

The other guy was older, had white hair with a sharp widow's peak. The skin on his face looked like an afterthought, a light coat of beige paint over a chiseled rock substrate. That was the way the rest of him looked, too, lean to the bone. Just enough flesh to cover long cords of muscle.

Todd had been about to joke that the two guys had been in the bathroom together so they didn't have to pull their own meat, but he reevaluated. He was nowhere near as strong now as when he'd been captured. Regular workouts hadn't been part of his day. He'd almost shriveled up to the point of being the scarecrow he'd been as an academic.

If he wanted to get strong again, he'd have to survive.

He told the older guy, "I was working toward a build like yours."

"You get close?" the guy asked.

The guy with the scar stayed silent and motionless like a well-trained dog.

"Yeah."

"My name's Arn Crosby," the older guy said. Nodding at his friend, he added, "This is Olin Anderson. We've done terrible things for our country. This is our retirement villa."

Todd heard Crosby's every word, but part of his mind was listening for the footfalls of men racing to grab him while his root identity was still available. If anyone had been assigned to watch him, he must have been asleep at the switch. Todd didn't hear any commotion.

Didn't hear anything alarming at all.

Until Anderson laughed. That was fairly creepy.

He said, "Must be Judgment Day. The dead are rising."

Todd looked at the fourth bed. The man who'd been lying there as if comatose was sitting up with his feet on the floor. He was staring at Todd.

Gesturing at Crosby and Anderson, he said, "Those guys are the patriots. My name is Stanwick. I'm the traitor. And you are ...

not the same person who entered this room."

Todd told them, "I'm the guy who's going to get out of here soon or die trying."

The other three looked at one another.

As if they couldn't have asked for anything more.

They signed him up for the team.

Easier than killing him and having to hide the body.

Salvation Path Administration Building

Reverend Burke Godfrey drew his right index finger across his throat, a sign to videocam operator Art Dunston that he should stop recording. The camera's light went out and the interview was over, before Ellie Booker could ask her last question: "Are you fucking nuts?"

Godfrey had gone on for hours. Fidel Castro would have been impressed by the length of the rant. Any perceived flaw in the federal government, generally, or Patricia Darden Grant, specifically, was addressed, excoriated and judged to be grounds for damnation. Neither life in prison nor capital punishment was sufficient for those who stood against Godfrey's vision of the way things ought to be. His enemies had to become rotisserie roasts in hell with the oven timer set on forever.

He'd spoken well of the Catholic Church, despite its theological errors, for having the foresight to establish its own sovereign state, Vatican City. He advocated that every state in the union have "an equivalent evangelical moral center free from the heavy hand of government" where the righteous might come to live, worship and educate their children as scripture demanded. Big states like Texas should have more than one such free and virtuous city. As soon as the forty-eight contiguous states were linked by these cities, the *princes* of faith who led their congregations would meet, say right there at Salvation's Path, and elect a leader.

Good God, Ellie thought, the man wanted to be the Protestant *pope* of America.

She asked him as much.

And he had the brass to admit it. "If it comes to that, so be it."

"Should the president and Congress bow to you or whoever was chosen to lead this new league of holy cities?"

Godfrey smiled. "The League of Holy Cities, what a fine name that is. Thank you."

Meaning, Ellie was sure, that he was going to swipe it.

The reverend continued, "The president and the Congress, of course, would do what they consider to be politically advantageous, but in time I'm sure they'd come to see the wisdom of following the guidance of those closest to God."

"How do you measure that?" Ellie asked.

"I beg your pardon."

"How do you measure how close you are to God, and how do you compare your distance with anyone else's?"

Godfrey frowned, and that was when he drew his finger across his throat.

Before Ellie could ask him if he was nuts.

Godfrey slumped back in his chair, Ellie's inconvenient questions already forgotten. He looked at Dunston and said, "You'll get that video right down to the editing bay, Art?"

"Yes, sir, Reverend. You want me to do the first cut?"

"Just the obvious stuff. Any place I might have scratched my nose or paused too long searching for a word. Make sure you've got a nice balance for the lighting, keep my skin tones even throughout."

"Lay in a music bed?"

Godfrey nodded. "You've got a good ear, Art. Give it a try."

Dunston smiled, said his goodbyes and left.

Godfrey followed him to the office door and locked it. Ellie wondered how many times he'd done that with a woman in the room, and how many of them had felt threatened by it. She found it convenient, saved her the trouble.

Still, she had a role to play.

"If you don't mind, I'm tired. I think I'll go down to my car and get some sleep."

Godfrey ignored her. He sat behind his desk and said, "You think I'm mad as a hatter."

Ellie made no effort to evade the accusation.

"In a word, yeah. In a few more, maybe crazy as a fox."

The reverend leaned forward. "Meaning what?"

"Your home movie could be your insanity defense."

"You don't believe in your own words, a league of holy cities?"

Ellie leaned in, further narrowing the distance between them.

"You know what would happen if you actually got something like that up and running? Each of your *princes* would claim to hear something different from God, something that benefitted him individually and you'd be at each other's throats in no time, begging for the heavy hand of government to save your precious backsides."

Godfrey sat back and smiled. "I was just about to ask if you're a believer. Then I was going to ask if you're a Democrat. Now, I'm wondering if you voted for that damn Patti Grant."

"I didn't, but you and some other people are making me think I might next time."

"You're a very independent young woman."

"You don't know the half of it, Reverend. You, Sir Edbert Bickford, Hugh Collier: I don't take crap off anyone. Now, I'd like to get some sleep. You want to unlock the door?"

Godfrey said, "You don't have to sleep in your car. I've got a bed in the next room."

"Okay, as long as you're going to join your friend in the editing bay."

"Am I really that unattractive?" he asked with a smile.

He really was, Ellie thought, but it was still time to play along. Stay in character.

"At the very least, after the sweat you worked up, you need a shower," Ellie said.

"I also have one of those in the next room."

"Good. Turn it on nice and hot. Use a lot of soap."

Ellie almost added, *See if you can wash the ugly off.*

But she knew about editing, too.

As it was, he saw her as a challenge, and there was no end to the guys who liked that. Two minutes later he was in the shower. She had declined the inevitable invitation to join him. She did, however, step in close from behind when he got out and clocked him with the Beretta. He couldn't have dropped faster if she'd shot him.

She took the roll of duct tape out of her bag and secured his wrists behind his back. Taped his ankles together. Tore off one last strip to seal his mouth. Hoped, mildly, he didn't retch and choke on his own vomit.

Ellie went back to the reverend's office. Did *not* sit in his chair. She pulled the one she'd used up to the other side of the desk. If Art Dunston was in on Godfrey's little scheme to drag her off to bed, he wouldn't be back until morning. If he were simply doing the editing he'd talked about, he'd still be gone for hours.

It was Ellie's guess the feds would make their call before then.

She was right; it came at 11:59 p.m. She made a mental note of that and answered on the first ring. Unable to resist cracking wise, she said, "Salvation's Path, have you been saved?"

There was a beat of silence before a man said, "This is Acting President Mather Wyman. May I speak with Reverend Godfrey, please?"

More good material, Ellie thought, but what the hell had happened to Patti Grant?

"Mr. Acting President, my name is Ellie Booker. I was formerly a producer with WorldWide News. I was being held here against my will. Every word of what I'm about to tell you is true. I hope you'll believe me. I've turned the tables on Reverend Godfrey. I've knocked him out and bound him with duct tape. He's in a bedroom off his office in the administration building. You can find a picture of me on the Internet. I have a gun I need to protect myself against Reverend Godfrey's men, but when the SEALs or whoever you're sending come, tell them I'll leave the office door unlocked. Please ask that they announce themselves. I'll throw my gun out to them, unloaded of course."

Wyman told her they had a picture of her. It would be relayed to the assault team.

They would arrive shortly.

But first things would get quite loud.

The Funny Farm

Damon Todd had heard of prison shivs, had even seen examples of the improvised knives on television. Most of them had been fashioned from metal. A small number, meant strictly for stabbing, had been made from hard plastic. Anderson had two shivs carved from wood. Masterfully carved from some unfamiliar fine grained dark wood. Each had a blade no more than three inches long with a sharply V'ed point and a serrated top edge.

Crosby's weapons were made from metal. They didn't have the same degree of finish as Anderson's knives, but they looked fearsome nonetheless. To Damon's untutored eye, they seemed to be some sort of hybrid hatchet with a broad sharp head on one side of a wooden handle and a triangular spike on the other side.

Todd's curiosity about the weapons was obvious.

Crosby told him, "These are called Vietnam tomahawks. Wicked for both slashing and stabbing."

Todd recalled a memory from childhood TV. "Can't you throw a tomahawk, too?"

The two men who had done terrible things for their country smiled at Todd.

Crosby said, "Man has a mind for detail."

Todd looked at the self-described traitor, Stanwick, who knew just what he was thinking.

"I don't have a weapon," Stanwick said, "and neither will you."

Todd understood the situation intuitively. "We're the bait."

"That we are."

Anderson liked that, Todd's awareness of his role and likely his fate.

"You said you'd die trying," Anderson reminded his new roomie.

"I will, if necessary. I suppose that's going to depend on how good *you* are."

Anderson's right hand was a blur, describing an arc in front of Todd's face. He didn't feel the knife make contact, but he was immediately aware of a drop of blood on the tip of his nose. His eyes crossed as he tried to confirm visually what he already knew; the bastard could as easily have slit his throat.

Crosby, as if he'd been prepared for such a moment, handed Todd a piece of toilet tissue.

"No worse'n a shaving nick. Olin likes to show off when people doubt him."

So did Todd, but he saw no opportunity to demonstrate that now, and he noted out of the corner of an eye that Stanwick had a fine scar just above and parallel to his right eyebrow. Explanation enough why Stanwick was willing to act as bait.

Obtaining raw material and crafting the weapons had to be why the escape attempt had been so long in coming because its choreography was a model of simplicity. Out the room door, down the stairs, out the back door, through the woods and cut the fence.

Anderson was first out the door and slit the throat of the floor guard. Crosby took the lead down the stairs. He drove a spike through the ground-floor guard's temple. Neither victim had the chance to make a sound. Their bodies were caught and lowered silently. Rushing out the back door, Crosby and Anderson collaborated on another silent kill.

At that point, the four men ran into the nearby woods. Once they were among the trees, Stanwick was told to take the lead. Todd was instructed to follow him. Anderson and Crosby brought up the rear. Anderson asked Todd, "You remember what we told you, smartass?"

Todd nodded. It was so simple he figured out what they *weren't* telling him.

Stanwick, looking nervous, picked his way through the forest.

U.S. Naval Air Station, Norfolk, Virginia

In theory, Admiral David Dexter's plan to comply with Acting President Mather Wyman's wish for the assault on the Salvation's Path compound to produce shock and awe without resulting in blood and body parts was simple. In execution, it required many highly skilled people doing difficult jobs precisely and with great speed.

State authorities in Virginia, much to the chagrin of the state's governor, were brought in to evacuate the church's neighbors for a radius of ten miles. Uprooting people from their homes and businesses on virtually no notice without causing either heart attacks or gun battles was no mean feat. Many people in the area had been preconditioned to think that their government might someday "come for them." Now, here it was happening.

If the effort had been made by anyone who didn't look and sound like the people being moved out of harm's way, there undoubtedly would have been casualties and lawsuits that would have lasted for years. On the advice of CIA psychologists, the state cops were advised to be unfailingly polite, tell everyone they'd be allowed to return in a matter of a few hours, promise them they'd be reimbursed for any inconvenience they suffered, and would have stories to tell family and friends for the rest of their lives.

The cherry on top was the assurance that their cooperation would be considered heroic by their fellow Americans.

Having been briefed on what was going to happen at Salvation's Path, the state cops were able to deliver their sales pitch with complete sincerity, making it compelling. Other than a few bruised feelings and one man who had to be Tasered, compliance was both unanimous and surprisingly gracious.

Far more so than the reaction to the grounding and diversion of civil aviation that went into effect for the entire Eastern Seaboard until further notice. Airlines moaned, private aviation bitched and some of the more impetuous media outlets threatened to send up their newscopters to see what the hell was going on.

What was about to go on would have knocked helicopters out

of the air if their pilots had been so foolish as to venture too close. A flight of six F/A-18D Super Hornets took off from Norfolk, formed up over the Atlantic and headed for the enclosed grounds of Salvation's Path.

The fighter/attack jets, capable of reaching a speed of thirteen hundred and sixty miles per hour, were going to come in very fast, one after another.

The speed of sound in dry air at eighty-eight degrees Fahrenheit was seven hundred and eighty-eight miles per hour. The sky was clear and bright that night and the temperature was eighty-five: close enough for government work.

Each military jet would break the sound barrier and lay down a sonic boom *carpet*. That carpet would extend over the entire flight path of the plane until it dropped to a subsonic speed. The boom intensity was greatest directly below the plane's flight path. Sonic booms were known to shatter glass and dislodge roofing tiles.

That was what could happen from a routine boom caused by an aircraft simply exceeding the sound barrier and continuing along its flight plan. If a military jet were to dive, accelerate and turn, it could *focus* the sonic boom it produced. That was the mission of the six Super Hornets.

The physical consequences of exposure to loud noises included: fear, anxiety, distraction, headache, hearing loss, fatigue, muscle tension and other impairments. Prolonged or repeated exposure only made matters worse. Hard surfaces such as roads, sidewalks and buildings reflected the noise causing still further aggravation.

Reverend Burke Godfrey's militia, untrained and unsuspecting, would likely suffer no fatalities from the aerial assault but it would be left staggering, far from fighting trim.

The flight leader radioed to the ground forces that he and his pilots were going in.

Salvation's Path Administration Building

Ellie Booker had taken Mather Wyman at his word. Things

were going to get loud. She sat in a corner of Reverend Godfrey's lair, opposite his unconscious form, with her index fingers lightly placed in her ears. The first thing she heard was a rattling from the room's windows. She had the feeling, though, that things were going to get a lot worse than that.

She took her fingers out of her ears and clamped her palms over them just as the roar of the first sonic boom hit. She drew her legs up and compressed herself into a ball. The windows shattered and blew into the room. The floor shook.

Waves rippled through the fat on Godfrey's torso.

Though still unconscious, he grimaced and moaned in pain.

Jesus Christ, Ellie thought, *the government was bombing the place.*

They were going to kill everyone. Ellie started to cry. Then the second boom hit and the whole building vibrated, a modern six-story structure. She looked at Godfrey. His eyes were open now, but it was clear he had no idea what was happening to him.

The guy had thought he was going to suds up, sluice off and get laid.

Instead he woke up in hell.

Maybe you didn't even have to go that far to find damnation.

Another boom hit. Ellie slumped onto her right side, hands still over her ears.

She never heard the guys in combat fatigues charge into the room.

The Funny Farm

Stanwick stopped and oriented himself. Todd saw he was looking for something. A point of reference? Stanwick bobbed his head, no doubt confirming something to himself, but answering Todd's question, too. He continued to pick his way through the trees, setting a deliberate pace, choosing each step carefully.

Anderson came up silently behind Todd and gave him a nudge.

"Get going, but watch your step."

That was all Todd needed to hear. The troll had told him not only what to do, but the value Stanwick had for the escape attempt. The traitor had learned the way through, what? A minefield? If not the explosive type of mine, then the sort that would set the hounds and their handlers loose upon them.

Todd moved as fast as he dared to catch up with Stanwick. If he tarried too long the man would be out of sight. Then he, Anderson and Crosby would be stuck. Getting stabbed in the back with one of Anderson's knives would undoubtedly follow.

He caught up, maintaining a prudent gap in case there was something in the ground that Stanwick might detonate. Todd's mind, though, raced ahead. What had he been told was at the end of this jaunt through the woods? A fence. The sort of structure that might enclose a suburban yard? No, the fence would be the final obstacle between the four of them and freedom.

It would be a smart fence. Electrified no doubt. Able to pinpoint any breach.

How could the fence be beaten? The inevitable first step had to be to take its reporting ability down or at least render it incapable of, what, frying anyone who tried to scale it? Linear logic yielded to an intuitive leap. The fence, like some bloodthirsty deity of old, would require a human sacrifice to win its favor.

Had Stanwick really been ready to sacrifice himself for Anderson and Crosby?

Maybe, being a traitor, he felt guilt, was ready to atone.

Maybe Stanwick's feelings were a mix of guilt and vengeance.

He could free the other two men and once again fuck over the CIA.

Or had he simply preferred electrocution as a means to end his life rather than be dismembered by his companions?

In any event, now that he, Todd, had stumbled into the escape, Stanwick had new hope to live and be free. The others could fling the newcomer on the fence as their payment for escape. Todd started to narrow the gap with Stanwick.

He couldn't close in on him immediately, not before Stanwick safely got them out of the woods. But he couldn't wait too long or Anderson might grab *him* from behind and fling him onto the fence. Todd's heart was in his throat as he continued to creep up on Stanwick foot by foot. He only wished the traitor had been given some weapon of his own.

He'd have loved nothing better than disposing of Stanwick and turning to disembowel Anderson. He turned his mind from thoughts of vengeance when he saw a barrier ahead. It wasn't the chain-link, barb-wire topped obstacle he'd expected. It looked like a camouflaged sheet of some sort. It would have been invisible in the night if it didn't possess a glow of its own.

Stanwick must have seen it, too, and he made a mistake.

He stopped and looked over his shoulder. Smiled. He'd done his part.

Now, he and the others would betray Todd.

Except Todd had broken into a run. He was no longer the extremely strong specimen he'd once been, but he still had that mindset. Stanwick had never been more than a data shuffler. He saw Todd charging him and horror filled his face.

He shrieked. "No, no. Not now. It's supposed to be you, not me!"

Todd hit Stanwick a double stiff arm blow to his left shoulder, spun him around and shoved him headlong into the barrier. The collision caused a flare of light like a firebomb exploding. The stench of scorched hair hit Todd. But both Anderson and Crosby shoved past him.

Stanwick had taken the charge out of the fence. Climbing the sheet would have been impossible, but Crosby's tomahawks made a great gash in the fabric, and he and Anderson slipped through it in a heartbeat.

Todd ran through the opening, too. He didn't know if —

Anderson and Crosby were going to let him live.

They had all four of their weapons pointing his way.

More woods, presumably free of mines, lay behind them.

"You're scary smart, pal," Crosby said, "figuring things out as fast as you do."

Anderson told him, "We have to wonder if you'll try to do a Stanwick on us soon."

Todd said, "You go your way, I'll go mine. I've got a safe house nearby."

That was a bold claim for somebody who had been brought in to be a sacrificial lamb.

But Todd had already demonstrated he was more than he might seem at first glance.

"It'd be only right if you returned our hospitality," Crosby told him.

Anderson nodded. They started off through the woods. Hadn't gone ten feet when a crushing wave of sound stopped Todd dead in his tracks. He clapped his hands over his ears. Crosby and Anderson grabbed his arms, pulled his hands down.

Crosby spoke directly into one ear. "It's just a fast-mover going over."

Anderson told him, "Best fucking cover we could ask for."

The three of them hurried off into the night.

GWU Hospital

McGill told Patti, "I catch the screws looking the wrong way, we make a break for it."

"Screws?" Patti asked.

"The guards. Aren't you up on your prison lingo?"

"I try to learn a new word every day but, no, I wasn't familiar with that usage."

"Grew up privileged and never watched Jimmy Cagney movies, that's why."

"My mother knew Mr. Cagney. They would bump into each other now and then on Martha's Vineyard. He told Mother she could have had a career in film."

McGill hadn't heard that tidbit before. He was tempted to say maybe he'd been thinking of Edward G. Robinson, but for all he knew "Little Caesar" had been Patti's godfather. At least he'd been right about the privileged childhood. Martha's Vineyard, la-di-da.

His family had summered at the Wisconsin Dells.

As he had many times before, McGill thought he was the luckiest guy in the world.

"Would you like me to ask if the hospital might roll in a cot for you?" Patti asked.

"That or a throw rug. I could curl up at the foot of your bed."

"The rug might be a possibility. I doubt they have any Milk-Bones, though."

Trading quips with Patti Grant was a no-win proposition, McGill knew. So he leaned over his wife and kissed her.

"I am so fortunate to have you and all the other people I love. At the start of this day, I thought —" McGill's voice caught in his throat.

Patti took his hand. "Looks like you're stuck with all of us a while longer."

McGill kissed Patti again. He sat in the chair next to the bed.

"I'll spend the night right here. I can see you better that way."

The two Secret Service special agents in the room had been studies in looking the other way, but there was no question they'd heard every word that had been said. Patti cleared her throat and they looked at her.

"If the two of you would please step outside now, I think I can fend off Mr. McGill on my own."

The agents said, "Yes, ma'am," without smiling.

But they couldn't hide the mirth in their eyes.

Once she and McGill were alone, Patti asked, "Do you remember the favor you did for me that night I was in London and you were in Paris?"

McGill said, "I sang you to sleep. Over the phone."

McGill's mother was a voice teacher, and he'd been an apt student.

"Bob Seger," Patti told him.

"You'll Accomp'ny Me."

"Do you think you could do a light rock medley for me tonight?"

"Start with Rod Stewart?"

"You're the maestro."

Patti was asleep and breathing evenly before McGill got to his cover of Dylan's "Lay Lady Lay." He started to drift off moments later, counting his blessings. Only one niggling thought disturbed him. He hadn't seen Sweetie all day.

Where the heck had she been?

2

August 22 – August 31, 2011
Florida Avenue NW — Washington, D.C.

Sweetie just couldn't bring herself to do it in Vegas.

She had accepted Putnam Shady's proposal of marriage without hesitation, which was something of a surprise, though maybe it shouldn't have been. Ordinarily, deciding to make a commitment she held to be sacred and lifelong would have required a lengthy period of careful consideration. Then again, she'd never imagined that any man she might have married would have had a gun pointed at his head the day before he popped the question.

Not only had Putnam's life been threatened by Speaker Derek Geiger, Sweetie had been present to see it happen and, along with Jim McGill and Special Agents Kendry and Latz, she had thrown herself on Geiger. Putnam had done his part by losing the will to stand upright and falling to the floor.

That night she and Putnam had stayed awake at his townhouse, sitting close and holding hands. Sweetie had managed to spend part of that time thinking of Kenny McGill and offering silent prayers that he would recover his health and have a long and fulfilling life.

Uncharacteristically, though, the majority of her thoughts had focused on herself and Putnam. Geiger, in his final moments, might have killed either of them. Or Jim. Or one of the special agents. Latz had been wounded and rushed to the hospital.

Sweetie spared the time to pray for his recovery, too.

The thought of losing Jim McGill had shaken Sweetie to her core. She'd once stepped in front of a bullet meant for him. Jim was the keystone to both his marriage and his family. But unless he was killed outright, Sweetie was sure he would regain his strength and meet his every obligation.

If she had been killed, though … It was a strange thing to say of a grown man already on his way to becoming wealthy, but she wondered what would have become of Putnam. Not in terms of simple physical sustenance. He wouldn't miss any meals; he'd likely eat too many. That kind of overindulgence lay at the heart of her concern. Putnam had grown so much in the time she'd known him. He was still shrewd, sophisticated and even conniving, but now he was also levelheaded, dependable and showing signs of developing a moral center.

She worried all those virtues might slip away without her.

Attagirl, Margaret, she thought, pat yourself on the back.

Maybe you could leave just a little room for the rascal in Putnam to survive.

She wanted it to. He made her laugh. Softened some of her more rigid attitudes.

His company had made *her* a better person, too.

God, the thought that either of them might have been killed was reason to —

Say, "Yes," when Putnam asked, "Margaret, will you marry me?"

But she couldn't see doing it in Las Vegas. Yes, that was where they could get married without delay, but Sweetie believed that a good start was the most important part of any endeavor. It set the tone for everything that followed. She didn't want the tone of their lives together to be characterized by casinos, neon marquees and all-you-can-eat buffets.

Sweetie wanted a natural setting. That was what she told Putnam.

"Adam and Eve had a garden," he said. "Welborn Yates and Kira Fahey had a parklike setting. Things can still go amiss."

"Yes, they can, but be honest. Be the son of a famous handicapper." Which Putnam had told Sweetie was exactly what he was. "Would you like the odds of things going better after being married in Las Vegas or somewhere outdoors and pretty?"

"Outdoors and *beautiful*," he said. "No half measures."

"All right, beautiful. Can we narrow that down a little? Mountains or seaside?"

"Seaside and warm."

"Big or small wedding?"

Putnam said, "Small. You, me and the padre — and we frisk the padre."

Sweetie smiled. She'd have liked Jim McGill to be present. But you couldn't invite the president's henchman without inviting the president, and everywhere Patti went hordes of people went with her. Maybe Putnam would give in and allow a photographer to be present so they could send pictures to people.

Putnam saw she was thinking things over, and like any good prospective husband he made a preemptive concession.

"We can always throw a party when we get back to town," he said.

"I'd like that," Margaret told him.

He took matters one step further.

"I want to buy you an engagement ring, right away."

"I'd like that, too. Should we wait for the stores to open or go window shopping now?"

The sun was just coming up.

"Let's have breakfast first," Putnam said. "I'll cook."

Sweetie nodded. He was far better in the kitchen ... and the bedroom. She had the edge in the gym and on the street. They both had a lot to learn.

She said, "But let's settle on a location first. Somewhere warm near the water. California or Hawaii? The Caribbean?"

Putnam shook his head. "We met, got to know each other and fell in love right here on Florida Avenue. Why not go with what's worked so far?"

"I like that," Sweetie said.

They discussed a number of places in Florida and settled on Key West.

Third Street — Bloomington, Indiana

Sheryl Kimbrough was driving to her new job at Indiana University when her phone rang. She'd been hired to teach the lessons outlined in her book *Cutting Through the Bull-Puckey: Reporting Political News in the Age of Double-talk*. That Monday was the first day of classes. She pulled her car to the curb on East Third Street two blocks from campus.

Sheryl had taken her bachelor and master degrees from IU in journalism and political science respectively. She figured she'd done the equivalent of earning a doctorate by putting in ten years as the press secretary to the state's retiring senior United States senator, Charles Talbert.

A careful woman, she never carried on a phone conversation while driving.

Nine times out of ten, she simply let voicemail take the call.

Last night, however, Tal, as precious few were allowed to call the senator, had phoned to tell her to expect an important call from Neal Drummond, the chairman of the state's Republican Central Committee. Tal hadn't told her what Drummond wanted, but if he or any of his friends was looking for a press secretary, they would hear a polite but unshakable no thank you.

Sheryl was looking forward to starting a new life in academia. She liked the idea of teaching. Yes, she'd heard there were no politics pettier than those of a university, but having spent a decade in Washington, she refused to believe that. She looked forward to dealing with bright young minds that had yet to be calcified by ideology and greed.

If she could help create just one great journalist, one great statesman or woman and one great bar owner — because, after all, in Washington, you had to have a place to unwind — her labors would not be in vain.

Nah, she never went for that doing just one of something stuff.

She wanted to send swarms of young people to D.C. to knock the place on its ass.

Not that she'd expressed that opinion during her job interview.

She answered the call, "Chairman Drummond, a pleasure to speak with you, sir."

"Pleasure's all mine, Sheryl," the chairman's gruff country voice told her. "How're you and that sweet girl of yours?"

"I'm fine, sir, and Cassidy makes me more proud of her every day. Senator Talbert told me to expect your call. What can I do for you?"

"You can tell me how you'd like to elect the next president of the United States."

"I beg your pardon."

"Senator Talbert thinks highly of you, Sheryl. He put your name in nomination to be a Republican elector. The central committee took a look at your CV and liked what we saw. I imagine when we take a formal vote, we'll respect the senator's wish. All you have to do is say yes. Then you'll not only be a teacher at IU, it won't be long before you're a member of the Electoral College."

Sheryl Kimbrough was overwhelmed. She never expected to have such an honor. She felt tears well up in her eyes. Wouldn't that be something to tell Cassidy? To tell her students, if she could get to class on time.

"You there, Sheryl?" Drummond asked.

"I am, sir," she said, her voice husky, "and I'd be honored to be an elector."

"I know just how you feel. I'll be an elector for the fourth time this year, and every time it's a thrill. We are the people who actually elect the president. Hoo-wee, that's a feeling you don't forget. Well, I know you've got honest work to do now, so I'll just say we'll be sending you all the information you need to know. But if any old question comes to mind, you give me a call."

"I will, sir, and thank you very much."

Sheryl took a deep breath and pulled back into the flow of traffic.

Just before her phone rang again.

This time, she let it go to voicemail.

Hart Senate Office Building — Washington, D.C.

Senators John Wexford and Richard Bergen, the Democratic majority leader and his assistant, and representatives Marlene Berman and Diego Paz, the Democratic minority leader and her assistant, sat at the conference table in Wexford's office suite. Paz had the floor.

"My wife has a friend who works at GWU Hospital," he said.

"Mrs. Paz is a retired nurse and now works for the American Nurses Association," Representative Berman added.

"That's right," Paz said, "and her friend Barbara Marcos was part of the medical team treating Kenny McGill."

"How's he doing?" Senator Bergen asked.

Paz said, "Good. It's still early, but it looks like he'll be okay."

Wexford nodded, glad to hear good news.

"Anyway," Paz said, "Barbara Marcos confided something to Yolanda that she really shouldn't have; Yolanda told me, and she shouldn't have."

"Now, you're going to tell us," Wexford said.

"Yeah, but if it goes any farther, there's going to be a special election for my seat because Yolanda is going to have my ass," Paz said.

"Lucky for you we can't afford to lose anyone in the House," Bergen joked.

The minority party could never afford to lose a seat.

Berman told the assistant leader, "Don't keep the senators in suspense, Diego."

"You guys ever hear of something called mitral valve prolapse?" he asked. "No? Well, Patti Grant experienced it while under anesthesia at GWU Hospital for her bone marrow donation. There was a possibility she might have had a stroke or even died."

Wexford said, "Jesus!"

Bergen saw the subtext. "Wait a minute, Diego. You said Kenny McGill is doing okay. Do you mean that when the president experienced this condition the doctors still let her go through with the donation?"

"Jim McGill's call. Word is, he had to choose: risk the president or watch his boy die."

Both senators shuddered. Paz and Berman had, too, when first they heard of it.

The minority leader turned the focus back to politics.

She said, "The question is, gentlemen, what do we do now? We're not supposed to have this information, but we do. Do we back away from making Patricia Darden Grant our party's nominee to be president? Do we take a chance with her and hope she doesn't suffer a stroke or worse? Do we go through a normal primary election process? Do we kick ourselves if the president runs as the head of a new party and whips both us and the Republicans?"

Wexford looked bleakly at Paz.

"Diego, tell your wife she *really* has to keep these things to herself."

The White House Residence

Patricia Darden Grant was released from the hospital on the second day following her bone marrow donation to Kenny McGill only because a team of heart specialists would be on hand at the White House to keep resident physician Artemus Nicolaides company. Short of major surgery, they would be able to provide any sort of medical attention the president might need on site. If the situation rose to the point where hospitalization was required, well, the good woman had her own helicopter and a Marine flight crew parked out back.

Having made sure that Kenny was continuing to recuperate, and promising his son that he would visit him again later that day,

James J. McGill accompanied his wife to the residence. The fact that the First Couple wasn't in a working area of the White House didn't stop people from wanting some of their time.

Acting President Wyman asked if he might have some of Patti's time, if she felt up to receiving him, so he might tell her the details of the successful raid at Salvation's Path. Chief of Staff Galia Mindel also said she had important news to share with the president. Galia assumed if Patti was back in the building she was ready to talk. Special Agent Elspeth Kendry urgently requested a meeting with McGill.

All the above had been relayed through Nick. The White House physician shook his head.

"Madam President, I must insist that you rest — preferably sleep — for an hour before seeing anyone, and then limit yourself to thirty minutes of discussion."

Patti looked to McGill for a second opinion.

He backed up Nick.

"Very well," she said. "I'll be good. For now."

"I'm cleared to see Special Agent Kendry?" McGill asked Nick.

"Of course, but if I might see you privately for a moment …"

McGill nodded, uneasy now that Nick might have some disquieting information about Kenny. He tried to push the fear aside as he accompanied Patti to their bedroom, waited for her to change into pink cotton pajamas and get in bed. He pulled the covers up for her.

"You'll tell me whatever it is Nick has to say to you?" she asked.

"What, you want me to break doctor-patient confidentiality?"

"You're not his patient, I am."

"That's why you're president; just can't slip anything past you."

"You haven't answered my question."

"I'll tell you." He confirmed his promise with a kiss.

"I am kind of tired," Patti said.

"You want a song?"

"We have to be careful about that. It could be habit forming."

She settled for another kiss. McGill dimmed the lights and left.

Looking back from the doorway, he saw Patti was already asleep.

He found Nick waiting in the hallway. The White House physician asked, "The president is sleeping peacefully?"

"She is."

"Has she shared any complaints with you? Discomfort or pain, particularly in the area of her chest?"

"No, none of that."

"Would you tell me if she had, if she asked you not to?"

McGill said, "Anything you have a need to know, Nick, I'll make sure you do. Is there anything else?"

"Two things. You're due for your annual physical soon."

In the past, McGill had not always been prompt about attending to that obligation. Now, with both Patti and Kenny on the mend, he thought he'd better not give anyone cause to fret over him.

"I'll set up a date soon, and keep it."

"Good."

"I'm not looking pale, am I?" It was an old joke between the two of them.

Nick chose to ignore it this time. "You are looking tired, understandably. So it might be easier for you to accept the other thing I have to say to you."

"What's that?"

"For the immediate future," Nick said, "no activity for you and the president."

"Activity?"

"Do I need to be more … earthy?"

"No, you don't. A little smooch now and then is okay?"

"Most likely beneficial."

McGill asked if Nick had anything new on Kenny.

He didn't, so McGill went to his Hideaway and called for Elspeth Kendry.

Wondered what her sense of urgency was all about.

***

"Damon Todd has escaped from CIA custody," Elspeth Kendry

told McGill.

He blinked as if he hadn't heard her right. He'd been stretched out on the long leather sofa in his private White House retreat. He'd sat up as Elspeth entered. Or thought he had. Now he wondered if he was asleep and dreaming.

"Escaped?" McGill asked, not wanting to ask a female agent to pinch him.

See if he really was conscious.

"Yes, sir. I was notified as you and the president were on your way here. I thought it best to tell you personally."

Not share the news where Patti would hear it; that's what Elspeth was saying.

"Thank you for that. Do you have any details?"

She said she did and McGill told her to have a seat. She sat, almost as reluctantly as Celsus Crogher would have, McGill thought.

Elspeth told him, "From what the CIA was able to reconstruct, Dr. Todd and two other prisoners, Arn Crosby and Olin Anderson, also fled. A fourth inmate, Arlen Stanwick, was found dead at the security feature bordering the property."

"Security feature?" McGill asked. He was used to hearing government jargon substituted for plain English, but that was a new one. "Is that supposed to mean a fence or a wall?"

The special agent struggled to contain her disgust. "The CIA doesn't use anything that prosaic, sir. They put up something called a hot sheet, a synthetic fabric that conducts electricity. The way it was explained to me, it's something that can't be climbed and because the weave of the fabric varies in density from the ground to ten feet in height, from ten to twenty feet and twenty feet to thirty feet, the jolt you'll get from touching the thing varies, too. Touch it down low, you get knocked on your backside; middle range knocks you out; the upper range fries you."

"How about if you have something, an inanimate object, that can blast through it?"

Elspeth said, "It's supposed to stretch but not tear."

McGill detected a fly in the ointment. "Supposed to?"

"The fabric was cut, sir, by an edged tool."

"Not while it was hot though, right? It was cut after this guy Stanwick ran into or was thrown into the sheet. That did what, cause a need for the system to reset itself? And unless Mr. Stanwick was very small and the others were very strong, they didn't fling him twenty feet up the security feature."

"No, sir. Apparently the hot sheet doesn't have all the bugs worked out."

McGill tried to repress his anger by working out the escape in his mind.

"Getting to the barrier had to take some doing."

"The personnel who were supposed to prevent that have been killed."

Damn, McGill thought. The news kept getting worse.

"How long had Todd known these other two, Crosby and Anderson?"

"He didn't. He'd been transferred into their housing unit only the night before. We think he just fell into an escape plan that had been in the works."

McGill had to agree with that assessment, only …

"If Todd hadn't shown up," he said, "would Stanwick still have been the one to get electrocuted?"

Elspeth nodded. "That's the working assumption, sir."

"So why didn't the others use Todd instead, after he showed up? Personal enmity against Stanwick or something else?"

The frown on Elspeth's face showed she didn't have the answer.

But McGill thought he had a good guess. "What if the plan was to use Todd to short out the electrical system? Then he saw it coming and forced Stanwick into the sheet."

"Is Dr. Todd that smart and capable of being that ruthless?" Elspeth asked.

McGill nodded. He certainly was.

Then a jolt that felt electric hit McGill.

With Todd on the loose, he wasn't the only one in danger.

He told Elspeth, "I've got to get in touch with Chana Lochlan."

Having read the file on Todd, Elspeth knew whom he meant.

"Yes, sir, right away. Also, the FBI is hoping you can help them find Dr. Todd."

After her nap, a shower and a quick once over from Nick, Patti Grant received Acting-President Mather Wyman in the sitting room off her bedroom. She wore pearl gray sweats with the presidential seal on the shirt and fuzzy pink slippers. Wyman was impeccably dressed in a Brooks Brothers suit and looked every inch of what the American people might expect a president to be.

The thought didn't cross Patti's mind very often, but she wondered if, at some subliminal level, the electorate didn't miss having a man at the head of government. If she were to serve a second term, would that longing rise to the surface? Might a successor even campaign on that issue? *It's time to put a man back in the Oval Office.*

Didn't have to be a white guy. An African-American, a Latino or an Asian-American might make a case for himself. Mentally surveying the current political landscape, Patti couldn't think of anyone she'd rather have succeed her than Mather Wyman.

Well, whatever would happen would happen.

Her job was simply to make sure she was a damn hard act to follow.

"You're looking very impressive, Mr. Acting-President," Patti said.

"For an old man who hasn't gotten much sleep lately? Thank you, Madam President."

Patti smiled and gestured Wyman to sit in an armchair.

She sat opposite him, tempted to curl her feet under her, but keeping them on the floor.

Mather Wyman was giving her a look of blunt appraisal.

Patti was sure none of her doctors, certainly not Nick, would have blabbed about her episode of mitral valve prolapse. Jim wouldn't have told even Sweetie without her permission. So —

"Please pardon me, Madam President," Wyman said, "but when you spent an extra day in the hospital, I had a staffer contact the Surgeon General's office and ask, without specific reference to you, what might extend a bone marrow donor's time as an inpatient."

Patti nodded, an appropriate and thoughtful approach for a man who might wonder when the boss would return.

"What did you find out, Mather?"

"I was told a complication from anesthesia would be the most likely cause."

"Smart people in the Surgeon General's office."

"I didn't want to pry, but I plan to make a statement about the assault on the Salvation's Path property today, and I feel certain that I'll be asked how you feel about the matter and when you will resume office."

Patti thought Wyman had assessed the situation precisely. Which was more than she had done. She didn't think she was impaired in any permanent way, but for the moment she felt as though … she had lost a step, to use a sports metaphor. Her energy was low. She was able to focus on the moment, for the most part, but looking ahead to see what might come next was harder.

Her mind kept returning to what Jim had told her last night.

Kenny had said he could feel her inside him.

For a woman unable to have her own children …

"Madam President, are you all right?"

She looked up and saw Mather standing in front of her, extending his handkerchief to her. She took it and dried her eyes. To reassure Mather, she told him what had given rise to her emotions.

Wyman returned to his seat and said, "What a wonderful thing to hear. I can see how that would make you very happy."

"It does." She dabbed her eyes again. "I'll try to pay closer attention now. What can you tell me about Burke Godfrey? Where is he being held?"

"At Walter Reed in a guarded room."

"What's his condition?"

"Concussion and headaches. The doctors say he needs close observation."

"Please tell me how the assault went," Patti said. "Were there any deaths or injuries?"

"No deaths, I'm happy to say. One man broke his back when he fell off the roof of building. The prognosis is he'll be paralyzed from the waist down."

"How did that happen?" Patti asked.

Wyman told her of the military's use of low-flying fighter jets to create prolonged and intense sonic booms. The man who fell was a sniper who had covered his ears to protect himself and lost his balance, according to a witness, another would-be sniper.

"Did Godfrey's men shoot at military personnel?"

Mather Wyman smiled. "Not a round, Madam President."

He told her about Ellie Booker having taken Godfrey hostage.

"I talked to her myself when I called to give Godfrey his last-chance warning. I relayed Ms. Booker's message to Admiral Dexter. He talked to the SEALs' commanding officer. They took my word that I felt Ms. Booker was telling the truth. They changed their plans on the spot, deciding to go in, grab Godfrey and get back out without engaging anyone else if possible. That's exactly what they did, using the tunnels Godfrey had dug for his own purposes. They brought Ms. Booker out along with them. Once that was accomplished, they reported the sonic boom attack was so intimidating that no one in the compound offered the least resistance."

Patti smiled and offered brief applause. "Bravo, Mather, bravo."

"Thank you, Madam President. After we had Godfrey, we photographed him standing between two SEALs, with their faces concealed, of course. Then we restored power to the compound and broadcast the image. When the people inside saw we had Godfrey, they surrendered. We confiscated their arms and transported them to the disciplinary barracks at Fort Leavenworth."

"Maximum security," Patti said, "but a hospital room for Godfrey?"

Patti thought she might have done things the other way

around.

"Yes, ma'am," Wyman said. "I can have Godfrey sent to Leavenworth, too, if you like. My thought was to have him closer to hand, but if you disagree ..."

"No, no, Mather," she said. "You've handled the situation brilliantly. I'm not going to second-guess you now."

She might have, if she'd felt more certain of her mental acuity. That would have to wait for the moment.

"Please give everyone involved in our efforts my compliments on a job well done."

Mather Wyman beamed. "I will, Madam President."

"When you make your announcement to the nation, please say that I completely support your decisions and the execution of them by our armed forces. You may say that I will make a statement about my return to office in the near future, and the nation should rest assured that it is in good hands with you in the Oval Office until I return."

Now, Wyman got emotional. "Thank you, Madam President. There is one other issue I feel compelled to discuss with you."

"What's that, Mather?"

"The charges to be filed against Burke Godfrey and his leadership at Salvation's Path."

The president looked puzzled. "He'll be charged with the murder of Andrew Hudson Grant."

"Yes, of course. I meant in addition to that, for his actions at Salvation's Path."

Patti nodded. She should have thought of that. "What did you and the attorney general decide?"

"We agreed that only one charge is appropriate: treason."

Before Patti could respond, there was a knock at the door.

Nick stepped into the room, telling the president she needed to rest now.

30,000 Feet over the North Atlantic

Sir Hollis Rudd asked Welborn Yates, "Do you think you could fly this bird?"

The bird in question was a Gulstream G550 that belonged to Sir Hollis. It was carrying the newlywed Mr. and Mrs. Welborn Yates back to the United States from Barcelona on the third day of what was supposed to be a two-week honeymoon. The duration of that nuptial holiday was reinforced by a presidential order; it was not supposed to be cut short.

Welborn could, conceivably, face a court-martial for disobedience.

If the president could be bothered with such a trifle.

Once Mather Wyman had launched the attack on Salvation's Path, the news spread around the world, even to El Mansou, Spain where Welborn and Kira saw a report on the television in a café. When another bulletin reported that President Patricia Darden Grant had remained in the hospital an extra day, without explanation, after making a bone marrow donation, Welborn and Kira started packing.

Kira asked, "What's the fastest way to get home?"

Flying commercial was not the answer. Welborn said, "I'll call my father."

Sir Robert Reed had lent the young couple the use of his villa in Catalonia. He knew everyone in the British community there. Among them was the billionaire entrepreneur Sir Hollis Rudd. Sir Hollis happened to be leaving for New York the next day and was only too happy to let Welborn and Kira accompany him on his executive jet.

After making Rudd's acquaintance and thanking him for his hospitality, Kira took him up on his offer to "kip a bit" in his private cabin. The men sipped soft drinks and Rudd asked Welborn about his military career, learning with great interest that Welborn had been a fighter pilot.

Answering Rudd's question about flying his bird, Welborn said, "I might need a minute or two to familiarize myself with the controls but, yes, I'm sure I could."

Rudd said, "I can give you a run-through. I'm rated to fly the G550."

Of course, he was, Welborn thought. First generation wealth was hands on.

Rudd said, "I asked because, although you and Kira have been very gracious, I feel a sense of urgency in the two of you. If I'm not mistaken, you'd both like to be home now. I thought you might feel better if you took matters into your own hands, so to speak. Fly this bird from the left-hand seat. With me as your copilot."

Welborn got the feeling he'd just stepped into a job interview, but he didn't care. He felt almost as excited as he had the first night in Spain. When Kira had made sure their honeymoon exceeded expectations.

The executive jet was a far cry from an F-22 but it would be great to fly again.

"I'd like that very much," he told Rudd.

Welborn got goosebumps when Rudd added, "I think we have sufficient fuel to fly full throttle."

The Hay-Adams Hotel, Washington, D.C.

Reynard Dix, the chairman of the Republican National Committee, had decided to err on the side of caution and move the party's offices out of the presidential suite when Patti Grant left the party. Despite the urgings of party stalwarts to stay — the hard cases saying the GOP was entitled to stay for a full term even if the turncoat had abandoned them — Dix didn't want any barbs thrown their way over a symbolic issue. They had bigger fish to fry.

Besides, moving into the Federal Suite wasn't exactly slumming it.

Dix was joined that day by House Majority Leader Peter Profitt of North Carolina and Senator Howard Hurlbert of Mississippi, the first declared candidate for the GOP nomination to be president.

He'd announced the day Patti Grant was donating her bone marrow cells.

In jest, Dix, a Georgian, rapped his knuckles on the table around which they sat and said, "I declare this meeting of the Sons of the Confederacy open."

Profitt, who was all business and smiled only when his job required it, replied, "Sorry, I don't qualify. My family didn't arrive in this country until fifty years after the close of the Civil War."

One of the things that kept Profitt from cracking even the slightest of jokes or saying anything that might be considered remotely incriminating was the warning he'd received from his father upon deciding to go into politics.

"Never say anything you wouldn't want to repeat in front of a grand jury or your mother's garden club."

Keeping that thought in mind, Profitt spoke as if his every utterance was being recorded by some hostile cabal.

Howard Hurlbert was far less inhibited. He laughed at Profitt.

"You were a late arrival because you slick British fellas down in Trinidad got rid of slavery in the 1830s but you made do with *indentured* help you brought in right up into the twentieth century. When that game was up, *that's* when your family and all its money came to America."

Hurlbert had his facts exactly right. That told Profitt he had somebody competent doing opposition research for him already. Must be his wife, Bettina, or his chief of staff, Bobby Beckley, pushing the cause forward, Profitt thought, because the senator just didn't work that hard.

"Now, now, Howard," Dix said. "I was just joking about the Stars and Bars, and I'm sure Peter was just keeping the record straight, didn't intend any offense."

Profitt said, "I also don't intend to run for president so Howard can turn his oppo research efforts elsewhere."

"You don't?" Hurlbert asked, not sure if he could believe his House colleague.

"I don't, I won't, nobody can make me."

Hurlbert seemed relieved, but Dix brought up the obvious question.

"You do intend to become the next speaker, don't you?"

With the death of Derek Geiger, the most powerful job in Congress lay vacant.

"I'm leaning that way, but I haven't made up my mind."

"Why not?" Hurlbert asked.

He wasn't one to ignore a prize that dangled in front of him, free for the taking.

Profitt said, "What's going to happen the moment a new Speaker takes the gavel?"

"We're going to get to the bottom of how Derek Geiger died," Hurlbert said.

"Exactly," Profitt replied. "And if we don't like the direction in which that inquiry is heading, we'll have to impeach the testimony of two Secret Service special agents, explain how it was that Speaker Geiger came to be at a wedding to which he had no legitimate invitation and …"

"And what?" Dix asked.

Profitt sighed. "And it's been whispered in the House that Harlo Geiger had dirt on the speaker that she intended to use against him in her divorce proceedings. If we were to go after the other side in any Congressional investigation, I'm sure that dirt would come out. That whole circus makes the job less appealing than it ordinarily would be. Thinking about things now, I'd have to say my interest is no greater than fifty-fifty."

Hurlbert said, "Without a Republican Speaker, George Mossman becomes the second in line for the presidency."

Mossman, the senior senator from Hawaii, was the president pro tem of the senate.

Couldn't fool Howard, Profitt thought.

"The party's a mess," he said. "The president leaves, the speaker dies …"

And fools run for the White House, Dix thought, making sure he didn't look at Hurlbert. He thought it might be time to update his résumé. Maybe he could speak with Profitt privately. As Hurlbert had pointed out, Profitt's family knew when it was time to find greener pastures.

That was when the House majority leader showed just how smart he was.

He said, "You know, there is one way we could solve most of our troubles at a stroke."

"How?" Dix asked, uncertainty in his eyes.

"Well, there is an eminent Republican the party could draft to be president," Profitt said.

"Draft?" Hurlbert almost choked on the word.

He had no doubt that bastard Profitt didn't mean him.

"Who?" Dix asked, thinking he knew but wanting to hear it from Profitt first.

"Mather Wyman. He's still a Republican, isn't he? He's been on a winning presidential ticket. He has White House experience. He just captured Burke Godfrey without losing a man."

Senator Howard Hurlbert got to his feet, his face red.

"Burke Godfrey is a friend of mine, goddamnit! He, Doak Langdon and I wrote the Support of Motherhood Act together."

Profitt told him, "As I recall, that piece of proposed legislation failed, and the last poll I saw said that seventy-seven percent of the American public approved of Acting President Wyman's actions in Richmond."

"I won't listen to another word of this," Hurlbert said.

A promise kept, he walked out.

Dix looked across the table at Profitt.

"Do you think Wyman would accept a draft?" he asked.

"We won't know unless we ask. What I'm sure of is if we run Howard Hurlbert or anyone like him against Patti Grant, we'll lose."

"I've heard rumors the president isn't well. Something happened to her when she was in the hospital for that bone marrow donation."

Profitt bobbed his head. "I've heard that, too, but I wouldn't bet against Patti Grant if she lay in her grave with a stake through her heart."

The party chairman laughed nervously. "I don't think I would either. But what about the twenty-three percent of the people who hate what happened in Richmond? They're our base."

The majority leader said, "Our party has been moving to the right for thirty years or more. Seems to me it's time to tack to the center. Campaign from there and then *govern* from the right. I seem to remember Patti Grant's predecessor winning two elections that way."

"So do I," Dix said. "Who do you think should make the first approach to Wyman?"

Profitt placed a hand over his heart.

"Well, I believe I am the ranking Republican in Congress."

Dix smiled. "Yes, Mr. Majority Leader, you are. You'll let me know when you make your move? If the acting president were to accept, I'd have to forestall others from getting into the race. It would be best if we could keep too many people's feelings from getting hurt."

Other than Howard Hurlbert's, he meant.

"Of course," Profitt told Dix.

They shook hands and the majority leader departed, feeling he had played things just right. He was a senior member of his party selflessly looking out for the GOP's best interests. If Mather Wyman were to choose him to be his vice president, so be it.

Charlottesville, Virginia

Crosby and Anderson had a simple plan for Damon Todd after the three of them escaped from the Funny Farm: They would kill him the minute he stopped being useful. If it turned out he was bullshitting them about having a safe house nearby he'd become roadkill. Fling him in front of an eighteen-wheeler doing eighty and watch him become a stain on the blacktop.

He wouldn't be the first guy they'd done in that way.

So they were taken aback when Todd told them, "The first thing we need to do is steal a truck."

"What for?" Anderson asked.

He'd started to wonder if the little fuck was some kind of mind-dreader.

"Transportation," Todd said, waiting to see if his companions could grasp the concept. Feeling they were keeping up with him, he added, "We'll also need to keep the truck driver alive and un-marred."

Anderson lost traction on Todd's last three words.

"No beating the shit out of him," Crosby explained. "Or killing him."

"Exactly," Todd said.

"We're going to kidnap someone and we're *not* going to kill him? We're not even going to muss his hair, so he can look neat when he goes home to his old lady?" Anderson asked.

"That's right," Todd said.

"You have a reason for doing things that way?" Crosby asked.

"I do. You'll like it when you see how it works."

Crosby shrugged; Anderson went along grudgingly. If they had to kill a trucker along with Todd, that was no big deal. Being in the wrong place at the wrong time was always a capital offense for everyone.

Todd had one more detail to share. "You will have to intimidate the driver, get him to do as he's told until we get where we're going and I can take over."

"Yeah, about that," Crosby said, "just where is this nearby safe house?"

"Charlottesville," he said.

Virginia wasn't a big state and its major college town was reasonably close. Crosby walked point keeping to woodlands; Anderson walked drag to keep Todd from trying to ditch them. They double-timed it and took little more than an hour to find a truck-stop and kidnap a driver returning to his rig from a trip to the men's room.

The driver was a bearded man who had to go at least two hundred and fifty pounds, but Crosby and Anderson manipulated him like he was a toddler learning to take his first steps. They got him into his cab and behind the wheel in a matter of seconds. All three of the driver's unscheduled passengers sat in the seat behind the driver where they'd be unlikely to be seen by other motorists.

Anderson controlled the driver with a grip that had a thumb on his cervical spine, an index finger on a carotid artery and the remaining three fingers positioned around the driver's windpipe. Crosby saw Todd studying his partner's technique.

"No harder than playing a B-major chord on the guitar," he told Todd.

The instrument under Anderson's hand drove exactly how and where he was told. He parked the truck behind a home improvement store on Woodbrook Drive in Charlottesville. Anderson finally let go of the driver's neck, but grabbed a hank of hair with his other hand. Anderson shook some feeling back in his strangulation hand as the driver found his voice.

"Please don't kill me, I'm —"

Todd leaned forward, put his head close to the driver.

"I don't want to know about your life quite yet," he said in a soothing voice, "but we will get to that. If you do as you're told, you'll not only live, you'll be on your way to wherever you were going within a few hours. Do you believe me?"

"I want to," he said, trying not to whimper.

"Good. That's an honest answer and a smart one. Stay that way and you'll live, I promise you."

Crosby and Anderson spared each other a glance. They both admired Todd's technique. But they hadn't promised anything to anybody, except each other.

"What do you want me to do?" the driver asked.

Having accepted in some measure that he had a chance to live, he wanted to be helpful.

Todd told him, "Your rig wouldn't look right where my friends and I need to go. So the fellow holding your hair is going to stay with you. He's the testy sort, short-tempered, given to spasms of violence. Just sit still and be silent and you'll be all right. My other friend and I will be back within an hour. We'll all go for a short ride in a car. Within two more hours, you'll be back on the road following your normal routine. Can you manage that?"

The driver wanted to nod, but Anderson's grip on his hair was too tight.

"Yeah, I can do that."

"Good." Todd turned to Crosby. "Shall we go?"

Crosby looked at Todd, then shared a silent exchange with Anderson.

Both of them thinking Todd had them arm-barred, proned and at his fucking mercy.

Metaphorically, yeah. But easier, even, than they'd grabbed the trucker.

Unless they wanted to kill him right now. Having seen what he'd already accomplished, getting them this far, they didn't. It would be to their advantage to do it later, if the prick didn't outsmart them.

Crosby said to Todd, "Well, yeah, we better, if we're going to keep to your schedule."

He opened the cab's door.

Before leaving, Todd told Anderson, "Be nice."

Todd and Crosby were back in fifty-five minutes, Crosby driving a late model Range Rover Evoque, shiny and black. Anderson wanted to keep on disliking Todd, and he succeeded, but he couldn't contain a growing respect for the guy. There had been missions he and Crosby had been on where someone as smart as Todd would have come in damn handy.

Crosby lowered his window and gestured to Anderson to bring the driver to the Rover. The man was nervous being transferred to a new vehicle, but he didn't do anything stupid and Anderson managed to get them both into the back seat without any problems.

Crosby said, "You're going to like this, my friend."

"Me?" the driver asked.

"Yeah, you, too." Crosby's voice was full of good humor.

The driver relaxed. Anderson got a bit of a grump on. Things were going too damn well. It upset his fundamentally pessimistic worldview. Some bad shit *had* to happen soon.

If it didn't, how was he supposed to have any fun?

The big house sat on one hundred and seventy acres of wooded land. It was a white two-story Colonial with a horseshoe drive-way. Of the four men in the Rover, only Todd had ever stayed in any home approaching the grandeur of this one, and even he had never owned anything so nice.

He had a key to the front door, though, and he opened it to the others.

Inside, sitting in the lotus position before a fireplace burning a blue gas flame, was Fletcher Penrose, a gray-haired man wearing white silk pajamas. He was oblivious to the strangers who entered his home. His silence and immobility scared the trucker; Anderson put his hand on the trucker's neck.

Lightly, Todd was pleased to see.

Even better, that was enough to calm the fellow.

Todd said, "There's no need to feel alarmed, Mr. … You may tell me your name now."

"Lydell Martin," he said turning to look at Todd.

"The man you see in front of you, Mr. Martin, was once a bright but underachieving graduate school student. After work-ing with me, he learned how to apply himself. To want to succeed. Now, he teaches both economics and computer science at the uni-versity nearby. He's a renowned academic and a highly successful day-trader in stocks or other instruments. He owns this house, the car we arrived in and many other things. He's single, but he enjoys the company of a number of accomplished women, without com-mitting to any of them. Do you have any questions, Mr. Martin?"

"Is he alive?"

Todd chuckled. "Very sensible. All the riches in the world aren't worth a damn, if you can't enjoy them. Go ahead. Look at his face. See if he looks alive to you. Touch him, gently, if you want. See if he's still warm."

Martin took advantage of doing just those things.

Anderson paid particular attention to him as he did.

"He's alive all right. So what do you have planned for me?"

"Do you like to hunt, Mr. Martin? Are you any good at it?"

The trucker nodded. "I like to go out in deer season. I get my share."

"How would you like to hunt for opportunities to improve your life and be even better at it than you are at killing deer? I don't know if you'll ever be able to buy a place like this, but I guarantee your life will improve substantially."

Now, things seemed to be going too well to Martin, too.

"You ain't the devil, are you?"

Todd laughed. Even Crosby and Anderson grinned.

"No, I don't want your soul or anything else, except your friendship. Ninety-nine percent of your life will remain yours. You won't even remember anything that happened tonight. But sometime in the future I might call on you, and then you'll do everything I ask of you."

If only Todd had been present, Martin might have tried to squirm out of any deal. With Crosby and Anderson on hand, the trucker understood that killing him was still an option. There was only one thing for him to say.

"Sign me up."

Todd administered an injection of ketamine-hydrochloride to Martin. Fletcher Penrose, like all of Todd's *friends* had firm instructions to keep a supply on hand at all times. The accepted use for Special K, as it was known on the street, was as an anesthetic, but Todd had found it to be ever so useful in hypnosis.

He took the trucker deep into a K-hole, a state likened to an out-of-body experience, and learned his most secret longings and instructed him as to the best psychological approaches for achieving his goals. Martin was told to forget everything that had happened to him after arriving at the truck-stop. He would tell anyone who asked that after he got back on the road he started to feel dizzy so he pulled off to sleep. He would pass any physical he was asked to take and the episode would be passed off as a one-time thing. He would go about his life with a brighter attitude and fresh insights. His relationship with his wife and children would improve and …

The only thing he had to remember from that night was a phrase that would place him entirely under the control of Damon Todd.

Crosby came back to Fletcher Penrose's house after getting Martin back on the road and saw Todd was working on Penrose. The professor was talking back, but clearly not in a conscious manner. He told Todd he had no complaints; he had everything he'd ever wanted.

Anderson had been watching, but he broke off to join Crosby.

In a soft voice, looking back at Todd, Anderson said, "This guy is fucking spooky. You really let that damn trucker go?"

"Sure did. Sucker looked like he had his brain washed, dried and permanent pressed to me. He'll check in with the story Todd gave him; he doesn't know shit about you and me. We just fucking vanished."

"Yeah, if everything works right." Anderson couldn't embrace optimism no matter what.

Dropping his voice further, Crosby said, "We could kill both those guys in ten seconds. Take whatever money's in the house and be gone. Is that what you want?"

"That's what I *should* want," Anderson responded. "But, as usual, that smartass has a better idea. He says he has *friends* all across the country. We should just tell him where we want to go and he'll set us up. All these people, he says, will be as happy to help us as this guy here is."

Crosby said, "That's damn impressive. What does he want to do?"

"Stay right here. The professor has a smaller house out in the woods, only two bedrooms, but it's almost right on the James River and we're real close to the Shenandoah National Forest."

Crosby said, "Lots of wilderness. Guys like you and me could hide out a long time."

"Yeah, and there's one last thing."

"What?"

"Todd's got a job for us."

"That being?" Crosby asked.

"He wants us to kill someone for him, only he says it won't be easy."

Crosby grinned. "That'd make it a mission."

"It would," Anderson said, "but he had me at kill someone."

Casa Marina, Key West, Florida

Carina Linberg sailed her fifty foot Hunter, *Irish Grace*, solo from Newport, Rhode Island to Key West. The vessel had been purchased with the money she had received for listening to a pitch from a Hollywood producer. He'd told Carina he wanted to make a movie of her autobiography, *Woman in Command*, the story of a female Air Force bomber pilot and the political-sexual struggles she had faced. He'd pay her a million dollars just to hear him out. Before the producer could get so much as one word into the substance of his pitch, she told him he had to put every detail of the proposed deal in writing, sit down with her lawyer, and put the million dollars she'd get for listening to him into an escrow account.

The producer said, "Talk like that makes me hot."

"Start a phone-sex company for masochists," she told him.

The guy loved that, too. He followed through on the idea, using a front company.

After the producer had jumped through the specified hoops and her lawyer told Carina the money was hers as soon as she listened to what the man had to say, they took a meeting at the

Grille in Clarke Cooke House, Newport. She listened earnestly to what the producer had to say. The idea of someone making a smart movie from her book did have its appeal, but in the end she had to say no.

Carina wanted final approval for both the script and casting.

The producer said he couldn't do that. Those decisions were the perquisites of the director.

"As you envision things," Carina asked, "would the director be a man?"

The producer said yes. He said the man he had in mind was bankable.

Carina thanked him for his interest but said she'd never again let any man make important decisions regarding any aspect of her life. She might have agreed to working with a female director who had a collaborative attitude, but she saw no sense in giving the producer false hope and kept that to herself.

To his credit, the producer was gracious in defeat. He wished her well and said he hoped they might meet again under happier circumstances. Better yet, word never got back to Carina that the producer had bad-mouthed her in any way.

Almost made her wish … nah, no point wishing for the fall of Hollywood's *auteur* system.

The Pentagon would become a matriarchy first.

So Carina used the million dollars she was sure had been intended as a down payment on her movie deal and bought her boat. She took two years of sailing lessons from a master female mariner who wanted to become her lover and was also sent away disappointed. When Carina's contract with WorldWide News came up for renewal, she put that off, too.

She'd been a special consultant on issues of women in the military.

And was oh so bored with all that. She wanted to move on, not be trapped by her past. *Woman in Command* was her version of the adultery charge that had been brought against her by the Air Force. She'd had an affair with Navy Captain Dexter Cowan. She'd told the investigating officer, Lieutenant Welborn Yates, that Cowan had told her he was single. But Cowan had said he'd told Carina he was married but separated from his wife. It was a classic case of he said, she said. After Captain Cowan had died in a car wreck, the matter of a court martial for Colonel Linberg was dropped in the outgoing trash.

So was any chance for her career advancement.

She resigned her commission, was honorably discharged, and signed a three-year deal with WWN that left her with seven-figure assets, but hadn't made her appreciably happier. She was single, getting older — not that most people would notice — and at a loss about what she wanted to do next.

She decided to take a month off, August being a good time to do that. With the end of the month fast approaching, she got her lawyer to buy her another month of grace with the network. She set off alone on a voyage to Key West. She'd never gone farther than Charleston, South Carolina before, but she felt confident she could make it to the far point of Florida.

She'd keep an eye out for hurricanes, oil tankers and any Somali pirates who might have drifted off course, and she'd be fine. One thing did take her by surprise during the voyage: a story in the on-line edition of the *Washington Post* about the death of Speaker Derek Geiger at the official residence of Vice President Mather Wyman during the wedding of Kira Fahey and Captain Welborn Yates.

Sonofabitch, she thought, little Welborn had grown up, got married and been promoted. She'd bet he would become a major the day after Patti Grant's second term began, assuming she got reelected.

Carina knew Welborn had a barely restrained case of the hots for her when he was investigating the adultery charge against her. She'd felt more than a little attracted to him as well, despite their difference in age. But she'd felt certain Welborn was the type of Boy Scout who, had he slept with her, would have turned himself in because he felt guilty.

She hadn't thought she could beat two charges: adultery and

subverting an investigation.

But she had two nights alone on the ocean dreaming of Welborn.

Seven days out of Newport, she pulled into the Waldorf Astoria resort in Key West, Casa Marina.

Determined to think of the future not the past.

McGill's Hideaway — The White House

Before Elspeth Kendry left, McGill asked her to send for Deke Ky and Leo Levy. He intended to talk with the two people most immediately responsible for his personal well being before he spoke with the FBI about hunting down Damon Todd and friends. He was on the phone with Edwina Byington when the two of them appeared in his hideaway. He gestured to them to sit, and they did so reluctantly.

It was as if they thought it best to be on their feet and on their guard even in the White House, which was protected by a legion of uniformed Secret Service agents and Marines. Maybe Deke and Leo were right, McGill thought. Attitude might count for more than multitudes. Better safe than sorry was now more than ever the operative state of mind.

McGill asked Edwina, "Are you handling the acting president's schedule, if that's not being too nosy?"

"It might be," Edwina said, meaning it, "but I'll go out on a limb for you. Yes, I am."

McGill thanked her and said, "Will you ask him if I might have a minute or two of his time? A phone call will be fine, if that's all he can spare."

Edwina said she'd make the request at the first opportunity.

McGill thanked her again and hung up. He turned to Deke and Leo.

"Did Elspeth inform you guys about Damon Todd's escape before she talked to me?"

They nodded.

McGill said, "And?"

"Pulling a jailbreak on the CIA is a pretty good trick," Leo said.

Deke said, "Scary, if you're the kind of person who gets scared."

"Something nobody here would ever admit to," McGill said.

Deke said, "Not part of my job description."

"I *like* riding someone's bumper at two hundred miles per hour," Leo told McGill.

"But *you're* the one who's married to the president," Deke said.

"The one with three kids," Leo added.

At the mention of his children, the word *hostages* leapt to McGill's mind.

The expression on his face was enough for Deke to hold up a hand. "The Secret Service doesn't overlook the obvious. SAC Crogher is working up new protection for everybody."

"Including me?" McGill asked.

Deke said, "Sure. We see someone whose looks we don't like, we now have permission to *snarl* at them."

Leo grinned at the joke. McGill saw the larger truth behind it.

He said to Deke, "Celsus knows he can't overtly force a platoon of agents on me. So what's he going to do, reinforce Elspeth's outer ring?"

Deke sat mute. He wasn't going to blab.

Leo shrugged. He wasn't privy to Secret Service plans.

Someone else might be, though, and McGill asked, "Deke, did Mather Wyman sign off on whatever it is Celsus has in mind?"

Deke nodded.

Well, wasn't that a kick in the ass? There was a new *de facto* president in the White House and he didn't have McGill's back. No, that wasn't quite right. Wyman had his back far more oppressively than McGill ever would have wanted.

Unfortunately for him, he couldn't in good conscience ask Patti to rap Wyman's knuckles. She had to focus on getting better, just like Kenny. So he'd have to sit tight for a while. Let himself be boxed in. Help the FBI catch Todd, if he could.

God, he hated the situation already.

There was only one thing to do: talk to Sweetie.

Maybe the two of them could … he saw Deke and Leo staring at him.

Trying to read his mind. See what sort of plan he might be hatching.

Maybe tattle on him?

The idea caught him by surprise. Rubbed him the wrong way, too.

McGill asked, "You guys remember our agreement, right? Nothing I do or say gets back to SAC Crogher or anyone else."

Leo looked very uncomfortable; Deke looked the other way. It was plain they'd received other orders. Crogher must have laid down the law to Deke and … McGill had no idea who headed up the White House Transportation Agency, Leo's direct employer, but an order from Wyman would bring Leo's complicity.

Not hearing an answer, much less a satisfactory one, McGill got to his feet, his temper also rising, and said, "Fine, I'll ask to have both of you reassigned immediately. You're no longer working for me. Not if you can't keep our agreement."

Deke only narrowed his eyes. Leo said, "Sumbitch."

They both stood and looked McGill in the eye.

He repeated, "We had a *deal*. If you can't keep it, for whatever reason, we're done. It was a pleasure working with you. If you need letters of reference, I'll be happy to provide them."

McGill sounded anything but happy. He opened the door for Deke and Leo.

Before they could leave, McGill told them "I'll need a new driver to visit my son at the hospital this afternoon. If Elspeth wants to ride along with me, that's fine." Then he had one last point to make, emphatically. "But you tell SAC Crogher and *Acting* President Wyman that Elspeth is the only Secret Service protection I'll accept. If they have any objections, remind them that I do *not* work for them. I am *not* subject to their wishes. I —" McGill bit his tongue.

He'd promised Patti at the start of her presidency he would not embarrass her.

If he let his temper burn any hotter, he might go too far.

He stood aside so Deke and Leo could leave. He felt as if he'd just discarded two friends.

He got Edwina on the phone and canceled his request to speak with Mather Wyman.

He sat alone in his hideaway, feeling as if he was the one who needed to make a jailbreak.

Galia Mindel caught McGill before he could go anywhere, nabbed him in his hideaway.

"I'd like you to repay the favor you owe me," she said.

McGill took a deep breath. He still hadn't completely calmed down.

"Would you like a light drink or snack, Galia?" he asked. "You wouldn't believe the service in this place."

He was stalling, trying to collect himself and figure out what the chief of staff wanted. There was no question that he would do whatever it was she asked. He owed her, and he paid his debts.

"Thank you, no. What I'd like you to do is …" She gave him a once over. "Are you all right, Mr. McGill?"

He saw no reason to evade. "I had a difference of opinion with SAC Crogher and indirectly with the acting president. I dismissed my personal bodyguard and driver."

Galia took that in and started to process what the consequences might be, but she tabled the matter for later consideration. She had to focus on her issues first.

"I'd like you, sir, to take a quick shower, put on a suit and talk to the press."

"The White House press corps?"

"That's the only one we allow in."

For most of his wife's first term, McGill had kept a deliberately low profile. He attended state social functions with Patti and got good reviews for looking spiffy when he put on a tuxedo, but the only time he'd done a press conference was shortly after the inauguration when he'd accepted the necessity to formally introduce himself to the American public.

"You cleared this with Mather Wyman?" he asked.

"I cleared it with the president and the acting president." Galia's tone told him he should have known better than to ask.

"What would you like me to say?" McGill asked.

He didn't want to be coached and would refuse to use canned responses, but knowing a general direction would be helpful.

"I'd like you to reassure the nation that the president is resting comfortably, is on the mend and will return to office."

"Isn't that something Nick should handle?"

Galia frowned. She was expecting a greater degree of cooperation.

"Dr. Nicolaides will precede you in speaking to the press. What I hope you will provide is a more personal assessment as the president's ..." Galia almost said henchman but she caught herself. "Husband."

McGill thought about that, apparently a moment too long.

"Are you going to repay my favor or not?" Galia asked.

He did owe her, and not knowing if someday he might need another favor from the chief of staff, McGill said, "What color suit would you like me to wear?"

McGill wore a navy blue suit and a marigold tie. The suit was sober but not funereal; the tie evinced a note of optimism. Galia had selected both items of clothing from his closet. In the White House press room, he stood to one side as Nick gave a concise unemotional recitation of Patti's condition. The plan, simply, was to give the public a full disclosure of what had happened to the president at GWU hospital.

Nick finished by saying he felt the president's prognosis was good.

He refused to take any questions, saying that going beyond what he'd already said would violate doctor-patient confidentiality.

That ethical shield was allowed to remain in place because

McGill stepped forward and shook Nick's hand and took his place at the lectern. Press Secretary Aggie Wu stood to McGill's right. She'd pick out the newsies who would be allowed to ask questions, and smack anyone who forgot his or her manners.

McGill began, "The American people deserve to know the condition of their president's health. That's what my wife tells me. If anyone other than Patricia Darden Grant were president, I would feel the same way. As her husband, though, I'm somewhat uncomfortable discussing what feels to me like a family matter.

"I'm sure those of you who have experienced medical crises in your own families will understand what I'm saying. If you're caught in the middle of a life-or-death situation, the last thing you need or want is someone looking over your shoulder.

"That's an entirely reasonable position to take, if you're a private citizen. When you're the president, though, the only things that outnumber your powers and perks are your obligations to the people who put you in office ... and to those who wish you'd just go away."

The newsies gave McGill a laugh. More in sympathy than anything else, he thought.

"My wife is a remarkable woman. She's done her best for our country from the time she entered Congress to the present. During her years in public office, she experienced the tragedy of losing her first husband, Andy Grant, to a horrific act of violence. In recent days, Patti and I, along with Carolyn Enquist and her husband Lars, all faced the possibility ..."

McGill needed a moment to compose himself and took it.

"The possibility that we might lose our son, Kenny, to leukemia. Kenny's best treatment option was a bone marrow transplant. Patti, as God or fate would have it, was a perfect match for Kenny. During the course of administering general anesthesia to the president, the medical team discovered the condition Dr. Nicolaides just described to you. I was called on to make the decision whether to continue with the transplant process or to stop it. I chose to proceed."

McGill paused to take a sip of water.

"That was the hardest decision of my life. I believe I did the right thing. The president's health is being closely monitored and she has shown no further sign of any heart irregularity, and Kenny's transplant seems to be working. As long as I'm here speaking to you, I ask that those of you who believe in the power of prayer remember the president and Kenny in your prayers.

"Within the limits of matters of public interest, I'll take your questions now."

From the forest of hands that immediately sprouted, Aggie Wu picked a reporter from the *Washington Post*.

"Mr. McGill, were you informed of any risk the president would face by continuing with the transplant process, and did you think to consult with anyone else before you made your decision?"

"I was informed of the risks. You may talk to experts of your choosing to find out what they were. I did not consult with anyone. I was told time was of the essence, and I was the only person involved who was both the spouse to the donor and the parent of the recipient. Who else might have made the decision?"

The *Post* reporter followed up. "If there was no time for consultation, your decision must have been all the more difficult. In retrospect, though, if you'd had the time, do you think you would have owed it to the American people to consult a medical ethicist?"

"No," McGill said. "The obligations I mentioned that the president owes the people of this country are not infinite, and the ones I owe them are far fewer than hers."

Aggie called on the reporter from the *Chicago Tribune* next. "Mr. McGill, I can't speak for anyone else's religious convictions among the media, but I feel comfortable saying everyone here extends their best wishes to the president, your son and your family."

"Thank you."

"My question is," the reporter continued, "have you spoken with the president about the decision you made to continue the transplant process, and if you did will you tell us what her response was?"

McGill looked down at the lectern for a moment. When he

raised his eyes, it was clear that he had decided to answer both halves of the question.

"I have talked with the president about that, yes. She supported the choice I made. The president and I both work in risky occupations. If you're a politician or a cop these days, there's a chance someone might take a shot at you. It might seem strange to most people, but you learn to live with that possibility. You consciously come to accept that there are reasons for which you'll risk your life. The president and I have both made it clear to each other the circumstances we consider justifiable for self-sacrifice."

The reporter from the *New York Times* wanted to know, "Do you think the president will be up to or even want to make a run for reelection?"

"The answer to both parts of your question is yes. I expect her to recover, run for reelection and be returned to office."

WorldWide News' White House reporter asked, "If you had *your* choice, would the president run for reelection?"

"Not if I have to do any more press conferences."

The newsies all laughed.

McGill continued, "If I thought there was anyone who had the vision, the intelligence, the charm and the determination to do the job as well as Patti, I'd be doing my level best to persuade her to leave public life. But I don't see anyone who comes close."

"Not even Acting President Wyman?" the *Wall Street Journal* called out.

McGill had anticipated the question. "Mather Wyman is a good man. He did a terrific job resolving the difficult situation at Salvation's Path, and he would be a good president. You'll have to allow for my bias, though, when I say Patricia Darden Grant is in a class by herself."

Aggie Wu decided that was enough and thanked the newsies for their interest.

She walked McGill out of the room — just as an idea occurred to him.

There was someone he needed to see.

Charlottesville, Virgina

From the cabin in the woods they were now calling home, Todd, Crosby and Anderson all had watched McGill's press conference. The two former CIA agents looked at each other and then they both looked at Todd.

He asked them, "What do you think?"

Crosby said, "I think you're right, he won't be easy to kill."

"Not impossible, though," Anderson added.

Todd said, "Is it true there's nobody who's impossible to kill?"

Anderson said, "Nah, that's bullshit. Plenty of assholes die rich and in bed."

"Stalin died from a stroke," Crosby said, "in bed, but also in a lot of pain."

Giving the matter further consideration, Anderson added, "I will say it's harder to keep a well funded, planned and executed assassination attempt from succeeding these days than it was even twenty years ago."

Crosby said, "That's because both information and weaponry are so accessible. It's just about impossible for anyone, especially big shots, to keep their movements secret, and if you know when, where and how someone will be traveling, and you can lay your hands on the right hardware, you stand a decent chance of making your kill."

Todd asked, "Without the benefit of study, what would you say the major difficulties would be in an attempt to kill James J. McGill?"

Anderson snorted. "The Secret Service."

"Those guys are good," Crosby said. "They learn from history. The Kennedy assassination taught them about long-range shots; the attempt on Reagan's life has taken away the chance to walk up and plug a guy."

Todd told them. "I got McGill to come to me alone. He didn't bring anyone with him."

The two former agents exchanged another look.

"How'd you do that?" Crosby asked.

"Without saying so, I made him think I'd taken his landlord hostage."

"His *landlord?*" Anderson asked.

"He considered the man a friend."

"You got lucky you were only locked up," Crosby told Todd.

The psychiatrist stiffened. "What do you mean?"

Anderson said, "What Arn means is hostage takers are a sniper's favorite target. Pop the sucker and celebrate with a beer. And that's if the hostage doesn't get the drop on the guy who grabbed him." He paused briefly and added, "I bet McGill had a chance to kill you, didn't he?"

Todd took a deep breath and let it go slowly.

"I thought I had the chance to kill him first, but yes. He could have shot me."

Both former agents nodded their heads.

"The SOB was quick, wasn't he?" Crosby asked.

"Did he show a preference for a weapon other than a gun?" Anderson wanted to know.

Todd told them, "He was very quick. I tried to hit him with a baseball bat. I aimed for his ribs, but he got inside my swing."

Crosby went to the desk in the room and found a pad of paper and a pen. He started making notes. "What about what Olin said? Did he use other weapons?"

Forcing aside his embarrassment, Todd admitted, "He threw a boxful of pushpins at me. Some went into my open mouth, and he swung a stapler at me and hit me on the head."

"An improviser," Crosby said, adding to his notes. "A good one is limited only by his imagination."

"I hate those fuckers," Anderson said.

Finally, something he and the thug had in common, Todd thought.

Something of a dismaying revelation, really.

Crosby looked at his compatriot.

"You think he's started?"

"If they've told him, yeah," Anderson said.

"Started what?" Todd asked.

Crosby laid it out. "If your friend McGill knows the three of us are on the loose, he's hunting us."

"Lucky for you," Anderson told Todd, "we like a good challenge."

The White House — SAC Crogher's Office

Special Agent Deke Ky had been told to report to Crogher's office after his meeting with McGill. He was to report anything McGill had said to him. In other words, he'd been ordered to be a snitch. That wasn't an unusual requirement for someone in his line of work. The *bullet catchers* needed to know what their *packages* were thinking, what their next moves might be.

Sharing that information with superiors was a routine matter.

The problem was Jim McGill was anything but a routine package. He wasn't a politician, an appointee or a government employee of any kind. He was a private citizen and the spouse of the president, the woman who could fire anyone in the executive branch at whim.

Beyond the matter of his clout — which for the first time in over three years he had chosen to exert — McGill was a former cop. He was used to being the guy with the gun who took the risks, who protected other people. It only made sense he wasn't going to roll over and let someone else force him into a passive role.

Hell, Deke thought, he wouldn't have put up with that crap either.

Even so, it stung that McGill had literally shown Leo and him the door.

Quick as a wink, too. No appeals. You can't do things my way? Goodbye.

Now, Deke had been forced to cool his heels waiting for over an hour in Crogher's office. The SAC was going to be pissed off when he heard what McGill had done, especially the part about allowing only Elspeth Kendry to provide —

A knock at the door interrupted Deke's train of thought.

Crogher would have just walked in. So who …

He got up and opened the door, professional paranoia requiring him to put a hand on his weapon and be ready to dive out of harm's way. But it was only Leo. He had a sheaf of paper in one hand.

"I was told I might find you here, Deke," he said, "and you were waitin' on your boss." Leo peeked over Deke's shoulder, saw Crogher wasn't present. "Can you spare a minute?"

"Yeah," Deke said, glad to have the break in waiting for the SAC. He stepped out into the corridor and closed the door behind him. He asked Leo, "What's up? You get reassigned already?"

Leo shook his head. "I decided to go proactive."

Deke frowned. "Meaning what?"

"Meaning I quit my job."

Not much surprised Deke, but that did. "You're leaving the White House? What are you going to do?"

"Well, I've gotten a bit too old to go back to NASCAR, and even if I tried, that would still distress my mother. But before I took on government work, I tried being a driver for rich guys. You know, the kind who might get bushwhacked and need a driver who could get them out of tight spots. Problem was, I couldn't stand any of those jerks. But, now, what I thought was —"

Deke said, "You quit so you could work for Holmes as his private driver."

Holmes being McGill's Secret Service code name.

Leo smiled. "That's it. I took it to heart when the boss said he wasn't subject to anyone else's wishes. Right now, I've got enough money put by that I don't *need* to work for anyone else. But I do like to drive, so I thought I'd see if he'd take me back if I promise to keep my mouth shut. You know, the way you and I said we would."

"He'll take you back in a heartbeat," Deke said.

"I got my fingers crossed on that one. If he does, I'll still be in and out of the building here, and I thought you should be the first to know. Here's a copy of my resignation." Leo handed Deke a sheet of paper from the half-dozen in his hand.

Deke read it at a glance. Leo had been succinct. He was leaving his job to pursue other opportunities.

"You sure Holmes can afford you?" he asked.

"I might have to forgo stock options, but we'll work something out."

Deke extended a hand to Leo, and the two men shook.

"I'm happy for you, Leo. I'm also glad Holmes will have you behind the wheel."

Leo didn't say Deke might consider the benefits of working in the private sector, too.

You had to let people come to decisions on their own.

White House — South Portico

Taking the time to give Deke a heads-up left Leo standing in the driveway watching McGill ride off in the armored, super-charged Chevy that Leo had driven to work that morning. He thought he'd seen Elspeth Kendry in the back seat with McGill. He wasn't sure who was driving.

Damnitall, now what was he going to do for a ride?

He knew. He'd call Margaret Sweeney.

Some friends of his had souped up that mint-condition Malibu of hers.

Next best thing to the car he watched pull out through the White House gates.

Welborn Yates was behind the wheel of McGill's Chevy. McGill had done a double-take when he'd seen Welborn at his desk in the West Wing. He'd just come from Galia Mindel's office to get one of the two reviews of his press room performance that would matter to him.

"I did okay, Galia? The quid was worth the quo?"

She nodded and gave him a long look.

"What?" he asked.

She said, "You were fine. You looked good. You spoke well. You were honest but you set clear boundaries."

"Didn't even use a TelePrompTer," McGill said.

Galia responded, "You joke, but that's important, too. The truth was, you had much of the same presence, the same command of the room, as the president."

McGill saw where she was going and got the best laugh he'd had in long time.

"Only if a voice comes to me from a burning bush, Galia," he said. "Only then would I go into politics, and first I'd whine, 'Do I have to?'"

The chief of staff smiled. "It is something of a calling."

McGill decided to see if the moment was right to ask for another favor.

"Do you remember a fellow by the name of Daryl Cheveyo?"

Galia's recall of names was equal to that of any politician who had ever lived and she was faster on the draw than most of them.

"The CIA psychiatrist who was the agency's contact man with Dr. Damon Todd, the fellow you put away working your first private case."

"Technically, a judge put him away. Todd managed to escape recently."

Galia leaned back in her chair, as if retreating from bad news.

"Is he a danger to you?"

"That's a possibility. I'd feel better about things if I took the initiative."

"You want to find him before he finds you."

McGill said, "I think things would work out better that way."

"Or you could rely on the Secret Service for a change." One look at McGill told her that wasn't going to happen.

"You should understand," he told her. "You're just like me that way. You want to chart your own course, not just book passage."

Galia thought of her recent scheming with three governors.

She still hadn't told the president about that.

It might be a good idea to have McGill in her corner, should she need an ally.

"What can I do for you?" she asked McGill. "Contact Dr.

Cheveyo for you?"

"All I'll need is a phone number where I can reach him."

Galia unlocked a desk drawer and took out a laptop computer. She opened the lid so he couldn't see the screen. Her fingers flew over the keyboard for what had to be a dozen-character password. A few more flurries of touch typing had Galia nodding.

"Daryl Cheveyo," she said, "took a disability retirement from the CIA. He now teaches at Georgetown University."

"Huh," McGill said. "Abbie's school. Small world."

"Official Washington is the most incestuous village in the world." She gave him a phone number. Then she added, "Being an authentic Jewish mother, I have license to tell you to be careful. The president and your family now depend on you more than ever."

"Thank you, Galia," McGill said and left.

GWU Hospital, Washington, D.C.

Kenny was busy getting a once over from Dr. Jones when McGill arrived at the hospital. He filled the time by talking with Special Agent Elspeth Kendry in the lounge down the hall from Kenny's room. McGill kept one eye on Elspeth and the other watching for the summons that his son was ready to receive a visitor.

He didn't have any reason to think Kenny was doing anything except continuing to make progress in his recovery. Still, he felt the need to see that was the case. It reminded him of the times when his children were newborns. All of them had been healthy, but he'd always wakened at least twice a night to tiptoe over to their cribs, look at them and make sure they hadn't forgotten how to keep breathing.

Such paternal impulses seemed to have returned with his teenage son. Your kid bumped up against the Grim Reaper, you had to make sure the bastard wasn't reaching out to haul him back. For now, though, it looked like the old GR would have to wait some more.

McGill turned his attention fully to Elspeth and gave her a quick rundown of what had happened with Deke and Leo. Then he added an evaluation that he hadn't shared with the two men of his former protection detail.

"You've probably already noticed SAC Crogher and I have an element of antagonism in our relationship. Used to be we couldn't stand each other. Then we reached a point of understanding if not agreement. Now, with the president convalescing and Mather Wyman filling in, Crogher has tried to seize the opportunity to have things his way. You need to know that isn't going to work."

Elspeth thought about that and said, "You understand why he's doing it, right?"

"Sure. It's what he's been taught and what he thinks is best."

"Pretty much all of us would. My guess is that's why Special Agent Ky fell in line. He thinks SAC Crogher is doing what's in everyone's interest."

McGill did his best to give people the benefit of the doubt, but he'd really been stung by what he considered Deke's violation of his trust. He felt as if Deke had been playing him for a sucker the past three years.

He tried an approach with Elspeth he thought she might understand.

He asked her, "Do you know when it was that women were first permitted to join the Secret Service?"

She did. "Nineteen seventy-one."

"Who do you think had it easier, you or that first female special agent?"

"Me. The institution has evolved."

"Right. Well, I'm the first of my gender in my position. If you've read the file on me, and I feel sure you have, you saw that from the start I never described myself as the 'First Gentleman.' I called myself the president's henchman. It was meant both as a joke and a declaration of independence. I was going to keep on being me, not try to become some ideal figure other people might want me to be."

Elspeth said, "Reading between the lines, you're saying there will be other men married to other presidents and the institution will have to adjust."

"Right. I could say I'm doing things for them, too, but I'm not. I'm just saying nobody's going to put a straightjacket on me."

Elspeth thought she might be assuming too much, but she decided to try acting as if James J. McGill wanted someone to test his arguments. Might get her reassigned to Tierra del Fuego; she was sure Deke Ky was still reeling from getting bounced. But risk be damned, she didn't like to be penned in either.

"Mr. McGill, do you think you ever would have met someone like Damon Todd if you weren't married to the president?"

"Possibly but not likely," he said.

"You handled Dr. Todd without any help, but now he has escaped in the company of two former covert operatives whose records the Agency still hasn't released to us but has informally described as extremely dangerous. If Dr. Todd were able to enlist their help, how do you think you'd deal with the three of them? On your own, that is."

"I wouldn't try to deal with them on my own. I have friends."

"Margaret Sweeney?"

"First and foremost, yes." He also thought he might see what Gabbi Casale was doing. Maybe even Odo Sacripant and Harbin. Them and one or two other tough guys he knew. As he was running down a list of names in his mind, he saw the look of doubt on Elspeth's face.

McGill knew what she was thinking: No local cop was a match for a fed.

Elspeth was adept at reading people, too. Knew she was about to be given her walking papers. Didn't want to go, not yet.

"You're right," she said. "I don't think the Vegas betting line would favor your side. But I'm willing to listen to a contrary point of view."

McGill didn't really feel the need to provide it.

Only reason he did was he didn't want to get a bad rep and

have it rub off on Patti.

"Who got to Speaker Derek Geiger first when he was about to start shooting, you or me?"

"If I remember correctly, sir, Special Agent Latz got there first."

"He did. He was a lot closer. You were closer, too, but which of us got there first?"

"You did," she admitted.

"There's a monstrous thug in a French prison by the name of Etienne Burell. I had help with him from some very able people I can call on again, but who was it that set M'sieur Burell on fire and sent him scurrying into the Seine?"

"You sir."

"And as you say I subdued Damon Todd when he was a fearsomely muscled specimen. You can also ask Special Agent Ky and SAC Crogher if they've ever seen anyone with a faster gun draw."

"I've already been informed about that, sir."

Most times McGill would have told her to can the *sir* stuff.

Not now. He'd had his fill of the Secret Service for one day.

And he saw a nurse coming his way, smiling, thank God.

"Find another ride back to the White House, Special Agent Kendry. I'll be safe with Captain Yates for company."

Elspeth thought to object, but she knew what would happen if she did.

Hola, Tierra del Fuego.

"Yes, sir."

Having mentioned Welborn, McGill thought he might be someone else who —

No, he couldn't do that. Welborn was just married. He shouldn't be asked to take the risk.

McGill went to see his son.

"Dad!" Kenny said. His bed had been inclined so he could sit up slightly.

McGill's heart swelled with joy at seeing Kenny. It seemed almost as if he were coming into sharper focus right in front of his eyes. A 3D Polaroid photo. He wanted Patti to see this; Carolyn, too. Abbie and Caitie. He wanted all of them to tell him he wasn't just imagining things. Kenny was looking visibly better.

He wanted to throw his arms around his son and kiss him.

But Kenny's visitors still had to wear caps, gowns, masks and gloves.

He contented himself by saying, "You're looking good, champ."

Kenny tilted his head in surprise. "You never called me that before."

"Things change. If you don't like it though ..."

"No, no. I do like it, kind of. Maybe, though, we could keep it between us."

McGill put a gloved hand on Kenny's shoulder, and looked over at the room nurse.

"I won't tell," she told them. "Though I do agree."

The two McGill's smiled at her. Then the elder McGill felt a tug at his sleeve.

"Dad," Kenny said in a soft voice, "Dr. Jones just told me she's never seen anyone make a better start on their recovery than me. Maybe I am a bit of a champ in that way. I'm actually starting to feel *good*. There was a time I didn't think I was going to feel this way again. There was a time I thought I might not feel *anything* again."

Tears came to McGill's eyes.

"You had a lot of people pulling for you, praying for you."

"I know. Man, do I have a lot of thank you cards to write. Thing is, I want to write more than that. I want to write how one day you're just going along the way you always do and the next day everything is changed. How you learn more about who you are than you ever imagined."

"You're going to be a writer now?"

"*And* a doctor. And who knows what else? I'm not going to fence myself in."

McGill and Kenny talked another thirty minutes, until exuberance gave way to fatigue. McGill stroked his son's head. Promised him he'd bring Patti next time. Watched him sleep for five minutes. Made sure he hadn't forgotten how to breathe.

The Mandarin Oriental Hotel — Washington, D.C.

Sir Edbert Bickford glowered at his nephew, Hugh Collier. The two of them occupied the end cushions of facing silk sofas. Sir Edbert had planted his flag in the presidential suite; it consumed thirty-five hundred square feet of the hotel's ninth floor. The suite included four bedrooms and a number of bathrooms that Hugh had yet to tally. Certainly more than Sir Edbert would need no matter how inelastic his bladder might have become.

"What did you say Ms. Booker told you?" Sir Edbert demanded.

Uncle's ears were not among his declining parts, Hugh knew. The old goat could hear the rustle of money during an artillery barrage. No, he was asking for an encore of the insults he'd heard only a moment before so he might more fully indulge his outrage.

"Ellie told me to sod off, Uncle. Then she said you should go fuck yourself."

She'd also said Hugh should bugger Sir Edbert, if he wasn't up to the job himself.

Some things, though, a chap kept to himself for his own amusement.

Sir Edbert, however, had heard enough. His head bobbed and his wattles wobbled.

His ire was at perfect pitch now.

He said, "I'll sue. I'll sue until she doesn't have —"

"Uncle, she doesn't have enough money to cover your lawyers' fees."

Ellie Booker had signed a contract with Center Ring Books, WorldWide News' publishing arm, to write an unauthorized biography of Patricia Darden Grant. Now she was telling them to stuff that, too. She'd also quit her job as a producer for WWN, and had left the aforementioned parting words for her former employers.

Sir Edbert sensed further treachery in his nephew's words of caution. He directed a look at Hugh that had made prime ministers around the world tremble. It might have concerned Hugh as well, if he hadn't been thinking of throttling the old bastard where he sat.

Might take a moment to force his fingers through all that fat and grab hold of his throat, but it would be worth the effort. Things were not looking up for WorldWide News. Uncle's attorneys had been advised that very day that the United States Department of Justice was looking at WWN for possible violations of the Foreign Corrupt Practices Act, the law that forbade the bribery of foreign officials by American companies.

WorldWide News, though global in its reach, was a Delaware corporation.

WWN also had more cops, court clerks and politicians on its payroll than the Mafia had ever dreamt of. It should have come as a warning to Uncle, Hugh thought, when the DOJ started looking at competing media empires for the same reason.

Delusions of the divine right of business moguls, however, were not easily pierced. Not if Sir Edbert had anything to say about it. He spent money furiously when threatened: witness his present surroundings. Hugh had heard Uncle had even taken to carrying outlandish sums of cash with him at such times. Doing in Uncle and scarpering with the loot had a real appeal, if only there hadn't been security cameras everywhere.

In the face of that reality, Hugh opted for logic and persuasion.

"Peace be unto you, Uncle," he said. "I think Ellie might still be persuaded to share her tales of adventure at Salvation's Path with us for the right considerations, those being contrition on your part and mine —"

Hugh held up his hand before his uncle could start a rant.

"Contrition, cash and courtesy. We admit that we were black-guards to leave her alone in the company of armed zealots; we make her a monetary offer no one else will match and we treat her as a peer not a vassal. That way we get what we want, we double-cross her as soon as we can and we dare her to spend the fortune we've given her on lawyers to sue us."

"She'd be a fool to do that," Sir Edbert muttered.

"Yes, Uncle, and our Ellie is anything but a fool. It might be that her crude language was just a bargaining ploy."

Sir Edbert raised his bushy brows. "Really?"

"Women these days, Uncle."

"Very well," he grumped. "See if you can strike a deal."

Hugh said he would. It was staggering, he thought, the amount of shit you had to shovel just to complete a publishing deal these days. But the tiff with Ellie was just a bagatelle.

The real battle would be the confrontation with the government.

If the Department of Justice truly sought to wound Sir Edbert, he would do his best to destroy Patricia Darden Grant in return.

Hillside Drive, Bloomington, Indiana

Sheryl Kimbrough interrupted her daughter's reading. The two of them were in the kitchen of their new home, a lovely old frame house with thirty-four double-hung windows. Old windows. On a late summer afternoon, the house was bathed in warm yellow sunlight. On a subzero morning in January, Sheryl could imagine the old furnace in the basement straining to compensate for all the drafts of arctic air.

The house had come at a great price, especially for its location in a wonderful neighborhood, but it had been accurately billed as a fixer-upper. Thing was, neither mother nor daughter was in the least handy with any tool that didn't include microchips. They'd found a retired gentleman who was skilled in the building trades, but he worked slowly and charged appropriately for his years of experience and meticulous craftsmanship.

Sheryl soon realized that she'd be working for him as much as he'd be working for her.

Even so, it felt wonderful to be home. She was an Indiana girl.

Cassidy, however, had spent all of her formative years in suburban Washington, D.C.

"How's school starting, honey?" she asked.

Couldn't keep herself from intruding on her daughter, even though she was doing assigned reading. She chided herself. She should have been content to marvel at the girl in silence. It surprised her anew each day at how comely her daughter was. So unlike her plain mother. She had her father to thank for her good looks, and for at least half of her shining intellect.

Blake was back in D.C., when he wasn't on the road. He worked for the State Department, recruiting college grads with fluency in critical languages. The truly gifted were given free rides to grad school to become multilingual so they might serve at embassies around the world throughout their careers.

In his spare time, he wrote books analyzing the state of the world. He had to submit them for State Department approval before they went to his publisher. But he'd never been told to delete more than a few words. His bosses knew he'd quit if they ever came down too hard.

He spoke six languages himself. Not bad for a kid from central Indiana. He'd taught Cassidy both French and Russian. She'd be ready to take paid internships with State when she got to college. By dint of grueling effort, Sheryl had learned Spanish so she could be more useful to Senator Talbert and so she wouldn't be the only one in the family who was monolingual.

"School's okay, Mom," Cassidy told her. "Pretty nice really."

Cassidy was at one of the best public schools in the state, but everything was relative.

"Not too white bread, mainstream, inbred?"

"Well, yeah, sure, all of that. Can't find anyone else who's read Tolstoy in Russian. Aside from that, though, everyone's pretty cool. My French teacher is actually Parisienne; she's helped me refine my accent."

"That's great," Sheryl said.

"You're worried about me?" Cassidy asked.

"Only when I'm awake. Or dreaming. I do a lot of REM worrying."

Cassidy laughed. "If you're going to ask if I miss D.C., yeah, I do. It helps to talk to Dad, ask him about the latest in world events. The kids at school are really friendly, but not … not exactly interested in the wider world."

Sheryl smiled and said, "Not everyone has a U.S. senator for a godfather."

Cassidy had been meeting the top politicians in the country since she was a toddler.

"Yeah, it's all your fault, yours and Dad's, that I'm a political junkie. That's what I miss the most, a good political debate. My class-mates like to talk about music, sports and each other. I understand that; I like it, too. But I miss talking about, you know, the big-ger things. The world. What other countries are doing. What our country should be doing."

"Maybe you could audit a class at the university. Plenty of political debate there."

Cassidy's eyes brightened. "That would be great."

"Who knows? Your old mom might even have some news to share with you."

Sheryl had been reluctant to tell anyone that she was going to be an elector, but then Cassidy was far from being just anyone.

"Like what?" her daughter asked.

"Can you keep a secret? I mean, really keep a secret."

Cassidy put a hand to her lips and mimicked turning a key in a lock.

"Okay," Sheryl said, "here's the deal."

Cassidy jumped to her feet and spun around when she heard.

She embraced her mother and …

Slumped back onto her chair as if her batteries went dead.

Alarmed, Sheryl asked, "What's wrong?"

"You're a *Republican* elector, right? Because Tal is a Republican."

"Yes," Sheryl said, waiting for the punch line.

"But Patti Grant *isn't* a Republican, not anymore."

"No, she's not. She left the party."

"But I *love* Patti Grant. It *kills* me that I'm too young to ever vote for her."

Cassidy would be only seventeen come the next presidential election.

Truth be told, Sheryl also had been crestfallen when the president had left the party.

She hugged her daughter. "I'm sure the GOP people in Washington know they have big shoes to fill."

Hart Senate Office Building, Washington, D.C.

Senator Howard Hurlbert sat at the head of the table in the conference room of his office suite. He was joined by thirteen of his colleagues in the Republican senate caucus. Neither the senate minority leader nor the minority whip was in attendance. It was a strictly rank-and-file affair. Hurlbert had been tempted to have a shot of bourbon to stiffen his resolve to go through with the announcement he planned to make, but he didn't want anyone to think it was just the liquor talking.

Hurlbert's chief of staff and campaign manager, Bobby Beckley, closed the door behind the last of the guests to arrive. Beckley knew what was coming. He was darkly amused by Senator Hurlbert's ambition. He never thought the old fart would have had the wit to come up with the idea or the balls to see it through.

But here they were and the train was about to climb that first big roller coaster hill.

Bobby gave Hurlbert a nod, thinking maybe he'd back down while he still had time.

He didn't, though. He got right to it.

Senator Hurlbert said, "I'd like to thank y'all for coming. I know your schedules are as busy as mine. What I've got to tell you today is the kind of thing you might want to tell to Fox or World-Wide News the first chance you get, but I'd appreciate it if you'd allow me to make my formal announcement first."

"C'mon, Howard," Senator Darrin Neff of South Carolina said. "I know it ain't been ten seconds, but the suspense is killing me."

"You're right, Darrin. No point in waiting. So here it is." Hurlbert shot a glance at Beckley and then took the plunge. "I'm leaving the Republican Party."

"You're retiring?" Senator Adel Wayne of Texas asked.

"No, I'm not retiring. I'm going to start my own party and run for president."

Senator Jim McKee of North Carolina said, "Never quite saw you as a political entrepreneur, Howard."

McKee's remark drew more than a few chuckles.

Senator Beau Brunelle of Louisiana, the senior member of those present, held up a hand requesting silence. He got it. If Brunelle had made the same announcement, it would have been a *real* shock.

"I thought you were going to run for the GOP nomination, Howard," Brunelle said.

Hurlbert said, "I was, until I saw the fix was in."

"A fix? By whom and for whom?" Brunelle asked.

"By Pete Profitt and Reynard Dix for Mather Wyman."

Brunelle saw the appeal. "That would be an astute move."

Around the table, other senatorial heads nodded.

"You see, you see?" Hurbert asked. "It's gonna happen and none of us can stop it. Mather Wyman is a moderate at best. He does not represent what we've worked so hard to make the Republican Party these past forty years. Somebody's got to stop him."

Senator Dan Crockett of Tennessee said with a grin, "The person best positioned to do that, if Wyman buys in, might be Patti Grant."

Few of those around the table found that amusing.

Brunelle returned to the subject at hand.

"You have a name for your new party, Howard?"

"I wanted to call it the Conservative Party, but Bobby tells me there's already a small party using that name in New York."

Crockett couldn't resist. "Imagine that, conservatives in New York."

Hurlbert ignored him. "So I came up with the name True South, and Bobby came up with a great tag line to go with it, true conservative."

Crockett continued to play the devil's advocate.

"Y'all are aware that the eleven states of the old True South, formerly known as the Confederacy, have only, let me see …" Besides his sense of humor, Crocket was known for a facility with numbers. "One hundred and sixty electoral votes. Even if you threw in Kentucky, West Virginia and Oklahoma, you'd get only another twenty. It seems to me your new party comes up short both geographically and numerically, Howard."

Crockett paused before adding, "You do know it takes two hundred and seventy electoral votes to win the presidency, right?"

"Of course, I do," Hurlbert said. He wished, though, that Bobby had provided him with those other numbers Crockett had brought up. He was starting to feel foolish. The only thing left for him to do was improvise.

"There are other states that are truly southern in their hearts."

"Maybe South Dakota," Crockett cracked to general amusement. "Other than that, name one."

Beau Brunelle took Hurbert off the hook. "Now, now, everyone. Let's not be too hard on Howard. There are interesting possibilities here. Were you thinking of recruiting candidates for Congress, Howard?"

"Well, I …"

"No? I think you should. In terms of electoral votes, our part of the country does not constitute a majority, but as a voting bloc in the Senate and the House, we would be a force that couldn't be ignored. If we didn't get our way outright with legislation, we'd certainly influence it or we'd kill it. In terms of an identity and a reason for being, I think True South could be quite powerful."

Dan Crockett shook his head and stood up.

"With all due respect —"

"Meaning with none at all," Hurlbert said.

Crockett said, "As you like, Howard. There is no true south as some of you might imagine it. The African American population would justifiably hate the name True South; the growing Latino communities would likely feel the same way. So would the Asian immigrants. The white people who've relocated from the North over the past twenty years are not going to pick up banjos and start singing 'Dixie.' Then there are the white people who were born in the South and have modernized their views a mite since 1865. Y'all do what you want. I'm not going to warn you. If you can't see why Howard's idea should die in this room right now, you're beyond my help."

"You're not going to run to the media are you, Senator?" Hurlbert said with a sneer.

Dan Crockett said, "Only if I hear my name attached to this madness in any regard other than to condemn it. True South, my ass."

Bobby Beckley let the senator out of the room.

"I guess we can't count on his vote," Beau Brunelle said.

Ten minutes later the other visitors had left Howard Hurlbert's suite, talking among themselves in clusters of two and three. Some of them even sounded enthusiastic. Unfortunately for Hurlbert, they were focusing on Senator Brunelle's idea of new voting blocs in the Senate and House rather than on winning the White House.

Hurlbert's clerical staff had been given the afternoon off to reduce the chance someone might leak the story to the media. The senator and his political mastermind slouched on opposite ends of the leather sofa in the outer office.

"Do you think I'm going to get support from *any* of them?" Hurlbert asked.

"Yes, I do. My guess is at least six, maybe eight."

"Because of Beau Brunelle not me."

"Does it matter?" Bobby asked.

"It does if Beau wants to replace me as the presidential candidate of my own party."

A large part of Bobby Beckley's job was keeping a straight face when the senator said something that revealed just what a hayseed he was. Beau Brunelle didn't want to be president. He saw himself as a lawmaker, a law*giver* after his third bourbon. He wanted to be the majority leader, but even if the Republicans recaptured the Senate, he was fourth in seniority. If he could be the top dog of a new party in the Senate, though, that might be a springboard to get him to where he wanted to be.

Howard Hurlbert should have known that, but he let Bobby do most of his thinking.

"The presidency is your personal turf," the chief of staff said. "I'll make sure of that."

Hurlbert smiled. "If you weren't so damn ugly, I'd give you a kiss."

"If you weren't so damn ugly, I'd let you."

They settled on having drinks and toasting their future.

Neither knowing Galia Mindel would learn of True South before the hour was out.

The White House

Edwina Byington was at her desk outside the Oval Office when the phone call from Senator Daniel Crockett came through. She'd met the senator on three occasions and had enjoyed his company, brief though their time together had been. Crockett possessed a wry sense of humor, not unlike that of James J. McGill.

"Good afternoon, Senator Crockett," Edwina said. "How may I help you?"

"I hear you're running a president-for-a-day show over there, Edwina. I just thought I'd ask if I could put my name in the running."

"Allow me to consult my copy of the Constitution, Senator. Let me see now. As the senior senator from the sixteenth state to join the Union, you're number thirty-one in the presidential line of succession — after the Secretary of Homeland Security."

"I shouldn't wait by my phone?" Crockett asked.

"It might be a while, Senator."

"And I suppose that new fella up there, Mather Wyman, is busy at the moment."

"Yes, Acting President Wyman is in a meeting."

"Would it be too much to ask for you to give him a personal message from me?"

"It would be my pleasure, Senator."

"Please let the acting president know there's a plan afoot to draft him to be the presidential candidate for the Republican Party."

Edwina hit her mental replay button on that one. She didn't hear any hint of a joke.

"I'll certainly do that, Senator. Is there anything else?"

"Yes, please tell the acting president I'll keep him advised of any further developments."

"That's very kind of you, Senator."

Edwina wondered what he'd want in return.

Mango Mary's — Key West, Florida

"I've been coming in here a while now," the man calling himself Jackie Richmond said, "and I haven't seen a single mango."

Jackie was really a car thief and a killer named Linley Boland.

"Do you even know what a mango looks like?"

"Sure, they're oval, yellow and red, sometimes have a high gloss finish."

"You know what they taste like?"

"Now, you've got me, Alice."

The owner of Mango Mary's was named Alice Tompkins, but she was open to letting anyone who so desired to call her Mary. Had she known, she wouldn't have objected to a car thief on the run using an alias. Most likely, she'd have been uneasy letting a killer live under her roof, whatever he called himself.

But Jackie's loan of ten thousand dollars on the night they met had taken her out of a very bad spot. So maybe she would have cut him some slack if he'd only killed a prick like the guy who had been very surprised to get all his money by its due date.

That guy'd had other plans, but now he was shit out of luck.

Not that Alice hadn't gotten the feeling that the bastard might try to find whoever had fronted her the money and express his pique to that person. She might have warned Jackie about that possibility, but she liked to keep her secrets, too. As it was, she'd repaid Jackie the money he'd lent her — no need to worry about that transaction — and had let him continue to live with her rent free and bought his drinks any time he came by the bar.

She'd expected he'd have made a move to get into her bed by now, but he hadn't.

He wasn't into other guys; she didn't get that vibe at all.

Jackie was just … well mannered. Like he didn't want to mess up a good situation.

Alice told him, "Once upon a time, these premises housed a three-cot bordello. The madam and number-one working girl was …" She extended a hand to prompt the answer.

Jackie said, "Mango Mary. *She* liked the fruit."

"No. Not that I know anyway. No, her philosophy was man *come*, man *go*."

"Okay, I get it. She'd been burned by more than one jerk."

"Not at all," Alice said. "She wasn't complaining, she was insisting. Man come, man go. No dawdling. That was her business model. But she got too old for that shit and sold the place to my dad for a song. He kept the name, made a bar of it and passed it on to me."

"Your dad still around, fishing on a pier maybe?"

"Be nice if that was the way things worked out after you died, but he smoked himself into an early grave. Luckies. There's an irony, huh? Anyway, this place went smoke-free the day I dumped Dad's ashes into the ocean, didn't wait for the new state law."

Alice looked at Jackie a minute, considering his question.

"You trying to find if I've got a man behind me someplace, in case I need one?"

Jackie grinned and said, "Not at all. I was just making conversation. What I really wanted to know was if you know anything about boats. I thought if I said your dad fished on a pier, you'd say, 'Hell, no. He fishes off his boat.' Something like that."

"Why didn't you just ask?"

"Sometimes I like being indirect."

Alice could understand that. She said, "Well, now that I know, yeah, I know a few things about boats. You live on a little island like this, you'd better. Are you looking for one?"

"I might be."

"What kind?"

"That's just it, *I* don't know much about boats."

"Well, would you want sails, a motor or both?" Alice asked.

Jackie's first impulse was to say motor, but he asked, "You can get one with both?"

"Just about any sailboat you don't put in a bathtub has a motor. Some of them can cruise a fair distance on their motors."

"Yeah, that sounds good," Jackie told. "What I'd like is a boat that can go a long way. One I could drive by myself if necessary."

"Helm, you mean. Drive is what you do with a car."

Jackie smiled. "See. I'm learning already."

The Oval Office

Acting President Mather Wyman looked at the note Edwina Byington had handed him as his meeting with Attorney General Jaworsky broke up. Both men were having second thoughts about bringing a charge of treason against Reverend Burke Godfrey. It had been Wyman's contention that Godfrey had raised an army to resist his lawful arrest. A member of that armed force fired a shot with hostile intent at an FBI helicopter. Any person aboard that aircraft might have been killed by that shot or everybody aboard might have been killed if, say, the fuel tank had exploded.

However, no one had been killed on either side. The U.S. military hadn't fired a round, and the army Godfrey had raised surrendered immediately upon learning of their leader's capture.

To suggest that Godfrey's army had represented a serious threat to the country was going to be a hard sell. Viewed in a historical perspective, the charge of treason became even more problematic. After the Civil War, Jefferson Davis and Robert E.

Lee had been indicted on charges of treason, but the government had declined to try them. Given that precedent, one that a defense lawyer was certain to raise, the attorney general was not hopeful about obtaining a conviction.

Wyman wasn't able to argue with him and didn't try. He was still damn mad, though. Things could have gone far worse than they had. The death toll could have been in the hundreds. There were too many groups of people in the country with short tempers, grandiose self-images and more firepower than a World War Two rifle company. A common thread among many of these groups was they denied the legitimacy of the federal government.

In Mather's eyes, failing to address the problem harshly was to enable it.

Michael Jaworsky's suggestion was to charge Reverend Godfrey as an accomplice to attempted murder, reasoning that it was his actions that led to the shot being fired at the FBI helicopter. Wyman had signed off on the idea immediately.

There was little satisfaction in that, though, as the precipitating incident of the siege of Salvation's Path had been the arrest warrant issued for Godfrey's participation in the actual murder of Andrew Hudson Grant.

It was maddening to Wyman that he could do so little on his own authority.

That had been when he was handed the note by Edwina.

Senator Daniel Crockett had called to say the GOP was planning to draft him to be their nominee for president. He hadn't known whether to laugh or cry. He crumpled the note, stuck it in a pocket and retreated to the Oval Office.

He was tempted to have a drink, but he knew better than to start down that path.

Instead, he picked up the phone and called the White House physician.

"Nick, this is Mather Wyman. Is the president up to taking a phone call?"

While the answer to that question was being pursued,

Wyman's mind went back to a message he'd spotted on Edwina's desk calendar. A request to take a call from Jim McGill. It had been struck through. Edwina wouldn't have done that without, what … McGill changing his mind?

The acting president had seen a video of McGill's press conference. He'd been polite in his assessment of the man sitting in the Oval Office, but to Wyman's ear it sounded as if McGill had given him a gentleman's C for his performance thus far. Sure, old Wyman, had pulled off the assault on Burke Godfrey … but it had been Galia Mindel who had found out about Godfrey's tunnels. Made the whole plan work. Not that many knew the whole story.

That was bound to change. Sooner rather than later.

Then the question would be asked: What could Wyman do on his own?

And that was when it hit him. There should have been a beam of heavenly light and a choir of angels singing. All the good stuff that accompanied an epiphany.

He could *campaign* for any issue he deemed important.

Not as a would-be freshman filling one of the four hundred and thirty-five seats in the House of Representatives, but as a man running to be president. He took Dan Crockett's message out of his pocket. His party wanted to draft him.

Serendipity.

That was the moment when a contrary thought struck.

He'd told the president he was gay.

McGill's Hideaway — The White House

"I got the word," Patti told McGill that night.

The two of them sat next to each other on the leather sofa holding hands.

The ambiguity of what the *word* might be made McGill uneasy. "What word?"

"I'm officially a medical mystery. The best heart doctors in the country can't figure out what happened to me. No, that's not right. They know what happened, the mitral valve prolapse. What stumps them is that there was no sign of a problem before the episode and there hasn't been any sign of a problem since. Consultation is now going global."

"Maybe it was an allergic reaction to the anesthesia," McGill said.

Patti laughed. "Very good. That's one hypothesis. Where did you study, doctor?"

"Mother McGill's kitchen apothecary shop."

"My compliments to Mom. Might you have any other theory?"

"God was busting my chops? Seeing how I'd react in a tough spot."

Patti leaned in and kissed her husband. "Passed with flying colors. My network of spies tells me Kenny is making very good progress."

"He is. He said he's looking forward to seeing you. Told me not to come back unless you're with me."

"He did not."

"Maybe I was reading between the lines."

Patti said, "I thought it best to let the family have the first crack."

"You *are* family," McGill told her, "now more than ever."

"I'll try to remember."

McGill's thoughts moved on to the other critical element of what his wife had just imparted to him: She'd heard from her network of spies — and she had several of them, operating worldwide. She hadn't been speaking figuratively.

"What else did you hear?" he asked.

"That Celsus overstepped and you, possibly, overreacted."

A spark of temper flared inside McGill. He quickly put it out. Not only had Patti proved her love for him beyond any doubt, saving Kenny's life at the risk of her own, she was also smarter than him. He'd be foolish not to heed her advice.

"I was steamed," McGill said, "but I'll try to follow the McGill family motto."

"That being?"

"Get over yourself."

"Words to live by. Leo quit his government job but would like to go to work for McGill Investigations, Inc."

McGill looked at Patti and smiled. "He got himself out from under any obligation to rat me out. That was a slick move."

"Only if you hire him."

"Of course, I will. He's the best driver in town. Your spies really found this out?"

"No, Sweetie called me. She and Putnam are engaged. They bought rings."

McGill's jaw dropped. "Sweetie is going to become … Sweetie Shady?"

The two of them laughed.

"Isn't love grand?" Patti asked.

"It is."

"At the risk of ruffling your feathers, may I ask a question?"

McGill nodded, waited, silently vowed to keep his feathers in perfect trim.

"Regarding Damon Todd, is the reason you want to go after him simply because you can? After you were unable to directly help Kenny, the thought occurs there might be a connection. You really don't need to revalidate who you are. Not to me. Not to anyone who loves you."

McGill hadn't worked that out for himself, not consciously.

But he couldn't argue with Patti's analysis.

"Chana Lochlan needs to be warned." Something he hadn't done yet, damn it.

"Agreed."

"Daryl Cheveyo, too."

"Yes."

"And what do you propose I do with myself?" McGill asked.

"Accompany me for a month in the country."

Camp David, he knew. The plan was to bring Kenny there, too.

He could do far worse than watch two people he loved get well.

Still, he said, "I could still help catch Todd on a consulting basis."

Holly G smiled. "I believe that was how Sherlock Holmes worked, Holmes."

3

September, 2011
The White House — Capt. Welborn Yates' Office

So much for cutting your honeymoon short and rushing back to work, Welborn thought. He'd had all of one day chauffeuring James J. McGill about after he'd dismissed Deke Ky and Leo Levy. Word on the grapevine was that he'd also passed the word to SAC Crogher and Acting President Wyman that they could lump it if they didn't like it, the way he'd sent the Secret Service packing. When the man went on a tear, he didn't take any prisoners.

Of course, then *the* president must have made McGill see the light of reason and bundled him and his son, Kenny, off to Camp David. Which left Welborn without much to do. Anything to do, really.

He came into the office each day and read law enforcement journals.

Hoping he might learn something useful and keep his brain from shriveling.

Kira, on the other hand, was thriving. Her *de facto* father was now the man in the Oval Office, and he seemed to enjoy talking with her. Welborn didn't ask if Mather Wyman was sharing any state secrets with Kira because he didn't want to be told he didn't have a need to know. When his eyes glazed over and refused to read any more articles on the proper escalation of force when placing someone under arrest ...

His mind returned to flying Sir Hollis Rudd's Gulfstream G550. Damn, but that had been fun. True, the civil aviation aircraft was a Clydesdale compared to a racehorse like the F-22, but just to take the controls from the pilot's seat again had been a thrill. Sir Hollis had been clear and concise in briefing him, and for that matter the plane's computer could have flown the aircraft to New York, but it hadn't. Welborn had, and he brought the bird in for a perfect landing.

The best moment, though, had been when Kira poked her head into the cockpit.

"Why, flyboy," she said, "you actually know how to fly."

Sir Hollis had laughed and promised them all the champagne they could drink once they were ensconced at the Waldorf, and he'd made good on his word.

"My, my," a female voice said, "someone's thinking happy thoughts."

Welborn blinked and saw not Kira but Elspeth Kendry.

"May I come in?" she asked. "I promise I won't pry."

"And I promise not to let any secrets slip," Welborn said.

He gestured Elspeth to a visitor's chair.

She told him, "I've been at loose ends lately, you may have heard."

"I have. I'm the same way."

"I've been trying to make myself useful, and it occurred to me there's this fellow Linley Boland still running around loose when he'd look so much better in a cage."

Welborn leaned forward, put his palms on his desk.

"You've found him?"

"No, but I've come up with some interesting information. I thought I'd get your take on it."

"Tell me," Welborn said.

"Well, not that I have any experience catching car thieves, but I thought maybe one thing they might have in common with, say, bomb-makers, which I do know a thing or two about, is they might have their own signatures."

"Some technique or target they prefer?"

"Right. So we know he went after your Porsche because you caught him trying to steal it. And I told you on your wedding day that on Monday, August fifteenth, in the Fels Point neighborhood of Baltimore, Boland grabbed a Bentley and left a dead body behind. And, of course, he left a hair behind in Leo Levy's garage when he tried to steal the Chevy assigned to Mr. McGill."

"I do remember all that," Welborn said, "and your new information is?"

"Well, I thought after his failed attempt at Leo's garage, Boland might have tried to grab one of his usual targets, a high-end foreign car, to console himself and prove that he hadn't lost his game entirely. Since he was already here in town, I checked auto thefts for D.C. on Thursday, August eighteen."

"You found one?" Welborn asked. "One of Boland's signature cars was stolen."

Elspeth held up a hand, tucking her thumb to palm. "I found four: a Porsche, a Mercedes, an Audi and a Tesla — an American car but still an exotic. What's really interesting is that same day somebody also stole a car-carrying truck."

Welborn shook his head. "The guy was doing some serious compensation."

"Yes, he was. Now, what else might we surmise from this situation?"

Welborn knew what Elspeth had in mind. "He stole the truck because he didn't intend to sell the cars here in town. But just maybe he knew where he could offload them in, say, Baltimore. Where he stole the Bentley and tried to take my car."

"Go to the head of the class."

"Do I get a gold star?"

"That or I could give you the names of the Baltimore detectives I talked to, the ones who think they might know the wholesaler up there who bought Boland's hot rides."

"Is *that* guy in custody?"

"Has been several times. Always calls for his lawyer and

dummies up."

"So ... I'm supposed to do what?"

"You're in the Air Force, right?"

"Yes."

"Tell him he gives you Boland or you'll call in an airstrike."

For something like that, Welborn thought, he'd better put on his uniform.

Whitehaven Street, NW — Washington, D.C.

The first Monday in October was not far off and the Chief Justice of the United States, Alberto Calendri, invited his most trusted colleague on the Supreme Court, Associate Justice Titus Hawkins, to dinner.

Mr. Chief Justice Calendri was married but had lost the company of his wife, Maria, to early onset Alzheimer's disease. He devotedly visited her care facility twice a week; not once since she'd been there had she recognized him. Before he would leave her side, though, he knelt next to her bed and said The Lord's Prayer. The first time he'd done that, Maria spoke the first words he'd heard from her in over a year. She prayed along with him, not missing a syllable.

His heart had soared, thinking he was the witness to a miracle, but his wife hadn't been restored to him. As soon as they'd both said amen, she'd lapsed back into the netherworld of her mind. The only time she ever spoke again was when they prayed together, and of late her voice rose barely above a whisper.

It gave Calendri some comfort that if Maria could remember nothing else, she still knew the Lord. He never told anyone else about this, but having seen a living example that his faith was more than mere superstition affected the way he voted on issues that came before the court and softened the tone of the opinions he wrote.

He now found room for a greater measure of compassion in his interpretations of the law. A man long considered a bedrock conservative had aroused the suspicion of some commentators that he was becoming a moderate, and who knew if the change might stop there.

Mr. Justice Hawkins, a taciturn bachelor, was often derided as Calendri's second vote. His confirmation hearings had been a spectacle of partisan politics. The Democrats had insisted they were only questioning Hawkins' professional qualifications to sit on the high court; the Republicans countered that the opposition was questioning the nominee's character. Hawkins, himself, had played the race card, asking the Senate Judiciary Committee members if they would have subjected a white judge to such an inquisition as he had been made to suffer.

In the end, Hawkins had been confirmed, a vote many Democrats came to rue. Hawkins, though he had never asked a question from the bench during his tenure on the Supreme Court, voted with Calendri ninety-five percent of the time. On the rare occasions when he'd strayed, the conservative wing of the court still won, having managed to snag a vote from the other side.

Hawkins' few harmless dissenting votes only made it look, more than ever, that he did what Calendri told him to do. Hawkins was easily the angriest man ever to sit on the Court. He was even becoming disgruntled with his mentor; seeing Calendri's leftward drift had inclined Hawkins' thinking, if not yet his vote, to tack farther to the right.

Looking at the court session ahead, Hawkins foresaw several cases on which he and Calendri would cast opposing votes. He intended to make his position clear that night, after dinner.

The two justices dined without company, as was their custom.

Calendri's cook had served the blood rare prime rib that both justices loved so well. Hawkins ate with gusto. He noticed with growing irritation, though, that Calendri was picking at his food, ignoring the meat and nibbling at the potatoes and leeks.

Damn, Hawkins thought, was the man becoming a vegan?

Couldn't he even *eat* like a Republican these days?

"Something wrong with your food, Alberto?" Hawkins asked.

"I don't have much of an appetite lately. I invited you here with the intent of enjoying a good meal, a cigar and an after-dinner drink, but ..." He shrugged.

"You don't want to discuss the upcoming docket?"

Calendri showed his associate the saddest smile he'd ever seen from the man.

"No, Titus, quite the opposite."

"The opposite being?"

"My imminent retirement. I thought you should be the first to know. I just don't have the heart for the job anymore."

Well, Hawkins thought, resignation would certainly keep Alberto Calendri from becoming another Earl Warren. That should have made him happy, but the thought of losing his only friend on the court left him feeling a bit lost. It wasn't subservience that led Hawkins to follow Calendri, it was a deep trust in his intellect and a complete faith in his character.

The times he'd disagreed with the chief justice, until recently, were honest differences of opinion. "Is it Maria?" he asked.

"Mostly. She's a little less with me every time I see her. I try to tell myself that means she's a little closer to God, but that comfort, of late, has proven to be inadequate."

"I'm sorry, Alberto."

Hawkins had never been comfortable around women; never saw a reason one of them would want him for company. He'd always tried to find comfort elsewhere. Not any illegal vice or even one that might be frowned on. No, his indulgence was the country's most socially acceptable addiction: food. He loved good food. It warmed him both physically and emotionally.

He speared the last piece of prime rib on his plate.

Tried to swallow it before it had been properly masticated.

Got it caught in his throat.

The chief justice saw the look of discomfort on his friend's face as the obstruction occurred, and how vexation became alarm as the blockage refused to be dislodged. There was always that moment of social awkwardness on such occasions. The observer's first impulse was to hope the moment passed without embarrassment on anyone's part.

When Titus Hawkins' eyes bulged, the moment for polite hesitation was over.

The associate justice opened his mouth, inserted an index finger and tried to pry loose the chunk of meat that was killing him, and Alberto Calendri knocked over his chair getting to his feet. He hurried around the table and hauled Hawkins to his feet. They were both solid-bodied men, to put it politely, standing less than six feet tall.

Al Calendri had been on the wrestling team at Colgate, but that had been a *long* time ago. Nonetheless, he still knew how to grapple with someone. He stepped behind Hawkins, forced his friend's arms into the air and locked his hands just above his friend's umbilicus. He pulled with all his might, hoping to execute the Heimlich maneuver and clear Hawkins' airway.

He succeeded but not without causing a lethal complication: a ruptured abdominal aortic aneurysm. A large volume of blood spilled into Hawkins' abdominal cavity. If the chief justice had kept up with medical literature with the same dedication that he read the law, he would have known the Heimlich maneuver had been largely discredited. The recommended response to help a choking victim was to give five strong blows to the back in the area between the shoulder blades, taking care not to injure the spine in the process.

The gap in Alberto Calendri's lifesaving education would never be explained to him. He was surprised that in his effort to save Hawkins he had managed to lift his friend into the air. He'd never have thought he still had the strength to do that, and then he had no strength at all. The sudden pain in his chest made him think he'd been impaled.

Both men were unconscious before they hit the floor and dead shortly thereafter.

The combined weight of the two justices totaled almost five hundred pounds, but Calendri's house was extremely sturdy in its construction. Their fall hadn't even rattled the silverware on the dinner table. By the time Hawkins' driver found them, the highest court in the land had two unexpected vacancies.

Charlottesville, Virginia

Damon Todd and his two fellow fugitives were getting to know each other. They came to a unanimous agreement that they'd been screwed by the CIA. None of them had ever been legally arrested, tried or convicted of any crime. Too bad those little niceties didn't matter a good goddamn in their cases.

"Working for a fucking spook shop is worse than being in the military." Anderson said. "You put on a uniform, they take away maybe half the rights you had as a civilian. You start doing covert ops for the Company, man, they own you from the asshole out."

Crosby said, "True, but we knew that going in. It's just that we were so jazzed about the idea of becoming badasses who didn't answer to anyone and got to kill other badasses without going to jail for it that, hell, we'd make the same deal all over again."

"Would you?" Todd asked.

"Damn right," Anderson said. "Only this time we'd be more careful."

"Leave no fingerprints on the unauthorized kills we made," Crosby said.

"Yeah, we called some of our own shots, but we didn't take down anyone who wasn't going to be targeted eventually." Anderson shook his head at the injustice of it all.

Todd said, "If you're right about that, you gave your superiors all the reason they needed to fear you. In a hierarchy, the structure maintains its integrity only if each member keeps to his own place. By showing those above you that you could do their jobs as well as your own, you might as well have pointed a gun to their heads."

Anderson laughed. "Now, there's an idea. Too bad we didn't have anyone like you to point out the big picture to us."

Crosby didn't crack any jokes. He turned contemplative.

"Just how much do you think you know about us, Doc? The kind of work we did and how we felt about it."

"I don't know about you; I only know about me."

Anderson smirked. "Like he'd have any idea what it means to kill someone."

Crosby reminded his friend, "He killed Stanwick."

"Oh, yeah. Must be getting forgetful," Anderson said.

Crosby studied Todd. "There are others, Doc. Stanwick isn't the only guy whose ticket you've punched."

Both former spooks looked at Todd. Waiting to see if he'd tell them.

Todd thought about it. He'd never thought confession was good for the soul ... but knowing he was still a potential target for his companions, it might make them feel more of a bond if they knew he was more like them than not.

On the other hand, he didn't have to let them know everything.

If they did come for him, he'd need as much surprise as he could muster.

He said to Crosby, "You're right."

"Someone you knew or someone you didn't?" Crosby asked.

Anderson wanted to know, "Were you playing offense or defense?"

Todd said, "Maybe later. If we get to know each other better."

The two rogue operatives nodded. They could buy that.

But Anderson asked one more question. "How'd you feel afterward?"

Todd thought about the man who had tried to rob him at gunpoint.

The man he'd strangled and watched die.

"Like there was something wrong with me," Todd said, "and that wasn't such a bad thing."

At the time, he'd glamorized it more than that, but Crosby and Anderson didn't have to know.

"Sonofabitch, he does know," Anderson said.

A feeling of kinship among them started to grow.

They set about planning how to get to James J. McGill.

Camp David, Catoctin Mountains, Maryland

With Nick and two paramedics pacing behind them, McGill and Patti set off on their morning three-mile walk around the grounds of the presidential retreat. After a week of taking things easy, they upped the tempo to moderately brisk. Actually, Patti was the one who determined their speed. The White House physician had told her as long as she could speak comfortably to her husband and did not experience any chest pain she would not be going too fast.

McGill kept a close eye on Patti, making sure her face didn't become flushed or her breathing labored. He consciously stayed a half-step ahead of her; if she suddenly pitched forward, she'd be easier to catch. If she fell backward, he'd have to be really quick.

Kenny had been moved to a bedroom in Aspen lodge, down the hall from his father and stepmother's suite. He had his own contingent of medical professionals nearby, but he'd been delighted to get out of the hospital, and the fresh country air seemed to be aiding his recovery. He'd told McGill that morning that he was looking forward to the day he could join him and Patti on their walks.

Meanwhile, he was happy to Skype with Liesl Eberhardt and other friends in Evanston.

Back in D.C., Abbie was attending classes at Georgetown with a reinforced cordon of Secret Service protection. Deke Ky headed the protection detail. McGill, despite lingering hard feelings, felt good about that.

Caitie was in Evanston, with Carolyn and Lars, and back in school. Caitie's security had been supplemented, too, and extended to McGill's ex-wife and her husband. Carolyn said it wasn't too oppressive. She admitted that Lars preferred having professionals keep them safe rather than have her continue to carry a gun.

McGill felt the same way.

Chana Lochlan had been warned and she and her husband, Graham Keough, had left Washington for parts unknown, accompanied by their own private security people.

It was a beautiful morning. The people closest to McGill's heart were all as safe as could be. The love of his life had just linked an arm with his and given him a peck on the cheek. He should have been a happy man, but he was restless.

Patti had been right. He wanted to find Damon Todd and neutralize any threat he might represent: because he could. But he couldn't right now. He had to be smart. Considerate. Not rock the boat.

Sweetie would be flying in that evening with Daryl Cheveyo and someone from the FBI. It would be good to at least get a start on throwing a net over Todd. Until they arrived, he'd spend time with his wife and his son — and work on staying fit with some of the Marines who guarded Camp David.

Patti gave a little tug on his arm. McGill jerked in reaction.

"Are you okay?" he asked. "You want to head back?"

"I'm fine," Patti said. "I'd just like to know if you're up for a little conversation."

"I was woolgathering, huh?"

"Three bags full."

"You now have my full attention, Madam President."

"Thank you." Patti took a moment to cock an ear in the direction of Nick and his acolytes. She continued in a soft voice. "I got some disturbing news this morning."

McGill made do with an inquisitive look.

"Galia called to let me know that Chief Justice Calendri and Associate Justice Hawkins were found dead."

"Foul play?" No assassinations, please God, he thought.

Patti shook her head and described the current medical assumptions as to the causes of death.

McGill shook his head in wonder. "That's still awful."

"Almost poetic, though, two men who worked so closely together dying together."

"Neither of them was your favorite member of the court," McGill said.

"No they weren't, though Calendri was starting to change, become less the ideologue. It would have been interesting to see if Hawkins had followed."

McGill couldn't begin to guess about that, but he knew something else.

"You're going to have an unprecedented opportunity, filling two Supreme Court vacancies at the same time."

Patti sighed and for the first time that morning she looked like she was still on the mend rather than fully recovered.

"You're forgetting," she told McGill, "that I'm not the person at the controls in the Oval Office at the moment."

McGill stopped dead in his tracks, bringing Patti to a halt, too.

From behind them, Nick called out, "Is everything all right?"

McGill held out a hand to keep the medical team from rushing forward.

"We're fine, Nick. Just discussing something."

"Are you telling me," McGill asked, "that Mather Wyman might try to make two nominations to the Supreme Court as acting president? Or even one, for that matter?"

Patti said, "I'm telling you, he could, and the only way I could stop him would be to resume office, let's say, today."

She gave McGill a tug and they continued with their walk.

He said, "You could pass the word through the attorney general that any judge who accepted a Wyman nomination might find himself or herself in the embarrassing position of having that nomination withdrawn when you resume office."

Patti laughed. "That's just what Galia said. The two of you are starting to think alike."

There was a time that would have bothered McGill. Not so much anymore.

"Maybe we're getting ahead of ourselves," McGill said. "I got ticked off at Mather because he sided with Celsus on subverting Deke and Leo. Before that, I always thought he was completely respectful of you."

Patti said, "He was, but he'd never sat behind my desk before. He was right to shut down Burke Godfrey's teapot rebellion fast, but his idea of charging Godfrey with treason was going a step too far. I didn't say anything because he was so new in the job and, really, there was nothing I could have done about it, short of returning. He called me to say he and Michael Jaworsky had thought better of it, but I could tell he felt embarrassed."

McGill thought he saw another concern in his wife's eyes.

"There's something else?"

"Celsus told me the CIA was being … unforthcoming about the service records of the two former covert operatives who escaped with Damon Todd. I told him to take his concerns to Mather. He said he had and was told the matter had been taken under advisement."

McGill laughed. "Celsus must have loved that."

"Not one bit. That's why he called me."

"Going over the acting president's head," McGill said.

"Yes."

"And?"

Patti said, "And I called the director of national intelligence and told him I wanted full copies of those men's records delivered to SAC Crogher immediately. He promised to do so … but if he called Mather to confirm that order things could get complicated. The country is not supposed to have two presidents at the same time."

"How soon do we find out who prevailed?" McGill asked.

"Galia is supposed to be on the helicopter due here this evening. Then we'll know."

"And if Mather is thinking of nominating a justice or two?"

Patti said, "Then I go back to work, ready or not."

Rock Creek Park — Washington, D.C.

White House Deputy Chief of Staff Stephen Norwood, wearing a Saint Louis Cardinals baseball cap, sunglasses, a polo shirt, jeans and sneakers, walked along a path in the park with Jean Wayburn, the chief political reporter for the online edition of the *Washington Post*.

Jean, also casually dressed, was a whip smart alumna of Vanderbilt. She had a sweet Tennessee accent that came and went with her mood and the company she was keeping.

She was laying it on thick with Stephen Norwood, a graduate of Washington University in Saint Louis, another elite non-Ivy.

"So what's the scoop, Steve," Jean asked, "and why tell me now if you don't want me to write about it?"

Norwood had mentioned an embargo date to her.

He said, "I'm running a test for the campaign I'm going to head. I want to see who we can trust in the media."

Jean's stride faltered. Norwood looked over his shoulder and smiled.

"Come on, Jean. You don't burn any calories standing still."

She didn't need to lose an ounce, but she hurried to catch up.

"You're telling me you're going to be Patti Grant's campaign manager?"

"I am."

"And by telling me this you're testing me?" Jean asked.

"I want to see if you'll honor the embargo date."

"What is the date?"

"I'll let you know."

Jean gave him a sidelong look.

"How's Andrea?" she asked.

"Mrs. Norwood is doing quite well, thank you."

"The two of you are still happy?"

"Blissful."

"No chance in the world you'd ever —"

"None. You should really —"

"You can't blame a girl for trying. You were the last sweet, good-looking guy God made."

"I seriously doubt that. So? You want to know what we're up to?"

"You and Patti Grant?"

"Yes."

"All right, I'll be good. Tell me."

"The president is going to run for reelection as an independent and put a billion dollars of her own money into the campaign. I think that's far more money than she'll need. Given the magnitude of her star-power, she —"

Norwood had lost Jean Wayburn again. She ran to catch up.

He was a happily married man, but he thought Jean looked quite fetching with a light sheen of sweat on her brow and her eyes sparkling.

"You better not be playing me, Stephen."

He was, of course. He was counting on Jean. Oh, she wouldn't publish the story. For one thing, she'd never find a second source for it, but Norwood and Galia Mindel would be grievously disappointed if the rumor of Patti Grant running as a self-funded independent candidate for president wasn't circulating far and wide through official Washington before the sun went down.

Galia thought the president's health problem might be causing doubts among the Democrats as to putting Patti Grant at the head of their ticket. The chief of staff wanted to make the Dems wet-their-pants anxious that they were about to blow their chance to recapture the White House. Neither Galia nor Norwood doubted they'd last forty-eight hours before making their entreaties to the president.

As for playing Jean, Norwood would make sure he found some special — platonic — way to make amends. He started by buying her a hot dog and a soft drink.

Mango Mary's — Key West, Florida

Jackie Richmond was working behind the bar when the woman came into the place and asked for a sparkling water with a slice of lime. Jackie had told Alice if he was going to keep living free at her house, he had to earn his keep.

He'd been tending bar for a month now and felt at ease doing the work.

Read the paper when nobody needed his attention.

The woman had taken the stool right in front of him during a lull in business. No one else in the joint. She could have sat anywhere she wanted and let him do the walking, but she hadn't.

Her light brown hair was streaked with blonde highlights that came from the sun not a bottle. She had bright blue eyes. She wore a butter yellow polo shirt and khaki shorts. Had an even tan and looked like she might have played sports in college. But that had been a while ago. She had little crow's feet at the corners of her baby blues. Didn't act like that bothered her at all.

He served her drink and asked, " Would you like to run a tab?"

She shook her head, paid cash, tipped him a buck.

Sat there and sipped her fizzy water and zoned out.

Jackie went back to reading his newspaper not five feet away. The best pick up technique in the world, he knew, was to be polite, safe and available. The worst was to be aggressive, self-important and wear gold anywhere you had body hair. Jackie, whose work required that he avoid notice and pay attention to the world around him, always went for subtlety.

He stayed alert to his surroundings by reading the *Key West Citizen* and the *Miami Herald* every day. He didn't think he'd find any headlines saying Cops About to Drop Net Over Linley Boland. But he might see something along the lines of Man Wanted for Questioning in Naples Deaths Thought to Be in Keys. That would be his cue to —

Take a good look at the punk walking through the front door. Face tight with anger. Gold chain around his neck diving into chest hair that might have required a weed whacker for grooming. No gun or knife in hand, but fingers half-curled on their way to forming fists.

He was heading straight for Jackie and, incidentally, the woman at the bar.

The guy didn't believe in introductions.

He just snarled at Jackie, "Hey, dickwad, where's the owner?"

The asshole was right behind the woman at the bar now. She turned to see who was breathing down her neck. She was none too pleased with what she saw.

The prick took notice of her, and Jackie's hand went under the bar.

"What the fuck you lookin' at?" he asked. Not waiting for an answer, he shoved the stool on which the woman sat aside with his leg.

"Hey!" she yelled.

The asshole pointed a finger at her as if to tell her to shut up and he —

Didn't get the first word out of his mouth. The woman grabbed his extended finger, sprang to her feet, bent the finger back so far she bounced the back of the jerk's head off the bar. Jackie caught him on the rebound with a forehand to the forehead. His blunt object of choice was a bottle of Seagram's V.O.

The guy somehow managed to keep his feet, but had lost all his hostility.

He staggered backward, toward the door.

Jackie offered the Seagram's bottle to the woman.

"Maybe he needs one for the road."

A clout on the head, he meant.

"I don't think so," she said.

As the prick neared the open doorway, he tried to turn and face the world head on. Instead, he tripped and did a face-plant on the sidewalk. Jackie tucked the Seagram's bottle out of sight. The woman returned her bar stool to its proper place. She received a fresh drink on the house.

Extending his hand to her, Jackie Richmond introduced himself.

Taking it, the woman said, "Carina Linberg."

When the cops showed up a few minutes later, both of them disclaimed any knowledge of the man on the sidewalk. The cops didn't push them. Someone falling down in public — drunk, stoned or stroked out — wasn't anything new in Key West.

They just hauled the guy off like they were collecting trash.

The Rose Garden — The White House

Acting President Mather Wyman ambled slowly along one side of the garden's central lawn. Walking with him was his niece Kira Fahey Yates. Wyman had been dismayed when Kira had returned from her honeymoon in Spain only a few days after she'd left. But when she'd told him that she and Welborn had seen the news of the assault on Salvation's Path and felt compelled to return and see if they might be of help, he'd never felt more proud of her.

She'd followed that by saying, "Mattie, I'll always be close by when you need me."

Kira made him smile, as she so often did.

The two of them came to a cast iron bench originally installed at the direction of Franklin Delano Roosevelt. Wyman and Kira sat on it and he took his niece's hand. With a wry note in his voice, he told her, "I was talking with Russell George today."

"Who's he?" Kira asked.

"The librarian of Congress."

"Time to renew your card?"

Wyman grinned.

"No, I asked if he might search his collection to see if there was any book of etiquette that applied to a sitting president and the fellow keeping her seat warm. I'm sad to say no such volume exists. Without any formal guidance, I find myself at a bit of a loss these days."

Kira knew the time for wisecracks was over.

"It's none of my business, Mattie, but are you and the president having any problems?"

"It's more a matter of ... the two of us are exploring uncharted waters and we might have run aground. I'm afraid I put a foot wrong by failing to understand the dynamic between James J. McGill and the Secret Service. SAC Crogher came to me and said Mr. McGill was at an increased risk of —"

"Being killed?" Kira asked.

"Imminent mortality, I believe, was the way he put it. He asked for permission to demand that Mr. McGill accept increased protection. I thought I couldn't be responsible for the president losing a second husband and told Crogher to do whatever he thought necessary. It didn't take long for me to receive an indirect rebuke from Mr. McGill and hear that he had discharged all of his protective detail. He said he didn't work for me and wasn't subject to my wishes."

Kira winced.

"It's hardly your fault, my dear."

"No, but I could have told you about Jim McGill and Celsus Crogher."

"How could you have done that?"

"Welborn and Deke Ky are friends. They talk. So do Welborn and I."

The acting president frowned.

"What?" Kira asked.

"It's not my place to come between a husband and wife," Wyman said, "but I hope you can keep our discussions private."

Kira smiled. "Of course, I can. Welborn speaks privately with his mother."

The acting president nodded. "An equitable privilege then. The situation with Mr. McGill was only the first difficulty. There's been a matter of national intelligence. I won't go into detail but I was considering what to do when I heard the president had already made a decision. I acquiesced because it would have been foolish not to do so. Now, there are, well, two more things."

"More secret stuff?" Kira asked.

"Yes and no. The secret is only a political matter so I can share that with you. I'm told the GOP, or at least some people in it, want to draft me as their nominee to run for president."

Kira's eyes got big. "Oh, Mattie, you'd make a great president!"

"You're not happy with the one we have?"

That poked a pin in Kira's balloon.

"Well, yes, of course, I am. I think the president has done a great job … all things considered. She would have gotten more done if … if her own party had gone along with her."

"Her former party," Wyman reminded his niece. "If I were to become the Republican nominee, I'd be running against my boss."

Kira thought about that. "Then I think it would be the first no-lose presidential election ever, but I think you could get the GOP to go along with you more often than Patricia Grant was able to do."

Wyman chuckled. "I don't know about that, but here's the other thing: A bright, ambitious fellow who undoubtedly has a long list of favors I might do for him has suggested that, in light of the tragic deaths of Alberto Calendri and Titus Hawkins, I draw up my list of candidates for the Supreme Court."

Now, Kira took her uncle's hand. "You think the president would let you do that?"

"Submit my choices to the Senate for confirmation? No. I could, however, let it become known who my choices would be if I were president. Who knows, if I were elected president, another seat on the court might come open. By simply composing a list, however, I'd show what my inclinations as president would be."

"Mattie, you *are* the president. For the moment anyway. I think you have no choice but to be prepared. It would be irresponsible not to start the process."

Wyman smiled. "Is there anyone you have your eye on?"

"Only Welborn and he wouldn't look good in a black robe."

"I'll take your word on that. You are a great comfort to me, Kira."

"I love you, Mattie." She kissed his cheek and stood. She told him, "Now, think some deep presidential thoughts and you'll know just what to do."

Easier said than done, Wyman thought as he watched Kira go.

He still had a secret he hadn't told anyone except Zachary Garner and Patti Grant. He'd revealed to them that he was a gay man. Zack had taken the news to the grave with him. But Wyman had told the president he intended to run for a House seat from Ohio as an openly gay man; he'd even asked for and received permission from the president to make his coming out statement while he was acting president.

She might be wondering why he hadn't done so already.

The immediate crush of business had kept him too busy to think about something that in the grand scheme of things was not so terribly important. Doing a good job for the country was what mattered. But having learned the GOP might draft him as their presidential nominee brought the matter back with a bang.

Running for a House seat as an openly gay man was one thing.

Doing it while running for the White House was quite another.

Running against an opponent who knew your secret and wondering if or when she might reveal it — that would require some very deep presidential thought.

Spaneas Import-Export — Baltimore, Maryland

Detective Harlan Greer of the Baltimore Police Department pointed to a red brick industrial building sitting behind a chain-link fence on a stretch of unimproved city waterfront and said, "That's the place."

His partner Herb Beekman nodded. He said, "Ring the bell on that post next to the gate. They give you any shit about opening up … I'm gonna be real interested to see how your plan works."

Sitting in the back of the unmarked police car, a BPD two-way radio in hand, wearing his Air Force uniform, Welborn Yates said, "Thanks for your help."

Greer said, "Guys like us have to take care of our own."

Beekman added, "Yeah, but don't shoot anyone if you don't have to. You wouldn't believe this city's paperwork on that."

"I'll try to restrain myself," Welborn said. He crossed the street and pressed the button as instructed. Doing so produced no sound that he could detect, but his fighter pilot's eyesight saw the red light of a camera on the near side of the building come on. The camera swiveled on its mount until it was pointing at him.

A voice came through a small speaker next to the call button.

"What?" The one-word query came with an accent.

Greek, if the name of the place meant anything.

"Captain Welborn Yates, Air Force Office of Special Investigations. I want to talk with Teddy Spaneas." Greer and Beekman had told Welborn that Spaneas was suspected of being the biggest wholesaler of hot cars in town. If anybody could handle a truckload of hot rides, it was him.

"Air Force?" the voice asked.

"The people who drop bombs on our enemies," Welborn explained.

The guy with the accent found that funny.

"That why you here? You're gonna bomb me?"

"Yes." Welborn could be succinct, too.

He saw the lens on the camera telescope. Someone wanted a closer look at him.

"You crazy maybe?"

"Might be."

"There's a car with two city cops parked across the street."

"They're with me." Welborn held up his BPD radio.

He overheard a brief exchange in a foreign tongue.

"I don't think you gonna bomb me. I think you're a cop playin' a cop game."

"I'm an *Air Force* cop, a federal agent, and you're about to change your mind."

"Yeah? Well, you go ahead and bomb us. We got work to do."

"Don't do it near any windows, cover your ears and your asses, too. Hiding under desks would be a very good idea."

"Hey! Are you *really* crazy? You can't bomb us!"

"You get one last chance," Welborn said. "One minute to let me in or send Teddy out."

Welborn keyed his radio.

Greer answered, "Call in your pals?"

"Yeah, tell them subsonic but up close and personal."

Allowing for civil aviation aircraft to clear the needed airspace, it would be a two-minute wait. Welborn thought that would work even better. The creeps inside the red brick building would be tense at first. Then they'd start to relax, maybe even crawl out of their hidey-holes and then, *bam,* three F-15s flying in tight formation would rocket past Spaneas Import-Export.

If one of the car thieves inside was peeking out a window and caught a faceful of flying glass, tough. The Air Force was hunting the killer of three of its own. Welborn was hunting the bastard who had killed his three best friends.

He kept his hands over his ears, and saw that Greer and Beekman had followed suit.

Welborn sensed the formation approach before he saw it, heard the approaching roar while the F-15s were still specks in the distance. A commercial jet engine at a distance of one hundred feet produced a meter reading of one hundred and forty decibels — the noise threshold at which even short term exposure *with* hearing protection could cause permanent damage.

Physical pain began at one hundred and twenty-five decibels.

Welborn pressed his hands harder over his ears.

At a glance, he saw the windows in the Spaneas building rattling in their frames.

Turning his head, he saw the three Air Force fighters closing fast, growing in size and definition so quickly, it made Welborn think they were going to take *him* like birds of prey. He wanted to throw himself to the ground. He wasn't the target, though, the building on the other side of the fence was.

What it must have sounded like to the men inside, he could only guess.

Exercising a level of skill that made Welborn swell with pride, the pilots of the F-15s put their aircraft into almost perpendicular climbs just as they came to the Spaneas property. The forty-six thousand pounds of combined thrust from the F-15's twin engines could hurl a city bus through the air like it was a ball of paper.

If that crushing power from three successive aircraft had been fully brought to bear against the old red brick building, it would have done a big bad wolf and blown the house down. But the pilots knew their mission was to scare not to kill.

In the wink of an eye, the fighters had climbed so high they were out of sight.

Welborn gave it ten seconds before he pressed the button on the post again.

Selling the plan to his Air Force superiors hadn't been hard.

He reminded them of the efficacy of air power at Salvation's Path.

Reminded them that Linley Boland had killed three Air Force pilots.

Asked if they were going to let Navy aviators have all the fun.

The accented voice came through the speaker and told him, "You *are* crazy!"

Welborn said in an even tone, "That's what happens when we *don't* bomb people. You want to see crazy, that's what comes next. Or you can send Teddy Spaneas out."

The gate in front of Welborn rolled open.

Camp David — Catoctin Mountains, Maryland

The two Marines, a first sergeant named Vasquez and a captain named Wolford, looked at the objects James J. McGill had placed on the grass in front of him. Then they looked at each other with the same question in their eyes: *Was this guy serious?*

Vasquez and Wolford were the men who had volunteered to help the president's husband get in shape for close quarters combat. The very idea of a civilian in his late forties fighting anybody for any reason had struck them as a joke. They'd anticipated injecting the dude with a quick dose of reality, not really hurting him and, if he was a sport, having a beer with him.

That and having a story they could pass along and laugh about for years.

Captain Wolford said, "May I confirm, sir, just what you have there?"

"Please, call me Jim," McGill said. "There'll be fewer inhibitions that way."

"You don't want us to pull any punches, Jim?" Vasquez asked. "Is that it?"

The first sergeant looked to be about thirty; the captain was maybe a year or two younger. They'd brought pugil sticks, helmets and rubber knives with them. The things McGill had brought were
—

"A shillelagh, a cane with a curved handle and a hockey stick," McGill said, answering Wolford's question.

"You've used these things before, Jim?" Wolford asked.

"The shillelagh and the cane, yes. The hockey stick is new, but I have some ideas I want to try with it."

"Never heard of the shill-thing before," Vasquez said.

"It's also called an Irish fighting stick. The Irish turned to the shillelagh after the English took the swords away. It's made of extremely hard wood and as you see has a bulge the size of a fist on one end."

"If you're not wearing ice skates, what kind of fight would require any of these things, Jim?" Wolford wanted to know.

McGill shrugged. "The kind where you can't get to your firearm and have to make do with what's at hand, facing an opponent who might have a gun, a knife or his own blunt instrument."

The Marines looked at each other again and shrugged.

"I take it we're not going to fight to the death here," Wolford said.

"No, we're all on the same side. Bruises to the body and our pride will be enough."

Vasquez and Wolford nodded, finding the rules of engagement acceptable.

Interesting even.

To be careful, though, Vasquez asked, "No courts martial, right, Jim?"

McGill nodded. He picked up his shillelagh. It had been a gift from his Uncle Ed, the man who had taught him the merciless, little known martial art Dark Alley. McGill wanted to polish his technique and had asked if he might spar with an enlisted man and an officer.

"How do you want to start, Jim?" Wolford asked. "Both of us at once or one at a time?"

"Let's start one on one. Is there any big difference between the two of you?"

"Vasquez fights dirty," Wolford said.

McGill smiled. "And you fight dirtier."

For his answer, Wolford grabbed a pugil stick and lunged at McGill.

Walter Reed National Military Medical Center
Bethesda, Maryland

The blow that Ellie Booker had delivered to the back of Reverend Burke Godfrey's skull with the Beretta she'd purloined had been sufficient not only to knock him out but also to land him in a guarded room at the military facility where U.S. presidents went to get their annual physical examinations. Invariably, the chief executives were pronounced fit to continue in office for another year. Burke Godfrey's outlook wasn't so sunny. Not at first. He'd been concussed at the time of his trauma and claimed to have suffered debilitating headaches ever since.

There had been some question whether he was malingering — pulling a Yossarian in the words of one DOJ prosecutor who'd read Joseph Heller — to avoid transport to less comfortable quarters, but the medical staff said Godfrey's pain was real. They were closely monitoring the patient's cerebral blood flow and pressure within his skull. The abundance of caution was taken despite Godfrey's injury being classified as mild. A complete recovery was expected.

As if to add to the clergyman's troubles, when he finally felt up to meeting with his lawyer, Benton Williams, he learned he was being dropped as a client.

"Why?" Godfrey groaned.

That morning, for the first time since Godfrey regained consciousness, the pain in his head had diminished somewhat and his jailers had agreed to call his lawyer. The hope that Williams would find some way to help him slip out of the trouble he was in had elevated Godfrey's sense of well-being another notch. Now that he'd heard he was being abandoned, he felt the crushing weight inside his head return.

Williams said, "I'm afraid the answer is this simple: You can no longer afford me."

"I wrote you a million dollar retainer check …" Godfrey couldn't recall the specific date. The way he felt it was a wonder he could speak at all. "Not long ago."

"Yes, you did. Looking at the situation you've contrived for yourself, though, that wouldn't be nearly enough. In addition to the charge of conspiring to kill Andrew Hudson Grant, you're now charged with resisting arrest and three counts of attempted murder of FBI personnel. The U.S. attorney who will prosecute you will also be asking for more than jail time for you; the court will be asked to have you pay for all the expenses you cost the government by resisting arrest. That amount, I'm led to believe, is staggering."

Godfrey asked, "How can they take more than I have."

"Burke, I don't know what possessed you to do what you did. If you'd told me what you had in mind, I would have found the men necessary to overwhelm you and deliver you to the FBI. You would have been so much better off that way. What they're going to do now is take your church from you. They'll probably subdivide your property and put up low-income housing and strip malls."

"Sow the ground with salt?" Godfrey mumbled.

Williams sighed. He'd heard whispers that Mather Wyman had wanted to charge Godfrey with treason before calmer dispositions prevailed. So, who knew? Maybe salt was on the menu.

He told his erstwhile client, "I refunded your retainer, but it went into an account the government has seized so that's unavailable to you, too."

"How about …" Godfrey began.

Williams saw Godfrey was really struggling to bring order to his thoughts, not just putting on an act. Maybe there was a defense for him there. Yes, he'd fucked up on a gargantuan scale, but if he was no longer competent to participate in his own defense, maybe a rehabilitative incarceration would be called for.

After that … well, John Hinckley had shot Ronald Reagan, nearly killed a sitting president, and by now he got day passes to see movies and visit his mother. There had even been talk that eventually he'd be freed.

As Williams thought about that, Godfrey gave him something else to think about.

"Who hit me?" he asked. "Not one of my people."

"No, it was Ellie Booker, the producer for WorldWide News. She said you were holding her prisoner."

Being very careful about it, Godfrey moved his head an inch to the right and to the left.

"Wasn't a prisoner." Now he had the idea that had eluded him a moment ago. "How about we sue Ellie Booker … and Sir Edbert?"

If Benton Williams hadn't been a master of masking his feelings, he would have beamed. Sue Sir Edbert Bickford? Now there were some deep pockets. If Ms. Booker, acting as Sir Edbert's agent, had wrongfully caused a lifelong impairment to Reverend Burke Godfrey, why the damages might amount to … enough to pay off the government's bill. With allowances made to pay appropriate legal fees.

The reverend wouldn't see any windfall … but wait a minute now.

Hadn't he read that Ms. Booker had taken the government's final give-up-or-else call and spoken personally to Mather Wyman, Williams asked himself. Yes, he had. Burke Godfrey hadn't answered the phone because he'd already been assaulted by Ms. Booker. It could be argued that Reverend Godfrey might have been brought to his senses by hearing from the acting president.

A wonderful legal mosaic formed in Benton Williams' mind.

Reverend Godfrey wouldn't stand trial because he wasn't competent to defend himself.

Ellie Booker and Sir Edbert Bickford would pay for the grievous physical injury caused to Reverend Godfrey.

The good reverend would be confined in a rehabilitative setting.

A large part of the damages the government wanted would have to come from WorldWide News. The DOJ could sue Sir Edbert, too.

Williams would safeguard the damages awarded to his … Oops. He'd just dismissed Reverend Godfrey as his client. Well, that was easy enough to remedy. The lawyer took a binding legal agreement out of his briefcase, something he always carried with him.

"Reverend Godfrey, your idea has some merit. Perhaps I can continue working for you on a contingency basis. I would receive forty percent of whatever damages you are awarded, and I can use those funds to support your defense in any criminal proceedings against you. Would that be satisfactory to you?"

Godfrey gave his attorney a minimal nod. He extended his hand, by way of asking for a pen to sign whatever papers Williams had for him. New hope was lifting just a bit of his pain.

He said something his lawyer couldn't quite make out.

Williams told Godfrey, "I'm sorry, I couldn't hear what you said."

He leaned in close as the reverend repeated his words.

Taking the signed contingency agreement in hand, the lawyer told Godfrey, "Yes, you're right. Miracles do happen."

Spaneas Import-Export — Baltimore, Maryland

Welborn had Teddy Spaneas step out onto the public sidewalk. It was just a precaution. No arrest of the alleged stolen car wholesaler was planned, but you never knew what might happen. The guy might get careless and blurt an admission of a crime. In that case, he would be hauled in and the leverage they'd have on him would go way up.

As a further act of prudence, and a show of federal-local co-operation, Welborn waved to Greer and Beekman to join him.

"Fuck," Greer told Welborn, "wish we had the backup you've got."

Beekman said, "Hell, I'd settle for a drone. Sitting in front of a video screen firing missiles at the bad guys, that's my idea of police work."

Welborn hadn't looked at either as they'd cracked wise.

He'd been watching Teddy take in their comments.

When the Baltimore cops fell silent, Teddy looked at Welborn.

"I don't speak English too good," he said with a shrug.

"No?" Welborn asked. "Maybe, with all the excitement, you forgot or didn't understand when I told you I'm a federal officer. You lie to me, it's just like you're lying to an FBI agent. I prove that you've lied you go to jail. Do you understand that?"

Teddy looked at the two cops. They both gave him crocodile smiles.

"Wish we had that going for us, too," Greer told Teddy.

"We'll help our federal friend here and find people who'll say you speak English just fine," Beekman added.

"What you want?" Teddy asked Welborn.

"I want the man who killed my three friends."

Teddy held up his hands in protest. "No, no, I don't know any —"

"I didn't say you *knew* he was a killer," Welborn said. "This guy also steals cars. Lots of them."

Teddy took a step backward.

Welborn shook his head. "Too late for that. I've already got you for lying to me, pretending you didn't have the ability to speak with me. I have two Baltimore detectives as witnesses. The easiest way out for you is to talk to me now. Otherwise, things will get *much* worse, and you've just seen what kind of people I have backing me up. You run, we'll find you, and we won't let you off with a warning next time."

Teddy looked like a man about to go to pieces. Every fast twitch muscle in his body was primed for flight, but he couldn't disregard Welborn's warning or the look in his eyes. If he didn't give the man what he wanted, his days were numbered and the number wouldn't have any commas.

"Tell me who you want," Teddy said.

Welborn said, "His name is Linley Boland, but I'm sure he didn't use that name with you. Here's a recent booking photo of him; he made the mistake of trying to steal *my* car."

"He was arrested, and he made bail?" Teddy asked.

"Guy not only speaks English, he knows how the courts work," Greer said with a sneer.

Teddy ignored him and looked at the mug shot Welborn had handed him.

He wanted with all his heart to deny knowing the man, but he didn't even have to look at Welborn to know he had no choice in the matter. He bobbed his head.

"Yes, I know this man but not by the name you say."

"What name did he use?" Welborn asked.

Teddy didn't want to be caught in another lie so he shrugged. "I do not remember."

Welborn sighed. He glanced at the Baltimore detectives.

"You guys want to hook him up? I forgot my cuffs."

Beekman smiled and reached for his handcuffs.

"Wait, wait! I know something about him."

"What's that?" Welborn asked.

"I have the number of his bank account. In Cayman Islands."

Teddy took a slip of paper out of a pocket and handed it to Welborn.

"Ain't that nice?" Greer asked. "He had it on him, ready to go."

Welborn said, "Why do you have this information?"

"I owed him money. He say pay to this number."

"Why did you owe him money?"

Teddy saw the trap immediately and said, "I forget."

"How much money did you send to this account number?"

"I forget."

Welborn asked Greer and Beekman, "You think you could babysit Mr. Spaneas while I check out this bank?"

"Happy to," Greer said.

"You arresting me?" Teddy asked, indignant. "But you say —"
Welborn said, "Did I? I lied. I can do that, but you can't."

Beekman smiled and told Teddy, "Nobody ever said life was fair."

Camp David — Catoctin Mountains, Maryland

The pugil stick was a military training tool conceived in the 1940s. The Marines were the first branch of the U.S. military to use them. The stick had a cylindrical pad at each end. It was used to train recruits how to use bayonets and rifles as close-quarters weapons. That was, to slash, stab and club the enemy. The pad at one end was marked to represent the bayonet; the other was marked to represent the butt of the rifle.

In training exercises, protective gear was worn. Helmets protected combatants against concussions and brain injuries. Torso padding helped to ward off broken ribs, punctured lungs and damage to other vital organs. Plastic cups shielded the genitals.

When Captain Wolford snatched a pugil stick off the ground and charged McGill, neither of them had a helmet or torso padding on; both had thought to wear a cup. Wolford's clear intent was to ram one end of his stick into McGill's midsection.

Knock him on his ass, give him a grin and help him back up to his feet.

Show him a civilian should never mess with a Marine.

Wolford was cat quick, but he wasn't the quickest cat in the fight. McGill had learned through stinging practice with Uncle Ed that, given the opportunity, it was always better to evade than parry. He sidestepped the captain's lunge.

His shillelagh also proved a far more agile weapon than a pugil stick. Starting with an overhand, two-hand grip on the Irish fighting stick, McGill stepped to his right, out of the line of Wolford's charge. To counterattack, he used his left hand to flick the shillelagh in an arc, moving it like a wiper blade clearing rain from a windshield.

The stick's arc ended on the meat of Wolford's left forearm. Judging by the captain's bellow, it stung pretty good. McGill wasn't done with the man, however. He assumed that a Marine had a lot of fiber in his diet. That and the mental toughness required to be an elite combat troop. So he paid Wolford the compliment of sliding behind him and using the knobbed end of his stick to deliver a moderate blow to the calf of his right leg.

Wolford collapsed with a thud, and McGill no longer paid him any attention.

Vasquez, he remembered, had been described as a dirty fighter, and with Wolford out of the way he was the next man up. McGill didn't expect the first sergeant would be polite enough to ask if he was ready.

He wasn't and his blood must have been up from seeing his superior officer disposed of so quickly. He swung his pugil stick at McGill's head like he was a lumberjack about to plant his ax in a tree stump. Damn guy might have killed McGill if he'd landed that blow, but he didn't.

With both hands back on his shillelagh, McGill raised a *roof* over his head just in time; his stick formed a horizontal barricade to Vasquez's vertical angle of attack. McGill followed through by swiveling his hips to the left and sliding his shillelagh down the shaft of Vasquez's pugil stick, raking the fingers of the first sergeant's left hand.

Vasquez managed to hold on to his weapon with his right hand, but was vulnerable for that moment. McGill might have stepped back and let the Marine recognize the fight was over for him, but his blood was up now, too. What the hell had the guy been thinking, coming at his head like that? He wanted to make a name for himself? Say he was sorry afterward, things just got out of hand. But, hey, that McGill guy, he promised there'd be no courts martial.

Too bad about him dying and all.

McGill flicked his fighting stick in another arc.

The knobbed end smashed Vasquez's right hand, breaking

bones.

The first sergeant howled, dropped the pugil stick and fell to his knees.

Sonofabitch, McGill thought, he was going to have some explaining to do now.

Probably a good thing they hadn't gotten to the knife fighting.

Aspen Lodge — Camp David

Patti Grant was going stir crazy. Sure, she still got her daily briefing. She was keeping up with the madness that raged throughout the world. Seen through the eyes of the country's intelligence agencies, the planet was a horrific place, Guernica in the round.

For any president who hadn't run to become a figurehead, keeping the country safe and helping it to prosper in an equitable way wasn't just a job, it was a compulsion. Otherwise there would have been no reason to put up with the endless bullshit of electoral politics. Patti, as compulsive as anyone who'd ever occupied the Oval Office, was determined to take one last plunge into that fetid maelstrom, if her suddenly uncertain heart allowed it.

Closing her eyes, holding still and letting her muscles relax, she listened for any untrue beat, but the rhythm of the muscle that kept her alive was steady, strong and seemingly effortless. She saw no reason why it shouldn't be. She'd never done drugs. Never smoked. Consumed alcohol only in moderation. Had exercised with regularity since she was introduced to hopscotch.

So where the hell had the damn mitral valve prolapse come from?

There was no family history of the problem.

More important, was there anything more than the tiniest chance it would come back?

God, she hoped not. She *had* to get back to work. Even if the voters, in their infinite wisdom, decided not to reelect her, she'd have to find something to do. Maybe go to work with Clare Tracy and raise money to get smart, progressive women launched into political careers. Wouldn't that be a hoot for Jim, his wife and his old girlfriend working together?

The two of them looking more alike than either of them would care to admit.

Patti heard a floorboard creak. Somehow the administrator of the General Services Administration had learned of the telltale board and had inquired of the White House when a convenient time to fix it would be. Patti's reply had been, "After I leave office."

So many people tried so hard to make everything perfect for the president, Patti felt, that it could really get on your nerves.

Having heard the creak, she opened her eyes and saw Kenny McGill.

"I'm sorry," he said. "I didn't know you were sleeping, Patti."

She smiled and said, "I wasn't sleeping. I was looking at the world with my eyes closed."

Kenny grinned. "That's cool. Sounds better than saying you were just resting them."

"I have to wait another five years before I'll be old enough to say that."

She patted a cushion on the sofa, inviting Kenny to sit with her. She loved Jim's children with all her heart, Kenny more than ever, but she was always careful not to overstep the line in her head that said certain behavior with them was inappropriate. Being physically affectionate in public, for example.

Even a kiss on the cheek might be televised and disconcert Carolyn.

Now, in private with Kenny, she felt she'd earned the right to give his hand a squeeze.

"You're looking good, kiddo," Patti said.

Kenny stroked his scalp. "Yeah, if you like fuzzy cue balls, I guess."

Patti laid a chaste kiss on the top of his head.

"That fuzz is going to grow out, and when it does Liesl Eberhardt will swoon."

Kenny shared a sly smile. "I was just Skyping with her, keeping up on things at home and …" He looked around, as if spies might be lurking. "Liesl asked me if I'll be home in time to take her to our school's Christmas dance."

"Does that work with your recovery program?" Patti asked.

"I should be all right to travel before the dance."

"Timing is everything. Well, almost. Sometimes it helps to have a friend who can guarantee you a seat on an airplane."

Kenny's eyes got big. "Your plane?"

"Well, maybe your father's."

That was an even bigger surprise. *"Dad* has a plane?"

"I can usually find one for him when he needs one."

"That is *so* cool."

"Being president has its moments, but it has more headaches."

"Like what?"

"I'd tell you but it'd make your hair fall out."

Kenny recoiled in mock horror and then laughed.

Patti took his hand again and kissed it. He leaned in and kissed *her* cheek.

"I want to tell you how grateful I am," Kenny said, "but I don't know the words. I'm going to find them someday and then you'll know."

"I think I have an idea, but I'll wait patiently."

Out of the blue, Kenny asked, "You think Liesl is being nice to me just out of … not pity since I'm getting better, but sympathy?"

Patti shook her head. "Not a chance. I think it's more like that old song lyric: You don't know what you've got 'til it's gone. Liesl didn't lose you but I'm sure she's smart enough to see what might have been. Now, she's glad to have a second chance."

Kenny nodded; he could accept that.

"You know, Patti, I don't worry about myself anymore. The only thing that scares me these days is the thought that something bad might happen to someone I love."

Patti nodded. "That's a threshold we all cross. You got to it early."

Kenny put his arms around Patti and whispered to her, "I

love you."

Hadn't taken him any time at all to find the right words.

Fifth Avenue — Midtown Manhattan

Ellie Booker, on her way to a meeting with her new literary agent and a prospective publisher for her book, told the figure she felt looming up behind her, "I've got a knife."

Be damn awkward if the guy turned out to be a cop, she thought.

She needn't have worried.

Hugh Collier told her, "And I have a rapier-like wit."

Ellie looked at him as he stepped up alongside her, matching her pace.

"What do you want?"

"Shouldn't there have been an 'asshole' at the end of that question?"

"Goes without saying," Ellie told him.

"True enough. To answer your question, I've come to ask how Uncle and I might beg your forgiveness."

"You can't. Not now, not ever."

"Very well. If forgiveness is off the table, how might we buy the story of what happened at Salvation's Path? Uncle said to offer you double the sum any other publisher might offer. Having seen how deeply we've hurt you —"

Ellie glared at him. "Pricks like you and your uncle can't hurt me. If you knew how I'd been worked over ..." No, fuck that, she decided. She wasn't going to tell him about her childhood. If she did, Sir Edbert would make a book out of that. She told Hugh, "You sent me into trouble and left me there. There's no forgiving that. There's no working with anyone who betrays me."

If I had any decency, Hugh thought, I wouldn't be bothering this woman. But decency was an alien concept to him and he asked Ellie, "Might it salve your feelings if I said we'd treble any offer you receive elsewhere?"

Ellie stopped and turned to face Hugh.

"Here's what I'd like you to do. Take a left at the next corner. Head for the East River. Along the way, grab the two biggest shit bags you can find. Tuck one under each arm and when you come to the river jump in. See if you can walk along the bottom all the way to Queens. If you don't make it, I'll write your eulogy. How's that?"

Hugh sighed. "I'll have to ask Uncle if I can quadruple any other offer."

With a shrug he walked off. Ellie watched him go. He crossed to the west side of the street and then continued to head south along Fifth Avenue. Giving him a decent lead, Ellie set off to get to her meeting. After yapping with Hugh, she had to pick up her pace to make it to her meeting on time.

She hadn't gone a quarter-block when she heard someone else coming up from behind.

This guy was moving fast.

Christ, she thought, had Hugh flashed a sign to someone?

The broad won't play ball, dump her *in the river.*

She wouldn't put it past Hugh or Sir Edbert.

She whirled and proved she did, indeed, have a knife. Not a switchblade. That would have caused her too much grief if a cop caught her with one. But the blade of her knife did release with just a flick of the wrist.

Anywhere else, someone rushing at a woman who pulled a knife might jump back. Not in New York City. Ellie found herself looking at someone who looked like he'd been born at the confluence of the Tigris and the Euphrates. He grinned at her knife.

Told her, "I got one just like that, lady. Only mine's twice as big."

Ellie was about to say, *Yeah, but it's not in your hand.*

But then the guy asked, "You Ellie Booker?"

Like a rube, she admitted she was.

The guy said, "You've been served."

And he impaled a subpoena on the blade of her knife.

Broadening his smile, he said, "Have a nice day, lady."

Ellie turned to watch him go.

And saw Hugh Collier had doubled back on the other side of Fifth Avenue.

He'd seen the whole thing.

Camp David — Catoctin Mountains, Maryland

McGill peeked through a living room window as he arrived at Aspen Lodge and saw Kenny embrace Patti and saw her hug him back. Even as someone close to both of them, he wasn't about to interrupt that moment. A Secret Service Agent posted outside the front door watched McGill do his Peeping Tom number, but didn't say anything.

Taking note of the guy, McGill gave a nod and got one back.

He stepped away from the building wondering if the word had spread to the rest of the presidential security detail that he'd fired Deke and told Elspeth to take a hike. Sure it had, he thought. You couldn't bottle up that kind of news. Not in Washington. Never at the White House. He'd probably caused no small amount of resentment among the troops.

Might even have affected their willingness to die for him.

Oh, well, he got along without them before he'd met them.

Have to get along without them now.

He headed off for a walk in the woods. Maybe he could bop a bear with his shillelagh. Drag its carcass back and have someone make a rug out of it. Outrage the environmentalists as well as the guys with the Uzis.

He chuckled at the idea. Hoped he'd be able to maintain his sense of humor in the coming days. He had the feeling he was going to need it. What he needed even more, though, was a long talk with —

"That some kinda club you got there, pal? You got a permit for it?" The voice was pure Chicago cop. Female variety.

McGill turned with a bright smile on his face.

"Sweetie! I was just thinking about you."

"Everybody tells me that, so it must be true."

She stepped forward and extended her left hand.

McGill took it, examined her ring and kissed her cheek.

"It's beautiful. I'm very happy for you, Margaret."

"Did you ever think you'd see the day?"

McGill nodded, "Yes, I did. You have too much heart to keep it to yourself."

"That's the way it works, huh?"

"If it's the real thing."

Sweetie bobbed her head. "It's real. So what are you doing out here, playing Mountain Man McGill?"

"Problem is, I haven't been playing well with others. Thought I'd stay out of people's way for a while. But you managed to find me."

"The special agent on the door at Aspen pointed me in the right direction. So other than firing your minions what misdeeds have you accumulated?"

McGill told her about his sparring misadventure.

"You're beating up on Marines now?" Sweetie asked. "Don't you know service people are very popular?"

"I respect them, too, but not to the point of letting one crack my skull."

"The guy was *really* trying to do that?"

"My widow and fatherless children would be weeping right now. You'd be hunting the guy down."

Sweetie thought about that. "I've mellowed some lately, but I haven't taken to wearing lace or letting a friend go unavenged. I guess you're right. A girl can change only so much."

McGill said, "Speaking of being protective, where do things stand outside of Shangri-La?"

That being the original name of Camp David.

"I put Leo on the company payroll."

"Good … and is Deke sulking?"

"No. He's happy heading up the security detail for Abbie. Says she's a lot more reasonable than her old man."

"Ain't that the truth? Now, Caitie on the other hand …"

Sweetie laughed. "She'd try to subvert her security people first. Then she'd be willful just like you. She seems to be doing okay though with the beefed up number of Evanston cops back home. One of the new guys is a former SEAL What I hear, Caitie thinks the two of them will co-star in a movie someday."

McGill grinned and asked, "Carolyn and Lars?"

"They're covered, too."

"Putnam?"

"I'm going home tonight. He's holed up in a five-star hideout until then."

"You've got to sleep sometime. I know this guy in France who might be able to lend a hand."

"He comes with your stamp of approval?"

McGill said, "Highly recommended. He's one of the guys who helped take down the Undertaker."

"Okay, we'll keep him in mind. Meanwhile, everybody's covered, and we'll see if we can't let the FBI catch Damon Todd and his new traveling companions. One of the Feebs' big guys is waiting for us along with that former CIA shrink, Daryl Cheveyo … and Elspeth Kendry. You're going to behave, aren't you, Jim?"

"I'll be good. I'm in enough trouble as it is."

They turned around and headed back to Aspen Lodge.

McGill told Sweetie something he wouldn't even share with Patti for the time being.

"When I saw this one Marine trying to bring this stick down on my head, I thought I can't let this happen. Not now. Not when it looks like we just pulled Kenny back from the brink. I didn't want my son and everyone else to lose me. I think that's why I reacted the way I did."

Sweetie questioned McGill in a way only she would.

"Did you feel like killing the guy?"

"Yes."

"Did you have an opening to do it?"

"Yes."

"So what you did was a measured response. You gave the guy a rap on the knuckles. That's no more than a nun would have done in the old days."

McGill smiled. "It's always a pleasure to talk with you, Margaret."

"Yeah, I get a lot of that, too."

Aspen Lodge

By the time Galia Mindel and Stephen Norwood walked in on the president and Kenny McGill they'd already broken their clinch. That only made it easier for Kenny to get to his feet and startle Galia with a hug.

"Thank you," he said, "for volunteering to help me."

"You're welcome, Kenny."

Galia fought off the first blush she could remember feeling in ages as Kenny let her go, extended a hand to Stephen Norwood and introduced himself. Norwood returned the favor.

"Well, I'll let you guys get on with making sure the trains don't go off the tracks. Thanks again, Patti."

The president, her face radiant with love, watched her stepson leave the room.

"Quite the young man," Galia said. "All is going well with him?"

Patti nodded and cleared her throat. "Yes, it seems so. Please, Galia, Stephen, have a seat."

They sat in arm chairs opposite the president. At the moment, the floor belonged to Galia. She and her deputy had made the trip to Camp David only because they had news too important to share by phone.

The White House chief of staff began by assuming responsibility.

"Stephen has informed me I can save myself by throwing him under the bus for what we're about to tell you, but all the blame, if it comes to that, falls directly upon my shoulders."

The president looked at Norwood. "Very gracious of you,

Stephen." Looking back to Galia she added, "You're really getting to be a bit of a drama queen, Galia."

Norwood muffled a chuckle but said, "This is fairly dramatic stuff, Madam President."

Patti gestured to Galia to proceed.

"Howard Hurlbert has followed your lead and left the GOP. He's forming a new party called True South and will run for president as the head of that party."

It was the president's turn to stifle a laugh. Seeing that her chief of staff was serious, she dispelled her mirth and said, "The last I heard, Hurlbert was going to challenge me as a Republican before I left the party. What happened? And *True South,* really?"

Patti was tempted to ask how Galia knew this, but one of the first things she'd learned from her chief of staff was that a degree of deniability for the president was usually a good thing.

If Galia had been asked, she would have told the president that one of her spies was Merilee Parker who had worked as Senator Hurlbert's press secretary and had been married to Bobby Beckley, the senator's chief of staff and campaign manager. Merilee had ended her marriage, and her job with Hurlbert, when she got tired of Beckley beating her.

The follow-on Mrs. Beckley, a friend of Merilee, had needed only one beating to knuckle under and become totally subservient, but she was always looking for ways to get even. When Merilee, at Galia's behest, offered money to know what Beckley and Hurlbert were up to, the new battered wife jumped at it.

"What happened, Madam President, was that RNC Chairman Reynard Dix and House Majority Leader Peter Profitt decided the wisest choice for their party would be to draft a candidate for president who was not Senator Hurlbert."

"And who might —" A thought hit the president with a jolt. "No, not Mather."

Galia nodded. "Who better, really? After you left, the vice president is the senior official in the Republican Party. He put down Burke Godfrey's insurrection quickly. His favorability rating is ten points higher than yours. It's just a bounce, but no one else in the GOP comes close."

But Mather had told her he was going to leave the White House, Patti thought. He was going to run for a seat in the House from Ohio. And he'd told her he was —

"There's more, Madam President. We have reason to believe the vice president is actively considering the idea. Senator Daniel Crockett walked out of Hurlbert's True South meeting, ridiculing the idea, but shortly after that he called the White House and left a message for Mather Wyman, saying if the acting president was considering the draft proposal the senator would be happy to keep him informed of further developments of which he might otherwise be uninformed."

"He's angling to join Wyman on the ticket," Norwood said. "That would give the GOP a nice north-south balance."

The president had to agree with that, thinking that Edwina Byington, God love her, must have shared Crockett's message with Galia.

"Stephen will cover the next point, Madam President, and if it's all right with you, I think Stephen would make an excellent manager for your coming campaign. I would be available to advise him on strategy and tactics, and I'd be watching your opponents and countering any of their less than ethical attacks."

The president assessed that idea, looking at the deputy chief of staff.

"Very well," she said.

Norwood nodded in appreciation and said, "Considering the new dynamic of Senator Hurlbert becoming a third-party candidate, Galia and I thought it might be better for you to run as a Democrat rather than as another candidate outside the two-party structure. But we've wondered if the Dems are getting cold feet about you given your health situation."

"I would, if I were them," Patti said.

"You can bet Roger Michaelson is laughing somewhere," Galia added.

"Yes, I imagine he is," Patti agreed in a flat voice.

Norwood continued, "What we thought we should do then is give the Democrats reason to worry. To that end, with an embargo date, I offered a tidbit to a reporter I know on the *Washington Post* that you'll be running as a self-financed independent candidate."

Galia said, "Not only will that make the Dems anxious, it will lay the foundation for an independent run if that would suit you better."

With a straight face, the president asked, "You think it's too late for me to make amends with the GOP and head off my vice president?"

Norwood, relatively young, took the question as being serious.

Galia just smiled and said, "Probably is."

Patti nodded. "The leak was a good move. Credit to both of you. No blame at all."

Galia asked, "Do you agree that the Democrats would be the best vehicle for your candidacy?"

"Only if they move fast. I won't wait long once I'm back in the Oval Office."

Galia continued the list of revelations by telling the president of her scheme to reorder the primary election system, displacing the importance of Iowa, New Hampshire and South Carolina, and putting New York, Illinois and California at the top of the list.

Patti said, "Everyone else is going to jump in the pool, too. We'll have a national primary."

Norwood said, "At that point, we can suggest counterbalanced regional contests, bundle groups of states so all points of the compass and the political spectrum are represented on any given Tuesday."

The president laughed. "I get the feeling the two of you enjoy your work."

Galia said, "We like to keep busy."

Patti said, "So much of what we've discussed depends on two things: when I return to Washington and what Acting President Wyman decides to do."

Galia and Norwood looked at the president.

She'd have to be the one to answer the first question.

Patti let her eyes close. She consciously slowed her breathing. Let her muscles relax.

Given everything they had just discussed, it wouldn't be unreasonable to expect she might be a bit keyed up. But she didn't feel her heart racing. Didn't hear her pulse pounding. On the contrary, she felt at peace.

Remembered Kenny McGill's whispered profession of love.

Was sure she could run again and not forget what was truly important.

She opened her eyes and told Galia and Norwood, "I'll be back sooner rather than later. I'll ease back into things. Work a Ronald Reagan schedule: early to bed, late to work and a nap in between. Limit my direct participation to a handful of the most important matters."

Galia wanted to leap to her feet and clap.

She contented herself by merely smiling.

"You know how we'll see what the vice president's plans are?" Galia asked.

"Of course," the president said, "he won't take the risk of nominating anyone to the Supreme Court, but he'll let it be known who his choices would be if he were elected president."

"That'll be the race's starting gun," Norwood agreed.

Camp David — Laurel Lodge

Laurel Lodge had a conference room, so that was where McGill and Sweetie met with Daryl Cheveyo, Elspeth Kendry and FBI Deputy Director Byron DeWitt. McGill, being courteous, let his guests enter the room first, and saw that was a mistake. The others arranged themselves two to a side and left the seat at the head of the table open for him. He gave Sweetie a dirty look as he passed her.

She replied with a smirk.

As long as he was occupying the position of power, McGill felt it acceptable to mention his wife. "The president told me she would have the CIA make available to us complete histories of the two former CIA agents, Olin Anderson and Arn Crosby, who escaped with Damon Todd."

"I have them, Mr. McGill, SAC Crogher forwarded them to me," DeWitt said. He put the briefcase he'd brought with him on the table. "I had copies made for everyone."

The willingness of an FBI poobah to share with others, including former local cops, had been a concern for McGill. But DeWitt handed out the copies with an air of geniality. He was the most laid back feeb McGill had ever seen. Even his haircut looked relaxed, and he had a tan.

McGill just had to know.

"Mr. DeWitt, any chance you might be from California?"

The deputy director smiled. He teeth could have starred on the silver screen.

"Is it that obvious?"

"Pretty much," McGill said.

Sweetie said, "Or he comes from South Boston with a great sense of misdirection."

"Now, there's a flexible thinker," DeWitt said. "But I was born in Montecito and went to college at UCSB. The thing most people overlook about me is I'm Chinese."

"One of those rare blue-eyed blonde Chinese," Elspeth observed.

"Our numbers are few," DeWitt admitted. "It was a matter of adoption. Not that I was taken in by another family. I adopted Chinese culture to a larger extent than most Westerners. That was after my father volunteered our guest house to a visiting professor from Shanghai University; Dad taught political science at UCSB."

Cheveyo asked, "The visitor decided to stay in the U.S.?"

DeWitt nodded. "After the Tienanmen Square massacre, he and his family requested political asylum and got it. My dad insisted Professor Chen and his wife and two sons continue to live as our guests, rent free, as long as they liked. The Chens insisted we be willing recipients of their hospitality for an equal period. As a result, I spent my formative years learning to eat, speak, read and to some degree think Chinese."

"So you bring several useful skills to your job," McGill said.

DeWitt bowed his head in modesty. Another thing not often found in the FBI.

"I try," he said.

With that, everyone turned to reading the files on Anderson and Crosby.

The two men had been extraction specialists or as they'd described themselves kidnappers who had the consent of the abducted. They didn't snatch people from their families, they took high value individuals from governments who hated to see them go. Shortly before the CIA ended their careers there was a joke going around the agency that Anderson and Crosby were going to make off with the entire roster of the Cuban national baseball team.

Then hold a bidding war and sell the players to major league teams.

Or wholesale the lot of them to the New York Yankees.

Bringing oppressed people with useful skills to the land of milk and honey had a long and honored history in American espionage. The problem was that Anderson and Crosby didn't go about things in the prescribed way. Instead of leading their would-be émigrés out of bondage by stealth, guile and, only if necessary, force, they hit upon the idea of assassinating a high official in the national security apparatus of the country in question while casting blame on local malefactors.

While the bad guys were distracted by chasing one another and blowing each other to bits, Anderson and Crosby would waltz off with the man or woman they were sent to liberate. They'd worked their dark magic from the Balkans to Burma. Each time, they were warned not to do it again. The blowback would be unacceptable if they were ever caught.

Both men had sworn they'd blow themselves to bits before they'd ever be taken prisoner. That kind of talk only worried their superiors more. Asked if they, too, thought they'd get a party boat filled with booze and virgins after their earthly demise, Anderson said, "Nah, all we expect to get is one last laugh."

Without much debate, it was decided Anderson and Crosby had gone *far* around the bend. It was only with meticulous planning and flawless execution that they'd been taken alive. They were committed to the CIA's psychiatric facility. Their term of treatment was listed as indefinite.

One by one, the people around the table finished reading.

McGill asked, "Thoughts?"

Cheveyo offered one that hadn't occurred to anyone else. "Anderson is a Swedish name. Crosby can be either Norse or Teutonic. It's Northern European at any rate. I read about these guys and one word popped into my mind: Berserker."

Sweetie said, "That's a new one to me. Does it come from mythology?"

Cheveyo said, "No, berserkers were quite real. Historically noted. They were the most feared of the Norse warriors. They fought like madmen. Once engaged in battle, they were uncontrollable. Some contemporary reports say they worked themselves into a rage before the battle; others say they used folk medicine, what we'd call drugs, to induce their ferocity. They wore wolf pelts and carried spears."

"An edged weapon," McGill said. "Like a knife. Their dossiers say they liked to start the trouble they caused by slitting someone's throat."

"Or taking off the occasional head," Elspeth added. "That might be the work of a big knife with some heft to it. Then again it could be a short sword or an axe."

DeWitt leafed though his copy.

He said, "Sharp steel does seem to be their preference, but there are a couple of long-range rifle shots in here. That would indicate some degree of calculation in how they approach their work, and proficiency in modern weapons."

Sweetie said, "So they'll do what's necessary, but their fun comes from close-up work."

Cheveyo nodded. "My surmise is they not only like it, they probably need it. Whatever forces shaped them as young men might have built deep wells of anger and resentment within them. The only way to relieve that hostility is by venting it upon others."

"By *ventilating* others," Elspeth said. "A pair of charmers, these guys. But if they bring knives to a gunfight, maybe they're not so smart after all."

McGill said, "At close quarters, a knife can sometimes strike faster than a gun."

DeWitt added, "Dr. Cheveyo mentioned berserkers used spears. They can be lethal at greater distances than a knife. Again, it's a matter of who can strike first, whatever the weapon in hand might be."

Remembering how her last debate with McGill had ended, Elspeth said, "I'll take your word for it, Mr. Deputy Director."

Sweetie had a question for Cheveyo. "How did guys like this ever get *into* the CIA? Don't they have to go through psychological testing?"

"Yes, it's part of a more general screening process, but generalized psychiatric exams do not fit all candidates. If you're looking for someone you expect to be able to operate efficiently in hostile environments you have to allow for variables that wouldn't be acceptable in someone doing a desk job."

McGill said, "If you're going to ask people to do crazy things, you have to accept they might be a little crazy, too."

Cheveyo nodded and looked at the faces around the table. "Secret Service agents are willing to be bullet catchers for their packages. Military personnel volunteer to disarm explosive devices. FBI agents and police officers volunteer to work undercover in murderous criminal cartels. None of these activities is something a *sane* person would do. Unfortunately, sometimes people who track a little too far over the line slip past the screeners."

Sweetie said, "I wonder how all of us would score on your battery of tests — not that I'm about to volunteer to take them."

"Neither am I," McGill said. "So what we're dealing with are people who don't mind and might even like spilling blood … and we're going to give the FBI the first crack at bagging them. We know the bureau has a long history of counterespionage, catching foreign bad guys operating in the U.S., but what about dealing with CIA-trained operatives?"

DeWitt looked at Cheveyo. "You want to tell them or should I?"

"I'll take a breather. You go ahead."

The deputy director nodded. "We don't publicize this, but it's not top-secret either. The last thing CIA candidates have to do before they're hired and receive real assignments is to run mock operations in U.S. cities. The FBI is tasked with keeping them from succeeding."

McGill asked, "Who's ahead on points, say the last ten years?"

DeWitt said, "There's a pendulum swing, as with most things. One or the other team might have an exceptional class one year with the reverse being true the next. But over the past four years the FBI has won hands down."

Sweetie asked, "Would that winning streak have anything to do with you?"

"I have something of an eye for talent," DeWitt said, "and I tend to take unexpected approaches to solving problems."

"That's a long way to go to say yes," Elspeth said.

"Immodesty rarely endears," DeWitt averred.

Cheveyo grinned at that. McGill thought the deputy director might be laying it on a bit thick, too. He asked, "You think you can avoid another pendulum swing on this one?"

"Yes."

A bow to Elspeth, everyone knew.

McGill turned to Daryl Cheveyo. "Doctor, do you have any ideas about how we … how the FBI might start looking for Damon Todd and his new friends?"

Cheveyo said, "The first thing I had to consider was whether Anderson and Crosby have killed Todd. I don't think they have or we would have found his body by now. There would have been no reason to hide Todd's body. They would have left it out in the open the same way they did with Arlen Stanwick."

"But that guy was found dead at the CIA's training facility. Leaving his body there wouldn't offer any clue as to which way they were heading," Sweetie said.

McGill said, "Margaret, you mentioned misdirection earlier. If they had killed Todd, they could have planted him one way and then gone the other. I have the feeling he's still alive."

"So do I," Cheveyo said. "Whatever his flaws, Dr. Todd is smart and resourceful. My feeling is he made his value to Anderson and Crosby readily apparent. Killing him would be discarding an asset. Even berserkers wouldn't do that."

"What's Todd's biggest appeal for these guys?" Elspeth asked.

Cheveyo said, "His network of *friends* and his facility with hypnosis, in equal measure, I'd say. Does everyone here know Todd's background?"

They all did.

"Very well," Cheveyo continued. "We know he's helped former students and others become successful in business, government and, my guess is, academia, the arts and philanthropy, too. The problem is, we never learned the extent of his network. Making another guess, I'd say it extends throughout North America and to more than a few foreign countries. It would be highly unlikely that he would not make use of his contacts to provide him and the others shelter and sustenance."

"You think they all stayed together?" Elspeth asked. "Once they got clear of the net that was first put out for them, maybe Anderson and Crosby wanted to strike out on their own."

Cheveyo said, "I think from this point on it might be more helpful to call them Crosby and Anderson. I should have put them in that sequence when I first mentioned them. From my reading of their files, I think Crosby would be the alpha member of that pairing."

The CIA shrink looked at DeWitt for his opinion.

"I agree," he said.

Continuing, Cheveyo said, "It's conceivable Todd might have gone one way, or hunkered down, while Crosby and Anderson headed off in another direction. If that happened, they might have been tempted to kill Todd, but I don't think they would have done that. Alive, he still might remain a resource to be tapped."

McGill said, "If they're being hidden by someone Todd knew and helped rise in the world, combing through Todd's past could give us a list of possible people and places to look at."

DeWitt nodded. "We can probably find most of the people he went to school with, taught and worked with."

McGill said, "Then you see how many of them are doing exceptionally well. Todd couldn't have done his Svengali act with everyone he ever met."

"Another good point," DeWitt said.

McGill and Sweetie exchanged a look. A helpful FBI guy was rare; a complimentary one was unheard of. They both came to the same unspoken conclusion. Patti Grant's shadow was influencing DeWitt. Who knew? Maybe he wanted to move up to the top job in the bureau.

Not crossing the president's henchman would be a smart move.

McGill asked Cheveyo, "Any ideas on how these guys got away without leaving a trace, Doctor?"

"Kidnapping. That's what Crosby and Anderson did after all."

DeWitt said, "There were no missing persons reports in the area of the escape for over two weeks in the aftermath of the breakout."

Cheveyo told him, "The kidnapped person wouldn't have to be gone long enough to be missed."

McGill understood what he meant. "Just long enough for Todd to do his hypnosis number. Grab some cluck and what … get to one of the people in his network who lives nearby. Put the guy, or the woman, into a trance, tell him or her to forget the whole thing ever happened and you haven't left any evidence behind for the cops to find."

Cheveyo nodded. "Todd worked with ketamine hydrochloride. It wouldn't be farfetched to think the people in his network had been instructed to keep some at their homes to be used whenever Todd might drop by. That way he can reinforce the personalities he crafted for them. Or in this case to build one for the kidnap victim."

Elspeth leaned forward. "You mean Todd would not only let the person they abducted go, he'd also help him to become more successful."

"Life is full of ironies." Cheveyo turned to DeWitt. "You might look for someone whose circumstances have improved dramatically since the breakout, not by luck but by dint of their own efforts."

"That's good, something we can work with." DeWitt said. "Here's something else. None of us feds or local cops who were out looking for these guys saw anything like three men trying to conceal themselves in a passenger vehicle. But if they coerced a ride for themselves in a commercial vehicle where the cab sits high they could crouch out of sight of police vehicles."

"Good cop thinking," Sweetie said.

DeWitt gave her one of his polite nods.

"Thanks. You put that together with what Dr. Cheveyo said about the abduction victim not being gone too long, what we might be looking for is, say, a trucker who experienced an unexpected delay in meeting his schedule."

"But he probably had a plausible reason to explain the delay, something Todd gave him," McGill said.

That time, Cheveyo did the nodding.

The meeting wound down with everyone agreeing to McGill's suggestion that they all keep the lines of communication open because they'd made a good start. Who could say, maybe a truly cooperative effort would be the way they'd put the clamps on Todd and his friends.

But it was only when McGill was walking Sweetie to the helipad without the others that he voiced the question that bothered him most. "What do we do with these creeps after we catch them? They've already escaped once."

Sweetie grinned and said, "We give them some of Damon Todd's medicine. Put them in hypnotic trances and convince them they're all lap dogs."

Aspen Lodge

"I'm going back to work soon, Jim," Patti said.

McGill had just entered the bedroom he shared with Patti. He'd been talking with Kenny, pleased by the steady progress his son was making, but he hadn't let himself look too far ahead and imagine it was all smooth sailing from here.

Doctor Divya Sahir Jones, Kenny's chief oncologist, had warned him and Carolyn that their optimism about their son's condition had to be guarded. The first hundred days after the transplant, also known as the graft, were critical. Kenny would need lots of rest and everyone had to be on guard against infection because Kenny's immune system was still weak.

If any sign of infection was found, the doctors would have to treat it immediately. External locations where infections were common were the site where Kenny's central IV line had been placed, his mouth and his rectum. Having that last area checked daily by a nurse was a continuing indignity that made Kenny grind his teeth.

Besides infection, there were two more possible complications. The first was called graft-versus-host disease in which the cells from the donated marrow attacked the body of the transplant patient. GVH disease was not uncommon. The second complication was even more serious: graft failure. That occurred when the patient's body did not accept the donated cells.

The rate of failure was low and there had been no sign Kenny's body hadn't accepted the bone marrow graft. Nonetheless, the doctors remained vigilant for any sign that all was not well.

McGill was watchful, too. He didn't have a medical expert's eye, but he knew his son's nature more intimately than anyone other than Carolyn. If something went wrong with Kenny, he wouldn't let it slip past him. So far, though, everything did seem to be going well.

For which McGill gave thanks daily.

At the moment, he had no problem seeing that Patti was a bit wound up.

He slid into bed next to her. She put down the iPad she'd been scanning. The screen now showed a scene of a tropical island, all sunshine, palm trees and translucent blue water. But it wasn't the thought of a South Seas vacation that was bothering her. It might be one of any number of disasters or tragedies that crossed a president's desk, or tablet computer, daily.

Patti's iPad had apps few others had.

"Your understudy is getting bad reviews?" McGill asked.

"No, he's polling ten points ahead of me."

McGill frowned. "We can't have that, now can we?"

"Galia assures me it's a temporary bounce."

"As all bounces must be."

McGill placed an ear against his wife's chest, listened and nodded.

"Your diagnosis, doctor?" Patti asked.

"Good, strong beat. Not even a sign of fevered reaction to my presence."

"So you're clearing me to return to the White House?"

"That or assert your authority in any other fashion you might choose."

He waggled his eyebrows at Patti and made her laugh.

Got a kiss for his efforts.

"How's Kenny?"

"Sleeping peacefully when I left him."

"He made me so happy today it was all I could do not to weep."

"Ah, the McGill charm, if only we could bottle it."

"We'll do something else with it momentarily, but Galia told me Sweetie, Elspeth, Dr. Cheveyo and the deputy director of the FBI visited Camp David this evening. Would you care to brief me on what the five of you discussed?"

"I'll tell you my secrets, if you tell me yours," McGill said. "As many of them as you comfortably can."

"We'd better turn the lights out for this."

They did and Patti and McGill exchanged their stories. Throwing in another at no extra charge, McGill told Patti about beating up two Marines.

"Dark Alley?" Patti asked.

"A variation thereof with an Irish fighting stick. I'm trying to decide how to handle things now. I thought I might visit Captain Wolford and see how he's doing, but I don't know what to do about Sergeant Vasquez. That guy honestly might have killed me."

"I'll have a word with the commandant," Patti said, her voice tightening.

"Are you mad at me or Vasquez?"

"You set ground rules before you started this … contest?"

"No fatalities, I said that quite clearly. Bruising was acceptable."

"Then I'm not mad at you."

"I also promised no courts-martial. So any kind of punishment for Vasquez would violate the spirit of that assurance."

Patti sighed.

"I try not to complicate your life," McGill said.

"You make me happy. I'll leave it to you to work things out with the Marines. You agree with my decision to return to the Oval Office?"

"After the thorough exam I just gave you, I think you'll be all right. You'll have Nick sitting on Edwina's lap, won't you?"

"I'll have him nearby."

"I have to take it on faith that both you and Kenny are going to be fine. How do you feel about things?"

"The same way. None of us can live in fear."

"That's my president. I would give things just a day or two, before going back."

"Make it easier for Mather Wyman to reveal his intentions?"

"Exactly. Then show up on the heels of his announcement. Make him think uh-oh."

"I like Mather."

"I do, too, more or less. But if he's going to run against you —"

"Hit him with my Irish fighting stick?"

McGill was silent for a beat. Then he said, "There's one more thing I have to tell you about that. In the heat of the moment, when I saw Vasquez had tried to kill me, I felt that I should kill him, and the opening was there. So was the temptation."

Patti reached out in the darkness and pulled McGill close.

"But you didn't yield to that temptation."

"I think I'm going to stay here with Kenny. Help him heal. Give the FBI a chance to catch Damon Todd and those other two mopes."

"A wise decision. I'll put a choice word or two into SAC Crogher's ear about respecting your prerogatives when you return."

"If Celsus gives you guff, whack him with your shillelagh, too."

"I have the feeling 2012 is going to be quite a year for us, Jim."

"No doubt. But before then you'll be able to visit me on weekends, won't you?"

Patti said she would, and showed him what he had to look forward to.

Number One Observatory Circle

Acting President Mather Wyman ate a late dinner alone at his official residence. Kira had invited him to dine with her and Welborn at their new house on Q Street, but that would have caused a huge inconvenience for anyone who wanted to enter or leave the neighborhood. At Patti Grant's insistence, his Secret Service detail cast an even larger shadow than hers normally did. The original intent of the extreme security measures surrounding him was to make sure there would be no chance the late speaker of the House, Derek Geiger, would move into the White House while the president was recuperating from her bone marrow donation.

With Geiger having shuffled off this mortal coil, and the Republicans in the House dawdling about replacing him, the next in line, after Wyman, for the presidency was Senator George

Mossman of Hawaii, a Democrat. A decent fellow with a record as a war hero and a reputation for honesty, Mossman presumably would have been a more acceptable fill-in than a schemer like Derek Geiger.

But it wouldn't have been good for the country to lose an acting president while the elected one was still laid up. So the super-sized security contingent stayed and Mather Wyman ate at home alone. The irony being he could have gone to Kira's house or just about anywhere else he liked with the smaller security detail he commanded as vice president.

Of course, he might have invited any number of guests to dine with him at the White House. A small family meal with Kira and Welborn would have gone uncriticized and probably unnoticed. A larger gathering with fellow politicians and celebrities would have caused an uproar and been deemed to be in bad taste. Too pushy by far.

The president, after all, was recovering from a lifesaving act. He might be leading Patti Grant in the polls at the moment, but he was sure that the minute she appeared in public his lead would disappear, and if Kenny McGill were at the president's side, she'd leave him in the dust.

With a mild sense of surprise, he realized this was the first time since his race to be reelected as governor of Ohio that he gave a damn about public opinion polls.

He'd enjoyed his two terms as governor. He'd balanced the state's budget without crippling services for the poor. He'd recruited businesses and well-paying jobs to the state the way the Buckeyes landed high school athletes for the university's football and basketball teams. Shame about the football coach crossing the line and having to resign.

A crying shame about the greatest player in the NBA leaving the Cavaliers.

All of a sudden, despite his best efforts, the mood in the state had turned sour. Then Patti Grant had won the GOP nomination and asked him if he'd like to join her on the ticket and be his vice president. She said she liked his record and his demeanor as governor, called him effective and gracious, a true gentleman.

He'd been charmed and was won over when she promised he'd be a working vice president with real responsibilities. She'd been as good as her word. He was the administration's political point man on education, energy and immigration. He thought he'd done a good job in each area, but he always stayed within the president's philosophical guidelines.

There had been more than a few times when he'd have liked to improvise.

Take more than incremental steps.

Lead the way.

A contradiction if ever there was one for a vice president. He had to be the ultimate loyal *follower.* He could offer advice certainly, but always defer *graciously* if his advice was ignored.

Then Kenny McGill had fallen sick and, wouldn't you know it, that led to Mather Wyman's return to executive power. Not just at the head of one state but of the entire union. And, God, did he love it.

Now, having heard that his party might draft him to be its nominee, he *wanted* it.

That surprised him no end. He'd never entertained the idea of running for the presidency. Having had a taste of what it meant to be president, power so pure it was like a drug, he could not resist yielding to the addiction.

Certainly, the president must have felt the same inexorable pull.

All of her predecessors, too.

In his lifetime, he could think of no one other than Lyndon Johnson who had stepped aside voluntarily when there was still a chance to hold on to power. Was there a lesson to learn from Johnson? He'd been a vice president, too. Had first sat in the Oval Office only after fate had placed him there.

Sure there was a lesson.

Don't start a war you can't win, and when you do win get out fast.

Johnson hadn't had Colin Powell around to articulate that for him.

Mather Wyman would follow the Powell Doctrine, should things ever come to that … and he would be sensible about everything else.

Including not coming out as a gay man before he was elected or even before he left office. Once he returned to private life, then he could go public. Having run the question through his mind innumerable times now, he'd come to the conclusion that the president wouldn't expose his secret.

If he'd misjudged her on that — or if she'd told James J. McGill — he was lost.

He finished his dinner and went to bed. Early the next morning, he called press secretary Aggie Wu. He told her he wanted to speak to the media at ten a.m. tomorrow.

Hart Senate Office Building — Washington, D.C.

"Galia Mindel called me at home this morning," Majority Leader John Wexford said.

Gathered with the Democratic senator in his office were his assistant majority leader, Richard Bergen of Illinois, House minority leader, Marlene Berman, and her assistant leader, Diego Paz. Coffee, tea, croissants and cinnamon rolls sat on a serving cart untouched.

Wexford continued, "The White House chief of staff said as a courtesy she was letting me know that the president will be returning to work in a couple of days."

"A couple?" Paz asked.

"In the literal sense, no more than two. I asked the same question."

The four leading Democrats in Congress looked at one another. All of them had heard the rumor that Patti Grant had decided to run as a self-financed independent. There hadn't been any hint that she would field or even endorse any independent candidates for seats in the House or Senate, but it was not hard to imagine that —

"If she does what we've all heard she'll do," Begen said, "we might be about to witness politics in this country becoming an entrepreneurial activity."

"Maybe even a venture capital enterprise," Marlene Berman suggested.

"People with money or access to it running for Congress without any party connections," Paz elucidated. "Talk about scary."

Wexford laughed with no sign of being amused. "I don't know. Isn't that what George Washington wanted? He said parties distract the government from its duties to the people."

"Guy must have had a crystal ball," Paz said.

"More likely human nature has persistent flaws," Bergen countered.

Asserting the voice of practicality, Marlene Berman said, "Gentlemen, let's table the history and philosophy discussions for the moment and ask ourselves whether Patti Grant and/or Galia Mindel is playing us. Those two sharpies have to know we're worrying about Patti Grant's health and the chance we'd be taking by making a commitment to the president to be our nominee."

Wexford said, "She may be playing us, Marlene, but I have no doubt we've just had a forty-eight hour deadline set for us. We confirm without reservation that we want the president to be our nominee and we do all we can to discourage any challenger to her nomination or she runs in the general election with her own line on the ballot."

"Galia Mindel would run her campaign, you think?" Paz asked.

Bergen said, "Might be her right-hand guy, Stephen Norwood, would do it. He'd handle all the nuts and bolts and that'd leave Galia free to scheme."

"Something at which she excels," Marlene offered. "You've all heard about the bills making their ways through the legislatures in New York, Illinois and California to piggyback their primary elections to the one in New Hampshire?"

Paz laughed. "I think that's great. It's about time the big states get to have some pull on who the presidential nominee is gonna be."

Wexford said, "You mean when we're not trying to put the fix in ahead of time."

"Damn political parties," Paz said with a grin.

Bergen suggested, "At least the new primary lineup should have a moderating influence on the Republicans. Wing-nuts aren't going to win in three big, diverse states outside the South."

Wexford thought about that and said, "Do you think the fix could be in on both sides of the aisle? Look at the polls. Everybody hates Congress. Who's the one Republican with a high approval rating right now?"

The other three said in unison, "Mather Wyman."

Wexford nodded. "And now Acting President Wyman has Oval Office experience. If the Republicans don't draft him, they're even crazier than we think they are. But if they do draft him and Patti Grant runs as an independent, our nominee will be facing a sitting president and a former acting president. How do you think we might do?"

Three glum faces were the only answer necessary.

"Me, too," Wexford said.

"We better make sure we get the first appointment to see the president whenever she gets back to the White House," Paz said.

Marlene Berman shook her head. "No, the thing to do is get to her while she's still at Camp David. If it's all right with you gentleman, I think I'd be the best one to get a true read on how the president is doing, health wise and otherwise."

The three men in the room were smart enough to agree.

And let the woman shoulder the blame if things went wrong.

Charlottesville, Virginia

"Little fucker has some grit, I gotta give him that." Olin Anderson said.

Crosby nodded and said, "From everything I've seen, the

Company should've welcomed him with a flourish of trumpets, like he was a sheik willing to sell us oil at half off."

The two former rogue operatives were playing hide and seek with Todd in the woods along the James River. Only in their version of the game they'd told the headshrinker they would kill him if they caught him in the first fifteen minutes. If they caught him in the first thirty minutes, they would give him a painful but not disabling beating. If he evaded them for thirty to sixty minutes, they would congratulate him and buy him a drink. If he remained undiscovered for more than an hour, he'd get the drink and the pleasure of watching the two of them go at it in close-quarters combat.

The game had been underway for fifty-five minutes.

With no sign of the prick.

Who was carrying both a knife and two Vietnam tomahawks.

Purchased off the internet. Weapon instructions provided by YouTube videos.

Crosby and Anderson looked for footprints, snapped foliage and frightened animal life. They listened for any sound that had no place in a woodland. A cough, a sneeze, a fart. They lifted their noses to the breeze, hoping to inhale human body odor or fear; they knew both.

Wouldn't be long before they'd have to call out, "Olli, olli oxen, come in free!"

Look like a couple of dicks not legendary badasses.

"You think we lost it?" Anderson asked.

"Sure as hell seem to have lost him," Crosby said.

"A few weeks ago, I might've thought he just drifted off with the breeze."

That was then. In the time since, Todd had been working out like a madman. Twice a day at first, then three and four times. Not for hours on end, but intense bursts of twenty to thirty minutes. In between, he'd run for both distance and speed. He stretched, too.

Shamed the two tough guys into keeping up with him.

Which was getting harder all the time.

Simple truth was, Todd was younger than they were. Not by

a lot but enough to show. You could work out and eat right all you wanted. If a younger guy did the same training regimen at the same intensity, he was going to get better results.

That led Anderson to wonder, "You think we should start using steroids? Take some human growth hormone?"

"I think what we ought to do is pull our punches with each other 'cause time just expired."

Each of them did a slow three-sixty, expecting Todd to step out from behind a tree, maybe descend from a cloud holding a lightning bolt, and sneer at them. It was going to be hard, they knew, to keep on scaring a guy who had made them look like chumps. If they tried, it might turn out he could kick their asses, too.

It was almost as if …

Crosby looked at Anderson and asked, "I know the bastard didn't hypnotize us, but is there any way he could have drugged us? Slipped something into our food or water. Slowed us down just enough to lose our edge."

Anderson told him, "If he managed that, we've *already* lost our edge."

"Maybe we should just *di-di*." Bug out.

"And go where? "

Crosby nodded. "Yeah, that was never a big part of our plan."

"Fuck it," Anderson said. He yelled, "You win!"

Adding under his breath, "You miserable little hemorrhoid licker."

As if to chastise him, a Vietnam tomahawk whistled past Anderson's head and stuck in a tree. He and Crosby turned and saw Todd had thrown the weapon from his knees. His face and arms had been smeared with dirt. Vegetation sprouted randomly from his clothes. He'd been underfoot the whole time. They might have tripped over him.

Crosby and Anderson just couldn't understand how Todd had gotten so good so fast, and how their games had gone to hell.

Crosby wanted to ask what Todd had done to them, but he said, "What'd we do wrong?"

"You both sleep at the same time."

There was only one thing to make of that: he'd fucked with them while they were unconscious. But neither of them could believe Todd had sneaked into the room where they slept and had messed with them physically. Professional pride demanded that they figure out what had happened on their own.

Failing that, they'd have to see if they could torture it out of the prick.

"You want us to fight now or later?" Anderson asked.

"Don't bother," Todd told him. "You can beat yourselves up metaphorically."

They watched him walk past and pull his tomahawk out of the tree.

"Yeah, we're real big on metaphor," Crosby said.

Todd smiled and told him. "You've seen how I can help people. If you'll trust me, I can do the same for you. One at a time, if you want, so you can make sure I'm not doing something I shouldn't."

Like introducing an aerosol into the ventilation system feeding your bedroom, Todd thought. There were more means to put a drug into a person's body than there were ways to skin a cat. Under sedation, he'd had Crosby and Anderson give him a primer on many of their skills. Give him a list of contacts for useful, if illicit, goods and services. That and blur the recall of the information they had provided to him.

Had they really told him those things or were they imagining it?

In many respects, they'd already become his creatures.

But there was no way to own someone like sending him down a K-hole.

"I'm just trying to be helpful," Todd said, heading back to their cabin.

The White House

Captain Welborn Yates sat behind the desk in his office just down the hall from the Oval Office. He had a laptop computer open on his desk and was staring intently at the monitor when Kira appeared in his doorway. She wore a frown.

Welborn looked up and read her expression. He told her, "I'm not looking at pictures of naked women."

"Of course, you're not. You've told me many times I blind you to other women."

"A compliment that's only somewhat fanciful," Welborn said with a smile. "What's the cause of your discontent, my beloved?"

Kira closed the door and took one of Welborn's guest seats.

"I was thinking of ordering monogrammed towels for my bathroom."

Their new home had his and hers sanitation facilities, something they'd agreed was a necessity not a luxury.

"And how might that have become a source of vexation?" Welborn asked.

"I thought it only proper to use my married name as the source of my initials."

Welborn needed but the blink of an eye to understand the problem.

"You think the initials KY are a mite too … commercial?"

"Goo from a tube," Kira said, "that's what those letters are for."

Ever helpful, Welborn said, "You might use KFY. Married women these days often add a name rather than displace one."

"I thought of that, but I'm still bothered that I hadn't foreseen this problem."

"I could change my family name to Smith, if you like," Welborn said. "Or you might tell me if there's something more substantial that concerns you. I believe baring your soul to me is now your prerogative."

Kira leaned over the desk. Welborn lowered the lid of his laptop and met her halfway for a kiss. They returned to their seats, each feeling better.

"What are you doing with that computer?" Kira asked.

"I'll tell you after you tell me what's upset you."

"Very well. I heard through the grapevine the president will be returning soon."

That struck Welborn as wonderful news.

"What's the problem?" he asked, but then he saw. "Oh. When the president comes back, the acting president exits the stage, his moment in the spotlight come and gone."

Kira nodded. "I *like* seeing Mattie in the Oval Office. He's done a good job. He'd make a wonderful president."

"I'm sure you're right, but you have to be elected or succeed to office as a result of death or resignation to hold the position more than momentarily."

"Thank you, Professor Yates."

"Logic isn't really much of a comfort," Welborn agreed.

"Mattie's going to hold a press conference in fifteen minutes. I'm going to watch. Would you like to come with me?"

Welborn lifted the lid of his laptop. Glanced at the monitor.

"I think, I hope, I should be able to make it. Why don't you go ahead and save me a seat?"

"What *are* you doing?" Kira asked.

"Promise not to tell? Anyone? Ever?"

Kira considered the conditions and nodded.

"With the help of some other government employees who shall remain nameless, and the approval of a court order, I'm robbing a bank in the Caribbean."

The idea struck Kira as unusual but not impossible.

"A court approved of that?" she asked.

"The judge is an Air Force veteran."

Kira's eyes widened. "The money belongs to that guy who —"

"Killed Keith, Joe and Tommy, yes. We found his money and we're going to —" Welborn smiled and made a fist. "We *have* just taken his money, a bit more than four hundred thousand dollars."

"But what good will that do you?" Kira asked.

Welborn told her, "The thinking is — and I bet it works — that the sonofabitch will show up at his bank and demand his money back."

"And you'll be there to catch him."

"That I will."

Welborn shut down his computer, closed the lid and locked it in his desk.

He gave Kira another kiss and took her hand.

"Let's go hear what the acting president has to say."

Kira opined, "Maybe he's going to announce a coup."

Welborn said, "If he's wearing camouflage fatigues, we'll know."

Sunset Marina — Key West, Florida

Carina Linberg sat in the stern of *Irish Grace* and looked out at the marina, seeing the other boats and the adjacent condo buildings. She'd been lucky to spot a slip-for-lease ad just as she decided that tying up at the Waldorf Astoria resort was getting to be a bit extravagant. The slip was fifty feet long, exactly what she needed, and the terms were far more reasonable than at the resort. She could have lingered at the Waldorf for several more months but she wasn't the sort of woman who spent money unnecessarily.

By living just a bit more modestly, she could give herself the peace of mind not to feel compelled to go back to work at WWN. Sir Edbert Bickford had called her personally. Hadn't even had his secretary place the call and make her wait while he came on the line.

He said he was disturbed that Carina had let her old contract lapse.

Had been unavailable when the network's business affairs people had tried to reach her.

He said he would give her a fifty percent bump over the previous offer WWN had made.

"Carina," he said, "you know how much I like you, but you also know I don't make business decisions based on sentiment. You have a high TVQ." Television's likability quotient. "We get a bump every time you're on camera. Please tell me you'll at least read the proposed contract."

"I will, Sir Edbert — after my lawyer reviews it."

The old man laughed. "Of course. You know, nosy as I can be, I learned how you made the money to buy your boat. So I thought it only proper to provide you with a small token of my esteem, just for considering this contract offer."

She thanked Sir Edbert for being so thoughtful and clicked off.

Money and gifts were all very nice, but she wanted to do something *new.*

As she was weighing her thoughts a young man approached her boat, made sure he was speaking to Carina Linberg and handed her the keys and the title to a shiny new black Porsche Cayman. He pointed out the car in the marina lot.

Compliments of Sir Edbert Bickford, he said.

Carina said thank you, not knowing whether she'd keep the car or send it back. She'd had an idea of what she wanted to try next. Having published an autobiography, she thought it might be fun to try her hand at fiction.

Not a novel, a TV pilot. About what she knew: women bomber pilots. She could reuse the title of her bio: *Woman in Command.* Working in make-believe this time, she could have the women come out on top. She'd start out with her heroine getting screwed in a divorce settlement. Have her commandeer a plane with a loaded bomb bay and go hunting for her ex. Knowing he and his new bimbo would be at a posh resort with others of their ilk.

There'd be one good guy she'd meet as she schemed. Always had to be *one* good guy. After all, she'd had Lieutenant Welborn Yates.

The sympathetic male would persuade her not to inflict mass casualties, but it would be a close thing. And, oops, she'd drop one bomb in the desert just outside the resort. To show her scumbag ex and his double scoop of silicone girlfriend what she could have done.

Carina had gotten excited enough about the idea to see if she could find a creative writing class, preferably right there on the island. She heard about a lady writer who lived nearby on Fogarty

Avenue, but while Susan Coates had been published and was willing to give lessons, she was a romance writer. Had a far different view of the male of the species.

Susan wanted the man in her life to tear her clothes off.

Not hit him with a thousand-pound bomb.

Even so, Susan had given Carina a few good suggestions. Read widely in the genre in which she wanted to work and then study how the best writers working in that field told their stories, built their characters, used language in exposition and dialogue. Once Carina did that, she could see if there were any TV shows that appealed to the same sensibilities and write to the producers and ask if she might have a sample script so she could study the format the shows used.

Carina had left Susan's house with a bounce in her step. Now, she had a plan.

On the way back to her boat, she'd stopped off at Mango Mary's for a drink.

And had teamed up with the laid back bartender to bounce the creep who came in.

That had really put her in the mood to start writing her TV show, but first she had to do the homework Susan had outlined for her. That was okay. She knew how to study and she liked to work. She hit the nearest bookstore and bought a half-dozen paperback books and an e-reader.

As for contacting the producers of TV shows, she was sure she could use her contacts at WorldWide News to help her out there.

She started her assigned reading aboard her boat. A Daniel Silva novel. The clerk at the bookstore had told her vengeance was a major theme in Silva books. Just what she wanted.

Sitting in the stern, she wore a San Francisco Giants baseball cap, sunglasses and zinc oxide on her nose. She made notes as she went along, analyzing how Silva took his story from one plot point to the next and copying down lines of dialogue she liked.

She was getting into a real groove when she got two phone calls.

One was from Sir Edbert Bickford. Not having heard from Carina in response to his previous offer, he was back with another. If she wanted to work a new beat, fine.

Carina had left it to her agent to pass that tidbit along to Sir Edbert.

He said she could do general interest news, politics, crime, whatever she wanted. She could work from Florida, file her stories from Miami, even make Key West her beat. Tell the rest of the country what it was like to live in one of America's far corners.

She'd need not do more than four stories per month. She could take up to three months to make up her mind. The money would be the same as the last offer, but as a favor to him she should keep the Porsche. He had no interest in becoming a used car dealer.

Carina decided not only would the gig Sir Edbert had proposed give her the time she needed to pursue her writing plans, but with a media tycoon behind her, the chances of getting her TV show on the air were probably just a bit better. She could become a writer-producer. Get the *created-by* credit for her show.

She told Sir Edbert to send the contract to her lawyer. As long as nobody tried to slip any funny clauses into the paperwork she'd accept his offer.

The second phone call had a whole different tone.

The general manager of the Waldorf resort called to report that he'd had an inquiry from a woman named Alice Tompkins who said she was the owner of a bar called Mango Mary's. She said she had something very important to talk about with Ms. Linberg.

Damn, Carina thought. She had mentioned her name to the bartender.

Why'd she have to do that?

What'd he tell her his name was … Jackie Richmond?

Whatever. The manager at the Waldorf had said he couldn't reveal who was or wasn't a guest at the resort and had hung up, but he thought Ms. Linberg should know about the call. She thanked him and said goodbye.

Considering the matter, Carina thought you never knew what

a bartender might get up to, but she hadn't gotten the impression the guy was a con man. Who knew about Alice Tompkins, though? Carina would have ignored the two of them except for a couple of concerns.

What if they wanted to talk with her about the jerk she and Jackie had driven out of the bar? Maybe he was a vengeful creep. Maybe he had friends who were tougher than he was. If there was any chance she was in danger, she ought to know about it.

Besides, as a wannabe writer, she thought she should always be on the lookout for good story material. There just might be some here. So she'd called Mango Mary's and told Jackie and Alice they could meet her at her boat.

In anticipation of receiving her guests, she stuck her Lady-Smith .38 in a pocket of her cargo shorts. And here they came now, eyeing the boats. Jackie did a double-take when he saw Carina's new Porsche, like it meant something to him.

As they walked the last stretch of jetty to where she sat, Carina saw it didn't look like they'd come bearing glad tidings.

White House Press Room

Acting President Mather Wyman wore the same Henry Poole navy blue suit he'd worn often as vice president, but he felt it fit him better since he'd moved into the Oval Office. For one thing, he'd lost three pounds in recent weeks, something he'd attributed initially to stress. In response to the increased demands of his new job, though, he'd taken to eating more sensibly: less red meat more fruits and vegetables. He'd also begun a light but disciplined exercise routine: cardio and strength. He thought he stood straighter; his shoulders seemed broader, too.

He also had his hair trimmed daily, got a barber's shave each morning and had his skin moisturized. The total effect was nothing shocking, certainly not outlandish, but he'd still managed to look subtly younger and more ... like a president.

"Thank you all for coming," he said to the gathering of newspeople.

As his eyes scanned the room, he saw Kira and Welborn sitting along the wall to his right. It touched him that his niece had come to see him speak. She and Welborn made such a handsome couple. He'd never wanted to be anyone other than who he was, but he'd often envied the easy social acceptance straight couples had, especially the attractive ones.

Wyman said, "In light of the recent tragic losses of two Supreme Court justices …"

Aspen Lodge — Camp David

The president and her henchman watched Mather Wyman on MSNBC.

"…there has been a good deal of understandable speculation as to who will replace them. This guessing game had been made more intense because the High Court has never before lost two of its members at virtually the same moment, and because the president has temporarily and constitutionally delegated the powers of her office to me.

"I hold as sacred both the trust Patricia Darden Grant has placed in me and the obligations I assumed when I became the acting president. Both of those considerations being equal, I nonetheless must take other factors into account as I go about my duties as acting president.

"The first of these is I must do what I believe is right; that is the obligation of any man or woman who occupies the Oval Office. The next thing I must take into account is that much of what I do will set precedents for anyone else who finds himself or herself in my position. That being the case I want to be very thoughtful about what I do. The last matter I must reckon with is to keep a sense of proportion.

"The length of time I will serve as acting president will be far shorter than the time I have been and will resume being the vice president. In matters such as the armed standoff in Richmond,

Virginia, where lives were at stake and where it had to be made clear that our Union will not abide an armed rebellion, I will act swiftly.

"That is not to say filling two vacancies on the Supreme Court is not a serious matter, but the Court is still able to operate and the odd number of remaining justices will be able to render decisions in which a clear majority will prevail. There has been some speculation in the media since the passing of Chief Justice Alberto Calendri and Associate Justice Titus Hawkins that I might nominate their replacements or at least suggest whom I think should be nominated.

"I will, in fact, do neither of those things."

Patti and McGill shared a glance.

White House Press Room

"My respect for the president forbids me from doing either of those things. To speak even casually of the matter would be a betrayal of trust. My fervent prayer is that the president is regaining her full health and will be here to speak with you from this very spot in the near future.

"Until that time, I will do my best to perform my job as she might do and has done these past three years. If there's any speculation to be done, let the question be asked, 'How would Patricia Darden Grant handle this matter?' Then see how closely I come to that mark."

Welborn leaned close and whispered to Kira, "So it looks like no coup."

Indiana University — Bloomington, Indiana

Sheryl Kimbrough and her fifteen students watched the television at the front of the classroom as Mather Wyman took questions from the assemblage of reporters at the White House. According to Sheryl's book, there was no bull-puckey like that spread at Washington news conferences — and the double-talk came from both the politicians and the newsies.

Objective reporting having withered to near extinction.

Advocacy and equivalency coverage having choked it out faster than kudzu.

Sheryl's journalism class had been given its place in the university's curriculum as a rear guard action in the hope that it might preserve islands of objectivity in a sea of partisan pro-paganda. Nobody was counting on one class and one teacher to reverse the tide. Not at first. The eventual goal, however, was the idea that all public figures would be made to respond clearly to fact-based reality.

Sheryl's students were expected to become the apostles spreading that gospel.

Everyone in the classroom leaned forward as the reporter from the *Cleveland Plain Dealer* was called on to ask the first question. No one believed it was merely coincidence that a newsie from the acting president's home state got to jump the queue ahead of the big names. Everyone was expecting a softball question that Wyman could knock out of the park.

They were fooled completely. About the first part of the assumption.

"Mr. Acting President, whatever your working relationship with the president, the oath you took on Inauguration Day was to the American people. Given that and the unique opportunity with which you've been presented, why shouldn't you nominate whomever you think is best qualified to fill the vacant seats on the Supreme Court and not worry about whether you might offend anyone else, including the president?"

His face deadpan, Mather Wyman said, "Alan, I can understand why you would ask that question, as you, like all your colleagues here, know that we politicians never miss an opportunity to offend as many people as we can." Wyman cracked a grin to let everyone know it was okay to laugh, and they did. He added, "We're also famous for taking risks and running about without covering our backsides."

That line played well in the Indiana classroom. Sheryl Kimbrough found herself warming to an old-time pol she'd always thought of as a bit of a stiff. She looked about and saw Wyman had engaged all of her students as well.

Turning serious, Wyman said, "I was elected to serve the American people as their vice president. Nobody went to the polls three years ago thinking, 'Let's have old Mather make all the big decisions.' Your question," he told the reporter, "while technically correct, ignores the reality of governing. It is a job best done cooperatively. Commandments from on high should be left to the Almighty. Edicts from someone holding a job temporarily should be left unspoken altogether."

Reverting to the normal pecking order, the *New York Times* asked the next question. "Mr. Acting President, there's little if any cooperation between the Republicans and the Democrats in Washington these days. The president has left the GOP while you have remained with your party. Don't you owe it to those Americans who voted for you to at least let them know whom you think should become the next chief justice and associate justice?"

Mather Wyman wanted to sigh, but offered no sign of displeasure.

"What would happen if I did that, Roger? It would make a situation that's difficult enough even worse. There would be those in my party who would say I should get at least one of my choices, and politicians, by their nature, would say that I should get my choice for chief justice. We'll let the president have the other pick, as long as the person she wants is acceptable to us. I won't play games with a court whose decisions can affect the lives of every person in our country. No one should."

The *Los Angeles Times* got the next crack at Wyman.

"Mr. Acting President, your party, after the death of Speaker Geiger and with the rumored defection of Senator Hurlbert leaving to become a third party candidate for president, is in disarray. My question is, how much have you grown as a statesman from your time as acting president and do you feel that your unique experience would give you an advantage over anyone else the Republican Party might run for president?"

Wyman allowed himself a chuckle. "Well, Lisa, I haven't even lit a White House Christmas tree yet." The press liked that one, too. "What I can tell you is that from the very first moment, this job is a real eye-opener. When you sit in the Oval Office behind the president's desk, you realize that the well-being of the entire country depends on you doing the right thing, and it's not a responsibility from which you can shrink. You have to rise up to meet it, and you'd better be quick about it. Having known a bit of that reality now, I would say I have some advantage."

The *L.A. Times* was quick to follow up.

"Have you made a decision to run, sir?"

Wyman said, "No, I haven't."

Nobody believed him for a minute. Not in the White House. Not in Camp David.

Not in Indiana, where elector Sheryl Kimbrough thought: Good.

I'd like to vote for this man and, lucky me, I get to vote twice.

Aggie Wu called on the *Chicago Tribune* for the final question.

"Sir, do you have any idea of when President Grant will return to office?"

"Soon, Rick. But that's just my feeling."

Camp David — Catoctin Mountains, Maryland

McGill looked at Patti and said, "He fooled us. Didn't give anyone except his own right wing anything to complain about."

"Most of them will be voting for Howard Hurlbert, so he didn't lose much there."

"Nice allusion to Lincoln with that line about defending the Union."

The president nodded. "Didn't even mention the great man by name but he got his point across. He didn't let any of the questions throw him off stride. He addressed the reporters by name."

McGill said, "Had fair timing when he cracked his jokes, too … but nobody's buying the idea he won't run for the Republican nomination."

"Of course not, but he didn't push it."

"This election looks like it will be tougher than last time," McGill said.

"Yes, it does."

Of course, Patti could have disqualified Mather Wyman simply by revealing that he was gay. But betraying his trust would be as dirty a political trick as the country had ever seen. She decided then and there she wouldn't do that. It would haunt her the rest of her life and taint her second term. She would win or lose the election on her merits. She could live with that.

Still, she couldn't help but wonder if anyone else might know Mather's secret and leak it.

The White House — Chief of Staff's Office

Galia Mindel looked to Stephen Norwood for his appraisal.

"Biggest surprise since Susan Boyle sang on that English talent show."

Galia nodded. "I vetted Mather Wyman to be on the ticket with the president. I watched hours of video on him and never saw anything to match that performance."

"It did have a touch of Pygmalion to it; should I look for Henry Higgins?"

"No, but review all my files on the vice president. Don't worry about dirt, you won't find any. At least, I couldn't. But see if any of his earlier political positions might look embarrassing in the context of what he said today."

"Are you sure you don't want me to rescan his personal life?"

"Waste of time," Galia said. "Even if you could find something I didn't, the president wouldn't let us use it."

Norwood knew better than to push the point too far.

Still, he thought he'd take a look. Just to satisfy himself.

Indiana University — Bloomington, Indiana

Sheryl Kimbrough asked her class, "Who spotted the bull-puckey in Acting President Wyman's press conference, and how much of it was there?"

"He's running," most of the class called out.

Half of them added, "He *knows* when the president is coming back."

A lively conversation followed about how Wyman's ambition and knowledge had affected the way he'd answered the newsies' questions. Just before the class ended, a question was posed to the professor.

"Ms. Kimbrough, did you ever meet the acting president?"

"Yes. He didn't make half the impression on me that he did today."

"So maybe the idea of personal growth in the presidency isn't bull-puckey?"

Sheryl laughed. The young were so optimistic.

"Most times that's just what it is, but something sure got into Mather Wyman today."

Camp David — Catoctin Mountains, Maryland

By McGill's estimation, House Minority Leader Marlene Berman called the president at Aspen Lodge less than a minute after Mather Wyman had left the White House press room. She inquired as to the president's availability to see her; Representative Berman said she would be happy to drive out to Camp David that very moment.

The president told her the White House was much closer and she could catch a ride on Marine One that afternoon. The minority leader was thrilled by that idea. The president knew that Mather Wyman would learn, sooner rather than later, of Marlene Berman's trip to Camp David. Let him ponder that while he was busy making his plans.

McGill didn't know precisely what Patti was thinking, but he said, "The campaign has begun? Skulduggery is in the works?"

Patti nodded. "It has and it is."

"Would you like me to take your pulse?"

"We'll get to that later. This will be my last night at Camp David."

"I'll try not to pine if you forget me in the crush of business."

"You'll keep busy. You're not one to have idle hands."

"That's true."

"You probably have something you want to do right now."

McGill said he did. "I'm going to see if Kenny's up for a little fresh air."

Patti smiled. "Go for a walk? I'd like to join you."

"Our pleasure. Then I'll see if Kenny's interested in what I was thinking about."

"What's that?"

"I'm going to teach him to play patty-cakes."

Patti arched an eyebrow.

McGill said, "I never told you before but that's the first step in learning Dark Alley."

The day was sunny, the pace was ambling and everyone enjoyed the walk. After Patti excused herself, McGill and Kenny stood facing each other in the living room of Aspen Lodge. They had both wiped off their faces with a damp cloth and washed their hands. Kenny was feeling better every day but they still had to guard against infection and they would be making hand-to-hand contact.

Kenny had been overjoyed by the idea that his father was finally letting him in on the family martial art. When McGill had told him patty-cakes was the necessary first step, he'd shown no skepticism and bought in immediately. His son's faith touched McGill.

"Okay," he said, "here's what we'll do: four claps high and then four claps low. Left, right, left, right. First high, then low. We'll keep the pace slow and easy, just find our rhythm. If you feel at all uncomfortable, you have to tell me."

Kenny nodded. "I will, Dad."

"After we're done, I want you to practice in your mind, but keep that slow, too, okay?"

"I can't even think fast?"

"You're old enough to know that certain thoughts can set your heart racing. I don't want Nick or Dr. Jones scolding me and nobody wants you back in the hospital."

"That's for sure. Okay, easy does it, but …"

"But what?" McGill asked.

"Well, you know how sometimes in movies when guys are supposed to be moving real fast they slow the film way down? How about if I think like that?"

"That's not a bad idea. You can keep a close eye on your form that way."

"Dad, whenever you had to use Dark Alley, back when you were a cop or after that, did it ever seem that way to you? Like you were going fast but it seemed slow."

McGill said, "When you're quicker than the other guy, it seems like *he's* going slow."

"What if he's quicker?"

"If he's quicker physically, you have to be quicker mentally. If he's quicker both ways, you'd better hope you can outrun him. Or avoid him in the first place. Okay, let's start. Four high, four low. Easy does it."

The went through the pattern high and low four times, thirty-two light hand claps altogether. McGill watched his son closely for any sign of fatigue or distress. Kenny's cheeks turned lightly pink but that only made him look healthier.

After they stopped, Kenny said, "Piece of cake."

McGill had liked the way his son had moved. Soft and supple, moving his hips and shifting his balance with each swing of his hands. Everything flowed just the way it should. Maybe Kenny was more of a natural athlete than either of them would have thought.

"Good," he said. "As we move along, we'll add points of contact and we'll go faster."

"How fast?"

"Fast within safe limits. When you're back to a hundred percent, we'll go all out, and being the younger guy, you'll clean my clock."

"Hah," Kenny said, "that'll be the day."

"It will be and it's not that far off."

Kenny embraced his father and asked the question that mattered most to him, "You haven't showed this stuff to Abbie or Caitie, have you?"

McGill said he hadn't.

He also didn't explain that the patty-cakes routine was window-dressing for intercepting an opponent's blow and delivering a counterpunch. That might have gotten Kenny worked up. He'd learn the purpose of what they'd been practicing soon enough.

They washed their faces and hands again and Kenny lay down for a nap.

Wearing a smile that made McGill's heart glow.

He'd just closed the door to Kenny's room when he heard the phone ring.

A call for Patti, he thought, but it turned out to be for him.

Deputy Director Byron DeWitt of the FBI.

"Mr. McGill, I just thought I'd let you know the bureau has been working hard on tracking down commercial drivers who'd fallen behind on their delivery schedules on the day that interests us. We allowed for tardiness ranging from one hour to one week. We've come up with twenty-three names. We expect to winnow that number down fairly fast."

"Don't forget to look for someone whose job approval is on the uptick," McGill said.

"I made a note of that, yes."

Telling McGill, politely, not to think he was a dope.

"Sorry. First time we're working together."

"Not a problem. What I'd like to know is whether you'd like to review our list."

The thought occurred to McGill that Celsus Crogher was not the only fed who'd heard from the president recently about how to deal with him.

"I'd appreciate that, Mr. Deputy Director."

Patti must have figured no harm could come his way doing a desk job.

Maybe he'd get a little eye strain.

"We'll transmit the files directly, sir," DeWitt told him.

"I'll be right here," McGill said.

Having some work to do made him feel better about that.

Aboard the Irish Grace — Gulf of Mexico

In calm seas, Carina Linberg dropped anchor little more than mile off Key West. Jackie Richmond and Alice Tompkins had told her they'd both feel better delivering their message out on the water. Carina had thought about that a moment, wondering if these two people were crazy enough to try stealing her boat out from under her. Weigh her down and toss her over the side.

That would be a lot harder to get away with anchored where there were all sorts of vessels, sail and motor, passing by within hand-waving distance.

"You wouldn't mind maybe going a bit farther out?" Alice asked.

"I would," Carina said. "I'm not a charter captain. This is all the ride you get for free."

Jackie told Alice, "It's all right. Nobody can hear us out here."

"Yeah, but they might *see* us," Alice said.

If the woman was acting, she was good, Carina thought.

Jackie was playing it cool enough, but that might have been male posturing.

Something more than a few guys were known to do.

Carina said, "You're worried, you two can go below. I can talk to you from here and no one else will see you."

Not only that, if they tried to make a move on Carina, they'd have to do it uphill.

Never an advantageous fighting position.

Alice took advantage of Carina's suggestion, extending her

hand to Jackie and leading him down into the cabin, going only far enough for the two of them to be out of sight of any passing vessel. Alice's upturned face looked at Carina like a waif about to beg for a crust of bread.

Jackie was still impassive, but he'd come to see her, too, Carina thought.

"Who's scaring you?" Carina asked.

Alice looked to Jackie to explain. He shrugged and said, "Alice has a sister named —"

"You don't have to get specific," Alice told him.

Jackie sighed and said, "Alice has a sister, her sister has a kid, a daughter." He looked at Alice. "It's all right to say we're talking about a girl?"

"Yeah, you gotta say that."

"Okay." Jackie looked back at Carina. "The daughter answered some kind of Internet ad."

"On FacePage."

"That's where it was then. The ad said a good-looking young girl could make a lot of money. Kid must've been raised sheltered because she went to check it out."

Carina frowned. "Just prostitution or white slavery?"

"Slavery," Jackie said. "She got beaten up and gang-raped. Told she belonged to this one dude and if she tried to run away she'd be cut up for chum and fed to the fish. Kid had guts, though, she ran and made it home. Told Mom what had happened. Mom put her on a boat to Naples and from there a bus to Georgia."

Carina said, "The assholes came looking for her? Had a talk with her mother? Threatened her?"

Alice looked at Carina in wonder. Jackie grinned.

He said, "You seem pretty wised up for a lady with your own little yacht."

That was when Alice leaned forward with a squint of recognition. "I've seen you on television, haven't I?"

Carina nodded. "WorldWide News."

"You're a reporter?" Jackie asked, tensing up a bit.

"A talking head. I got paid for giving my opinion, that's all."

"But what I remember," Alice said, "you were in the army or something."

"Air Force. I flew a bomber."

Now Jackie leaned forward. "You dropped bombs on people?"

Carina nodded.

"You've killed people?" Alice asked.

"Not anyone I knew personally."

That made Jackie smile again. He asked, "You know how many people you aced?"

"It's hard to do body counts up where I worked. Come to that, the weapons I dropped rarely left any bodies. So how did the assholes threaten your sister, Alice?"

"They told her by sending her daughter away she'd stolen their property. They wanted money for their loss. When they saw she didn't have much, she promised she could get them ten thousand dollars. They gave her two days to make good."

"Your sister came to you for the money, Alice?"

"Only for a short-term loan. My sister and I don't get on well, never have, but she's the apple of our grandpa's eye, him being up in Georgia."

Carina held up her hand. She wanted to process what she'd heard. See if she couldn't figure things out from there. That was what a storyteller would do.

She looked at Jackie. "You came up with the money for Alice. Where you got it is a mystery for the moment, but you didn't make it tending bar. So Alice took your money, gave it to her sister and everything was supposed to be cool with the bad guys. Sis got the money from Grandpa, repaid Alice and she returned it to you."

"Batting a thousand," Jackie told Carina. "What happened next?"

"That's easy. The assholes wanted more. Sis sent them to Alice's place and Jackie and I showed the tough guy who came calling he wasn't all that tough. So how bad was the next guy they sent?"

"Half again as big," Jackie said. "Real hairy. He was scaring

Alice pretty bad. She was working the bar alone."

Alice told Carina, "He said they were going to ask for another ten thousand but for hurting the other guy, now they wanted more than that. They want my place, Mango Mary's."

"Nice way to launder cash," Jackie said.

Alice added, "They also said they wanted to talk with Jackie … and you."

Maybe, Carina thought. Maybe Jackie and Alice were just trying to rope her in.

Not that she could say for sure. You embarrassed a creep, he'd probably want to get even.

Show he couldn't be pushed around by a woman.

She looked at Jackie. "How'd you get rid of *this* asshole?"

"I came behind him, put my gun up to his head. Asked if knew what a great job a forty caliber round did clearing out ear wax. Before he could answer, I kicked him on the back of his knee and laid my gun against the back of his head."

"Threw him out the front door like the other one?" Carina asked.

"Dragged him out back. Got him into an old grocery cart. Left him a couple blocks away."

"Any reason you didn't go to the cops?"

Alice said, "I'm too afraid. They burn down my bar or my house, I got insurance. But I don't want to be inside when the fire starts."

"What about your sister's house? She's not worried?"

"She rented; she used to anyway. She's up in Georgia now, too."

"But you don't want to go?"

"I might have to, but I don't want to."

Carina turned her eyes on Jackie. "You staying or going?"

"Haven't decided. I thought I might buy Alice's place. Someone comes in and I shoot them, I got more rights that way."

"No doubt. So the two of you just stopped by to give me fair warning?"

"The least we could do," Jackie said.

"And I thought maybe you'd like to buy my house," Alice added.

Carina laughed. "I still have a co-op in midtown Manhattan, but thanks for the thought. I'll run you two back in to the marina and you can make your plans."

Jackie said, "You have a gun on you, don't you?"

Carina took it out. "This is such a great boat I can steer with one hand and shoot with the other. Now, let me ask you a question, Jackie. Why'd you do that double-take when you saw my little black Porsche?"

He said, "That's *your* car? Small damn world. I had one just like it."

"And?" Carina asked.

"Somebody stole it from me."

Florida Avenue NW — Washington, D.C.

Sweetie looked at her fiancé as he cooked shrimp scampi for dinner in his ... in *their* kitchen. She still hadn't gotten used to that idea, that what had been Putnam's was or soon would be hers, too. She was anything but materialistic, but she saw that it would be wrong to deny partial ownership of the worldly goods that Putnam would bring to their marriage. To deny them would be to deny him.

There was precious little Sweetie would bring to the union. All she could think of was to let Putnam have her backup gun. If she could bring herself to part with it.

Without turning from the stovetop to look at Sweetie, Putnam asked, "You looking at my backside again?"

He would have said ass with anyone but Margaret.

"Just checking to see how the muscle tone is improving."

"That's what they all say."

"All of them, huh? And who would that be?"

He glanced over his shoulder and grinned. "The ladies at the gym you made me join."

"They spent less time ogling and more time moving, they'd

have better tone, too."

Putnam plated the shrimp over pasta and served it with a flourish. He poured himself a glass of chenin blanc. He held the bottle up inquisitively. Except for sacramental wine, Sweetie had been a teetotaler. After Putnam pointed out that even the Savior tippled at wedding receptions and that wine in moderation was good for a woman's heart, Sweetie would on occasion partake.

She held her thumb and index finger an inch apart.

That was exactly what she got. Sitting across the kitchen table from her, Putnam lowered his head in silence as Sweetie gave thanks. When she finished, he said, "Thank you, Margaret. You make me happy."

They touched their glasses. Putnam took a drink, Sweetie a sip.

He tried a bite of his cooking and smiled as he chewed.

After he swallowed, he said, "If you don't eat your food, I will, and my increasingly trim waistline might go into relapse."

Sweetie applied her fork to her dinner and ate without any apparent joy.

"Okay, I know the shrimp isn't the problem," Putnam said, "and my sinful ways aren't nearly what they used to be, so what's the matter?"

"I heard from Byron DeWitt earlier."

"The FBI guy, blonde and Chinese."

Putnam paid close attention when listening to Sweetie.

"Yeah, him. He said it was a courtesy call, which took a leap of faith to accept."

"The president told him to keep Jim McGill and you informed," Putnam said.

"Sure, I got that, but government employees can find a million excuses not to follow the boss's orders. Anyway, he seemed okay about sharing with me, and that caused me to start taking a new look at things. Realize the world is changing."

"You're not getting cold feet, are you, Margaret?"

She took his hand. "There was a chill, but it was my heart not my feet."

Putnam couldn't track that one. "Don't tell me something has scared you. I don't think I could believe that."

"Sorry to disappoint," Sweetie said, "but I am human. I've been worrying about you, that you might be harmed or worse."

Putnam said, "Yeah, it's that worse part that's the killer."

He lifted her hand to his lips and kissed it. Sweetie released his hand.

"I've also been worrying that I might become Carolyn Enquist."

"McGill's first wife? What's the connection?"

Sweetie told him the story of why Carolyn left Jim, how she worried about him being a cop, getting killed, leaving her a widow and the kids fatherless. She couldn't kick the anxiety until they were divorced.

"But I'm not a cop," Putnam said, "and you're only sort of one."

Sweetie agreed. "But I might be in danger and you might be, too, because of me."

"You mean from this Damon Todd guy and the other two crazies?"

"Yes. Deputy Director DeWitt told me the FBI will probably find the driver who helped Todd and the other two get away. He said it should be a matter of days."

"That's good," Putnam said.

"It's a step is what it is," Sweetie told him. "The file I read on Todd said the CIA was unable to crack his cover identity and they had three years to try. All the time they had Todd, they couldn't get him to admit he was anything but a young boy."

"So even if DeWitt's people find the driver it might not lead anywhere, and Todd could be running around free for a long time."

Sweetie nodded. "He could be patient. Wait until we let our guard down. Then maybe he tries to get at Jim through me or he tries to get at me through you, thinking I'd sacrifice Jim for you."

"Whoa," Putnam said. "You wouldn't do that, though, would you?"

"No. I wouldn't sacrifice you for Jim either."

"That's comforting, I suppose, but less likely than the other way around."

"You see why I worry. But where did worrying get Carolyn?"

Putnam emptied and refilled his glass. Sweetie declined his offer of more.

"What we'll have to do," Putnam said, "is emulate Jim McGill's *second* marriage. I don't know any of the details, of course, but I imagine both the president and her henchman know something bad could happen to either of them on any given day. They accept that, live with it, make the most of the present moment. Really, any day we pick up our car keys, we grab mortality right along with them."

He drank half his glass and added, *"Que sera."*

"You have that much faith?" Sweetie asked.

"I do and you have more."

"I used to think I did. You'd be all right if I wasn't with you all the time?"

Putnam said, "We might get on each other's nerves if you were. Besides, I'm going to Omaha, and no one would ever think to look for me there."

Sweetie gave him a look. "Why are you going to Omaha?"

"While you were at Camp David, I called Darren Drucker. You may have heard of him."

"The richest man in the country? The guy who thinks his taxes should be raised? Yeah."

"I pitched my idea for ShareAmerica, the mutual lobbying fund, to him. He loved it, wants me to go out to Omaha and run it from there."

"And when did you plan to share this news with me?"

"I wasn't. I told him I'd think about the move but I couldn't commit without talking to you. I was hoping you'd nix the idea, but after our little chat, maybe heading to the heartland would be a good idea. You can still veto the idea."

Sweetie shook her head. "No, do it. I like ShareAmerica, too."

"Patti Grant's second term will go a lot better, especially if she wins as an independent, if I can help shape the Congress for her."

"Absolutely."

"And you and I can steal away for secret weekends in, say, Kalispell, Montana."

"No one would look for us there," Sweetie said.

"But we won't let too much time go by before we go to Key West and get married."

"No we won't."

"If there are still madmen loose in the world at that time —"

"*Que sera,*" Sweetie said, and downed her chenin blanc.

Walter Reed National Military Medical Center
Bethesda, Maryland

The term splitting headache was usually thought of as something that cracked one's skull. In the Reverend Burke Godfrey's case, skull involvement was secondary — and literal.

What happened to him was a *shredding* headache, better known as a stroke, medically labeled as a cerebrovascular accident. A major blood vessel in Godfrey's brain ruptured. The sudden increase in pressure caused by leaking blood began to damage brain cells.

The stricken Godfrey weakly exclaimed, "My God!"

No one was able to ask if he'd had a vision of the hereafter. He lost consciousness immediately thereafter as brain function quickly diminished. He was rushed into the operating room. The on-the-fly diagnosis, later proved accurate, was a malignant cerebral infarction, so named because the chances for a happy outcome were less than minuscule.

Nonetheless, the surgical team removed a section of Godfrey's skull to relieve the pressure. The best hope at that point was that he would survive with significant disabilities. That hope was not realized. After the pronouncement of death, the detached segment of skull was put back in place, held there, pending an autopsy, by wires.

In short order, the surgical report was transcribed and transmitted to the White House.

Galia Mindel received it.

Without consulting anyone, she handed the hot potato to Mather Wyman.

Hart Senate Office Building — Washington, D.C.

Senator Howard Hurlbert, True South, Mississippi, was talking with old friends, fellow alums from Ole Miss and two of his bigger campaign donors, when Bobby Beckley rapped on his door and interrupted the conversation. Beckley was the only person on Hurlbert's staff who would have dared to do that.

"Senator," he said, "something urgent has just come up."

One of the good old boys visiting Hurlbert asked, "Soviet Russia's attacking?"

Beckley framed a thin smile. "Almost that bad. Senator?"

Hurlbert saw his chief of staff wasn't fooling around.

He told his friends, "I'll meet y'all for drinks at eight, if I can get away."

With handshakes and pats on the back, the senator ushered his friends out.

As soon as the door behind them was closed, he told his chief of staff, "This better be good, Bobby."

Beckley put on his campaign manager's cap. "How about this? You're gonna have two serious competitors, people with greater political stature, running against you to be president, and what just happened will let you hogtie at least one of them."

Hurlbert smiled.

Beckley told the senator, "A nurse I know from down home works at Bethesda Medical Center. She called me with the news. Reverend Burke Godfrey just died."

The senator looked stunned. Beckley was tempted to push his chin back up.

Before he could do anything so foolish, Hurlbert said, "That's terrible."

"For him, sure," Beckley agreed. "For us, it's Christmas come early."

"How the hell do you figure that?"

"Howard, Burke Godfrey died in a *federal* medical facility. Mather Wyman put him there. After he raided Godfrey's church compound. It's automatic we blame Wyman for the reverend's death. There's only one question we've got to answer now."

"What's that?"

God, this guy was dumb, Beckley thought. If he could somehow get the senator elected president, *he'd* be the one running the country. That sounded good at first. You thought about it, though, if there was any job in the world that could kill you, it was corralling all the assholes in Washington you needed to get something done.

"The question is, Howard, how do we blame Patti Grant, too?"

The Oval Office

Mather Wyman's first impulse after hearing from Galia Mindel that Burke Godfrey had died was to call the president and share the news. That thought was quickly elbowed aside by the realization that if Galia hadn't called the president with the news *before* she'd told him she would do so immediately afterward. Deciding the optics would be horrible if there were any delay in sharing the news with the public — the government was trying to cover up its responsibility for Godfrey's death — the acting president had Aggie Wu contact the TV networks and cable news outlets and say he would need five minutes of their time immediately before the evening news.

Politically, he had to be the one to pass the word. He'd ordered the assault on Salvation's Path. The consequences that flowed from that were his to bear. Trying to pass the buck to Patti Grant would only look cowardly.

As it was, there would be reverberations affecting the president. A fact that was not lost on her.

Two minutes before air time, a phone call reached the acting president in the Oval Office.

Patricia Darden Grant was on the line. "I trust you intend to be brief, Mather."

"Yes, Madam President. Just the facts as we know them and a promise that all post mortem proceedings will be completely transparent."

"Good. After you finish with that, please let the country know I'll be back at my desk in the morning."

Telling him he should be back at his desk in the East Wing by then.

"That's good news, Madam President."

"Thank you, Mather. Now, I have to squeeze in another call before you go on."

"Madam President?"

Who else did she need to call, he wondered.

The president said, "Erna Godfrey needs to know, before the rest of the world does, that she's lost her husband."

Charlottesville, Virginia

"You understand Olin will kill you if you fuck me up," Crosby told Damon Todd.

"I do," Todd said.

"You won't go easy," Anderson said.

"I understand," Todd assured them. "You don't have to do this if you don't want to."

The three fugitives were in their cabin in the woods. The sounds of the woodland's nocturnal animals and insects were muted. The doors were closed and the windows were covered with black curtains. The only light came from a low-watt ceiling bulb that would soon be extinguished and an iPad on a desk stand.

Not two minutes after Todd had appropriated the tablet computer from Fletcher Penrose, Crosby had taken it from Todd and inside of an hour had found and disabled the GPS and "Find My iPad" features. No one was going to track them through the computer.

There was an air of ghost stories around a campfire in the room. The two rogue covert ops were the edgy kids; Todd was the guy who got to say boo. It was starting to look like the big bad CIA dudes just might be scaredy-cats.

Todd sat on the desk chair, crossed one leg over the other and sighed.

He might as well have yelled, "Pussies!" at the other two.

Crosby and Anderson exchanged a look, knowing they couldn't back down. Todd had showed them that morning how a lame-ass civilian like him had already passed them by in hunt-and-kill skills. If any of their wet work buddies had seen that sorry exhibition, they would have put Crosby and Anderson out of their misery.

Come to that, Crosby and Anderson realized they were probably depending on Todd right now to evade recapture. Or death. Which didn't seem all that glorious at the moment. Knowing they probably weren't likely to inflict anything more serious than a stubbed toe on their pursuers.

Todd had said he could help them regain their edge. He said they'd have to be at the top of their games to get Jim McGill and he could help them get there. Then he offered to show them an example. He asked if they knew of the comedian, Tony Stone.

"Guy's got a fucking filthy mouth but he's funny," Anderson said.

"We've heard of him," Crosby said.

Todd told them, "He was a severely repressed young man when I met him. He was also filled with rage after a lifetime of psychological abuse from his father. He came to me when he was in college because he was afraid he'd start killing people in large numbers."

Crosby and Anderson didn't look at each other when they heard that. They knew guys like that, had worked with guys like that. They *were* guys like that. The only thing that had saved them — up to a point — was they had found a government approved outlet for their furies.

Todd said, "I'll call Tony. He'll take my call without hesitation. I'll have him tell you a few of his latest jokes, and then I'll have him speak to you as the young man I first met. Then you'll see what I can do. Fair enough?"

Crosby and Anderson nodded. They had nothing to lose from listening to a demonstration and, damn, if it hadn't gone *exactly* the way Todd had said it would. Tony Stone was blue from word one and hilarious, too. Then he became someone else entirely. His voice rose in register, became reedy and he sounded like he might either weep or scream. Maybe lose control altogether. Off himself or the first person he met. Then Todd calmed him down, brought the public Tony Stone back and everything was cool.

Except Crosby and Anderson were now afraid of just how *good* Todd was at his work. Who the hell knew what he could do to them? Turn them inside out. Make them his asswipes.

Todd knew that, of course.

"You two going to make up your minds or should I call it a night?" he asked.

"Do it," Crosby told Todd.

Then he directed another look at Anderson, silently reiterating the command that Anderson make sure Todd died painfully if anything went wrong.

Todd, calm as could be, sat Crosby down at the desk, swabbed his left shoulder with an alcohol-soaked cotton ball and injected him with ketamine hydrochloride. The drug could be introduced into a body either intramuscularly or intravenously. Todd went with the former, reasoning his subjects would find that less threatening. He did, however, shoot Crosby up with twice the recommended dosage.

Induction of full surgical anesthesia would follow more swiftly that way; it would also last longer. In a matter of minutes, Crosby would feel as if he were leaving his body very far behind, floating off into the distance. To help Crosby along on that journey, Todd brought up an app on the iPad called *Hypnotic Highway.*

It was remarkably like the video he'd created years ago. The view was of an endless stretch of interstate highway at night as seen from behind a steering wheel. Low beams illuminated lane-divider stripes. One after another, after another, after another passed by.

Just as in Todd's video there was the sound of a soft ceaseless wind rushing past.

Then somebody had to push the production values a step too far and added a quiet flute to the soundtrack. Too artsy by half, but it didn't seem to bother Crosby. Todd thought if anything should have been added it would be the hum of tires on a smooth road surface.

In a quiet measured voice, Todd said, "Keep your eyes on the road, keep your eyes on the road." Normally, he didn't need to repeat the instruction more than five times to induce the altered state of consciousness characterized by selective attention. In common parlance, a trance. The therapeutic values of working with someone placed in a trance included pain and stress management, control of anxiety and relief from nausea.

When Todd crafted a personality, he sought to heighten a subject's natural strengths and have him derive deep satisfaction from the successes that would flow from their enhanced abilities. That and be forever grateful and subservient to Todd.

With Crosby, he thought three reminders to keep his eyes on the road might have done the trick, but he stayed true to form. When he got to five, he looked not at Crosby but turned his attention to Anderson.

Anderson wasn't as far under as Crosby, but Todd had left a post-hypnotic suggestion with him from their aerosol-induced session. The suggestion: Keep your eyes on the road. Anderson was completely amenable to being injected with his own dose of Special K.

Before the night was over, Todd would own both men.

As promised, he would bring their skills to their upper limits. Just like the old army recruiting slogan, they would be all they could be. Better than that, they would die for Todd, and kill each other first rather than turn a hand against him.

Now, the challenge was to find the most effective way to turn them loose on Jim McGill.

State House Room 204 — Concord, New Hampshire

New Hampshire Secretary of State John Patrick Granby sat in his office well after the hour at which he usually went home to dinner. He was faced with an impossible task, was trying to accomplish it anyway and didn't know whether his heart or his head would be the first to explode. He blamed Galia Mindel for his predicament.

God *damn* that woman, he thought.

Earlier in the evening he'd completed a teleconference with his counterparts in Iowa and South Carolina, Paul Brandstetter and Charles Delmain. They were as outraged as he was that the legislatures in New York, Illinois and California had that day passed new laws mandating that their states hold their presidential primary elections "no later than one minute after the primary election in New Hampshire begins, whensoever that time may be." Added to that was the stipulation that "any political party that seeks to penalize the state of New York (Illinois or California) shall not have a line for its presidential candidate on the state ballot for the general election."

The situation had become impossible for Granby because New Hampshire law decreed that its presidential primary election must be the first in the nation by a margin of one week not one minute. In the past, that coveted head-of-the-line position had been protected simply by moving New Hampshire's election to an earlier date and by having the national committees of the two major parties threaten any would-be interlopers with a refusal to seat their state delegations at the national nominating conventions.

What had begun as a New Hampshire primary that had been held in late March had already been moved to early January. Now, it didn't matter when the primary was scheduled. Thanks to those bastards in Albany, Springfield and Sacramento, their states and New Hampshire were conjoined quadruplets. There was no getting away from them.

Not that Granby hadn't tried.

He'd called the chairmen of both the Democratic National Committee and the Republican National Committee, Henry Melchior and Reynard Dix, and screamed at them. "You've got to stop this shit! They're bluffing. They'd never leave the Democratic and Republican candidates off their state ballots. It's all bullshit. The Supreme Court —"

Granby got cut off right there by both men. They reminded him of the states that a majority of the justices, the ones still alive, called home: New York, Illinois and California. Those justices were going to be pro states' rights in their points of view on this matter.

"The people then," Granby argued. "Tens of millions of people will be disenfranchised. They won't stand for it."

Henry Melchior had told him, "Think about the point you're trying to make, John. Implicit in your argument is *seventy* million people should wait, hat in hand, to pick among the leftover presidential candidates while every four years a little more than *one* million people in New Hampshire get the full menu. If my party and the GOP were suicidal enough to bend a knee to you and our candidates weren't on the ballots in three of the most populous states in the nation, we'd soon be replaced in those states, probably by half-a-dozen new parties. I imagine any of the senators elected from those new parties would be inclined to filibuster any bill that so much as provided road salt to your state."

So said the chairman of the DNC, a lifelong resident of Central Park West.

He was firmly onboard with giving his home state more clout in choosing which Democrat got to run for president.

The chairman of the RNC, Reynard Dix, had listened to Granby's rant and concluded, "Maybe sticking to the old system would be the conservative way to go, but Jeez how could we not have our candidates on the ballots in New York, Illinois and

California?"

"You're not going to win any of those damn states anyway," Granby yelled.

"Not this time, but things change. Listen, I'll talk to some people. We'll get back to you."

"Bastard," Granby said after he hung up.

Then Brandstetter called with Charles Delmain already on the line.

The three of them switched to Skype. In varying degrees, they all looked like men who would face a firing squad in the morning. The thought made Granby regret giving up smoking.

Brandstetter suggested their states threaten to do what the others had done, refuse to list candidates who didn't go along with their way of doing things.

Delmain laughed. "Nice try, Paul. But quite a few of my fore-bears fought a war on the side of the small states against the side with the big states. It didn't turn out well for us. The other thing to consider is how much True South is going to cut into the GOP vote. Down here it figures to be substantial."

Brandstetter added, "They're liable to get a good chunk of the Evangelical vote here, too."

Granby snorted. "True South, no offense, Charles, is not going to play in New Hampshire."

"None taken, John, but I'm afraid you're going to have to carry the ball on this one. It looks like the world is changing and we just might get left behind."

With nowhere else to turn, Granby called all four members of his state's Congressional delegation and asked what they might do to stymie this insurrection. He was told, in a word, nothing. There were four of them and a hundred and seven members of Congress from New York, Illinois and California.

In desperation, so he could put a face on his enemy, Granby asked all four of New Hampshire's Washington cadre who might have been the architect of the hideous new plan. Their unanimous judgment was that it could be only one person: White House Chief of Staff Galia Mindel. Who, of course, was from New York.

Shortly after midnight, his fifth shot of scotch in hand, Granby realized he could not win.

As no one else ever had, he'd failed his state, his home, the place he loved above all others. He was sure his failure would kill him, and death would be no less than he deserved.

Reaching that conclusion, he decided Galia Mindel should die, too.

4

October, 2011
Department of Justice Building — Washington, D.C.

Benton Williams was ushered into the office of Deputy Attorney General Linda Otani, who greeted him with a polite handshake and a wary eye. She knew that Williams had been Reverend Burke Godfrey's personal lawyer. In light of Godfrey's death while being held in a federal medical facility, she suspected Williams was going to announce he would be filing a suit against the government for —

"I don't plan to sue the government," Williams said, "not unless I must."

The deputy AG asked, "Why would it even enter your mind to sue the government?"

"So I might obtain access to Mrs. Burke Godfrey."

The deputy attorney general was a lawyer who always read the fine print of any case she handled and she never forgot a word of it.

"You are not now, nor have you ever been, Erna Godfrey's lawyer," she said.

Williams nodded. "That's true, and I have not now, nor at any other time, claimed to be her lawyer. However, at the time of his unfortunate death, I was Reverend Burke Godfrey's lawyer, and we intended to file suit against WorldWide News for causing him great bodily harm, a debilitating blow to his head by one of WWN's employees, Ellie Booker."

"You don't intend to let a little thing like the death of your client stop you?" Otani said.

"Not if I can help it, no."

"So you're going to amend your suit to a wrongful death claim."

"Precisely," Williams said.

"Only you need a client, and that would be Erna Godfrey."

"Yes, it would."

"Now, you'd like the opportunity to ask Ms. Godfrey if she wants to pursue a legal action."

"I would."

"Do you have with you a letter addressed to Ms. Godfrey outlining your proposal?"

"I do, but I would much rather speak directly with Mrs. Godfrey."

"I'm sure you would. May I see your letter to Ms. Godfrey, please?"

Williams looked like he was going to object but Otani cut him off.

"This is not a criminal matter, Counsel," she reminded him, "and we've agreed you're not her lawyer. Mail sent to federal prisoners is subject to prior review. However, if you don't wish to pursue the matter after all …"

She shrugged and waited for Williams to make his choice. He took an envelope out of his briefcase and gave it to her. She took out the one-page proposal and read it quickly.

"Admirably brief and clearly detailed, Counselor."

"Thank you."

"The only plaintiff you name is WWN. You don't have it in mind to pursue a separate action against the federal government, now or in the future?"

"I don't contemplate that, no."

"But you reserve the right to change your mind?"

"Of course."

The deputy attorney general put the proposal back in its envelope and said, "If you like, I'll see that Ms. Godfrey gets this."

"But I won't be talking to her?"

"Not anytime soon."

"Madam Deputy Attorney General, might I raise a point?"

Linda Otani nodded.

"I've read in the press," Williams said, "that the government of the United Kingdom is looking into bringing possible corruption charges against WWN, the payment of bribes to police officials and possibly even a member of Parliament or two. That would raise the possibility of the DOJ also bringing charges against WWN under the Foreign Corrupt Practices Act. Caught in such a legal pincer movement, the company might declare bankruptcy."

"Making it judgment proof against your suit, is that what you mean?" Otani asked.

"That is my immediate concern, but there is another. If by pursuing your own action against WWN you were to foreclose a civil suit against WWN by the widow of Reverend Godfrey, that wouldn't look good in an election year, would it?"

Linda Otani laughed and tossed the envelope on her desk.

"Erna Godfrey is a convicted murderer serving a life sentence. Her food, shelter and clothing will be provided to her by the federal government. A huge judgment against WWN would benefit you but not her. Whether any of that becomes a political matter is not my concern." She spelled out why. "I'm not running for office."

"Thank you for sharing your personal plans," Williams said. "I'll assume your position also reflects the views of the Grant administration, but it is possible another president might see things in an entirely different light. Why it's even possible a new president might commute Mrs. Godfrey's sentence, release her with time served being her punishment. At that point, a decision to refuse to let Mrs. Godfrey have her day in court against WWN would look spiteful. It might even tarnish Patricia Darden Grant's legacy."

Linda Otani leaned forward and gave Williams her best prosecutorial glare.

"Any numbers of eventualities *might* occur, Counselor. A misguided future president might free Erna Godfrey, but I don't see any way a future president would be able to justify the release of a person who murdered the spouse of a predecessor. That president's legacy would be tarnished while he or she was still in office."

The deputy AG sat back and waited.

Williams could take her offer to deliver his letter to Erna Godfrey or leave it.

He took it, and once he was gone Linda Otani's anger vanished.

She'd had to appear hard nosed, of course.

But she sure hoped she hadn't just screwed up.

Push came to shove, politically, she could lose her job like anyone else.

Camp David — Catoctin Mountains, Maryland

McGill brought out the escrima sticks the morning Patti left for the White House. He'd planned to let Kenny sleep in and start their workout after breakfast, but his son had climbed out of bed early so he could say goodbye to his stepmother. Patti kissed and embraced both McGills and beamed at them.

"I couldn't ask for a better sendoff," she said. "Wish me luck."

They both did and waved as Marine One lifted off, watched until it was out of sight.

Kenny looked at his father and said, "Sometimes I think I'm living a dream."

"Me, too, but then I can't remember a dream this good. You want to eat first or do a light workout with the sticks?"

Kenny was excited about using the escrima sticks; that'd be much cooler than playing patty-cakes with your hands. "Let's do the workout," he said.

They went back to Aspen Lodge. McGill got two sticks for each of them, twenty-seven inches long, a half-inch in diameter and made of bamboo. They took them out back. McGill said, "Using the sticks helps to develop hand speed. Which is good. If one of us isn't careful, we can rap the other guy's knuckles. Which is painful. So the idea is to hold the stick low and make contact with the opposite end."

Kenny nodded, listening closely.

McGill continued, "We'll start with the same pattern as we did with our hands: two high, two low. We'll start easy, see how you feel. If it's not a strain, we'll pick up the pace just a bit. After each strike, remember to return the stick to your collarbone."

Kenny nodded. He concentrated to get the form right. Swung the stick in his right hand high. It clacked against the stick his father brought out to meet it. In an actual fight, the blow would be aimed at a shoulder or head. The right-hand stick was returned to the collarbone as the left-hand stick swung forward. That stick came back to resting position as the right-hand stick came out again, this time low, as if to strike a knee.

They ran through the pattern slowly until Kenny was in the flow of it and didn't need to think about what to do. McGill watched for signs of fatigue or other physical distress. Seeing none, he asked, "You want to pick up the tempo just a little?"

Kenny bobbed his head.

McGill put a bit more snap into each swing. Kenny matched him, keeping the flow.

"If you can," McGill told his son, "try to whistle a tune that'll match the rhythm of your motion."

Kenny licked his lips and began to whistle. McGill wasn't familiar with the melody, but he thought it was catchy and Kenny did a good job of rendering it. His son had let himself go, stopped thinking. He was laying down muscle memory, building reflexes that might serve him well someday.

McGill took joy in watching Kenny, alive, recovering his health and growing strong. What more could a father want? He'd have to train Abbie and Caitie, too.

Then, as if Kenny had come to the end of the first song, he switched to another. This one was more upbeat. Kenny's strokes came faster, keeping pace with the new time signature. McGill stepped up his responses.

The clacks of the sticks meeting were sharper now and nearly without interval. After a moment, Kenny stopped whistling, took a deep breath and stepped back. Sweat ran from his brow and he rubbed his eyes with the back of a wrist.

McGill moved toward him. "You okay?"

Kenny lowered his arm and revealed a broad smile. He laughed and said, "I guess I got carried away. All of a sudden I felt really tired, but I feel great, too. Better than I can remember feeling in a long time. The idea of whistling, adding music, that was great."

Kenny was breathing hard, but not struggling for breath.

He just seemed like a kid who was getting back into shape.

"What was that first song you whistled?" McGill asked.

"It's called 'Some Nights' by a group called Fun."

McGill nodded. A father could approve of that, pending review of the lyrics. He took Kenny's sticks from him and put an arm around his shoulders. "Let's go get some breakfast."

"Sounds good." As they headed into the lodge, Kenny said, "You know, Dad, we've heard some stories about you."

Looking at his son, McGill said, "Really?"

"Yeah, Sweetie's told us some things, Abbie, Caitie and me."

That had been part of a plan he and Sweetie had hatched, after McGill's divorce from Carolyn. Figuring the kids would learn the reason behind their parents' divorce at some point, and how Carolyn had been terrified that McGill would be killed, they thought some sanitized accounts of their father's activities should make their way to his daughters and son. Having Sweetie share these morsels privately would lend them greater credence.

Not that anything the younger McGills had heard was untrue; Sweetie would never lie to his children or anyone else. But the near instances of death and disfigurement were deemphasized, and the use of violence was always described as a last resort.

"We always loved hearing stories about you from Sweetie. It was like being let into some secret club. We weren't told not to share them with Mom, but we didn't. We held on to them as our own … possessions, I guess."

Kenny sat down in the lodge's kitchen. Navy mess specialists were available to cook for the president and her family, but McGill preferred to do his own cooking for his kids. Before moving to Washington, he'd shared custody with Carolyn and enjoyed making meals for his children. He poured two glasses of orange juice now and sat down across from his son.

"Are you fishing for something?" he asked Kenny.

"We haven't heard as much from Sweetie after she moved to Washington to work with you, but she did tell us one story."

"What was that?"

"About your fight in Paris, under the bridge, against the giant."

"I had three people helping me. You heard that part?"

"Yeah, but that only made me think how big that other guy must have been."

"He was very big," McGill agreed.

"Sweetie said you didn't just shoot him because you wanted to take him alive."

McGill nodded.

"So you used sticks like we just used."

"They were similar," McGill said.

"I kind of thought after you left the police things would be less dangerous."

"In general, they are."

Kenny nodded as if he wasn't going to dispute that point. He sipped his juice.

"Do you worry about me, Kenny?"

"I never did before I got sick. I thought anybody messed with you, it'd be their problem."

High praise from a son, but McGill didn't miss Kenny's use of the past tense.

"What's changed?" he asked.

"Well, I didn't think I was going to get sick. I never thought I might die anytime soon. Now, I'm not so sure about things. I told Patti I worry about the people I love, more than I do about myself.

She said that's something everybody feels."

"She's right. We all do."

"That's all I'm thinking," Kenny said. "I just joined the club." He finished his juice and gave McGill a hug. "Thanks for the lesson, Dad. I'm going to shower and take a nap. I'll eat when I get up."

"Okay."

Kenny started to leave, then turned around.

"I am glad you have Sweetie, Deke and Leo to help you."

He smiled and left the room.

McGill sat in the kitchen by himself, thinking Kenny wouldn't be the only one in his family who would be unhappy to hear Deke was no longer available to take a bullet for him.

Before he had too much time to beat himself up about that, the phone rang.

Patti calling to tell him the country was once again back in the best of hands?

"Mr. McGill, this is Byron DeWitt." The deputy director of the FBI.

McGill felt a ripple of energy pass through him.

"Good news?" he asked.

"We've found a trucker by the name of Lydell Martin. We're all but certain he's the man who transported Damon Todd, Arn Crosby and Olin Anderson."

"All but?" McGill asked.

"We haven't picked him up yet, but using the process of elimination, we think he's our guy. All our other leads for commercial drivers who fell behind on their delivery schedules have been eliminated. Martin pulled into his depot six hours late. He told his dispatcher he got dizzy while driving and had to get off the road. He couldn't remember whether he just pulled off to the side or into a rest area."

"Making his whereabouts impossible to either confirm or disprove," McGill said. "A very convenient case of amnesia."

DeWitt agreed. "Specialized, you might say. Martin was given a complete physical. No tumors, no neurological deficits, no defects of the inner ear. In short, no reason to get dizzy. The trucking company still didn't want to take any chances so they gave him a desk job that was supposed to last for a month. Inside the first week, Martin came up with two efficiency measures that the company says will save them millions of dollars. He's now on the executive track and expected to move up fast."

"Sounds like Damon Todd's handiwork to me."

"Yes, it does. The only other possibility is the bad guys highjacked another vehicle and killed the driver. But we've checked that angle and can't find either a missing person or stolen vehicle that works with our time frame."

"I think you can eliminate the *all but*," McGill said.

DeWitt said, "I think so, too. We're working out how far Martin might have taken the escapees and still get back to his depot six hours late. The first estimate covers four states."

McGill thought about that. "They could have been dropped off and used another of Todd's sleepers to move again or they might have found a congenial spot and are sitting tight."

"Depending on whether the just want to stay free or —"

"Hit back," McGill said, "at me or anyone else who has angered Todd."

"Or targets of spite for the former CIA operatives."

"Or both."

"Any suggestions for dealing with Lydell Martin, Mr. McGill?"

DeWitt's level of cooperation was almost too good to be true, McGill thought.

But he wasn't going to let old local cop prejudices get in his way.

He said, "The CIA wasn't able to crack Todd's assumed personality after three years of trying. There's no reason to think Martin's going to be any easier. But Todd might call him at home, at work or on his cell phone to make sure his new identity is holding up. If you can get a warrant to tap Martin's phones, you might hear something."

"I'm sure we could do that, but how long do we wait before bringing him in?"

"Maybe that's a last resort. If you don't intercept a call from Todd in, say, two weeks, then we could, if we want to be manipulative and nasty, begin a disinformation campaign."

"About Martin?"

"Yes," McGill said. "My bet is Todd takes great pride in what he does for people, making their lives materially better. How do you think he might react if he read, heard or saw on TV that one of his subjects went off the rails in a major way?"

DeWitt took a moment to consider the idea.

Then he said, "He might stop by to see what went wrong."

The White House

President Patricia Darden Grant stopped off at the residence to get a quick once-over from Nick and to change into a navy blue Chanel business suit. She checked the reflection in her bathroom mirror. Not a hair out of place, light makeup evenly applied and teeth sparkling white. So far so good. Now, if only the old ticker continued to beat as it should.

Nick said, "Madam President, you appear ready to resume your duties but, please, do your best not to let anything agitate you."

"Easy for you to say, Nick." Then she smiled and said, "I'll be good."

It helped her demeanor that every uniformed Secret Service officer she passed snapped to attention and saluted her, staffers came to their feet and applauded and Edwina stood behind her desk outside the Oval Office and said, "It is so good to have you back, Madam President."

"Thank you, Edwina. It's good to be back and see everyone again."

"How is young Master McGill?"

"Kenny is recovering strongly, thank you."

"I hope you won't mind, Madam President, but I've left a bit of a mess on your desk."

Patti raised an eyebrow.

Edwina told her, "After Vice President Wyman announced your return last night, messages of congratulations from heads of state around the world began to arrive. Ambassadors from almost every embassy in town have been delivering them personally."

Patti felt a catch in her throat. Then she remembered Nick's advice to avoid agitation. She hadn't expected such a warm welcome, but it certainly wouldn't do to let it make her swoon. She'd be whisked off to the hospital and there was no telling when they'd let her return.

Of all the people who had greeted her, three were conspicuously absent: Mather Wyman, Galia Mindel and Celsus Crogher.

Edwina cleared up one-third of that mystery.

"Chief of Staff Mindel is waiting for you in the Oval Office, Madam President."

"Thank you, Edwina. Please give me fifteen minutes and then ask the vice president to come see me."

"Yes, Madam President."

"No interruptions from anyone else except Mr. McGill."

As soon as the president entered the Oval Office and the door behind her had closed, Galia Mindel said, "I don't want to muss your appearance, Madam President, and I don't want to seem presumptuous, but I would like to give you a hug."

Patti extended her arms to Galia and the two women embraced, for just the right duration. Taking her place behind her desk, the president looked at the stacks of envelopes covering her desk. She turned her attention to Galia, sitting opposite her.

"Anyone significant missing?" she asked.

Galia said, "Madam President, do you think I —"

"Edwina said she'd left a mess on my desk. What I see here are neat stacks. Arranged alphabetically."

Galia smiled. "Sometimes I'm a bit compulsive, and, no, nobody important forgot their manners."

The president looked at one small stack. "You even separated well wishes from royal houses?"

"I thought they'd be more comfortable that way."

The president picked up an envelope from the Queen of England. She remembered meeting with Her Majesty in the gardens at Buckingham Palace. The queen had suggested to the president that she spare Erna Godfrey's life. Extend her sentence was the way she'd put it. The president was glad she'd taken that advice. She opened the envelope and found a handwritten note that made her smile.

She told Galia, "Nick tells me I have to limit my working hours, but I'm going to have to spend half my time writing thank you notes."

"Sure, it's not like you have anything pressing to do."

Patti returned the queen's message to its envelope and put it on the right stack.

"As I'm sure you know," she told Galia, "Marlene Berman came to see me at Camp David."

"Everyone in the building knows that, Madam President. I made sure of it."

"Well, here's what she told me. The Democrats want me. They'd like to make my switch to their party formal and public as soon as possible. They assure me that the party's power structure and a supermajority of their Congressional caucuses will pledge their support."

"But?" Galia asked.

"But I can expect primary challenges from two of their prominent names."

"Not just Roger Michaelson?"

Patti said, "Him, of course. We expected that. The other, though, is Jean Morrissey."

"The governor of Minnesota," Galia said.

"Yes. Marlene says I've inspired her. The governor was of the mind that a Democrat would have been the first woman elected president. She even thought it would be her. My run last time around caught her by surprise, before she was ready to take the leap herself. She's determined to try this time."

Galia nodded. "You've opened a lot of women's eyes as to what's possible, Madam President. From now on, there are likely to be serious female candidates in both parties for every presidential primary season."

Patti smiled. "Just a troublemaker, that's what I am."

"Certainly, Roger Michaelson would agree. With Governor Morrissey in the race, though, he's probably rubbing his hands together in glee."

"Figuring two women will split the female vote and he'll scoot all the way to the nomination on the strength of the male vote. What do you think, Galia?"

The chief of staff considered the question with the seriousness it deserved.

"I think," she said, "that it's not that simple. Things never are. The questions are how will you and Governor Morrissey divide the women's vote and which of you will attract more of the men's vote. I think you'll do better than either Michaelson or Morrissey with the African American and Latino communities. Jean Morrissey, being six years younger than you, might give you a run for the money with younger voters."

Patti agreed with all of her chief of staff's assessments.

"And the outcome?" she asked.

"You should win, but with another woman in the race, it will be a narrow win. You'd have to find a way to heal any rifts the primaries might cause to run a strong general election campaign."

"Still think the Democrats are a better choice than running as an independent?" Patti asked.

"I've given that question a lot of thought, and one name keeps coming to mind."

"Teddy Roosevelt," the president said.

"Exactly. We now think of him as one of our great presidents. But in 1912 with the new Progressive Party he lost to the Democrats and Woodrow Wilson, who is not one of the four guys on Mount

Rushmore. There were circumstances unique to that time that mattered, but thinking we can do better than Teddy Roosevelt ..." Galia sighed. "That would take some doing."

The president asked, "So whatever challenges we face with the Democrats, you think they are the better bet?"

Galia nodded. "Under the circumstances you've just described, Madam President, yes."

"And if I win the Democratic nomination with Jean Morrissey coming in a close second, do you think the country will be ready for an all-female ticket?"

Before Galia could answer, the intercom on Patti's desk buzzed.

Edwina Byington announced, "Madam President, Vice President Wyman is here to see you."

Mather Wyman entered the Oval Office with a smile on his face. He nodded an acknowledgement to Galia's presence. He offered a hand to the president.

"It's good to have you back, Madam President. I trust all's well with you and the McGill family."

Patti gestured to Wyman to take the seat next to Galia.

"Everyone is doing fine, Mather, thank you."

The social graces behind them, Wyman asked, "Am I here for a performance review, Madam President."

"Not specifically, no. Would you like one?"

Sparing a quick glance at Galia, he said, "Yes, to be honest, I would."

The president said, "You weren't perfect but you were close, Mather. You handled the Salvation's Path situation as well as anyone could have. We both owe Galia our thanks for finding out about Burke Godfrey's tunnels; that made things much easier for everyone."

The vice president gave Galia a small bow. "Madam Chief of Staff, thank you."

Galia returned the gesture with a nod.

"Your announcement of Burke Godfrey's passing was respectful and clear," Patti told Wyman. "Your pledge to make known all the medical information regarding the cause of his death was just what the situation called for. Your press conference regarding the passing of Justices Calendri and Hawkins, and your refusal to speculate on their replacements was also respectful of the presidency and of me. Thank you for that."

"You've more than earned my respect, Madam President."

"The one instance where you overreached was considering a charge of treason against Godfrey. In light of his passing, that would have looked very bad. Changing your mind was the smart thing to do."

Wyman asked, "Were you able to speak with Mrs. Godfrey before I spoke publicly?"

"I did. She was terribly hurt by the news, but she thanked me for telling her personally. She said ... it was very kind of me and it only renewed her sorrow for what she did to Andy."

"Remorse on her part is a good thing," Wyman said.

Patti thought so, too, but she wasn't about to share her private feelings.

The idea of forgiving Erna Godfrey still made her dig in her heels.

"Mather," she said, "Galia and I have just been looking ahead politically. I want you to know that I've been extended an offer by the Democratic leadership to run for reelection on their ticket. I've decided to accept that offer."

The vice president needed a moment to digest that news.

He finally said, "You're quite the history-maker, Madam President. I don't think I've ever heard of that happening before."

"It hasn't, as far as I know," Patti said. She turned to Galia for confirmation.

The chief of staff shook her head. It hadn't happened before.

"The change in party affiliation, will it be effective immediately?" Wyman asked.

"That's a very good question, Mather, the matter of timing. We haven't decided yet. But there's another point of discussion we need to get to first. I understand that I'm not the only one in this room who is being recruited to sit in this office."

"Madam President?" Wyman asked.

Patti nodded to Galia.

She said to Wyman, "Reynard Dix and Peter Profitt want you to be the GOP candidate and word of their interest has reached you, Mr. Vice President."

Patti picked up the ball. "At your press conference, Mather, you conceded your experience as acting president gave you an edge over other possible GOP candidates for the nomination. You said that you hadn't decided to run but, forgive me, you didn't sound very convincing."

Feeling he'd been set up by the president and her chief of staff, Wyman grew stiff.

"Would you like me to resign the vice presidency, Madam President?"

"No, not at all," Patti said. "We've worked well together. It would be a shame to let politics come between us."

Wyman looked for a sign that he was being played for a fool.

Before his inspection could go too far, Galia interrupted his search.

She said, "It would be the wrong move, Mr. Vice President, if you do want the Republican nomination. In your present position, you have superior status in the GOP. Resigning would diminish your standing."

"Galia's right, Mather," the president said.

"You want me to run against you?" he asked.

"Somebody from the Republicans is going to do it. Who better than you?"

He thought about that. "I'd run hard, give it my all."

Patti said, "I wouldn't expect anything else. But I think the two of us could keep the debate on a plane that most presidential elections never manage."

Wyman looked the president in the eye. He knew what she meant. She *wasn't* going to tell anyone that he was gay. In return, she'd expect him to play a clean game, too.

He told her, "Once you sit behind that desk, it's hard to leave, isn't it, Madam President?"

Patti only smiled.

Galia, watching both of them closely, had the uneasy feeling the president and her number two shared a secret that neither of them intended to share with her. She hated that. It would only make her job harder.

The president stood and offered her hand to Wyman.

"A clean, hard-fought campaign?" she asked.

Wyman stood and shook hands. "Agreed."

"Galia," the president said, "will you have the White House photographer come in, please? I think it would be a good idea to provide the media with a picture of Vice President Wyman welcoming me back. We'll show the American people how power can be transferred cordially in our country."

The chief of staff nodded and departed the Oval Office.

The woman and the man she left behind shared the same thought.

I hope I don't regret this.

The Mandarin Oriental Hotel — Washington, D.C.

Hugh Collier reclined on one of the twin silk sofas in the living room of the presidential suite and sipped from a flute of Krug Clos Du Mesnil champagne. The bottle sat in an ice bucket nearby. A second glass rested on an end table. He'd ordered from room service and had tipped generously. Putting both the bubbly and the gratuity on Uncle Edbert's tab.

Hugh had been given permission to enter the suite.

Making liberal use of the hotel's wine cellar hadn't been discussed.

From the look on Uncle's face as he entered his digs, Hugh may have overstepped. He wasn't sure if it was the champagne or his casual feet-on-the-furniture use of someone else's sofa. He thought the latter shouldn't have been too great a breach of manners. He had taken his shoes off.

"Sit up," Sir Edbert demanded.

Hugh sketched a mock salute and obeyed.

Both stockinged feet on the floor, he asked, "Have you had a pleasant day, Uncle?"

The expression on Sir Edbert's face said his mood might have been helped by whipping a servant. Lacking that opportunity, abusing an insolent nephew would have to do. He asked, "What have you accomplished with Ms. Booker?"

Topping off his glass, Hugh said, "I've learned she hopes she has seen the last of us, she will not be bought and, sorry to say, she will likely bring a great deal of aggravation and conceivably even suffering upon you."

Sir Edbert sat opposite Hugh and gave him a look so evil the devil might have envied it.

He hissed, "Do you think some jumped up clerk is a threat to *me?*"

"Alone, never. In the right context, with a smart lawyer at her side and the federal government in her corner ... Well, Uncle, the good lady in the White House deals in *trillion*-dollar budgets and shoots Hellfire missiles at chaps who annoy her. Private capital has yet to scale those heights."

"You're saying Ellie Booker is about to form an alliance with Patricia Grant and the two of them will target me for destruction?"

Having said those words aloud sent a tremor through Sir Edbert.

Hugh's manners could be those of a bushie but he was nobody's fool.

He might do well to hear his nephew out.

"Tell me what you think," he ordered Hugh.

"I think you've spent your waking hours today plotting with your lawyers. You've either heard or expect to hear momentarily that the Department of Justice will investigate WorldWide News for violating the Foreign Corrupt Practices Act. So you were plotting your defenses and if I haven't misjudged you, you're looking at which members of Congress you might blackmail into —"

"How might I blackmail anyone?" Sir Edbert blustered.

Hugh said, "Let me count the ways. Hacked cellphones. Surreptitious photos taken of politicians and comely aides on foreign junkets. Personal testimony of sex workers, especially if they're chaps who like things from the angle of entry I prefer. Shall I go on?"

Hugh took the grinding of Sir Edbert's teeth as a no.

"Now, to resume," he said. "You hoped to have enough dirt on someone in government who would have the weight to stop an investigation of WWN in its tracks. But from your vile mood it's apparent you don't. I'm afraid, Uncle, matters will turn darker still."

"Thanks to that strumpet who once worked for me?" Sir Edbert asked.

Hugh said, "She's not really a bad sort. In temperament and ruthlessness, she reminds me of the two of us. She's also the first woman who genuinely piqued my interest in a way I never anticipated."

"I'll alert your father," Sir Edbert said with a sour grin.

Hugh's father had put him on the street for being gay; Sir Edbert had taken him in.

"No need," Hugh told him. "I'm sure it was a one-time thing, and Ms. Booker would prefer to see me drown like a rat."

Hugh thought Uncle saw a certain appeal in that idea also.

He resumed, "What both of us missed is that Ellie has abandonment issues and leaving her at Salvation's Path when the fun began was the worst thing we might have done to her."

Sir Edbert made a dismissive gesture with a mottled hand.

"In any case," Hugh said, "Ellie was served with a subpoena on the street in Manhattan. I saw it. I also followed the process server and for only one hundred dollars he told me who required Ms. Booker's presence: Benton Williams."

"Burke Godfrey's attorney," Sir Edbert said.

"The very same. Having that information, I set a private

investigator to following Williams. My initial surmise was that Williams intended to sue Ellie and, more importantly, you for that bash on the head she gave Godfrey."

Sir Edbert shuddered when he heard that. An assault on any man at the top of his pyramid was a blow to the whole ruling class. Let things go too far and Bolsheviks might roam the land again.

"Then, of course, the gloom darkened when the good reverend died," Hugh said.

A spark of fear lit Sir Edbert's sunken eyes.

"Burke Godfrey is dead?"

Hugh nodded, thinking Uncle must've been burrowed deep in his scheming to have missed that bulletin. "He has expired."

"Might it be vengeance on Patti Grant's part?"

"It was a massive stroke. Trying to play it any other way would be suicide for us."

His fun spoiled, Sir Edbert grumped, "Go on."

"Benton Williams, my investigator tells me, went to the Department of Justice building today. I don't know whom he saw but a chap of his stature was bound to talk with someone high up the ladder. Can you guess what he might have had on his mind?"

With a grim nod Sir Edbert said, "He wants to make sure the government doesn't strip my carcass bare. At worst, he wants to make sure he has left a bone or two to gnaw."

Hugh was glad to see the old man hadn't lost all his faculties.

"Williams will pair up with a prosecutor and leverage testimony from Ellie for both criminal and civil proceedings. She'll get off with a slap on the wrist. WWN will take the body blow."

Uncle looked more desperate than Hugh had ever seen him.

"Do you think they truly mean to lock me away?" he asked his nephew.

"What could send a more powerful message?" Hugh replied.

"And what would your advice be?"

"The first bit is self-serving. Don't think you can sacrifice me and put your troubles behind you. I'd be a mere appetizer, and your foes are looking to feast."

Left unsaid, if Uncle were to ignore his warning that he wouldn't be made the fall guy, Hugh's earnest intent was to do the old bugger in. He'd thought long and hard on the matter.

"Beyond that?" Sir Edbert inquired.

"Moderate your editorial position."

As if he hadn't heard right, Uncle said, "I beg your pardon."

"There's a presidential election in the offing. Your natural instinct would be to destroy Patti Grant in print and on television. To attempt that now would be to tie a noose for the hangman. Still, you can't simply do a turnabout and be a shill for the president. That would be seen as tantamount to bribery. The last thing you'd need. So what you and WWN have to do, Uncle, is play things straight. Be responsible journalists. Play things so straight you set a code of conduct for all others to follow."

Sir Edbert Bickford couldn't have been more aghast if Hugh had told him he must pose bare chested on page three of all his newspapers.

Then the weight of reality overcame his combative nature and his face sagged.

"You're right. I hate you for it, but you're right. When do we begin?"

Hugh poured a flute of champagne for Uncle.

"First thing in the morning. Maybe after a few hours sleep you'll hate me a bit less."

The two men clinked glasses and drank.

One of the world's great champagnes pleased neither of them.

George Town — Grand Cayman Island

Welborn Yates had tried to persuade his new wife, Kira, to come with him to the Caribbean as a postscript to their truncated honeymoon, but she conveyed her regrets to him. Told him she had an obligation that would keep her in Washington.

"That obligation being?" he asked as he packed his bag in the bedroom of their new house on Q Street.

Kira said, "I can't tell you, not yet."

Welborn pressed the back of a hand to his forehead.

"The secrecy and evasion start so soon. The little white lies will come next."

Having bared his anguish to her, he counted out the pairs of underwear he'd need.

Kira told him, "I promise to tell you only the most horrid lies."

"Quality does matter."

"So does family."

He stopped his packing and looked at her. "I'll make a series of statements. You paw the floor once for yes, twice for no."

"How about instead of pawing I pinch you in tender places?"

"Within limits, that could be fun. Your concern is one Mather Wyman."

Kira stepped in close, put her arms around him and pinched his backside, once.

"He likes an oval office better than a rectangular one."

She pinched the inside of his right thigh, affirmatively.

"He might be considering how he could move up in the world."

She pinched the inside of his left thigh, a bit higher.

"Should he seek to make that move, you intend to help him."

Welborn anticipated where Kira might strike next and headed her off.

"If the time ever comes for a vasectomy, I'll see someone with a medical license."

He kissed Kira. "I'll also miss you terribly if you no longer work down the hall."

"Will you miss me while you're off in Paradise by yourself?"

"Paradise for one is a bit of a contradiction, wouldn't you say? But we're back where we started. I'd like you to come with me but you have your secret obligation."

"I could pinch you some more."

"Or you could give me a more traditional send off."

They had combined the two, and now Welborn in a marigold polo shirt, khaki shorts and stylish but functional running shoes sat in the shade of a Cinzano umbrella in Pennyman's Café on Shedden Road, just up the block from the Marlborough Bank. He was careful to introduce himself at both establishments as a good natured fellow and a man of means. He'd deposited two hundred thousand dollars in the bank — half of what he'd taken from them — and had bought the house an eye-opener at the café. Fortunately, the hour had been early and his bonhomie had extended to only half-a-dozen souls. Even so, the gesture had been appreciated. As was the generous tip. He was welcome to linger, reading his newspapers.

The consensus of the Air Force team that was covering Welborn's tab was Linley Boland would show up within a matter of days. He wouldn't send a surrogate because it wouldn't look right for a bank customer whose account had been siphoned to have anyone else do his complaining for him. Once Welborn had spotted Boland, he was to maintain visual contact and call the U.S. embassy in Kingston, Jamaica, which had consular authority for the Cayman Islands. The ambassador there would prevail upon the officials in George Town to have its cops make the arrest. Boland would be held until he could be extradited, indicted, tried, convicted and locked up for the rest of his miserable life.

On paper, the plan was simple and straightforward.

In the tropics, though, events followed their own rhythm and logic.

This fact became apparent to Welborn the first morning he sat down at Pennyman's Café.

He wondered how much time he might spend sitting there. How long the memory of his last night with Kira would hold the same joy it did now. Whether he might end up alone and forgotten in the tropics like some minor character in a Graham Greene novel.

Charlottesville, Virginia

Damon Todd wanted to know, "Is there any way the two of you could infiltrate Camp David?"

He was guessing that was where McGill would retreat if things got too hot for him.

"No," Crosby said.

"Not a chance," Anderson confirmed.

"Wouldn't even be able to get close," Crosby added.

"What do you mean? Why couldn't you get close?" Todd asked.

The two rogue ops grinned at each other. They'd spent the whole day sneaking around in the woods. Shadowing recreational hikers as if they were enemy military. Getting close enough to count freckles on bare shoulders or slit a throat, without anyone being the wiser. But they hadn't done any harm. Well, they had messed with a couple of guys' heads. After coming close enough to yank them off their feet, they'd faded back and hit them with thrown pebbles.

Both those dudes knew they'd been deliberately struck, but when they turned around hadn't been able to spot anyone. They'd both cursed, angry at the abuse. But both of them had strong enough survival instincts to realize the threat was still there and they'd *di-di-ed.*

Crosby and Anderson were laughing and patting each other on the back by the time they got back to the cabin. They were feeling as strong, swift and silent as when they were in their prime. Ready to take on the world, kick its ass and drink all night long.

They knew they owed it all to Todd. Whatever the hell he'd done to them, God, it was like getting a head-to-toe hard-on. The feeling was better than any drug they'd ever had, and they'd had everything from grain alcohol to zacatecas purple.

That and blind devotion to him were what Todd wanted them to feel.

So —

Crosby saw where Todd was going and said, "Camp David is protected by Marines and Secret Service agents, and those are just the guys you see. There are others you don't see."

"Guys who are just as good in the woods as we are, only there are a lot more of them than there are of us," Anderson told Todd.

Crosby continued the tutorial. "You walk past the White House, you see the fence all the way around the place. You see the uniformed guys guarding the grounds. You look up you might see the guys on the roof, but they're pretty good about keeping their sniper rifles out of public view."

"But they've got their long iron handy, you can believe that," Anderson said.

Crosby nodded. "What's a lot more subtle is the guys on other rooftops, outside the White House grounds, looking in at it. Them and the plainclothes people, men and women, mingling with the tourists and the office workers."

"They watch for people with compact automatic weapons under their suit coats or windbreakers. That or suspicious packages that might be left in a litter basket and be detonated by a cell phone," Anderson said.

"That or an amped-up SUV filled with a thousand pounds of explosives that's ready to make a suicide run at the fence. Or an ultralight aircraft that might try to get over the fence," Crosby elaborated.

Anderson nodded. "There was even talk of bad guys trying to work up their own flying drones, making the whole aircraft a flying bomb, and that was before we got sent to our room at the Funny Farm. Who knows what the assholes might be working on now?"

The recitation left Todd agog, and more than a little indignant. The idea that these terrorist assholes would even think of … Then he realized he might be considered a terrorist, a guy with a major grievance against the CIA and the president's husband.

That was true, but his complaints were personal not ideological.

From a defender's point of view, though, he could see that the distinction wouldn't matter.

"You get the idea?" Crosby asked. "Any place that really matters to the government is going to have layer upon layer of defense, most of it in places you'll never see."

"And if you go looking for their defenses, they'll see you first,"

Anderson said.

"So what would you advise?" Todd asked. "To get to someone you want dead."

"Patience," Crosby said.

"Or you draw them out of their safe place to where their protection can't be as comprehensive," Anderson said.

"A combination of the two works best. You want this McGill guy? Wait until he goes stir crazy and thinks the threat is no longer real," Crosby instructed.

Anderson agreed. "Then take out someone who means a lot to him and is more accessible. That gets him super-pissed off and he's not functioning at top form. His security people will be scrambling to keep up with him as he goes charging around. Makes the whole job a lot easier."

"You know anyone who fits that bill for your target?" Crosby asked.

Todd thought about it. When he'd gone to confront McGill the first time at his business office, he'd taken the building's owner, Dikki Missirian captive. He hadn't used him as a hostage, but had learned from him that McGill had a business partner, a woman. Entering McGill's offices, he'd seen a photo on a wall, McGill and the woman, both wearing the uniforms of the Chicago Police Department. The desk in the outer office had a woman's name on it.

Had to be the same person.

In a moment of epiphany, Todd made a connection. He'd seen the woman in person. She'd been the one he'd seen running on the Mall, the Amazon who had reminded him of the woman in the old Apple computer TV commercial, the one who flung her hammer and smashed Big Brother.

She was McGill's colleague, a friend of many years. Someone near and dear.

Crosby and Anderson saw the smile appear on Todd's face.

"He's got someone," Anderson said.

"Somebody good," Crosby said.

Todd nodded. "Her name is Margaret Sweeney."

The White House — Helipad

"Good to see you again, boss," Leo Levy said as McGill exited Marine One-A, the call sign for the aircraft when he was aboard but the president wasn't.

Elspeth Kendry waited with Leo, not speaking.

"Good to see you, too, Leo. Special Agent Kendry."

"Sir," Elspeth responded crisply.

"Doing your best Celsus Crogher imitation, Special Agent?"

Elspeth stifled a smile. "Sir, I'm here at the president's direction."

McGill turned his gaze on Leo.

"I'm just tryin' to earn my pay, boss. I'm real tired of watchin' daytime TV."

"You have my Chevy ready to go?"

Leo nodded and said, "I'll go fetch it right now."

Leaving McGill with Elspeth. "Would you care to share the specifics of what the president told you?"

"Of course, sir, but the president asked me to relay to you her desire to keep this information private."

McGill nodded. "I'm very good at keeping the president's secrets."

"Yes, sir."

"Elspeth, please. I'm not angry at you, even if our last conversation wasn't all that pleasant. Feel free to talk to me like a human being not an inmate at her parole hearing."

Elspeth studied McGill for a moment and then bobbed her head.

"All right," she said. "The president, after consulting with the Secret Service director, has decided to make some changes in the White House security detail."

McGill was mildly surprised he was hearing of this after the fact.

Then again Patti didn't tell him how to work his cases and he didn't tell her how to run the country.

"Those changes being?"

"I'm to replace SAC Crogher after next year's presidential election. Assuming the president wins the election, I'll head the detail in the next term."

McGill, despite his recent contretemps with Elspeth, liked the idea.

"The president also would like, with your permission, for me to be your personal protection agent."

Now, that one truly surprised him. Last time around, he'd been the one to select his bodyguard. Maybe, though, Patti had made her plans only that morning. He'd have to find out.

"How are things supposed to work, Elspeth? Do you still have to report to SAC Crogher for the time being?"

"No, I don't. I've been promoted. I'm free to confer with SAC Crogher on matters where his experience and insight might be helpful to me, but I do not have to share everything I know with him."

McGill kept a straight face, but he was smiling inside. Patti's solution for providing him with Secret Service protection was a triumph of both politics and marital harmony. He got what he wanted; she got what she wanted. It was … he wondered if Galia had a hand in this. She was another master conniver.

He saw Leo pull up in the Chevy on the driveway adjacent to the helipad.

"That being the case, Elspeth, I'll assume you'll be the soul of discretion."

"I know how to keep secrets, too, but if the president wants me to talk …"

McGill could live with that. "Of course. The president but no one else."

"Not even Ms. Sweeney?"

"All right. Sweetie, too."

"Anyone else?"

"Not until further notice." A thought occurred to McGill.

"Does Celsus know about all this?"

Elspeth glanced at her watch. "He should be getting the news right about now."

The Oval Office

The president, seated behind her desk, asked SAC Crogher, "Would you prefer to sit or stand?"

"Stand," Crogher said.

Just once, the president thought, it would have been a hoot to have Celsus Crogher crack wise with her. In the present circumstances he might have asked if he was entitled to a blindfold and a last cigarette. But that wasn't who he was. He didn't smoke, for one thing.

"Very well," she said. "If you're agreeable, Celsus, I'd like you to remain in your present job through the presidential election. At that point, I'm going to have Elspeth Kendry assume the SAC duties of the White House security detail."

"Yes, ma'am."

Crogher showed neither anger nor relief. Not that the president could see.

"Might I hear your opinion of Special Agent Kendry, Celsus?"

Now, he gave the president a bit of a look, asking for his opinion *after* she'd made her choice. "She's smart, she's watchful and she's holds up well under fire."

He might have been describing a police dog, Patti thought.

One who, maybe, deserved to be tossed a bone.

"Do you want to stay on through the election, Celsus?"

He thought about it. "Yes, I do."

"Because you'd have made it through virtually a full term that way?"

"Yes, ma'am."

Jim had once cracked to her that Celsus Crogher wasn't fully human, Patti remembered. She'd thought he was awful, saying that. Now she began to wonder if he hadn't been more than a little correct. It made her want to see if the SAC could hold up under another sort of fire.

One neither his training nor his temperament would have prepared him for.

"Celsus, within the bounds of the law and common decency, would you do anything for me?"

"I'd die for you."

"Other than that."

Now, suspicion crept into his eyes. "What do you mean?"

"Do you dance, Celsus?"

She might as well have asked him if he baked cookies.

"No, ma'am."

"Would you learn, for me?"

"May I speak frankly?"

Patti nodded.

"What the hell are you talking about?" he asked.

"Assuming I'm reelected, Mr. McGill and I will be attending all the usual inaugural balls. My husband and I will dance the first dance together. In gratitude for your years of willingness to sacrifice your life to preserve mine, I'd like to dance the second dance with you."

That did it. She finally got to him. Celsus Crogher blushed.

The president would bet the last of the billions of dollars Andy Grant had left to her that no one had seen Crogher do that twice in the same year. Possibly in the same lifetime. She was very careful to keep a straight face.

Still, Crogher asked, "You're kidding me, right?"

"I am not."

"But I … don't know how."

The SAC was desperately looking for a way out of the trap when a thought hit him like a hammer blow: *Holmes would be there.* McGill would see Crogher dancing with his wife.

The thought so captivated him he did something else the president had never seen.

He smiled in the Oval Office.

"I'll take lessons, ma'am." He quickly added, "You won't tell anyone?"

"It will be our secret. Of course, it would be a shame if I lost the election by one vote."

The woman's cunning was not to be believed, the SAC thought.

He said, "You've got my vote, Madam President."

McGill Investigations, Inc. — Georgetown

Sweetie was waiting for McGill in his office on P Street. So was the building's landlord, Dikki Missirian. He beamed at McGill and shook his hand.

"You are well, my friend?" he asked. "The president, your son, your family?"

McGill said, "We're all fine, Dikki. How are your wife and son?"

Dikki showed McGill, Sweetie and Elspeth two wallet photos of his family.

They were professionally taken shots of smiling people, but they left McGill with a sudden chill. Three years ago, Damon Todd had used Dikki as bait to lure him into an ambush. And McGill still hadn't gotten around to warning him.

"Dikki, not to alarm you, but do you know how to use a gun?" McGill asked.

Despite McGill's cautionary words, Dikki uneasily took his hand back as if he might need it to fend off bad news.

"I am a peaceful man. I have always been. Before I go into business, I wish to be a poet."

McGill saw Sweetie and Elspeth were giving him looks, Sweetie's knowing, Elspeth's questioning.

"Do you know anyone who knows how to use a gun?"

"My father. He is, was, a colonel in the Armenian army, a hunter of terrorists."

"Your father is still alive?"

"Yes, of course. He is in Washington. I bring him here after he retires. May I ask why —"

McGill said, "Damon Todd has escaped. Your father is still fit?"

News of the breakout hadn't reached the media yet.

"Vigorous," Dikki said, bobbing his head. "He has friends in the Armenian community here, also former soldiers." He leaned forward, closing the distance with McGill. "Do you really think …" He didn't want to complete the thought.

Being at the mercy of a madman was not a memory easily revisited.

McGill said, "I think it would be a good idea for you to have some protection until Dr. Todd is back in custody."

"Yes, yes, I agree."

"I should have thought to tell you earlier," McGill said. "I'm sorry."

Dikki waved off the apology. "I talk with my father immediately." He started for the door, then stopped. "Will you and your friends require refreshments?"

"We'll make do," McGill said.

"Dumb," McGill said, sitting behind his desk. "I don't know how I could have forgotten to warn Dikki."

Sweetie and Elspeth sat opposite him.

"Maybe you had one or two other things on your mind," Sweetie said. "I did, too. But you're right, the two of us would be kicking ourselves if something bad happened to Dikki."

Elspeth asked, "Do you think Mr. Missirian's father and friends will be up to the job?"

"We'll have to rely on you to check that out, Elspeth. Military counterterrorism sounds like a pretty good credential, but somebody at State or the Pentagon should be able to tell you if Armenia is any good at it."

"Dikki seems to think well of his father," Sweetie said.

Elspeth told her, "Parental respect is pretty automatic over there. I'll see what I can find out. I'll be in the outer office."

She left McGill and Sweetie to themselves.

"You've made peace with Elspeth?" Sweetie asked.

McGill told her about the new arrangements Patti had made.

Sweetie liked them. "Smart woman, that president." Switching gears, she asked, "Kenny was all right about you leaving Camp David?"

"Once Carolyn arrived, he was. She asked if she could have a little private time with him, and then you called. Lars is going to bring Caitie out this coming weekend. I'll pick up Abbie from school. Patti will come if the world doesn't intrude. We'll all be together. You're welcome to join us, of course."

"That'd be good," Sweetie said.

McGill asked, "We're not forgetting about anyone else who needs to be protected, are we?"

"I don't think so. Chana Lochlan has made herself scarce. Daryl Cheveyo shows up for his classes at Georgetown and has otherwise made himself invisible."

McGill thought about that. "I don't think Todd would try anything at the university, not with Abbie's Secret Service detail on campus."

"Maybe he would," Sweetie countered. "Two potential targets in proximity with only one security detail between them. Divide and conquer is always a popular way to go. I'll talk with Deke about it."

McGill said, "No, I will. I don't want to leave things between us where they stand now."

Sweetie nodded. "Good idea. Just make sure the two of you don't have a shootout."

McGill grinned. "Do my best. Now tell me about this new potential client of ours, the one you didn't think we should take on without my in the flesh approval."

"She should be here any minute now," Sweetie said. "Her name's Ellie Booker. Remember her?"

McGill sat back, surprised.

"You and I never met her, but Welborn told us about her. She and Hugh Collier tried to do that ambush interview with me here.

She's a WorldWide News producer."

"Used to be," Sweetie said. "She quit."

McGill knew of Ellie Booker's subsequent claim to fame.

"She was the one who clocked Burke Godfrey and took the call from Mather Wyman."

"Uh-huh, and now that Godfrey has died and Ms. Booker has been subpoenaed by Godfrey's lawyer, Benton Williams, she thinks she's going to be sued for wrongful death and maybe prosecuted for manslaughter. She wants us to find exculpatory evidence and pull her out of both fires."

McGill shook his head. "Not for all the money on K Street."

"That was my feeling, too. But she said she has something else to offer."

"What?" McGill asked.

Sweetie said, "Ms. Booker says if we help her, she'll tell us just how Sir Edbert Bickford, Hugh Collier and WorldWide News plan to smear Patti during the presidential election."

"Damn," McGill said.

The flea-bitten cliché was true. Everybody had his price.

Mango Mary's — Key West, Florida

The Florida legislature, like all the others in the U.S., was in the pocket of the gun lobby. The difference was Florida's legislators loved being there. In the face of the shooting of an unarmed teenager by wannabe cop cum neighborhood watch crazy, protestors around the nation demanded that the state rescind its "stand your ground" law. That, however, did not deter one good ol' boy in Tallahassee from sponsoring a "notches in your gun" resolution that would give an official commendation and a plaque to any citizen who had "permanently taken three or more bad guys off the street with righteous shootings."

The gun lobby's top man at the capitol advised the legislature's leadership that maybe they should wait on that idea a little while. Not kill it, mind you. Just table it.

That being the milieu in the Sunshine State, nobody stepping into Mango Mary's was in the least alarmed to see bartender Jackie Richmond take out a Beretta M9, field strip it between two paying customers and clean and lube the semi-auto handgun. There were nods of approval. A clean well-maintained gun was one you could count on in an uncertain world.

As long as Jackie had raised the subject, eight other patrons at the bar and nearby tables took out the weapons they carried as a practical exercise of their second amendment rights, and they moved on to use the first amendment the way it was intended, by discussing the relative merits of their choice of firearms.

The tourists present, those who didn't know if Florida had reciprocal concealed carry agreements with their home states, felt left out.

Except for the few, probably from San Francisco, who got up and departed.

The guy with the Landshark Lager to Jackie's immediate left suggested, "Probably be best you don't cut off anybody's drinking privileges for a while."

Jackie saw the twinkle of humor in the beer drinker's eyes and grinned.

The guy to his right knocking back shots of José Cuervo told Jackie, "You ought to take care of your weapon before you open. What'd happen somebody came in here lookin' to rob you right now?"

Jackie looked around at all the weapons on display.

"One or more of you guys could shoot him," he said, "and I'd buy the house a round."

All the guys at the bar and several more at tables who'd heard that raised their glasses and their guns in salute. Jackie said, "See, we're all playin' on the same team."

"Okay, you got a point, but let's say maybe you picked a slow moment to clean your weapon," the Cuervo drinker said.

Jackie had his M9 back together by now. He jacked a round into the chamber and set the weapon on the bar. For the sake of discussion, though, he said, "Yeah?"

Cuervo said, "The bad guy comes in at exactly the wrong moment. What're you gonna do? Ask him to wait up a minute?"

"I might," Jackie said, "if he looked like his mama taught him some manners."

Landshark chuckled.

Jackie said, "If he looks like some low-life, shoot-first asshole, I'd grab for this."

The moment Jackie reached under the bar, three morons wearing Bus Milbaugh masks, sporting the bloated physique of the radio ranter, too, and holding Glocks with extended clips stepped into Mango Mary's in a neat little V-formation.

The way they came to an abrupt halt, it seemed they were not expecting to be met by a roomful of guys with their own weapons. For a frozen moment, darting eyeballs were the only things that moved. Then from under a table a spunky mongrel belonging to a drinker growled and dashed toward the intruders.

The lead Bus Milbaugh saw the animal coming his way and pointed his gun at it.

"Oh, hell, no!" the dog's owner shouted, reaching for his revolver.

By that time, Jackie held the Winchester carbine loaded with .44 caliber rounds that he had stashed under the bar. He got the first shot off, dropping the Bus in the one-pin spot. After that, the whole room erupted in gunfire. Jackie listened from where he'd dived on the floor behind the bar, his arms crossed over his head.

The firefight probably lasted only a matter of seconds, but it seemed to Jackie as if the shooting went on for most of the day. After it stopped, he heard a dog woof and then whine as if its heart were broken. As the dog continued to keen, Jackie counted to sixty. Then he took a peek over the bar top.

All three Bus Milbaughs were down and motionless. Other than leaking blood.

The dog was licking the face of a guy with a gun in his hand who looked dead, too. Counting from left to right, Jackie saw at least three more patrons who'd bent their last elbow at Mango

Mary's. Six more, including two women, were bleeding and moaning. Eight more appeared unhurt, and four of those held smoking guns in their hands.

"All clear," Jackie said, hoping he had that right.

In the distance, but getting closer fast, he heard sirens.

What the hell was he going to do now, he thought.

That was when he saw Alice gesture to him from the hallway that led to the office in back where she'd been taking a nap. Grabbing both the Winchester and the M9, he rushed over to her, hurried her toward the back door.

"Listen close now," he said. "I've got to get these guns out of here. I'm not supposed to have them." He squinted in thought for a moment. "Not even in Florida, I don't think."

Alice looked at him, surprised that anyone couldn't own a gun. Then she remembered: "You got a criminal record? You're a felon?"

The thought that she'd been working, living and sleeping with someone like that almost made her swoon. Giving Jackie time to think of a lie and take hold of her so she didn't fall.

"A criminal? Of course not. Baby, I'm in the witness protection program."

He kissed her and then ran out the back door, promising to call her.

McGill Investigations, Inc. — Georgetown

Jim McGill was on the phone with Galia Mindel. She'd been in a meeting with Stephen Norwood, but when McGill told her the matter was urgent, she gave him her full attention.

McGill said, "I'll have Ellie Booker coming into my office any moment now. She wants me to help exculpate her in the matter of Burke Godfrey's death. I wouldn't do that for the money, but Margaret Sweeney has told me Ms. Booker can give me the details of how WorldWide News intends to smear the president during the campaign. What I'd like to know, Galia, is whether you already have a good idea of what they'll do. If so, I won't have to help Ms.

Booker."

"Of course, I know," Galia said, "in broad strokes. It would be helpful to know specifics, but having you work for the woman who will be accused of killing Godfrey would look very bad for the president. She's going to get none of the evangelical vote in any case, but the damage could extend to enough moderates and independents to hurt us."

McGill hated that he had to make political calculations regarding his work.

Still, he asked, "You think it's going to be that close?"

"It's going to be razor thin," Galia said.

"So I'll tell Ms. Booker to find another investigator."

"That would be best, and it was a good idea for you to call me. I know this isn't easy for either of us, working closely together, but we do have a mutual interest."

"Yes, we do," McGill said.

"So you won't mind if I have to call you with either a suggestion or a question?"

"Anything that helps the president, Galia, you've got it."

"We're becoming strange bedfellows, as they say."

Sweetie rapped on McGill's door and poked her head in. "She's here."

"Gotta go," McGill told Galia.

He hung up, and Sweetie ushered Ellie Booker into his office.

McGill got to his feet and took her measure. Not yet forty, he guessed. Thin and full of nervous energy. There was apprehension in her eyes, but there was intelligence, too, and the set of her jaw was firm. She knew she was in a tough spot and was determined to get past it. Ordinarily, McGill respected such grit and would have done his best to be of help, but nothing was normal when your wife was running for reelection to be president.

Ellie Booker extended her hand to McGill. He took it. Sweetie stayed in the room, providing McGill with a witness to anything that might be said or done.

McGill came straight to the point. "I'm sorry to say, Ms.

Booker, that I won't be able to help you. The situation makes it impossible."

Ellie looked at McGill. It was the first time she'd met him in person. The man had a presence. Looked a bit like an old time movie star. He also had the decency not to try to con any information out of her and then send her packing. She appreciated that.

"By the situation you mean the politics," Ellie said. "Well, I can't blame you if you think I'd cost the president some votes."

McGill didn't respond.

"Here's the thing," Ellie said, "the way things are shaping up, I hope your wife wins again. Really. So I'll give you a free taste of what I was going to tell you. Sir Edbert's a dinosaur. He hates any woman he can't control, the president being the prime example. His nephew, Hugh Collier, is as ruthless as the old man but he's smart. He'll try to be a moderating influence. But if Sir Edbert sends Hugh back to Australia or fires him, look out. He's got a special project in mind. He'll launch it two to four weeks before the election."

McGill wanted to ask what that would be, but he wasn't going to pay the price to find out.

Ellie Booker continued, "If Sir Edbert moves onto his yacht, that will mean all out war."

"His yacht doesn't come equipped with cannons, does it?" McGill asked.

Ellie laughed. "Not the old fashioned kind, but it has the electronics aboard to launch a broadside media attack. Barrages of mud and slime. Vicious stuff. Nobody will be spared. Not your wife, not you, not your family."

Seeing McGill's eyes narrow, she added. "I can expect a small-scale version of the same. I'm not number one on Sir Edbert's hit list, but I'm in the top five. He'll sail up and down the Eastern Seaboard, just outside the twelve-mile limit, firing off orders to his TV and radio networks, his newspapers and magazines, laying waste to the reputation of anyone he considers an enemy."

"The guy thinks he's a pirate?" McGill asked.

"He always has, but no one's ever given him a good fight."

"Sir Edbert starts in with us," McGill said, "we'll see if he has the courage to go down with his ship. Thank you for the heads-up, Ms. Booker."

Number One Observatory Circle — Washington, D.C.

Mather Wyman put his hands on Kira Fahey Yates' shoulders and looked his niece in the eye.

"You'll need to find a new job, if you side with me," he said.

"I already need a new job. I resigned my position at the White House this afternoon."

Wyman lowered his hands. "Politely, I assume."

Kira nodded. "With sincere gratitude, too. I appreciate the opportunity I was given. I thanked the president and everyone else with whom I worked. I'd still be there if anyone but you was running against the president."

Wyman said, "This won't cause any trouble for Welborn, will it?"

"At work? No. He's Patti Grant's pet; Mr. McGill likes him, too."

"How about between the two of you?"

Kira shook her head. "Not only do we love each other, we're *stuck* with each other and we know it. I won't go into any intimate details —"

Wyman held up his hands and said, "No, please don't."

"What I will say," Kira told her uncle, "is that it would be impossible for either of us to get conversation as good from anyone else."

"That is important."

"Essential," Kira said. "The physical part is wonderful, but a well turned word from my flyboy can melt my heart, steel my will or lift my darkest gloom. When Welborn and I have children, I'll tell them to look for someone they can talk to endlessly without the conversation ever growing tiresome."

Kira saw the sudden effect her words had on Mather Wyman. His eyes grew misty.

She put a hand on his arm. "I'm sorry, Mattie. I made you think of Aunt Elvie, didn't I?"

"Thinking of Elvie has never been anything but a joy for me. I do miss seeing her, but what I miss most of all is what you just mentioned. I miss *talking* to her, *hearing* her voice."

Hearing that made Kira decide to call Welborn right away.

Wyman dabbed his eyes with a handkerchief and pulled himself together.

"Well, now, I'm having three gentlemen over as dinner guests tonight. I don't know how sparkling the discussion will be, but it will be important. To me anyway."

"I'll be happy to chat with you afterward, if you'd like," Kira told him.

Wyman kissed his niece's cheek and said, "I look forward to it, my dear."

The University Club — Washington, D.C.

The four tall wingback chairs in the bar were arranged so that drinks might easily be served but conversations might easily be kept private. Senator Roger Michaelson (D-OR) and Governor Jean Morrissey (D-MN) were the heavyweights present. Their seconds were Bob Merriman, Michaelson's former chief of staff, now a candidate to fill the senate seat Michaelson was leaving to run for president, and Frank Morrissey, the governor's brother, chief of staff, personal lawyer and confidant.

The three men had eschewed alcohol and were drinking sparkling water.

The governor was sipping Bushmills neat.

She was also, by ten years, the youngest person at the table.

Jean Morrissey was blonde and despite her Irish name looked Scandinavian. Roger Michaelson was glad about that. He liked blondes, was married to one. If he'd had to compete against another brunette like Patti Grant, a second brunette since he *was* going up against Patti Grant again, he didn't know if he could —

"You could drop out, Roger," Jean Morrissey said, "let the president and me have a cat fight. That would be fun for everyone."

When had women become such ball-busters, Michaelson wondered.

Or had they always been that way?

He said, "Fun, sure, if all you like to do is watch. I'm more of a doer."

"What makes you think you'll *do* any better than the last time you ran against Patti Grant?"

Michaelson knew he was being tested. There would be primary debates. If Jean Morrissey could get under his skin in the quiet corner of a private club, she'd make him look like a chump in front of the TV cameras and the nation. Without looking at them, he knew Bob Merriman and Frank Morrissey were watching to see how he'd react.

"I've upped my game," Michaelson said. "I've been here in Washington competing against heavyweights, not overseeing farm bills in St. Paul."

Jean Morrissey grinned and raised her glass to Michaelson.

"Nicely played. I'll have to keep you in mind as a possible VP pick."

Republican Central Committee Meeting
Indianapolis, Indiana

The conference room in the Canterbury Hotel wasn't filled with smoke, but the gathering that formally voted on the GOP's slate of electors wasn't customarily one that welcomed children, even those who would be within a year of being able to cast a ballot in the next election. In deference to retiring Senator Charles Talbert and in recognition of a decade of service from his former press secretary, Sheryl Kimbrough, an exception was made for Cassidy Kimbrough.

She was allowed to see her mother approved by unanimous

consent to become a GOP elector, pledged — but not legally bound — to vote for the party's nominee in the Hoosier State's delegation at the Electoral College.

All of the nominees were approved by unanimous consent.

When it came to central committee votes, the fix was always in.

Even so, once the formalities were concluded, Cassidy said, "Yessss!" She hugged her mother hard enough to make her wince and kissed her on both cheeks. "This is so cool!"

She turned to Senator Talbert to thank him for sponsoring her mother for such an honor, but he held up a hand and put on a look of mock terror.

"Now, now, Cassidy, I'm older than Moses and not up to grappling anymore."

Taking her cue, Cassidy politely kept her arms at her sides and gave the senator a polite peck on just one cheek. He beamed in appreciation.

"This experience might make for an interesting college essay, don't you think?" the senator asked Cassidy. "You'll be applying to IU, of course."

Cassidy said, "I was thinking the same thing, about the essay, and I will be applying to Indiana."

What she didn't say was that she saw IU as her safety school.

She'd been praying she would be admitted to Stanford for years.

Sheryl put an arm, gently, around her daughter's shoulders.

She was so proud of Cassidy, and she knew about her daughter's Stanford dream.

Sheryl had pledged to vote for anyone who might win the GOP's nomination.

But she was praying that person would be Mather Wyman.

That was her secret.

Darnall Hall — Georgetown University

Abbie ran to McGill the moment she saw him. It wasn't the

cool thing to do, especially with a dozen or so of your new friends watching. College students, even freshmen, were supposed to be more reserved than that. You didn't show obvious emotion to a parent.

When Abbie threw her arms around her father and he lifted her off the ground, though, a cheer went up in the corridor. Young men and women leaned out of their dorm rooms and raised their voices and whistled in approval. McGill lowered his daughter. They faced their audience and just as if they had rehearsed it, took a bow. The gesture received a round of applause.

Abbie whispered to her father, "A standing ovation. This would make Caitie green with envy."

"We'll keep it to ourselves," McGill said.

A young woman stepped forward and Abbie took her hand.

"You remember Jane Haley from home, right? She's my roommate."

McGill smiled, "Of course, I do. How are you, Jane?"

"I'm well, and we're all so happy about Kenny. Everyone here was praying for him."

McGill felt a tug at his heart. "Thank you." He looked at Abbie. "I was thinking I'd take you out to dinner, but if you'd like we can go downstairs to the Epicurean, bring as many of your friends as you like and I'll spring for pizza and soft drinks."

Abbie bobbed her head. "That'd be great."

McGill said, "Give me just a minute to talk to the Secret Service, let them know what we have in mind." McGill walked back the way he'd come and saw Elspeth Kendry standing next to Deke Ky. He extended his hand to Deke. The special agent hesitated only a moment before taking it. McGill told him, "I'm sorry about losing my temper. I'm very happy you're overseeing Abbie's security. Everything is working out okay?"

Deke nodded. "It's good."

McGill told them what he wanted to do, him and the kids.

Elspeth said, "Give us ten minutes to get set up in the Epicurean."

"Right." McGill went back to talk with Abbie and the young

people now clustered in the hall.

Number One Observatory Circle — Washington, D.C.

Vice President Mather Wyman and his guests had finished dining and had moved into the sitting room. They were ready to get down to business. Wyman held an unlit Cohiba from the Dominican Republic — the Cuban variety would have been impolitic — in his left hand. His three guests, Senator Crockett of Tennessee, House Majority Leader Peter Profitt of North Carolina and Republican National Committee Chairman Reynard Dix of Georgia had each accepted the gift of a cigar from the vice president but had tucked them into their coat pockets and would smoke only if the vice president lit up.

All four men were partaking of the bottle of George Dickel Tennessee sipping whiskey Senator Crockett had brought as a gift to the vice president.

Without preamble, Wyman said, "I'll do it, be the nominee, but only my way."

Crockett lifted his glass, but Profitt and Dix looked at each other.

The RNC chairman asked the question. "What way would that be, Mr. Vice President?"

"Think Eisenhower with just a dash of Reagan," Wyman said.

"The party has moved on quite a bit, especially since the 1950s, sir," Profitt pointed out.

"If he hadn't been paranoid, corrupt and nearly impeached, I might have mentioned Richard Nixon from the '60s and 70s. He recommended a national health insurance plan, if you'll recall."

Senator Crockett, who'd served as a 19-year-old in Vietnam, nodded.

The chairman and the majority leader looked at each other again.

Dix said, "I was born *after* President Nixon resigned."

Profitt added, "I was in second grade at the time."

"Well, gentlemen, then you might want to read a little of your party's history. I agree that by today's lights, Eisenhower, Nixon and even Reagan might be viewed as liberal to moderate. If we were to go back farther and look at Teddy Roosevelt and Abraham Lincoln, they would be considered liberal to radical."

"Your point being, Mr. Vice President?" Dix asked.

"My point is that for our party to survive, let alone prosper, it's long past time for the pendulum to swing back the other way. That's what I meant by saying I'd do things my way."

The majority leader turned to Crockett. "Would you care to comment, Senator?"

"Sounds good to me so far. Short of Candidate Wyman promising to nationalize the Grand Ole Opry, I'm sure I can deliver Tennessee for the GOP. Probably North Carolina and Virginia, too."

Wyman smiled and said, "I promise to leave Nashville alone, unless some worthy group there might need a grant from the National Endowment for the Arts."

Crockett touched up Wyman's glass of Dickel.

Profitt, however, defended his home turf. "Why don't you leave North Carolina to me?"

The senator said, "I bow to the gentleman from Raleigh. But tell me, Peter, don't you think all those bright, well edu-cated families moving into your Research Triangle from other states might be changing the traditional character of North Carolina?"

Profitt made no denial. Didn't comment at all.

"You really think we can win Virginia running as moderates?" Dix asked.

"Gentlemen," Wyman said. "We need to look beyond any one region of the country. Our party's choices are plain. We can try to run to the right of Howard Hurlbert and True South, which will guarantee that we marginalize ourselves. Or we can stake out a position between Senator Hurlbert and President Grant, which, for me, is the only choice."

Senator Crockett added, "That's where the independents and

most of America will be."

The majority leader said, "It's never a comfortable moment when a new reality drags you away from old habits."

Shaking his head, Dix said, "I just don't know. It's more than discomfort for me. Moving to the right is what I think is right."

"Think of it this way, Reynard," Crockett said. "Hard right is where road builders put their ditches."

Wyman grinned. He was coming to like the senator's folksy humor. If he were to have Crockett on the ticket with him, it might well take some of the stiffness off his own image. He could play the self-deprecating straight man.

But not at the moment.

"Think of this, too, Mr. Dix. If you want to have a nominee who's comfortable on the far right, it won't be me. Who will that leave you? Beau Brunelle? I hear he's already committed to True South, hoping to recruit candidates for Congress and to be their leader in the legislative branch. Darrin Neff? True South isn't far right enough for him. The joke is he's waiting for the Confederacy to make a comeback. Even if you do find somebody who's remotely plausible, all you'll be doing is duplicating True South. Dividing the same slice of the pie."

A pout appeared on the face of the RNC chairman.

He looked as if he might like to kick the vice president on his shin.

"We can *not* run a liberal candidate to be president," Dix said. "That would duplicate Patti Grant."

"President Grant *won* the last election," Wyman reminded Dix with heat in his voice. "I was there and had a front row seat. If it hadn't been for the members of the party ..." The vice president took a moment to rewrite his thoughts. "If it hadn't been for people driving our car toward the ditch, President Grant wouldn't have left our party. Then, again, maybe the party left her first."

Crockett took a sip of Dickel and said, "Well, I think the three of us have made our sentiments clear. How do you feel, Peter?"

"I want to win, and neither Beau Brunelle nor any of his toadies is going to have any say over the House, if I can help it. I think Vice President Wyman is our only chance to win the White House."

Reynard Dix got to his feet and looked at the other three.

"I'll submit my resignation first thing in the morning."

The door had barely closed behind him before Crockett added, "But you'll start working for Howard Hurlbert this very night."

Georgetown University

What had begun as an impromptu social gathering ended as a political rally. McGill kept his word and picked up the tab for the eats and drinks. He thanked everyone for their kind thoughts and prayers for Kenny. He wished them well with their studies

McGill kissed his daughter goodbye, drawing another cheer, and told her he'd be back on Friday to take her to Camp David. He and Deke Ky stepped outside.

"I'm sorry, too," the special agent told McGill.

"Yeah?" McGill asked.

Deke nodded. "I gave you my word; I went back on it. Problem is, I wasn't supposed to make a side-deal with a package. I'm supposed to follow the rules."

McGill and Deke walked the campus by themselves after dark. Elspeth Kendry was back at Darnall Hall watching Abbie.

"So what happened?" McGill asked. "You got caught up in the excitement of shadowing the president's husband?"

"Yeah, you know me, giddy all the time."

McGill laughed.

Deke said, "I should have told SAC Crogher I needed to be reassigned."

"Would he have gone along?"

"No offense to the president, but I think SAC Crogher fell in love with Wyman. Having a new, inexperienced guy in the Oval Office gave Crogher an edge he'd never have had otherwise. I think it went to his head and, no, he wouldn't have given me an easy out."

"So you decided to be a good soldier."

"Must be genetic or something, on my dad's side."

Deke's father had been an army man and later a cop. His mother was a successful criminal, currently residing in Hanoi.

He asked McGill, "The president tell you about Crogher yet?"

"I heard Celsus leaves the White House after the election."

"Word is, unofficially, he's going to retire."

"And do what?" McGill asked.

Deke looked at him. "We're working up a pool on that. I'm betting he goes on display in a diorama somewhere."

McGill grinned. "A speaking tour would seem unlikely."

"You hear about Elspeth Kendry moving up?"

"Yeah. What do you think about that?" McGill asked.

"I'm okay with it. Never was my ambition. Elspeth is smart in ways most of us aren't. Probably comes from growing up in the Middle East. She'll be good."

A moment later, Deke added, "The other thing is, there's going to be a rotation of Secret Service personnel in the White House detail."

"Including you? I feel good having you watch out for Abbie. I can put in a word for you if you want."

Deke shook his head.

"I'll make sure my replacement can do the job. Then I think I'm going to call it quits, too."

"Leave the Secret Service?"

Deke nodded. "They'll probably start a betting pool for me, too. Maybe I'll just live off the ill-gotten but squeaky clean bequest my mother left me."

McGill said, "Leo found employment in the private sector."

"Maybe after I get tired of living the life of the idle rich. Ought to take at least a week."

They left talk of the future there.

Got down to planning how to protect both Abbie and Daryl Cheveyo.

Dumbarton Oaks — Washington, D.C.

Galia Mindel and Stephen Norwood were ignoring the pitcher of orange juice, basket of croissants and bowl of fresh strawberries that might have been their breakfast to pore over piles of lists, charts, opinion polls and maps that would be turned into the campaign infrastructure needed to win a presidential election.

Because the work was political in nature and Stephen had resigned his White House post to become Patti Grant's campaign chairman, their activities had to take place on private premises, and there were no premises Galia felt were more securely private than her own home.

As was necessary, the first point of discussion was money.

Norwood said, "We can describe our donations compared to this time in the last cycle in two words: holding steady. That's true for both small and large donors, men and women, young voters and old, whites, African Americans and Latinos. We're even on a par with where we were last time with white men."

White men usually skewed conservative.

Galia gave a knowing grin. "We'd never admit it publicly, Stephen, but there's something compelling about having a gorgeous woman running for office."

Norwood asked, "You think that would hold true across lines of ethnicity and skin color?"

Galia said, "Let's put it this way: If you took Patti Grant and applied any human hue to her, she'd still make men look twice and more of them would vote for her than would vote for me, even if we advocated exactly the same agenda."

"Only because they don't know what a sweetheart you are, boss."

Galia laughed and swatted Norwood affectionately.

"Yeah, well, that's another closely guarded secret," she said.

They went on to vet the campaign chairmen and chairwomen for all fifty states, reviewed requirements and deadlines for placing their candidate's name on ballots, added and deleted names from the list of media people who would be granted exclusive interviews, who would be denied all but the most perfunctory access and in the case of a select few who would be favored with major leaks. Galia joked that if the careers of talking heads were traded like shares of stock they could do some serious insider trading.

As if her ears were burning, Press Secretary Aggie Wu chose that moment to call Galia.

"Sorry to intrude," she said, "but I thought I'd bring you up to date on a few things, in the way of general news."

"Please do," Galia said.

"Governor Eugene Rinaldo of New York just signed the legislation fixing the time of New York's presidential primary election to one minute after that of New Hampshire. Governor Edward Mulcahy of Illinois will sign identical legislation for his state in an hour, and Governor Lara Chavez of California will follow that by two hours."

"And?" Galia asked.

Aggie said, "And Democratic National Committee Chairman Henry Melchior has sent advance word to media outlets that after Governor Chavez signs her bill and makes her statement, he will announce that the party will recognize the move by the three states but urge others to wait until the next presidential election to move up their elections."

"No word from Reynard Dix on the Republican reaction?"

There was a pause on Aggie's end of the conversation before she asked, "You haven't heard?"

"Heard what?"

"Dix has left the Republicans for True South."

"Oh."

Galia wanted to say more, like, "Do you think Mather Wyman engineered that?" But Aggie had called from the White House and that hallowed ground was off limits to such speculation, even voiced on a phone.

"There's one more thing," Aggie said. "John Patrick Granby called."

"To curse my name?" Galia asked.

She had to think the secretary of state for New Hampshire knew by now who was responsible for stealing his state's thunder.

"No, he was pretty good natured, all things considered. He wanted to know if the White House would get behind an idea he has."

"That we should all drop dead?"

"Galia, come on. What he'd like is to make the most of the minute head start you've given him. He's going to ask voters in his state to select one worthy citizen, not a pol or a poobah, to have the honor of casting the nation's first vote live on television and streaming on the Internet. There'd be maybe a thirty-second intro, then the selected person would drop his or her ballot into the box and, bang, everybody could follow along with their votes coast to coast."

Galia smiled. She liked the idea.

"Give some old sweetheart, colorful character or local hero the first vote, that's great. I'll talk with the president, but I'm sure she'll agree."

"Good. That'll make the last part easier."

"What last part?" Galia asked.

"Granby said he'd like to meet with you. Show you there are no hard feelings."

J. Edgar Hoover Building — Washington, D.C.

FBI Deputy Director Byron DeWitt had offered to come to the offices of McGill Investigations, Inc. to brief McGill and Sweetie on the bureau's plan to interview Lydell Martin and persuade the upwardly mobile former truck driver to go along with the plan to draw Dr. Damon Todd into a trap. The gesture was in keeping with DeWitt's air of geniality and cooperation. But neither McGill nor Sweetie had ever been to FBI headquarters. They wanted to see the place and observe how DeWitt behaved in his native habitat.

Both of them were surprised upon entering DeWitt's office to see an Andy Warhol serigraph of Chairman Mao on the wall. Declining an offer of tea or soft drinks, McGill and Sweetie sat opposite DeWitt in a grouping of leather arm chairs.

"I thought you guys were supposed to hunt Communists," McGill said.

DeWitt nodded. "We still do, but the big threat has moved to cyberspace these days. China has more than a few extraordinary hackers. The print on the wall is a reminder that they're always trying to snoop on us."

"You didn't get any grief about putting it up?" Sweetie asked. "The ghost of J. Edgar hasn't haunted you?"

DeWitt said, "Given my personal history and the director's support, the bureaucracy has humored me, and I had the office spiritually cleansed before I moved in."

Sweetie looked at McGill. "Maybe we should have Francis Nguyen bless our place."

He smiled and asked DeWitt to bring them up to speed.

The deputy director said, "We did background checks on Martin and the principals of the company that employs him. Everybody came up clean. Nothing more than traffic violations and one drunk and disorderly on a VP of marketing. Otherwise, the executive suite is composed of solid citizens. We found only one person who'd been married more than twice, so they're pretty stable in that way, too. We have every reason to believe the company will readily assist us in approaching Martin, and that he will be willing to help out, too."

"I've been thinking about that," McGill said. "The way that Todd avoided prosecution last time by slipping into the identity of a child shows that he's both clever and cautious. He might have left some safeguard tucked away into Lydell Martin's mind. Push Martin or probe him too hard, he might become somebody else, adopt an identity of which he's unaware."

DeWitt said, "That would be a complication, but wouldn't necessarily throw a monkey wrench into the plan."

"You mean we can still run the disinformation campaign,"

McGill said. "As long as Martin doesn't come out and personally contradict the lies we tell about him, we can still suck Todd into our trap."

DeWitt nodded. "If we grab Todd, he can bring Martin out from behind any mask he places on him."

"You can do that if you can keep *Todd* from slipping into another identity again," McGill said.

"We've thought about that, consulted with our own psychiatric specialists. One of the problems you faced with Dr. Todd was that he was conscious when he was taken into custody. Our thinking is to zap him, say with a taser, before he can make a shift. Then before he completely regains his senses we start talking to him. Tell him if he goes away again he gets locked in a rubber room for good."

"You mean that?" Sweetie asked.

"At a minimum, we have to make him believe we do," DeWitt said.

McGill took the next step. "So the person delivering the message has to believe it's true."

DeWitt nodded.

"But it's not true, right?" Sweetie was a devout believer in redemption.

DeWitt said, "That's a very good question. We've yet to achieve a consensus around here. What do you think, Mr. McGill?"

McGill replied, "I don't want Damon Todd or any of his people to be a threat to my family, my friends or me ever again," McGill said.

"So the rubber room it is?" DeWitt said.

McGill said, "There's no question Todd tried to kill me with a baseball bat. This time instead of handing him over to the CIA we go to trial and ask a jury to find him mentally incompetent but guilty of attempted murder, and lock him up in solitary confinement in a supermax prison. See if that can hold him."

The deputy director nodded. "Legal, ethical and —"

"A threat that will really scare Todd," McGill said. "Make him face up to who he is and what he's done."

DeWitt asked McGill if he wanted to be present when the trap was sprung.

He said he'd trust the FBI to get it right.

Leaving unsaid but understood three words: Don't blow it.

Key West, Florida

Jackie Richmond never had a better idea of the shock and distress he must have caused by stealing people's cars than when he checked his account in the Marlborough Bank on Grand Cayman Island and found that the balance was one hundred dollars. There should have been more than four hundred thousand dollars. Seeing most of his life savings gone — like he'd been some chump hustled by a financial scammer — left him feeling so hollowed out he had to sit down before he fell.

He sat for hours on a park bench trying to figure out what the hell he should do next. He'd been thinking of leaving Key West anyway. He didn't need any more bullshit from a gang of white slavers. He was sure those pricks had put a bounty on his head by now.

Probably had done the same for Alice.

He'd been thinking of jetting off to Isla de Margarita. He'd heard it was a pretty place belonging to Venezuela, just off the coast from the mainland. He thought he could set himself up there, make some contacts, start a business. Get an order for a specific vehicle from somebody in Caracas, fly up to Florida, bag it, ship it and head back to his island hideaway.

Who the hell would ever look for him in Venezuela?

So the thing to do was get away soon.

He still had better than twenty-five grand in cash …

That, goddamnit, he'd tucked into a hidey-hole at Alice's house.

Meantime, he knew a good-looking woman who had a nice big boat. Ought to be able to sail down to Grand Cayman so he could raise hell at his bank, get some kind of compensation, and then cruise on to Isla de Margarita no sweat.

And he really should throw a scare into that pretty woman. Tell her how dangerous Key West had gotten.

George Town — Grand Cayman Island

Welborn couldn't get his conversation with Kira out of his mind. She had quit her job at the White House. Just like that. He snapped his fingers. Who knew what other drastic changes she might make on impulse, a new wife without the stabilizing influence of her husband? He felt a compelling urge to —

Willa Pennyman, the daughter of the café's owner, was looking at him like she was the Queen of Hearts about to issue her favorite command, "Off with his head!"

She'd figured out the second day Welborn had plunked himself down at the table in Pennyman's Cafe, that he soon came to think of as his own, that he was no ordinary tourist.

"You're some kind of crook or copper," she told him that second day.

Made the accusation quietly enough that no one else had heard.

Welborn had dismissed her appraisal and said, "I'm an astronaut."

She considered that possibility but only briefly. "Too young," she said.

Willa said she figured him for about her age, twenty-seven.

"A bit younger than that," Welborn told her, "and it's true I lost my chance to go into space after suffering damage to my inner ear, but I still hold astronaut status."

Willa laughed and told him, "You're a pretty boy and you tell a pretty story, but I'll figure you out."

Their relationship had become amicable, to the point that Willa would reserve Welborn's preferred table for him, but now she was furious at him because … the light dawned for Welborn. She thought he'd snapped his fingers to summon her to his table, reducing her status from a budding friend to a menial serving person.

He waved his hands at her to dispel the idea that he'd behaved improperly.

That didn't stop Willa from storming over to his table and glaring at him.

She said, "People don't do that sort of thing on this island and they especially don't do it in this establishment. Have I made myself clear?"

"Completely," Welborn said, "but I didn't intend my manner to be peremptory. I was merely providing a sound effect to accompany a passing thought."

Willa took the seat across from Welborn, temporarily obscuring his view of the Marlborough Bank. Not that he was about to complain. Not if he could help himself. Keeping any misplaced impulse in check was aided by the fact that Willa, even angered, was easy on the eyes.

"Peremptory, you say," Willa said. "Did you go to one of those posh American universities?"

"Mine was highly selective," he said, "and it has produced the most astronauts."

Actually, the Air Force Academy came in second to the Naval Academy in that distinction, but Welborn was willing to fudge the truth for the moment.

Willa wasn't interested in space travel. She had another question.

"What was the passing thought?" she asked, a note of suspicion clear in her voice. "The one that got you to ..." She snapped her fingers.

"Oh, that. I was thinking about a woman."

Now, Willa smiled, and she made a guess that was half right.

"Things change with women, sometimes just like ..." She snapped her fingers again.

Welborn cautioned, "You might want to stop doing that. People might think it has become acceptable behavior."

Willa studied Welborn for a long moment.

"I like you," she said. "I bet you could talk a lady right out of her knickers."

There had been times, but Welborn didn't want to send the wrong message.

"The woman I was thinking of," he said, "she surprised me but she's still very much in the picture."

Willa sat back in her chair. "As in you're very much married?"

"I am."

"You're not wearing a ring."

Not when I'm working, Welborn thought. Wouldn't do to let any bad guy know where a reprisal might be taken.

"I behave as though I do," he said.

Willa sighed. "Sad but true. We can still talk, right?"

"Of course."

A thought struck Welborn just then, an idea that had never made an appearance in the curricula of his federal law enforcement training classes at Glynco, Georgia. He wondered if James J. McGill would approve of it. Cops used snitches, didn't they? Of course, they did.

"What's going on under all your pretty blonde hair?" Willa asked.

"I'm trying to think of how I might ask a favor of you."

"While remembering you're married."

"Always keeping that in mind. I can't tell you what I'm doing here, but I'd like you to help me do it. You and any of your people working here. I'd be happy to offer monetary compensation for your efforts, if that's an appropriate thing to do."

Willa thought about that. "You wouldn't put me into any trouble with the police?"

"Never. What I'd be asking is perfectly legal."

"How much money would you be offering?"

The alumni association of the Air Force Academy had a standing offer of one hundred thousand dollars for information leading to the arrest and conviction of the person or persons responsible for causing the deaths of Keith Quinn, Tommy Bauer and Joe

Eddy. Welborn considered what he might add to that bounty as seed money.

He told Willa, "At least five thousand dollars and perhaps as much as one hundred thousand dollars."

The young woman's eyes widened and then she became suspicious again.

"Tell me true," she said, "this has nothing to do with drugs or hurting people."

Welborn said, "It doesn't. If things work out, you'll learn what I'm doing and you'll be glad you helped."

"You know what I think?" Willa asked.

"What?"

"I think you could sell turn signals to fireflies."

Welborn grinned. "You just made that up."

"Heard it from another Yank not long ago. Had to explain it to me, he did."

Welborn took a photocopy of Linley Boland's likeness out of a pocket. He laid it on the table between them. Willa moved it to a better angle for her to examine.

"Now, this bloke's a proper villain."

Welborn nodded. "He steals things and he kills people."

"And he's coming to George Town?"

"Yes."

Willa had the wit to turn and look in the direction Welborn always faced. She saw the bank first thing. Everyone in the Cayman Islands knew how their banks were often used. Not everyone approved. She looked back at Welborn.

"Now we're at the part you won't tell me about."

Welborn nodded. "The proper villain is a wanted man in the United States. All I want is for your police to take him into custody until he can be extradited."

"So you are a copper."

"My interest is personal."

"And this man, this villain, he's going to show up at the bank?"

"I think so."

"But he's got to fly into the airport or sail into a marina, yes?"

"Yes." He thought he saw where she was going.

Willa told him, "One man can watch just one place, but if you know a lot of people …"

Welborn said, "You can watch a lot of places. That would be helpful."

"And all anyone has to do is call the police, have this man arrested?"

"Yes. That'll get you five thousand dollars."

"He gets sent to prison in the U.S. we get the rest?"

"Yes."

"What if the police don't want to cooperate?"

Welborn gestured to the pad on which Willa took food orders. "May I?"

She handed the pad and a pen to him. He jotted his name and a phone number.

"If the cops aren't interested, nobody acts like a hero. Just hand the bad guy this information."

"You think he's going to call you? Cop or not, you're the bloke hunting him."

"That's right. So you tell him one thing."

"What?"

Welborn said, "Tell him I've got what he wants."

Sunset Marina — Key West, Florida

Carina Linberg was working on the synopsis of the idea for her TV pilot. She sat in the stern of *Irish Grace* working on a Mac-Book Pro. Her boat had WiFi so she could go on the Internet to do research as needed. The sounds of the marina had become second nature to her and usually didn't disturb her concentration. But that day it sounded like someone a few slips over was using a power saw. That made creative thinking difficult.

Only until she dug out a set of earbuds, plugged them into the computer and clicked on the Mary Chapin Carpenter channel on

Pandora. Dialed up the volume until the sound of the saw became a soft buzz. You couldn't beat technology for isolating you from the —

Asshole standing on the jetty yelling at you and waving his arms to catch your eye.

It was Jackie Richmond, the bartender. The guy was becoming a real pain.

She was tempted to go below and button up. But it was such a damn nice day. And, Christ, he might have more news about that mess she'd stumbled into. There might be more story material she could use somewhere down the line.

Make the sacrifice for your art, she told herself.

She pulled the buds out of her ears and was relieved to find the saw had gone silent.

Jackie said, "You got a minute?" Catching the look on Carina's face, he added, "It might take a little longer than that."

Carina responded, "I bet it's not something you want to talk about from a distance."

Jackie looked around to see if anyone was paying attention. No one was.

Even so, he said, "Best not to."

Carina's study of writing for TV had advanced to the point where she'd learned about pitches and log lines. You had to nail the interest of a producer or a studio executive in one sentence. Otherwise it was, "Thank you for coming. Next."

"Give me a brief summary," Carina said.

After looking around again, Jackie told her in a quiet voice, "There was a shooting at Mango Mary's, three dead."

Carina had to admit that wasn't bad. Hooked her. A couple of ways. One, it *was* good story material. Two, she wanted to find out what her own liability, if any, was. She waved Jackie aboard. She took it as a good sign that he didn't smile as he set foot on the boat.

He wasn't running some scam; he was serious about the shooting.

Carina told him, "Tell me everything that happened, but keep to the point the way you did just now."

She opened a new file on her word processing program. She wanted to get down both Jackie's narrative and any dialogue between the two of them. From where he stood, he wouldn't be able to see what she was typing, but if he wasn't a total dope, and she didn't think he was, he'd be able to guess she was making a record of their meeting.

What he couldn't know was that if he made a move to grab the computer or assault her, she could send everything she'd transcribed to a cloud server with the touch of a button.

That and pull out her LadySmith with her free hand.

Jackie told her what had happened at Mango Mary's. He kept his voice down and his sentences short. Blue collar Hemingway. When he finished, he said, "That's it."

"So you shot a guy and killed him?" Carina asked.

"In self-defense. Three guys in masks charge in with Glocks with extended clips, and one points the damn thing at you, what else you gonna do?"

The logic was inarguable, but there were a few points to clear up.

"You recognized the make of the guns they had?"

"I *thought* they were Glocks. They were sure semi-autos. The clips were long as a dog's leg, it seemed."

"Okay, and you just happened to have a rifle in hand?"

"I told you, we were talking guns at the bar. Everyone had theirs out. You got one yourself; you should know how it is. Especially after the trouble we already had at the bar."

Carina thought that was reasonable, too.

"So, out of the goodness of your heart, you decided to come and warn me?"

Jackie said, "My heart's only middling good, if that. I want to ask you about doing a job for me."

That caught Carina off guard. "What kind of job?"

"Sail me down to an island off South America. I'll pay. Can you make it in this boat?"

Carina nodded and asked, "Where's Alice? She's okay, isn't she?"

"The last I saw, but the longer we stick around here …"

He left it to her to imagine the rest. She was already working on that.

"You're writing all this down, aren't you?" Jackie said.

"I am, but I'm not using any names."

"Why not?"

"When I write a story I like to make up my own names."

She was tempted to say the way you made up Jackie Richmond, but she didn't want to push it. Instead she asked, "What do you expect to pay for a charter to South America? Keep in mind I have the expense of making the return trip."

"Would ten grand do it?" he asked. He figured he needed to keep at least fifteen for himself.

"That's a bit modest, but worth considering."

"Does that mean yes?"

Carina said, "Tell you what. You go get Alice and bring her along, I'll have more faith in you. Do it for ten thousand."

"Long as we're adding conditions," Jackie said, "if I bring Alice, can we make a quick stop at Grand Cayman on the way?"

Carina liked a plot with twists. She said, "Sure." Then she added, "I'll need to get fuel and provisions for the voyage. That'll take a little while. Can you remember a phone number?"

Jackie nodded. "Yeah."

"Call this number before you come back." She gave Jackie her mobile phone number. "I'll want to talk with Alice when you call. I'll want to see her walking down the jetty with you."

"You think I'd leave her behind?"

"I know what guys do to women," Carina told him.

"What if she doesn't want to come?"

"Find yourself a travel agent." Carina took her LadySmith out of her pocket.

"I'll call first and I'll be with Alice. We'll be back with the money."

That, Carina had learned, would be what people in the writing biz called a plot point.

She watched Jackie depart the marina. He took another look at her Porsche as he left. He'd said somebody had stolen his Porsche. She had the feeling it was more likely the other way around. Then, maybe, somebody took the car from him.

Once Jackie was out of sight, she called her agent.

Told him, "Call Sir Edbert. Say I've got a TV show I want to pitch him."

The White House Residence

McGill and Patti called Camp David from McGill's Hideaway. They both spoke with Kenny and were heartened to learn he was in good spirits and continuing to gain strength. He confided to his father that he was eager to resume his training in Dark Alley. Patti, listening in on another extension, raised her eyebrows when she heard that. McGill said they'd get back to it that weekend when he brought Abbie up for a visit.

Patti said, "I'll be there, too."

Which was the first McGill had heard of that.

Patti said hello to Carolyn when she joined the call, but then left McGill to speak privately with his former wife. Carolyn said she thought Kenny was looking well. "Almost back to normal. I keep holding my breath that there are no setbacks."

"Me, too," McGill said. "Remember, faith is what keeps you going through *tough* times."

"I'm not as tough as I should be, as you well know. Maybe I should start pumping iron."

McGill laughed "There you go. Do that and start talking with an Austrian accent. You could get into movies and become the governor of California."

"Kahl-ee-forn-ee-uh," Carolyn corrected.

"You're on your way."

"Only if I promise to bring Caitie along."

They ended the call feeling the mutual comfort of seeing

Kenny on the mend, and knowing each of them would continue to pray as hard as they could for all of their children.

McGill picked up the house phone and told Patti it was okay to come back.

She brought Blessing, the White House head butler, with her. He came bearing a cold Sugar Hill Golden Ale and a frosted mug for McGill. The president was refreshing herself with a White House Ice Tea.

McGill raised his mug to Patti, "To my dear wife, a better woman than I deserve."

Patti clinked her bottle against McGill's mug of beer. "For an undeserving guy, you seem to do pretty well with any number of women."

"I'll drink to that," McGill said.

And he did, joined by Patti.

"I had my daily once-over with Nick," she said.

"All's well?"

McGill prayed hard for Patti, too.

She nodded. "The doctors are calling the episode of mitral valve prolapse I experienced an idiopathic event."

"Fancy way of saying they can't figure it out, right?"

"Unknown cause arising spontaneously, if you'd care to be more precise."

McGill said, "Nobody likes an unsolved mystery, but Nick and friends aren't worried beyond that, are they?"

"Caution is still the watchword, but I've been given the go-ahead to bump up my schedule by twenty percent. I've decided to take it up only ten percent."

"How come?" McGill asked. Patti wasn't exactly a slacker.

"Because I've decided to give you the other ten percent."

To avoid any possible misunderstanding, she batted her eyes at him.

McGill beamed. "Maybe there's more to recommend me than I thought."

**

"Surely you've heard of an October Surprise," Patti said to McGill an hour later.

"It's a Halloween prank, isn't it?" he asked, adjusting his pillow.

He got an elbow to his ribs for that, but it was barely more than a nudge.

No point in ruining the easy-does-it mood of what they'd just enjoyed.

Having considered the matter now, Patti said, "You may be right. It could have been inspired by the idea of trick or treat. Politics being what they are, though, it's more like trick and treat. You play a dirty trick on your opponent just before the election and enjoy the treat of watching him scramble desperately to recover, only to come up short and lose the election."

"If the truth comes out a little late," McGill said, "there are no do-overs."

Patti gave a laugh with a cynical tone.

"What?" McGill asked.

"Of course, there are do-overs. They're called recounts. In many cases, they're mandated by law. If the first count falls within certain prescribed margins, you count again until everybody's satisfied — or you have a majority of the Supreme Court in your pocket and they stop the recount. You know, just in one special case. Not setting a precedent or anything."

"Oh, yeah, I forgot about that."

Patti said, "Anyway, I'm sure that was what Ms. Booker was telling you."

"She not only told me what, generally speaking, she told me who — specifically, Sir Edbert Bickford. Kind of rankles having a Brit meddle in American governance. Next thing you know, they'll try to burn down the White House again."

"We have a fire suppression system these days," Patti reassured him.

"All to the good, but I still think Galia should send out her minions to see what Bickford is up to," McGill said.

"You think Galia has minions?"

"Somebody had to hire all those displaced KGB workers."

The elbow this time was just a touch sharper. McGill took it as a sign Patti was still feeling playful. He rolled over, stroked her cheek and kissed her.

"It's probably for the best you don't know about your chief of staff's spy network," he said. "Gives you plausible deniability. I think."

"You've been studying political science again," Patti accused.

"Only as it applies to you. As your henchman, I have to protect you in every way I can. I'll tell Galia what Ellie Booker told me. When would be a good time to see her or should I ask Edwina?"

"I can tell you that. Tomorrow morning before the press conference."

"Galia is conferring with the press?"

Patti nodded. "She'll be talking about the schedule of presidential primaries."

"That," McGill said, "was a pretty slick move."

Patti said, "Slick always looks good at first. But you have to see how it shakes out."

Alice Tompkins' House — Key West, Florida

Jackie Richmond entered Alice's house only after taking a series of precautions. He passed by Mango Mary's before heading to the house. The bar was still standing, front door tight in its frame, front window intact, Landshark Lager sign still alight. He stopped at a hardware store for a few necessary tools. He circled Alice's block three times.

He didn't seen any sign of slavers lying in wait.

Jackie entered the house by removing the window air conditioner in the kitchen from the outside and crawling through the opening. He took the Beretta M9 out of his waistband, waited for his eyes to adjust to the ambient light. There wasn't much of it at the back of the house.

As he waited, he listened. The kitchen wall clock ticked. Farther into the house, he heard water dripping. The sink in the bathroom next to Alice's bedroom. Damn thing had kept him up nights until he got used to sleeping with a pillow over his head.

Jackie eased into the dining room, half expecting to find the place wrecked, but it wasn't. It was pin-neat, the way Alice always kept it. He moved into the living room. The curtains were drawn but there was a street light directly outside. He could see everything was orderly there, too. He was beginning to get the feeling Alice had bugged out.

Maybe not, but if he couldn't find her and get her onto *Irish Grace* he was fucked.

Maybe not, but that was the way he felt.

He could just take his cash from Alice's house and steal Carina Linberg's Porsche. Maybe he could get away clean. Or maybe he'd get caught again because that particular car was his *bad* luck charm.

He checked Alice's bedroom. Her bed was perfectly made, pillows arranged just so … but one of them was missing. There should have been two rows of three, the front row just off center from the back. But there were only two pillows in front.

Maybe a slaver had used one to smother Alice, Jackie thought.

He pointed the Beretta at the door to the bedroom closet.

Could Alice be dead in there, he wondered.

With her killer just waiting to pounce on his ass.

Jackie was getting ready to unload half-a-clip through the closet door when he heard a soft buzz. Softer than usual. The way Alice snored was musical compared to the ruckus he put out; he knew because his only ex-wife had recorded him. Alice, being a more practical sort, had simply bought ear plugs. No big fuss.

The sound of the sleeping bar owner came, he realized, from *under* the bed. He lowered himself to his knees without making any noise. Picked up the coverlet and there she was, sleeping like a baby on the missing pillow. Now, the question was how did he wake her up without giving her a heart attack or even pissing her off.

You made somebody mad it was hell getting them to be cooperative.

Best way he could think of was to show her the money.

He tiptoed back to the kitchen and looked at the fridge. Every burglar in creation knew about hiding valuables inside a refrigerator, but damn few wanted to move one and look under it. Jackie had done a little carpentry one day when Alice had left for the bar first. Moved the fridge and cut a hole in the floor, built a little homemade safe box that sat down into the crawl space beneath the house.

He tugged the fridge out of its usual niche, taking care not to make any noise. His money was right where he left it, all of it. On the way back to Alice's bedroom, he stopped in the bathroom. Got a bottle of Alice's preferred fragrance, Opium. He spritzed ten Ben Franklins and went back to the bedroom. He tucked the first one six inches away from Alice's nose, and laid out a trail to the chair where he sat opposite the bed.

Five seconds after he sat down, he heard a sneeze. Another five seconds and Alice's hand poked out from under the bed, grabbed her third hundred dollar bill. There was a pause while Alice tried to figure out who was reeling her in, but from her point of view she could see there was more money waiting to be had. Inside of a minute, she poked her head out for a look.

In a soft voice, Jackie said, "Bet you never had anyone wake you up like that before."

The White House Press Room

The press room was filled to capacity. It wasn't every day or even every month that the White House chief of staff deigned to talk with the newsies. She was pleasant enough about it when the need arose, but it was also clear that given a choice she'd prefer to have her teeth drilled. Without anesthesia.

The topic of Galia's announcement, that she had been one of the architects of changing the presidential primary system, was enough of a draw to pull in every warm body with a press pass to the White House, but the word that John Patrick Granby, the secretary of state of New Hampshire, would be present heightened the drama to the point where the reporters were almost giddy in anticipation of what might happen.

Press Secretary Aggie Wu had tried to calm the media munchers down, saying that Granby had been gracious about his state being dethroned by Galia Mindel's plan. Aggie said that Granby had even come up with a face-saving plan to make good use of the one-minute head start the Granite State still retained over New York, Illinois and California.

Not a reporter in the room believed that Granby was happy.

They were sure they would witness fireworks to make their day, maybe even their careers.

What the newsies did take to heart was the bulletin that James J. McGill would be present at least for the outset of the chief of staff's remarks. He would be on hand strictly as an observer. Anyone who so much as said more than good morning to him would have his or her White House credentials reviewed and most likely yanked.

Aggie overheard some of the schemers among the media try to advance a plan in which the entire press corps would rise as one when McGill entered the room and say, "Good morning, Mr. McGill," in the singsong cadence of a kindergarten class greeting its teacher.

The press secretary thought that was funny, and wouldn't have objected if it happened. The president's henchman, she knew, was quick with a quip. It'd be interesting to hear what his response might be.

Before unanimous consent to the prank could be reached, John Patrick Granby arrived. He was well into middle age with a gray widow's peak, a red face and a barrel chest. His suit coat was unbuttoned and didn't look as if it had enough cloth to cover Granby's middle expanse. He wore a blood red tie that dangled unfashionably long.

The man could have used a fashion stylist, Aggie thought, but maybe he didn't worry about such things. He didn't seem to need the security of an entourage either. He'd come alone.

The newsies jumped out of their seats upon seeing Granby. Then they sat right back down when Aggie glared at them. She'd been a dragon press secretary long before anyone had ever heard of dragon mothers. Cross her and you never got called on to ask a question.

"Mr. Granby," she told the chastened reporters, "will take questions after he and Ms. Mindel have made their statements."

The New Hampshire secretary of state bowed to Aggie and took a seat at the side of the room. Two minutes later, James J. McGill entered the room, gave the press corps a friendly wave of acknowledgement, shook Granby's hand and did him the courtesy of leaving an empty seat between them as he sat.

He'd always thought that sitting too close to someone the first time you met was a bad move. He also felt it was strange that in a well air conditioned room Granby should have a sweaty palm. He leaned closer to Granby so they might talk quietly.

"Mr. Secretary of State, I need to have a word with Ms. Mindel before the two of you speak to the media, but if you have anything to say to her before that, you can have the first crack at her, if you like."

Granby thought about that for a moment and bobbed his head.

"I do and I would. Thank you, Mr. McGill."

McGill said, "You're welcome," and left it at that.

Other than watching Granby out of the corner of his eye. There were beads of sweat on the man's brow as well as his hand, and he fiddled lightly with the end of his tie. McGill wondered if Granby was experiencing stage fright. He might have been comfortable speaking with local reporters in Manchester but ill at ease speaking in front of the national media crew.

Maybe, McGill thought, Granby was worrying about more than just flubbing his lines. He might have led Galia to believe he was going to be gracious about his state being usurped, but he was going to come out and blast her, make some sort of threat, hope to overturn the new order. If he was going to try that, he'd have a

— PART 1: The Last Ballot Cast —

reason to be ill at ease.

Back home in Chicago, McGill knew, mayors had been known to kill the power to the microphones of any city council member who dared to speak out of turn. He didn't know if that sort of thing would play in the White House press room. But he wouldn't put it past either Galia or Aggie to make the attempt.

If things turned into a circus, he'd better be on his toes and ready to make a quick exit.

Galia entered the room. McGill saw that she held a sheaf of paper in her left hand. The text of her remarks, he assumed. Knowing Galia, he was sure she had committed the main talking points to memory. She was probably doing a quick review right now.

McGill watched Granby get to his feet and wipe his palms on the legs of his pants.

The guy was keyed up, no doubt about it.

Galia, though, smiled as she saw Granby approach, extended her hand to take his. The two of them exchanged words that were inaudible to McGill, but Granby must have said something that was at least intended to be funny because he saw Galia laugh politely. Then Granby graciously gestured to her to precede him to the podium where Aggie Wu stood ready to introduce them.

The moment Galia stepped in front of Granby his public mask changed to an expression of loathing — and McGill launched himself from his chair. Galia saw McGill hurtling toward her, the look on his face enough to make her knees wobble, and she reflexively backed away.

Granby pulled a thin transparent length of what looked like plastic wire out of his tie just as Galia bumped into him, and he draped it around the chief of staff's neck. By now, everyone in the room was focused on the drama, most of them were also on their feet. Videocams recorded every frame of what happened next.

Secret Service special agents were moving in, but McGill was closer and going to get there first. Granby's intent was clear: He wanted to garrote Galia and have the whole world see what he'd done. Galia reacted as most people would, she tried to escape the agonizing pressure on her throat by running away from it.

McGill knew that was exactly the wrong thing to do. You had to escape the trap by backing up as fast as you could, relieving the constriction and applying unexpected force against your assailant. McGill hit Galia and Granby, wrapping his arms around both of them, like Brian Urlacher crushing both a running back and his blocker.

The three of them went down in a heap, Granby's hands losing their grip as the back of his head slammed into the floor. The impact of being caught between two bodies knocked the wind out of Galia, leaving her dazed and gasping for air. McGill tore the ligature away from her throat and discarded it.

As Galia continued to struggle to breathe, McGill turned his head and, hoping the White House physician somehow would hear him, shouted, "Nick!"

Charlottesville, Virginia

Damon Todd, Arn Crosby and Olin Anderson watched the freeze frame image of McGill yelling for help. It would go viral on the Web within the hour. Cable news and broadcast TV had it on the air about the same time. Newspapers across the country and around the world would carry the picture by the following day.

Of the millions who saw McGill in action, the three men in the cabin in the woods along the James River in Virginia would prove to be among the most important viewers.

"Sonofabitch is quick," Crosby said.

Anderson nodded. "Strong, too."

Todd went with his specialty. "His decision making was right. He knew that if he didn't react immediately and effectively the woman would have died. That being the case, he didn't allow himself to be inhibited in the least in his application of force. He slammed into the woman as hard as he could and —"

"We don't know that," Crosby said.

Anderson bobbed his head in agreement.

"What do you mean?" Todd asked Crosby. "Did you see McGill hold back in any way?"

"No, he went balls out, in context."

Anderson elaborated. "Look at how he was dressed, in a suit and leather soled shoes. Started from a sitting position. Didn't have much room to build up speed, quick though he was."

Crosby continued the analysis. "A guy his age, he might have had a bit of foot speed in reserve over a short distance, but everybody starts slowing down after a certain point."

"Including the two of you?" Todd asked.

They nodded together like bobble-head dolls.

"It's inevitable,"Crosby said.

"Hand speed is another thing that slows down, but you can help offset that by experience," Anderson added.

"What do you mean?" Todd asked.

Crosby said, "It's like when you're a kid learning to drive. You're going down the street and don't have a clue what the car in front of you is going to do. You're just trying to stay in your lane and not sideswipe somebody or miss seeing a pedestrian stepping off the curb. The better your skills become, you start noticing the *drivers* around you, front, back and sides. You know if they're paying attention, talking on the phone or jerking around some other way. You can feel if they're going to cut you off or make a turn without signaling."

Anderson asked, "You *can* do that, Doc, can't you?"

"Of course," Todd said.

The truth was he didn't drive all that often and wasn't comfortable in heavy traffic.

"Same thing applies when you're going hand to hand with somebody," Anderson said. "There are only so many moves someone can make on you and only so many countermoves you can make in reply."

"But there must be infinite degrees of skill," Todd said.

"Yeah," Crosby agreed, "skill *and* experience. Experience is what lets top-end guys know what's coming intuitively, get a head start on reacting, an edge, even if the other guy's a bit quicker physically."

"And your assessment of McGill in both areas?" Todd asked.

"Must've been a blur in his prime," Crosby said. "Still looks like he hasn't lost much."

Anderson said, "We can't say what techniques he knows just from seeing this one video."

"But from the *way* he moves, we can make educated guesses at what disciplines he might be good at," Anderson added.

"We'd have to watch this video a lot more to pin it down for sure, though," Crosby said.

Todd said, "At the risk of sounding like an adolescent in a schoolyard, do you think you could take him? Could you teach me to cope with him?"

"What could *we* do against him?" Crosby asked. "Not knowing anything more than what we've seen today, all I can say is maybe we'd come out on top."

"That's disappointing," Todd replied. "You were CIA, he was just a cop."

Anderson addressed that point. "We were trained, and he was, too. Doesn't matter where the training came from."

Crosby said, "More to the point, he hasn't been locked up for years. He's been free to practice; we haven't."

"As for you, Doc," Anderson said. "We'd be better off teaching you how to shoot over long distances."

Learning sniper skills had a measure of appeal for Todd, but he said, "I'd still like to acquire some martial arts skills."

Crosby told him, "We call it close quarters combat because combat is on the mark, art isn't."

Todd wasn't dissuaded. He told them he wanted to learn how to fight hand to hand, whatever label was attached to it. Having implanted post hypnotic suggestions in the two men's minds that they should aid him in any reasonable way, they shrugged and said okay.

Told him the best way for any of them to start was to watch the way McGill moved over and over.

That's what they spent the rest of the day doing, watching McGill, thinking about how to attack him and defend themselves against him. They continued to survey live broadcasts hoping to find videos with differing angles of McGill in motion.

The rescue of Galia Mindel wasn't the only news that day, of course, and inevitably they saw some of it.

On one evening newscast, they saw the story of Lydell Martin, a trucker who had become an overnight success as an executive at his transportation company. The segment showed Martin as a bearded trucker and later as a clean shaven executive. It was said he had instituted efficiency programs at his company that had won him a six-figure bonus. The sad part of this Cinderella story, the anchorwoman told her audience, was that Martin hadn't thought he'd been sufficiently rewarded and had been caught embezzling money from his employer.

Martin had been questioned by the police but had been released pending a company decision whether it would press charges or seek alternative reconciliation.

The broadcast went to commercial after that story, and Crosby and Anderson turned to look at Todd. Crosby said, "That's the guy you said it was okay to let go."

"He is okay," Todd said, "he has no conscious memory of us."

"What about his subconscious?" Anderson asked.

Todd reminded them, "The CIA had me for three years and couldn't crack me."

Crosby said, "But this guy seems to be falling apart on his own, unless you put a streak of greed and larceny in him."

Todd shook his head. "No, I didn't do that. I'd better go take a look at him."

Anderson said, "We'll come along."

Indiana University — Bloomington, Indiana

Sheryl Kimbrough had never liked to run, but she'd done it

ever since Cassidy had first shown that it was her preferred form of exercise. There had been many a cold morning when they'd gone out to pound the pavement that Sheryl had wished Cassidy had preferred indoor swimming. That morning, though, with the first cool breath of fall in the air, she almost enjoyed running with her daughter.

She always loved being with Cassidy, had to consciously refrain from looking at her too often or too intensely. It just amazed her that she'd given birth to this beautiful young woman. The odds against it had been high. But the love of running, that had come from Cassidy's father. The ways heredity could play out always impressed her, too.

Still, all the roadwork she'd put in with her daughter had left both of them trim and strong with fantastic resting heart rates. Running in the early morning also gave them the opportunity to tour the IU campus before most of the student body was up and about. They cruised through the Old Crescent section, past the Memorial Union, across Dunn Meadow. The school grounds were beautiful in all four seasons.

Sheryl knew of Cassidy's desire to go to Stanford, and it was a source of pride that her daughter's classwork in high school made reaching for an elite college a reasonable ambition, but some of Sheryl's best years had been, and most of her heart remained, at IU. She was so happy to be home again.

"Is your Hoosier pride showing again, Mom," Cassidy asked as they jogged side by side, "or is there some other reason for that silly grin you're wearing?"

Sheryl looked at her daughter and broadened her smile.

"I'm just overjoyed to be in my favorite place with my favorite person."

Without breaking stride, Cassidy gave her mother a peck on the cheek.

"Will you keep running when I'm in college?" she asked.

"I will if you're here," Sheryl said. "If you go off to Palo Alto, I'll sit at home in a house dress and eat bonbons any time I'm not teaching."

Cassidy laughed. "You will not, and besides I'm thinking about adding Georgetown to my list of college choices."

"You want to go back to D.C.?"

"Blame it on growing up there, Dad being there and … James J. McGill."

Sheryl cast a look at her daughter.

"You're kidding, right, about Mr. McGill?"

Cassidy's step faltered. "You know him?"

"I met him once, briefly, when Senator Talbert asked me to accompany him to a dinner at the White House."

A note of both excitement and complaint entered Cassidy's voice.

"You never told me that."

"I did. It was three years ago. You were unimpressed."

"Well … I was just a kid then. Barely out of middle school. Now —"

"You have a young woman's crush on a much older man?"

Cassidy turned her face away from her mother but her blush covered her neck, too.

Keeping her eyes on the path ahead, she said, "Okay, yeah. I recognize it for what it is, something silly. But what he did, saving the White House chief of staff and then holding her while he called for help … it gave me an idea of what I should look for when the time comes."

Sheryl nodded. "I wouldn't object if you brought someone like Mr. McGill — only a generation younger — home someday."

Cassidy looked at her mother and waggled her eyebrows.

"I wouldn't either."

Both of them laughed as they left the campus and headed for home.

"I think it says something good about President Grant that she has a husband like him."

"Yes, it does. It says she's a *lucky* woman."

"She's a terrific president, too. It so bums me out I'll never get to vote for her."

The subtext came through loud and clear to Sheryl.

She would have the opportunity to vote for Patricia Darden Grant.

Including the time it would matter most, in the Electoral College.

Never mind that her vote was pledged to the Republican nominee.

As they neared their new house, Sheryl slowed her pace, let Cassidy go on ahead and sighed.

Q Street — Washington, D.C.

Having left her job at the White House and not needing to rise early for her new job with Mather Wyman's presidential campaign, Kira Fahey Yates was sleeping in. The curtains in her bedroom were drawn and the only light came from the clock radio. When a warm nude body slipped under the covers and cozied up to her, she purred.

"Mmm," she said, "you feel almost as good as my husband."

"Would you like me to send for him?"

"No, he's off in some island paradise, no doubt consorting with native girls."

"What does consorting involve, specifically?"

"Letting them see how gorgeous he is, charming them silly, leading them right up to the brink and then blithely stepping aside as they fall head over heels in love with him."

"Not high heels, surely. I have it on good authority that island girls usually go about barefoot."

"You keep a sharp eye on women's feet, do you?"

"That's where I start. If the pedicure passes muster, I work my way up."

Kira pressed her bottom against the visitor.

"I start in the middle, then decide which way to look."

"Depending on whether you're in the mood for thighs or abs?"

"Depending on which direction the gentleman is facing."

The visitor snuggled closer. He kissed Kira's shoulder.

"Deltoids often go unappreciated," he said.

"Only by those who don't know better. I like to bite them."

The visitor brushed Kira's hair aside and kissed the back of her neck.

She shivered. "How did you know to do that?"

"There was a note on the bedroom door."

"Of course. The maid leaves hints for first-timers."

"That was the only one I saw. Do I have to figure out the rest for myself?"

"Do your best, but try not to be ordinary."

The visitor let a lock of his hair fall forward and used it to trace the length of Kira's spine. She shuddered, rolled over and took the visitor's face in her hands.

"Oh, it's you, Welborn," Kira said.

"So glad you remember me."

"Couldn't stay away, flyboy?"

"After hearing you'd left the White House, I thought it best to visit before you made any other life-altering decisions."

She pulled him to her and said, "We can talk politics later."

Sitting at the breakfast table sipping orange juice and nibbling a *pain au chocolat* he had brought home, Welborn asked Kira, "So you're a … spy?"

"In effect, though that does sound overly dramatic. A snoop with portfolio might be more accurate."

"The duties of your portfolio being to get Uncle Mather elected president."

"*Exactement,*" Kira said, biting into her own French pastry.

"You do recall I work for the current and future president?"

"I'll concede the present to you; we'll see about the future."

"Moving on," Welborn said, "your current responsibilities are to vet prospective vice presidential candidates who might join your uncle on the Republican ticket?"

"Unofficially. There are rafts of lawyers, accountants and doctors to look into the obvious nooks and crannies. Do the wannabes have criminal records of any sort? Might their tax returns raise a stink? Is there a family history of kleptomania? You know, the sorts of things that are committed to writing."

"Whereas you will deal with what exactly?" Welborn asked.

"Before pen and paper, there was an oral tradition of story-telling."

Welborn smiled. "Ah, you're the campaign's gossip columnist."

"Gossip to be shared with a select few," Kira said.

"People often lie, you'll remember."

"Men especially, but I'm quite discerning about such things."

Welborn ignored the sexist gibe.

"You do have the social standing and graces to move in the highest circles."

Kira said, "In my case, social circles to the right of the political spectrum. Mattie said Democrats would find me suspect. I won't be snooping on the president's side of the aisle."

Welborn experienced a small measure of relief.

Until Kira pointed out, "You, however, might be tainted, sleeping with the enemy."

"I'll tell everyone it's just a physical thing."

"Speaking of which, do you have to get right back to your barefoot girls?"

"They're very patient. What do you have in mind?"

She showed him. As they were about to drift off to sleep in each other's arms, Welborn said in a tone that was unusually serious, "I won't ask you to give away any secrets, but just in case you overhear something that rises above and beyond political chatter —"

"You mean a matter of national security?" Kira asked.

"Mock me if you will, but if you hear anything that scares you, I'll want to know."

"If things get to that point, flyboy, I'll keep you fully informed."

She kissed him and began to doze.

Realizing just before she fell asleep that she might have missed taking her birth control pill that day.

Department of Justice Building — Washington, D.C.

Attorney General Michael Jaworsky sat behind his desk making his way through the reports that called for his immediate attention. The stack of paperwork led him to think he'd become the victim of one of history's great curses. The original malediction was thought to be either Chinese or English. Might have been either. Curses traveled well.

May you live in interesting times, that was the wording.

The meaning was: May you experience much vexation and upheaval.

Jaworsky's secretary buzzed and announced his first challenges of the day in two words, "They're here."

"Please send in Mrs. Godfrey first."

"Mr. Williams would —"

"He can wait," the AG said.

"Yes, sir."

Erna Godfrey was escorted into Jaworsky's office by a female correctional officer. Both women wore off-the-rack pantsuits, the officer's from her closet, Erna's courtesy of the federal government. The widow of Reverend Burke Godfrey also wore handcuffs and leg restraints.

"Please have a seat, Mrs. Godfrey," Jaworsky said.

"Thank you, sir."

The officer helped her into a visitor's chair.

Jaworsky said, "Officer, please wait outside."

The woman didn't like that but was in no position to argue.

She did step forward, picked up a letter opener lying on the AG's desk and handed it to him.

He nodded his thanks and put the pointed implement in a desk drawer.

Once he and Erna were alone, the AG said, "We have two

matters to discuss, Mrs. Godfrey. I'd like to start with the medical report on your husband's cause of death."

"I was told it was a stroke," Erna said, suspecting correctly she was about to learn more. "Benton Williams, outside, wanted to talk with me, but your people wouldn't let him."

"You'll have the opportunity to speak with him, but I wanted you to hear from me first."

Erna bobbed her head. "All right."

"Just before the siege of Salvation's Path began, your husband was being interviewed by a woman named Ellie Booker, a producer of television programming for WorldWide News. Ms. Booker claims she was being held prisoner by your husband. She managed to lay hands on a pistol and used it to hit your husband on the head."

"She killed Burke?"

"No, she injured him, seriously enough to require hospitalization, but he was recovering from the trauma when the stroke that killed him occurred."

Erna frowned. "Did the one thing lead to the other?"

Jaworsky kept himself from sighing. "The truth is, no one really knows. As I said, your husband was making clear progress in recovering from his injury, and the medical examiner's report says that your husband suffered from several risk factors for stroke: age, obesity, high blood pressure, high cholesterol and atrial fibrillation. The medical consensus is that in his later years your husband was a prime candidate for a cerebral vascular accident at any time."

The AG opened the medical examiner's report and placed it so Erna might read its conclusion. As she read, tears formed in her eyes. Jaworsky handed her a tissue.

"The president called me," Erna said. "Told me Burke was gone and she was sorry everything had to come to this."

"I've heard that, yes."

"I only hope he had the time to beg the Lord's forgiveness before he went."

"We should all be so fortunate," Jaworsky said. He gave Erna a moment and then asked, "Mrs. Godfrey, I need to know the extent to which you wish to cooperate with the government in prosecuting the people you've named as committing illegal acts against abortion providers and clinics. If you do wish to provide ongoing cooperation until the last of the prosecutions is concluded, you'll be kept —"

"Outside of prison?" Erna asked. She shook her head. "No, I want to go back."

Jaworsky took that to mean Mrs. Godfrey's cooperation was at an end.

"Do you realize the fact that you've already helped us means you'll be at an increased risk of danger while you're incarcerated? That being the case, the government is obligated to offer you solitary confinement for your own protection."

Erna said, "I have no fear of death, sir. I won't try to kill myself again, but if I can't start a ministry in prison and try to help other women, there won't be much point of going on."

Jaworsky looked closely at the woman, searching for any sign of deceit.

Finding none, he said, "I'll have to ask you to sign a statement saying you were offered protective custody and declined it."

"I'll do that right now, if you let me start my ministry."

"That will be up to the Bureau of Prisons, and I'll need witnesses when you sign the statement. Now, I need to inform you that Mr. Williams would like to talk with you about bringing a wrongful death suit against Ms. Booker and WorldWide News. Whether you allow Mr. Williams to pursue that suit is up to you, but you should know you won't be allowed to benefit monetarily from any judgment or settlement."

A smile appeared on Erna's face. "Why would I care about money?"

"There's no reason at all, but I have to make the situation clear."

"Mr. Williams doesn't want to sue the government, too?"

"He said no, but I don't believe him."

"You're a very honest man, Mr. Jaworsky."

"I go to confession every Saturday with my mother, Mrs.

Godfrey."

"So you understand the comfort the clergy can bring. Maybe you could have a word with the Bureau of Prisons about my ministry. All I want to do is help poor women."

The AG thought he'd need to speak with the president first.

"Will you reconsider helping me to prosecute the people you've named?" he asked.

"I'll pray that they see the light and sin no more."

Jaworsky nodded. "Pray that they beg the Lord's forgiveness, too."

He called for Benton Williams to be admitted. With the lawyer came the correctional officer watching over Erna, the AG's secretary and a videographer. Discussing the possibility of a federal prisoner initiating a civil suit, as Jaworsky had informed Williams earlier, was not a matter covered by attorney-client privilege.

Everyone got to hear, and in the case of the videographer, record the lawyer's conversation with the prisoner. Erna flatly refused to become a party to any suit. Her concerns, she said, were celestial not civil.

Perhaps as a matter of pique, Benton Williams agreed to be one of the witnesses to Erna Godfrey signing the statement saying she wished to be housed among the general population in whatever correctional facility was chosen for her by the Bureau of Prisons.

Before Erna was taken away Attorney General Jaworsky told her, "I will consider your request to start a ministry, Mrs. Godfrey."

Once he was alone again, the AG took up the next matter on his schedule.

A Super-PAC and a TV station in Mississippi, per the president's directive, were going to be tried for fraud for running an attack ad against the president that was substantively false. A whistle-blower would also state that, contravening FEC regulations and a Supreme Court decision, the ad had been a coordinated effort between the Super-PAC and Senator Howard Hurlbert's True South campaign.

More interesting times ahead for me, the AG thought.

The Super-PAC and True South, though, would be facing their

own classic curse.

May you come to the attention of those in authority.

The Mandarin Oriental Hotel — Washington, D.C.

Hugh Collier told Sir Edbert Bickford, "I could flog you, if you like."

The media tycoon cast a sour look at his once favorite nephew.

"In a strictly non-sexual way," Hugh added.

Sir Edbert turned his attention back to the oversized flat screen television.

The clip of James J. McGill saving the life of Galia Mindel played on a continuous loop. As it had all day long. As it had for more days than Hugh cared to think about. Uncle would sit and watch and drink Scotch. Hugh couldn't recall the old tripehound getting up to relieve himself.

Made him think the old saw about having a hollow leg had some truth to it.

Also that it was possible to survive without one's liver.

All one had to do was persist on pure bitterness.

Hugh tried again as he saw the televised McGill leap up from his chair yet again. "You'd think the least the blighter could do is rip off his clothes and reveal himself as —"

Sir Edbert clicked the TV off.

"Superman," Hugh finished.

"Would you have had the courage to do that?" Sir Edbert asked his nephew.

"Uncle, James J. Bloody McGill was never in any danger. What courage was re —"

Sir Edbert held up a hand and said, "He might have *failed*, with the whole world looking on. He might have arrived after the woman's head was halfway removed. He might have wound up *causing* her death despite his best intentions. He might have put a foot wrong and broken his own damn neck."

Hugh had watched the loop more times than he'd bothered to

count.

McGill had barely put a hair amiss, much less a foot wrong.

Coming 'round to Uncle's question, Hugh said, "Yes, I think I would have done much the same thing. If I'd failed, the blokes I know, back in Oz anyway, would still have stood me to drinks all night for trying."

"Taken you home and tucked you in?"

Twitting him about being gay. Hugh grinned. The old man's supply of bile was endless.

"Kissed me nighty-night, too."

Sir Edbert shook his head and moved on. "You think we've been wrong, not joining the mob in singing hosannas to the beggar?"

Hugh nodded. "It makes *us* look small, and you know as well as I do that judges are human. When WWN goes to trial, we'll want all the good will we can gather, both inside and outside the courtroom. Praising McGill's courage, no matter how we feel about him, would simply be good politics. I *told* you that, even if all your toadies were too fearful."

Hugh thought Ellie would have told him so, too, but one battle at a time.

"Are we too late now?"

"To use an Americanism, we'll look like we're playing catch up. Still, it's better to be on the record than not. I also told you what we *really* need to do."

"Set new standards in practicing objective journalism."

Sir Edbert looked as if he was ready to call room service for a cup of hemlock.

"That's right, and you won't be able to do it with the same pack of hacks who spout the party line right now."

"Change the talent?" Apparently, the notion came as a complete surprise to Sir Edbert.

"Start with O'Dell," Hugh said.

"He has the highest ratings," Sir Edbert protested.

"You don't even like the Irish, and he's a sod." This time, Hugh held up a hand, forestalling further objection. "He also has the highest salary on the network. Get rid of him and you can hire *three* first-class journalists for the same price. After O'Dell is gone, start knocking off the other marquee names. Put the resources into honest news gathering. You'll knock the competition on their arses."

"And our friends in Washington?" Sir Edbert asked.

"Your *pawns* in Washington? They will have to find new masters."

"And the sweetener?" Sir Edbert asked.

Hugh always saved his best arguments for last, the media tycoon knew.

"You'll displace McGill as the hero *de jour*, you'll be in a much stronger position when you have your day in court and if, by chance, one of your new people finds real dirt on Patti Grant, it will be seen as a scoop not a smear."

The dear boy. He finally put a smile on his old uncle's lips.

"You're feeling better, Uncle?" Hugh asked.

"I am … so well that I've just decided to approve Colonel Linberg's TV show."

Aboard Irish Grace — 20° North, 82° West

Carina Linberg was sailing the Caribbean for the first time, making way ahead of a steady wind from the Northwest. Grand Cayman Island lay ahead, a blurry speck in the distance. So far, the passage from Key West had been a piece of cake. Clear skies and seas with nothing worse than moderate swells. She'd been careful to stay outside Cuba's territorial waters as she'd skirted the western tip of the island. No patrol vessels from the *Marina de Guerra Revolucionaria* challenged her.

Upon reaching the twelve-mile limit of Cayman waters, she'd called Island Port Security, identified herself and her vessel and requested permission to proceed directly to the Barcadere Marina where she'd rented a slip. Permission was granted for her to clear customs at the marina. As she approached the island and watched it grow sharper and larger in her vision, she wondered how her life might have been different if Captain Dexter Cowan, USN, had been a decent guy or even just a horny Navy man instead of a Pentagon provocateur who'd set out to ruin her military career.

Dex, though, had been nothing more than a handsome pawn. Former Air Force Chief of Staff General Warren Altman had been the man making all the moves. He'd dumped Carina as his lover after she'd reached the rank of colonel; he'd feared that if she got even one star on her shoulder she might become too independent for him. There would no fun in that. It was so much more enjoyable when the woman under you in bed was also under your thumb.

Altman had told her that to her face, the bastard.

He'd also said she had lost sex appeal as she rose in rank.

Carina had hit back, hoping to wound Altman as deeply as she could. Her idea had been to show the bastard that *all* the women in his life had screwed him only to get ahead. Including his wife, Cheryl. Given a choice, Cheryl would even prefer another woman to him.

It had turned out that Carina didn't need to seduce Mrs. Altman. She needed only to get Mrs. Altman moderately drunk before the general's wife admitted knowing that Carina had been one of her husband's many lovers. Cheryl Altman thought it laughable that Carina had conceived the idea of seducing her. She had long thought she should see for herself what was so great about all the whores her husband screwed.

The forty-five minutes the two women spent in bed together was nothing more than an exercise in mutual debasement. Carina still cringed when she thought about it. Wanted to put it permanently out of mind. She'd never imagined that Cheryl Altman would go home and gloat to her husband about what she had done, and what a mistake he'd made leaving Colonel Linberg.

If the general was any kind of man, Mrs. Altman said, he would take both her and the colonel on at the same time. Altman, who followed only his own orders and had already targeted his next military mistress, slapped his wife so hard he knocked her out. When she regained her senses, Mrs. Altman called Carina to warn her that retribution would surely be coming her way, too.

Not that it could take the form of a beating. The Uniform Code of Military Justice forbade corporal abuse. The general didn't want to ruin his own career. So he'd sent Captain Dexter Cowan, posing as a divorced man, Carina's way. After Dex and Carina had slept together, their affair was *discovered,* and only then had Carina learned her new lover was a married man.

Adultery was also forbidden by the UCMJ.

At least for those without four stars on their shoulders.

Carina faced not only losing her rank but also being imprisoned at Fort Leavenworth. She learned without question that a chief of staff's revenge could go far beyond anything she might conceive. Then the possibility of Carina standing before a court-martial fell apart when Dex Cowan got himself killed. No witness, no prosecution.

Dex had been told that General Altman's connections would help land him a lucrative post-military career in the defense industry. The irony was both Carina and General Altman soon left the Air Force and went to work as military analysts for competing media outlets. In television, though, military rank took second place to other considerations; a good-looking woman got better ratings and bigger money than a grumpy old man. In that way, at least, she'd trumped the bastard.

If Carina had anyone to thank for squeaking through a very tough situation and coming out a free woman, it was the young Air Force investigator who had been assigned to her case, Lieutenant Welborn Yates. It might have helped that he'd developed a crush on her. That and, according to the rumors she'd heard, having James J. McGill give him uncredited guidance.

As she struck her sails and motored slowly toward the marina, she received a text message from her agent. Sir Edbert Bickford had approved her idea for a TV pilot. Discussions regarding finding a director, casting and a production budget would begin at her earliest convenience.

Carina beamed, feeling as if she'd just been reborn. Again.

She wanted to celebrate, but her mood ebbed when she realized she had no one with whom to share her good news. Then she though to hell with that. She'd find —

Welborn Yates. He was standing at the end of the breakwater watching *Irish Grace* arrive.

He brought himself to a posture of attention and gave Carina a crisp salute.

Without a second's hesitation, she returned it.

Pennyman's Cafe — Grand Cayman Island

Welborn Yates had spent less than twelve hours with Kira before he turned around and went back to the Caribbean. George Town was in no way a hardship posting, and after a brief discussion with the president, he had been given permission to stay there at government expense for as long a time as he thought reasonable, but he missed his bride. The irony of whiling away time alone in what for many couples would be a honeymoon destination — after he'd cut his own honeymoon short — was not lost on him.

In fact, it grated.

So did the fact that Kira had acted unilaterally in making her decision to leave the White House. He couldn't blame her for supporting Mather Wyman. The man was her uncle, her *de facto* father, really. Welborn knew he would do almost anything for his mother and was feeling progressively better about his own father, whom he'd met only recently. So, considering matters on a rational plane, he could hardly blame Kira for ...

Aligning herself with the second best candidate in the presidential sweepstakes.

Welborn wouldn't vote for his mother ahead of Patricia Darden Grant.

Maybe it was just the lack of consideration that bothered him.

Would it have been so hard for Kira to at least give him fair warning?

He took a deep breath and got a grip on himself. The bastard responsible for killing his three best friends was bound to show up soon. If he wasn't too busy sulking, he'd put Linley Boland in handcuffs and take him back to Washington. March him through the streets and put him to the sword on the National Mall as thousands cheered.

Welborn grinned at the flight of fancy.

"About time your storm clouds blew over. You were scaring off the tourists."

He looked up and saw Willa Pennyman give him a wink. The café bearing her family name was operating at capacity. The only open chair on the terrace was the one opposite Welborn. Willa took it and asked, "The villain you're chasing didn't get nicked by someone else, did he? That's not what's causing your tropical depression?"

Welborn shook his head.

"He's still out there. I'm sure you would have told me if you'd turned him in for the reward."

"I'd have my hand out, if I did. Actually, I have the Pennyman family watching the whole bloody island for your bloke."

"There are that many of you?"

Willa nodded. "We're a fertile lot."

Welborn wasn't going anywhere near that one.

"So he couldn't have nipped into the bank and slipped out unnoticed?"

She shook her head.

"I have a cousin drives a taxi. He could give you a tour of the island. Maybe you'd see your villain coming in at the airport or sailing into George Town harbor. Meanwhile, we'd get our table back. Turn it over a few times, make some money."

"You'll have someone watching the bank?"

"Luv, we have someone in the bank. A hundred thousand dollars goes a long way among working folk on this island." A thought crossed Willa's mind and she took Welborn's hand in a way that wasn't at all flirtatious. "I hope you're not having me on about all that money."

"No, ma'am," Welborn said.

Willa matched his words to his eyes, and patted his hand.

With a summoning gesture, she brought a taxi to the curb next to Welborn's table.

"Eddie'll take you anywhere you want to go, charge you only standard fare. Go see what the tide brings in."

Stretching his legs on the breakwater at Barcadere Marina after hours in the taxi, Welborn was surprised to see the tide bring in former Colonel Carina Linberg, suntanned and looking like the million dollars it must have cost to buy the boat she was helming.

Reacting to the presence of a superior officer as he'd been trained, he saluted her.

He was pleased when she returned the salute.

It would be rude, Welborn thought, not to welcome the colonel ashore.

Camp David — Catoctin Mountains, Maryland

"No good deed goes unpunished," McGill told Patti.

He was sitting in the whirlpool in the master bathroom at Aspen Lodge. Patti had just flown in from the White House that Saturday morning. McGill had picked Abbie up from school a day early, Thursday, and they'd made their way to the presidential retreat to escape hounding from the media.

The final straw had been when WorldWide News had contacted Aggie Wu to request an interview with McGill, and had made assurances that it wouldn't be a hostile piece.

Following the instructions McGill had left, Aggie declined on his behalf, explaining as she had to all the other newsies that, "Mr. McGill injured his lower back in coming to the aid of Chief of Staff Mindel. He'll be recuperating for the foreseeable future."

"Coming to the aid" was the official language used to describe McGill's actions.

He might have helped an old lady cross the street.

A soft sell might be peddled to the press, but it didn't hold up when Aaron and Joshua Mindel called to thank McGill for saving their mother's life. He could hear the two young men choke back the fear of having almost lost Galia. McGill wasn't going to disrespect that, didn't try to deny the significance of what he'd done.

"Your mother and I are the closest of rivals," he told Aaron and Josh. "Each of us thinks we know what's best for the president. I have the upper hand, but I need Galia to keep me honest."

Galia's sons laughed and Aaron said, "Mom loves you, too, Mr. McGill."

McGill joined in the laughter, and then turned serious. "Galia was also tested as a potential bone marrow donor for my son, Kenny. I'll never forget that."

"A mitzvah," Josh explained.

"For me, too," McGill said.

He told Galia's sons he wished her a swift recovery. She'd suffered a laceration of her esophagus that had been surgically repaired. John Patrick Granby had done the damage with the length of fishing line he'd secreted in his necktie. Galia was recovering in New York. She had made news from her hospital bed when, following doctor's orders not to speak unnecessarily, she'd allowed a pool photographer into her room.

In her right hand she'd held up a photo of General Douglas MacArthur bearing a caption of his famous vow, "I shall return." In her left hand, Galia held up a handwritten note, "Me, too."

Various talking heads had sniffed that if Galia could throw them a bone, McGill could, too.

McGill wouldn't play ball with the media. He had tweaked his back.

The muscle strain, however, hadn't been so bad that he'd failed to honor his promise to Kenny to continue his Dark Alley lessons, but with both Abbie and Caitie on hand for the weekend they insisted on being included in the instruction, too. Having no reasonable way to exclude his daughters, McGill gave in. Teaching three students, showing them proper technique, making sure none of them did any unintended harm to the others, he'd aggravated his back.

Took it for a hot, swirling soak in Aspen Lodge, where Patti found him.

Then he'd complained about the back pain being reverse karma.

"Your good deed has not gone unrewarded," she told him.

"How's that?" McGill asked.

Patti held up a printout of a computer screen capture.

"Your public approval rating across five major polls is a cumulative eighty-nine percent."

McGill said, "Whoop-ti-do."

"A likable spouse is a decided plus for a presidential candidate. That would be me. You were helpful last time, too."

Last time. McGill had an abiding regret about not being able to save Andy Grant's life. Finding Andy's killer, he thought, was a poor substitute. The public, however, had found Erna Godfrey's swift arrest compelling. If Patti still found comfort in it, he wouldn't argue.

"Thank you. Whatever I can do for you, I will. Short of talking to WorldWide News."

"Something's going on over there," Patti said.

"Like what? Sir Edbert has renounced his title?"

"Close. He's fired Mike O'Dell."

"Mike Odious, gone? The madhouse won't be the same without him."

"Aggie says the rumors are there will be a wholesale change of on-air talent."

"The apocalypse nears. Or it's one big fake-out."

Patti asked, "What do you mean?"

"As you know, I normally don't read more than the sports section, but I thought I saw the DOJ was going to take World-Wide News to court, something about bribing cops in England."

"That's right," Patti said.

She started to take off her clothes. McGill gave her a look.

"I'm a little stiff myself. I believe there's room enough for two in there."

"Sure, there is, but I've already lost my train of thought."

Patti slipped into the swirling water next to McGill.

"There, now you can't see a thing other than my smiling face."

"Yeah, but there's what I've already seen."

"You were saying an editorial change at WWN might be a ploy, and when we're done talking shop we might turn to personal matters."

The former actress having clearly explained his motivation, McGill moved on.

He said, "You were the one who told me the October Surprise is a classic move in a presidential campaign. So what if Sir Edbert is only pretending to make himself look like a good corporate citizen, an evenhanded supplier of news instead of a partisan propagandist, to bolster his position in court. Then, once the verdict comes in, he's free to either revert to form or get revenge for being found guilty. In either case, that October Surprise would really *be* a surprise."

Patti put her head on McGill's shoulder and thought about that.

She looked up at him and asked, "By any chance, are you channeling Galia these days?"

"Are my hips getting big?" McGill asked.

He got an underwater pinch for that one.

Securing his wife's hands, he said, "I can be a devious thinker, too. You Washington types don't have a monopoly on that."

"No, but we're pretty good at it. May I have my hands back?"

McGill let go, but didn't relax until Patti kissed his cheek.

"I'll be good," she said.

"What sort of deviousness were you referring to just now, if it isn't a state secret?"

"It's only politics, but let's keep it between us."

McGill nodded his assent.

"In my talks with the Democrats, I allowed them to think I'd select Roger Michaelson as my vice president."

McGill said, "And you promised I wouldn't pummel him again?"

"That topic didn't arise; I think it's understood."

"So you're about to pull the rug out from under old Roger?"

"Not overtly. But here's something that's not general knowledge yet. Governor Jean Morrissey of Minnesota is also considering a run for the Democratic nomination. What would you think if I, quietly, through third parties, directed resources her way?"

"To what end, that she'd come in second to you but ahead of Michaelson?"

Patti nodded.

McGill said, "That'd be a fine needle to thread, wouldn't it?"

"I think I can do it."

"You'll run the idea by Galia?"

"Yes."

"And the result would be the first all-female presidential ticket?" McGill asked.

"How's that for a shocker?" Patti replied.

"You've got my vote, of course. Better Morrissey than Michaelson. I imagine it would have lots of women cheering, but how —"

"Will it play with most men? It won't with any man who wouldn't vote for me anyway. Of the rest, like you, I think most will stick with me. I should pick up more female votes than lose male votes."

"Could give you a powerful lobbying position with Congress after the election, too. You could rally most of the women in the country for issues you'd claim will directly affect their well being."

Patti smiled. "You're really becoming quite the student of politics."

She swung a leg over McGill, sat astride him.

"We're done talking shop?" he asked.

"Just about. You're not going stir crazy up here at Camp David, are you?"

"I love the time I spend with Kenny but, God willing, he'll be returning to a more normal life soon. Once he goes home, I'm not going to hide out here. I can be useful to others. See Ms. Galia Mindel for a reference. I *do* hope Byron DeWitt and company can catch Damon Todd, but there's any number of bad guys who need an application of justice."

"Deputy Director DeWitt has informed me that the first move has been made to snare Dr. Todd."

McGill held up a hand and crossed two fingers.

"Anything else?" he asked.

Patti leaned into McGill and told him, "I've lost my train of thought."

Dude's Sports Bar — Wilmington, Delaware

The following Monday evening, Damon Todd, Arn Crosby and Olin Anderson had their coming out party at a "great little local bar," according to the review on Google, on the corner of Union and Fourth. The beer was cold, the service was friendly and nobody paid untoward attention to the three men from out of state. But then as Anderson had put it, "Nobody'd ever think of looking for anyone in Wilmington. Bin Laden would be alive today if he'd hidden out in Delaware."

Nonetheless, they'd all taken precautions to alter their appearances. Dye, facial hair, baseball caps and in Anderson's case makeup to render the scar on his forehead less obvious were all put to use. To Todd's surprise, the former covert operatives did a passable South Boston accent to go with their Red Sox caps. Todd's cap featured only a Nike swoosh. So he went with inflectionless California tones.

They hadn't left their retreat in the Virginia woods because of cabin fever.

Well, not *just* because of growing claustrophobia.

They were out trying to learn why Lydell Martin wasn't behaving the way Todd had programmed him. That was of particular concern to Crosby and Anderson as Todd had made them new and improved versions of their former selves. They liked the fact that they felt mentally sharper and physically stronger than they had in years, but the idea Todd might have installed faulty software in their heads, too, was not comforting.

They hadn't talked about it, but Crosby and Anderson each had the idea they should kill Todd, leave his body on a bench next to a bus stop and hope their offering to the powers that be would buy them a measure of leniency if not outright forgiveness. Thing was, they weren't able to conspire. That should have been the most natural thing in the world for two guys like them. As much blood as they had shed together, they couldn't tell their barbarities apart.

Each time one of them came close to acting on the idea a question popped up in his head: *What if this fucker has set a booby-trap in my brain that only he can defuse?*

If that was the case, and they killed Todd, then where would they be?

Todd had, of course, left that warning in their minds, while they'd been drugged on ketamine hydrochloride. Not that they could recall that. Things that happened in the K-hole *really* stayed in the K-hole.

Despite everything, Crosby and Anderson both thought it would be a good idea to see just what had gone wrong with Lydell Martin. That might help them determine how much trouble they were in. Might give them a clue what they could do about it. So they all went to Wilmington.

The waitress, a honey who had to be pushing forty but was still looking good, especially to two guys who hadn't enjoyed any female company in years, brought their burgers and fries and another round of brew.

"You guys need anything else, give a yell," she said and walked away.

Todd was the only who didn't watch her backside depart.

Crosby and Anderson noticed his lack of interest.

"You don't play for the other team, do you, Doc?" Anderson asked.

"Am I gay? No, but I set my sights a bit higher."

Todd's thoughts — other than those directed at Lydell Martin and James J. McGill — were focused on Chana Lochlan. He definitely wanted to renew acquaintances with her.

"Why be fussy?" Crosby asked. "Couldn't you fix up any old girl?"

Todd chose to ignore the implicit criticism.

He said, "We're here to do business, remember?"

Both of his companions nodded. Truth was, Crosby and Anderson were impressed by what Todd had set up. Damn CIA had been dumber than shit not to make use of Todd's talents.

Todd wanted to see what Lydell Martin's problem was, but maybe some bright guy at the Agency had made a good guess how the three of them had gotten away from the Funny Farm. As a next step, the hunters might have spotted the truck driver who'd made those big career moves, figured he'd had some help getting ahead in the world. That would have taken sharp thinking, but it could have happened, and it was always a mistake to underestimate the opposition.

So unless they wanted to be dicks who got caught easy, they had to take precautions.

They wouldn't go poking around the truck depot where Martin worked, just up the turnpike in New Jersey. They'd stayed in Delaware where they were only three guys having a bite to eat. Not bothering anybody, blending right in.

What Todd had done was send four of his *friends* to birddog Martin. Each of them, two men and two women, was a successful person with no criminal record. All of them drove different makes of upscale cars. Each car was painted a shade of gray meant to deflect attention rather than attract it. Each friend had a smart phone with a video camera.

The four of them — coming from different directions, separated by quarter-mile intervals — had been instructed to cruise past the depot as the office staff left work.

They emailed their video clips of workers departing the depot to the iPad Todd concealed behind the open newspaper he was pretending to read. Once the clip was received it was acknowledged and the friend deleted it from his or her phone. Then he or she circled back from another direction and made another pass by the depot, taking more video.

The great thing was, even if some cop, fed or spook nailed one or all of Todd's friends, they would have no conscious recall of what they'd been doing. They could be water boarded and they wouldn't give up anything. Their root personas, the upgraded versions of whom they'd been since birth, the ones the authorities would find, were dissociated from the covert personalities doing all the dirty work.

Crosby and Anderson thought this was the greatest thing since complimentary call girls.

"Got him," Todd said softly.

The two former spooks had been contenting themselves with their food and beer — Todd hadn't touched his — but both were eager to see the video that was coming in. Like children who had been well drilled in table manners, though, they'd waited their turns.

Todd sent a musical cue — the melody line from Sting's "Every Breath You Take" — to all four friends, instructing them what they should do next. After making sure the waitress wasn't hovering nearby, Todd slid the iPad over to Crosby and Anderson.

Concealing the computer between them, they hunched over and watched the video. Sure enough, there was Lydell Martin. He was wearing a suit, not jeans and a flannel shirt. He had a new beard now, one of those three-day shadow things. Whatever he'd had before as his personal wheels, a pickup maybe, had been traded in for a Mercedes sedan — painted gray.

That was when it clicked for Crosby and Anderson. They looked at each other, thinking the same thing: Mistake. Martin's car fit too neatly with those the friends were driving. The one they were driving, too. The pattern was easy to see now. They should have picked it up right off. Would have if they weren't so rusty. Their oversight told them something about Todd, too.

He might have been smart as hell in his own way, but he was an amateur in fieldcraft.

Thing was, they couldn't bring themselves to say anything

about it. Not to each other. Not to Todd. That didn't mean Todd couldn't see the looks on their faces.

"What is it?" he asked. "Is something wrong?"

They should have told him. They *wanted* to tell him. They couldn't.

Todd's own safeguards were preventing him from gaining information he needed.

"Nothing's wrong," Crosby said. He slid the tablet back to Todd.

"Not a thing," Anderson confirmed. "We got the bastard."

The four friends would follow Martin home, watch every move he made, rotating positions as they tailed him. They would relay Martin's address to Todd. Tell him if it looked like anyone was with Martin in his dwelling or watching the place. Then they'd go their separate ways, retire for the night and wake up thinking they'd spent the prior evening at home.

If there was no sign of a trap at Martin's house and he appeared to be home alone, Todd, Crosby and Anderson would pay him a visit. If he had company they'd come back another time.

Crosby settled their bill with cash. Anderson got Todd's permission to chug his beer and ask for a doggie bag for his uneaten burger and fries.

Crosby felt things were starting to come apart and didn't like it. He made a move sly enough for Todd not to notice. He left a big tip. The kind that would make any serving person take a good look at a customer. Crosby was able to call attention to the three of them because there was no prohibition in his head about conspiring with a third party.

Learning he had some freedom of movement made Crosby smile.

When the waitress saw the size of her tip she smiled back at him.

Told all of them to come back again real soon.

As they reached the gray Omni that they'd borrowed from Fletcher Penrose, their host in Virginia, Todd stopped dead in his tracks. He'd been gnawing at the looks of doubt he'd seen on Crosby and Anderson's faces. Something was definitely wrong.

Crosby opened the driver's door to get behind the wheel.

The dome light went on, illuminating the interior.

That was when Todd saw the problem.

Fairfax Road — Drexel Hill, Pennsylvania

Deputy Director of the FBI Byron DeWitt sat at the kitchen table of the house on Fairfax Road. The house sat at the rear of a large lot. It had spacious yards in front and to each side. Close behind the house was a thick stand of trees, separating it from the neighboring house on Lakeview Avenue. The bureau owned both houses. The two structures were connected by an underground passageway that didn't appear on any building permit records.

The houses were used as temporary shelter for witnesses testifying on behalf of federal prosecutors in nearby Philadelphia. The protected persons would enter one house and exit through the other. Each house was guarded around the clock by a minimum of two special agents.

DeWitt stood up as Lydell Martin entered the kitchen.

He shook the man's hand and said, "The government deeply appreciates your help, Mr. Martin."

Martin said, "I don't know what's going on here. I don't know how I stopped slacking off all the time and finally got my ass in gear. What I do know is I like the new me. My wife loves the new me. We want to keep things going the right way. So I'm trusting you to explain that this embezzlement stuff was all a ruse for … whatever it is you're doing."

"You have my word, sir," DeWitt said.

Martin added, "If it has anything to do with what turned me around, I hope you guys can bottle it. My wife wants to know where she can get hers."

"We'll keep that in mind." DeWitt opened a door to the basement. "You'll find a special agent downstairs. She'll see that you get home safely."

Martin gave DeWitt a wave goodbye and was gone.

The deputy director closed the door to the basement behind him.

He went back to sitting at the kitchen table, resumed studying the video feeds that had been sent to his tablet computer by his people in the field. For this operation, he'd chosen to use only female special agents. His guess was Todd and the two heavy hitters from the CIA would be watching for big guys with short hair trying to pass themselves off as civilians.

Female agents were much more credible posing as everyday people.

To be politically correct, of course, he'd said they were better actors.

They were also sharp enough to notice the four vehicles doing an automotive do-si-do around Lydell Martin's place of employment. At the far edge of probability, that might have been a coincidence. Looking at things more closely, noting that all the cars were of foreign manufacture, priced between sixty-five thousand and one hundred thousand dollars and muted gray in color, coincidence was dismissed as a possibility.

Especially after it was seen that Lydell Martin's car was a bird of the same feather.

DeWitt's people had captured both profile views of the four drivers in the suspect cars and their license plate numbers. Within minutes, the bureau had the drivers' names, addresses and occupations. Their lines of work included: managing partner of a Philadelphia law firm, publisher of an online financial newsletter, chief of surgery at an area hospital and a dean of admissions at a prestigious university.

Damn list read like —

DeWitt's cell phone beeped to signal the arrival of a text message.

A gray Audi sedan was approaching the house.

The deputy director was the stand-in for Martin. They were

close to the same size. DeWitt's head of hair was fuller, but he'd gelled it back tight. In silhouette, on a window shade, he should be able to pass. If Todd, his cronies or a combination thereof entered the house, they'd be captured, first on video and audio, and then by agents bursting in through the back door and up from below through the basement door.

Just in case that left any room for error, DeWitt held a gun on his lap, under the table.

He'd be able to shoot the legs out from under a man without moving.

But he received a call on his cell.

A special agent told him, "The gray Audi signaled a turn into your driveway, but it's just sitting there on the street. Looks like cold feet. We might have a runner."

DeWitt didn't hesitate. "Take them down now."

Mango Mary's — Key West, Florida

Alice decided to reopen for business, after she'd bought a Sig Arms P250 compact semi-auto and spent hours at a firing range getting comfortable and reasonably accurate with it. She wore the weapon openly in a Galco shoulder holster. She also donned, under her aloha shirt, a Savvy concealable body armor for women vest with three hundred and sixty degree bust protection. All in all, she felt ready to meet the public.

Thinking the Original Mango Mary, one tough woman, must be smiling somewhere.

Alice had alerted the cops that the door to her bar would be open again and they were keeping a close eye on the place. The broken windows, furniture, mirrors and glassware had been replaced, but there were still bullet-holes left, right and all over the place. So Alice put a sign outside the front door: *Shootout Specials, all drinks half price until repairs are made.*

The lure of cheap booze packed the place with both locals and tourists. People who hadn't been anywhere in the state much less in the bar were telling tales of the gunfight at Mango Mary's. Things got to the point where Alice thought if you could look past the unfortunate patrons who'd gone toes up in the conflict, drilling a handful of bad guys was a good business move.

She was struggling to keep up with the drink orders.

It didn't feel right to her to bring on any help just yet in case, you know, the assholes who'd sent the shooters last time parked a truck bomb out front. Still, she was going to fall over soon if she didn't think of some way to share the load with someone. As if he'd read her mind, Jackie appeared out of the crowd and stepped behind the bar with her.

She hadn't thought she'd see him again.

The last time they'd been together had been at the marina slip where Jackie had supposedly booked passage to South America on that rich bitch's yacht.

Looking at the empty slip where *Irish Grace* had been moored, Jackie had said, "I can*not* fucking believe this!"

Like no woman could ever change her mind about him.

Alice was having second thoughts about him herself right then.

Maybe she should take a solo cruise.

The idea of being one of two women out on the ocean with Jackie had been losing its appeal for Alice. Depending on what a guy's tastes were, Alice could see him preferring Carina — Jackie had said that was her name — to her. And Carina sure as hell had to have more money. Alice could imagine Carina telling Jackie, what'd they need Alice around for, anyway?

Alice would go to sleep one night and they'd throw her overboard.

"Did you give her part of the charter fee up front?" Alice asked.

"Hell, no! You think I'm stupid?"

Lots of smart guys got stupid around women, Alice thought.

The opposite was true, too.

"So maybe she just got scared," Alice thought. "Was too afraid to wait a minute longer, untied her lines and took off."

Jackie didn't think so. Carina had an attitude. Like not only was she smarter than the rest of the world, she was willing to plug you where you stood, if it came to that.

"You saw how she had a gun, didn't you?" Jackie asked. "Did she look like she was about to wet her pants anytime soon?"

Those two questions had made Alice flush with shame. Made her think of hiding under the bed in her own house. Daddy hadn't raised her that way, act scared as a kid with a nightmare. He'd had a gun in the house, but after he'd died, Mama had asked her to get rid of it. After Mama'd passed away, too, she'd thought of buying herself a gun, but hadn't acted on it.

Well, she would now. Get herself a gun and go back to work.

Jackie sat on the jetty with his legs dangling over the water.

The jerk just couldn't believe a woman had let him down.

Alice showed him it could happen more than once.

She had turned on her heel and walked off, being none too quiet about it.

Now, here Jackie was again, helping her out, not saying boo about it.

He'd colored his hair dark brown, got rid of all the gray. Must've paid somebody who knew her stuff. It looked pretty natural. Took about ten years off his appearance. She had to admit he looked pretty good, and just enough different the cops wouldn't take notice of him right off. Not from the description she'd given them. Which had been deliberately vague.

The cops wanted to sit down with Jackie and see if maybe he'd smoked one of those three guys wearing the Bus Milbaugh masks. None of the Milbaughs had carried any ID. The cops were working on the assumption they'd been a murder-for-hire crew. The guys with the badges weren't that worked up about bringing charges against anyone for shooting their likes.

After an hour of working so steadily they didn't have time to chat — but Alice had observed Jackie putting every dollar of tips he received in the kitty jar on the back bar — they finally got a moment to take a breath.

Jackie tapped a seltzer water for each of them.

"I found her," he told Alice.

"Found who?"

"Carina Linberg."

"Linberg's her last name? What is that, Swedish or something?"

Jackie frowned, thinking the question frivolous.

Then he remembered his manners and shrugged, letting his displeasure fall away.

"I don't know, Swedish or German, something."

"She's back here?" Alice asked.

Jackie shook his head. "She's in George Town, Grand Cayman."

"That's not so far, but how'd you find out?"

"I stopped in at the marina office, asked about her. She took off for the Caribbean, left her ports of call, satellite phone number. In case she needed to be reached before she came back."

"They told you all that?"

The clerk had pulled the paperwork. Then Jackie had suckered him out of the office for a minute. Copied down the information.

But he said, "Sure, why not?"

"So you going to wait for her to come back?" Alice asked.

"Unh-uh. I came looking for you so we could fly down to George Town, meet up with Carina and get her to sail us to South America from there."

Alice crossed her arms over her chest, a woman taking a stand.

Her right hand was close to the P250.

"I'm staying right here."

"Look, I've got her satellite phone number. I'll call her. She'll wait for us."

"What's the number?" Alice asked.

Jackie told her. Someone who could remember ten drink orders, Alice had no trouble holding a phone number in her mind.

"So, you'll come with me then? Leave as soon as you close up tonight?"

Alice shook her head. "I'm staying. Right here."

"Why'd you ask for the phone number then?"

"Wanted to see if you were bullshitting me."

Jackie's frown was back, deeper than before.

Alice dropped her left arm, let him see her right hand was on the P250 now.

Jackie put his hands up and backed off a step. He didn't want any trouble.

"Can you tell me just one thing, if you're staying *right here?*"

"What?" Alice asked.

"If I get Carina to sail me down to South America, let's say we head off, say, to Colombia. We're going along and something happens. A wave washes Carina off the boat. How long would it take me to learn enough to get me where I want to go?"

"You start right in helping her and watching her close, see how she raises and strikes her sails, how she plots her course and uses her navigation equipment, how she starts the motor when she needs to, it shouldn't take you more than a couple days to learn the basics — if you're a quick learner."

Jackie looked pleased, happy to hear what Alice told him.

Never thinking for a moment she'd handed him a load of shit.

"I'm a real fast learner. It's been a pleasure, Alice. I'm gonna miss you."

"Send a postcard," she told him.

He gave her a wave and said, "You ought to hire some help."

There was a break in the crowd as Jackie left Mango Mary's.

She saw him get into a black Porsche parked outside.

After he drove off, she wrote down Carina Linberg's phone number.

Stuck it in a pocket.

7 Prime Cuts & Sunsets — Grand Cayman Island

When Welborn Yates suggested to Carina Linberg that he buy her dinner as recompense for all the obvious suffering he'd caused her, she laughed and gave him a peck on the cheek. It took all of Welborn's self-control not to blush. Managing that feat, he went on to reclaim the rest of his savoir-faire.

"I'll take that as a yes," he said.

"No, I'll take you to dinner."

"A feminist statement?"

"An economic one. I just negotiated a new contract. I'm flush."

Carina's buying power and a craving for beef landed them at 7 Prime Cuts & Sunsets, a restaurant at the Ritz-Carlton. Their table was on the terrace with an unobstructed view of the beach, the sea and what they were promised would be a spectacular sunset.

Carina ordered a fourteen-ounce New York steak, after Welborn promised he would eat any portion she couldn't finish. Having obligated himself that way, Welborn chose the Irish organic salmon weighing in at a trim eight ounces. Carina was drinking Cabernet Sauvignon; Welborn went with pinot noir. Their choices met with the approval of the waiter.

Having a moment to themselves, Welborn said, "You're looking well. The private sector must agree with you."

"More so this week than last. You look like married life agrees with you."

Unlike Willa Pennyman, Carina hadn't needed to see a ring on his finger to know his marital status, leading Welborn to say, "You saw a media mention that my wedding was overshadowed by other events."

"I was in that line of work, still am to some degree. I read what happened at the vice president's house while I was sailing to Key West. If I'm not being too nosy, it's a bit early for you to be vacationing alone, isn't it?"

Welborn gave her a beat to work out the answer to her question.

She leaned forward and lowered her voice. "You're here on business. You're working a case for whom, the president or the Air Force?"

Welborn leaned in — and a little warning bell in his head told him what he and Carina would look like to any casual observer, not to mention Kira. He tried not to be bothered. His motives were pure and he had no intention of closing the distance between himself and Ms. Linberg any farther.

He said, "To what degree are you still in the news gathering business?"

"I just re-upped with Sir Edbert Bickford."

Welborn sat back as if she'd just confessed to an Ebola infection.

Carina leaned farther forward and seized a hand Welborn had carelessly left on the table. She pulled him back in her direction. It was only a lifetime of instruction from his mother on how to behave like a gentleman that kept him from making a struggle of it.

"I am *not* working now," Carina said. "I am having dinner with someone who is incorruptibly an officer and a gentleman. Someone, frankly, I wish was a bit of a rascal, as I'm certain he has an unspoken thing for older women."

The waiter arrived with aperitifs they hadn't ordered. Lillet red for Carina, white for Welborn. The man had been considerate enough to announce his approach with audible footsteps, something that otherwise never would have happened.

Setting their drinks before them, he said, "Compliments of the Ritz-Carlton."

Receiving their thanks, he departed silently.

"Somebody thinks we're dressing up the place," Carina said.

Welborn raised his glass, "To meeting each other again in better circumstances."

They touched glasses and sipped their drinks.

Carina said, "If you can't tell me what you're doing, I understand. But I am happy to see you again. I've had the time to think about things. I realize how decently you treated me when everyone else saw me as a pariah. There were even times, afterward, when I thought I should call you. I would have, if you weren't working at the White House, and if you hadn't gotten married."

Welborn filed the implicit compliment away for later review.

"You're happier than you were a week ago because?" he asked.

"I recently discovered I have a creative side to my nature. I want to tell stories. Loosely based on my life, but more about being a strong woman, generally."

They had to leave it at that for the moment as their dinners arrived.

Everything was wonderful, and Carina finished her steak unassisted.

The sunset was as stunning as it was promised to be. The dinner dishes were cleared. Complimentary after dinner drinks appeared, again compliments of the Ritz-Carlton.

"Who are they buttering up," Welborn asked, "you or me?"

"I took a suite for a week. I wanted to sleep ashore in a big bed."

Welborn pushed unbidden images from his mind.

"Another mystery solved," he said.

"There's no rascal at all in you?" Carina asked.

"It was pruned from the family tree generations ago."

"More's the pity." She picked up her glass and said, "To platonic reunions."

"Old friends," Welborn responded, touching his glass to hers.

They drank and watched the afterglow of the sun on the water disappear.

"Would you like to hear what I'll be up to in my professional life?" Carina asked.

"I'd love to."

She told him about doing intermittent news reports on topics of her choosing for WWN, and then with far greater enthusiasm she told him about the idea for her TV pilot, *Woman in Command,* that Sir Edbert had approved.

Welborn smiled. "Women usually are in command, as far as I've seen. My mother, the president, Kira."

Carina laughed. "You say that, but you look good enough to play a soap opera lead, and your manners are so smooth you'd make Emily Post hot. My money says you get your way at least half the time and you won't be pushed into doing anything you don't want."

"All that's true. The rest of the time I just follow orders. So how does your story begin? Your TV show, that is."

Carina thought about that. "I had one idea, about a jealous military wife getting even with her cheating husband, but …"

Welborn waited patiently for the creative process to play out.

Carina continued, "I met these two characters in Key West recently, one of them possibly shady, the other a woman who may have gotten in over her head. The man wanted to charter my boat to take him to South America."

A tingle ran up Welborn's spine, making the hair on the back of his neck rise.

"The man, did you get the impression he's running from something?"

"I know he is."

Carina told Welborn about the incident in Mango Mary's that had involved her and Jackie Richmond. She went on to tell him about the subsequent shootout at the bar. How Jackie and Alice came to her boat looking to take a long trip.

Welborn thought about what he'd heard. He was disappointed to learn this Jackie Richmond had a good reason — one having nothing to do with him — to get out of town.

Carina saw the chagrin on Welborn's face.

"What? You're looking for someone? Hoped I might have stumbled on him?"

"That would have been serendipitous," Welborn said.

Carina smiled. "I never heard anyone in the Air Force, cadet or officer, who talks like you. Are you sure you went to the academy?"

"Positive," Welborn said, his face falling as three lost friends came to mind.

Carina told him, "No blues allowed at five-star hotels."

Welborn summoned a small grin. "Not a bad line for a country song."

"I'll let you write it. Here's another thought I had about Jackie Richmond on the way down here. I think he may have been hiding out in Key West *before* he got in the trouble at Mango Mary's."

That idea brightened Welborn's outlook. He asked, "Just a feeling?"

"A couple of feelings. He's one of those guys who has a high sense of self-regard without any visible reason for it. Like he's got some big secret. The other thing was, I didn't like the way he looked at my car. Gave me the feeling he might steal it."

Welborn leaned forward and took Carina's hand.

She laughed. "If that's your idea of talking dirty ..." She dropped her voice to a whisper. "I thought he might even want to steal my boat. Conk me on the head and throw me overboard."

Welborn now took her hand in both of his. Carina liked that, too.

She said, "That's why I made myself scarce when he wasn't looking. Figured it was easier than shooting him. Sailed this way just so I could imagine what it would have been like to have him aboard. If you weren't working, I'd ask you to come aboard, keep me safe from all the other bad guys out there."

Welborn said, "You've got great instincts as a storyteller. If I show you something, will you promise not to tell anyone?"

"Are you talking dirty to me now?"

Welborn released her hand. "Promise?"

Carina nodded.

Welborn took a folded piece of paper out of a pocket, spread it out on the table.

"Is that Jackie Richmond?"

Carina didn't need more than a glance at the photo.

"Take away the creases in the paper, yeah. He's the guy you're looking for?"

Welborn nodded and explained the reason.

"He killed three Air Force pilots?" Carina asked.

"Them and some people whose cars he stole. He tried to take mine, too, but I got the cuffs on him. He made bail before we found out who he was."

"You mind if I write this down?" Carina asked.

"Be my guest, to be used only after Linley Boland is tried,

convicted and locked away."

"What kind of car do you have?" she asked. Hearing Welborn's answer, she said, "Damn, that's what I have, too."

Carina reached into her handbag, found paper and a pen and started making notes. She stopped and looked at Welborn. "You're here because he's coming here. How did you know that?"

"Can't say," he told her.

She wrote that down, too. "You know when he's coming?"

Before Welborn could answer, the phone in Carina's handbag rang. The ID screen said the caller was Alice Tompkins. Carina answered. The conversation was brief. Carina clicked off.

She looked at Welborn and told him, "Jackie will be here soon."

Mango Mary's — Key West, Florida

Closing time drew near. The crowd in the bar had thinned to a huddle of determined drinkers, a few gregarious talkers and a guy in a straw hat. Those folks and a white-haired guy with a lined face who stepped up to Alice and put a business card on the bar in front of her.

He said, "My name is Julius Miles."

His card said he was a lawyer from Miami.

"Pretty fancy introduction, if all you want's a drink," Alice said.

"I'd love a drink, but I have to drive home tonight and at my age even a little alcohol and getting behind the wheel would be a bad idea."

Alice always appreciated people who knew better than to be stupid.

"How about a club soda with a twist of lime?" she said. "On the house."

Miles smiled warmly. "Thank you very much. I'd like that."

Alice got him his drink and waited to hear what he was selling.

After taking a sip, Miles said, "I believe the gent near the door with the straw hat has a gun."

"A badge, too," Alice told him.

"I suspected as much. You might want to ask him over to hear what I have to say. Or not. Depending on how you feel."

Alice pointed a finger at the gun she was wearing openly.

"Oh, I'm no physical threat. Farthest thing from it. But I've been asked to deliver a message to you. I was contacted by phone and paid in cash, delivered by a courier, for my services, so I'm afraid, even with the police present, I couldn't identify my client."

"You do a lot of work like that?" Alice asked.

"Only when I like the message I'm being asked to convey."

"I've got an idea who sent you. The people who redecorated my place."

"Yes, that's what I was told, though I wasn't given a name."

"Neither was I," Alice said.

"In any case, my client asked me to tell you that pursuing their grievance against you is no longer cost effective. In fact, the client would like to compensate you for damages done to your business. If I may …"

Miles used two fingers to pull his suit coat open. An envelope projected from an inside pocket. The envelope bulged.

"Go ahead," Alice said.

Miles put the envelope on the bar. Alice could see now that it was stuffed with cash. She was sure the lawyer hadn't been hired to bring her singles, fives and tens. Or even twenties and fifties. Following that reasoning, there was a good chunk of money in front of her.

Not having been born yesterday or even last year, Alice said, "Looks like a bribe to me. What's it supposed to buy?"

"Without reference to the nature of his interest, my client said he'd like to speak to the fellow you had tending bar for you on the evening when … the peace was disturbed. If you could provide me with his name and his whereabouts, if you know them, my client would be grateful. He also promised you would never hear from him again."

Alice tapped herself a club soda and sipped while she thought about that.

Jackie had helped her the first night they'd met. He'd done an honest job working for her. Chased off the shitbirds who'd come calling. Then Carina Linberg had come in and there had been … what was it a lawyer like Miles would call it? An alienation of affection?

Alice didn't like the rich broad, but she thought Jackie had bad ideas in mind for Carina.

She didn't deserve that, but Alice didn't deserve having bad guys come after her until they got lucky or she got careless. The chance to be free of them changed the way she had to look at things. Still, she had to be careful she didn't work her way out of one bind only to get herself into another.

Alice pushed the envelope with the cash back toward Miles.

"I don't want the money. You say it's a gift now. Next week someone could come in and say it was a loan, and there's interest due."

Miles put the money back inside his coat, and looked at Alice with new respect.

"And the name?" he asked.

"Jackie Richmond."

"Any idea where Jackie went?"

Alice decided if Carina Linberg was with him at the wrong time she must not be living right.

She said, "For the next little bit, Grand Cayman."

The White House

McGill knocked on the door to the office Patti used for official business in the residence. He was given permission to enter and saw Patti sitting behind her desk, looking less than pleased. McGill closed the door. He sat in a guest chair and asked, "You, me or someone else?"

"Damon Todd."

"Not in custody or a body bag, I take it."

"No. Deputy Director DeWitt thought he had him, had lured

him into a trap, but Todd sent in a decoy. The trap was sprung on the wrong person."

"Is the decoy talking?"

"Won't stop talking, from what I heard. He's the son of a Delaware state senator. He was out driving Daddy's Audi when he was approached by a man wearing a Boston Red Sox cap and asked how he'd like to play a prank on someone and make five hundred dollars, half up front. The young man was assured that no one would be harmed and no property would be vandalized. All he had to do was drive to an address in Drexel Hill, Pennsylvania, use his turn signal as if he was about to enter a driveway, stay on the road, honk his horn twice and drive back to Wilmington to collect the rest of his money."

McGill said, "The kid didn't think that was a lot of money for doing very little?"

Patti sighed. "From your point of view or mine, that's obvious. When you or I were nineteen would we have jumped at the chance to make an easy five hundred dollars?"

McGill said, "Well, if you're going to be logical about it. How did Todd learn DeWitt fell for his trick?"

"The decoy had an open cell phone link to him. He got to hear the young man curse at him saying what a 'dickhead' he was."

"DeWitt couldn't even let the kid keep the cash, right?" McGill asked.

"Evidence," Patti said, "to be checked for DNA."

"The phone the kid used and the one he called were disposables."

Patti nodded. "Can't fool an experienced policeman."

"I might have set up the trap a little differently," McGill said.

"But you weren't going to interfere with the FBI."

"No. They do a lot of things well, but your average copper has more street smarts."

Patti said, "It's not hard to read the subtext there. No more relying on others to catch Todd."

McGill nodded. "Sweetie and I are going to find him."

"You'll take Elspeth with you?"

McGilled smiled. "Sure, me and my Amazons. If DeWitt wants to feel useful, he has resources I might like to use. If I can't charm him, you think you can?"

Patti nodded. "One nice thing about my job? People find me persuasive."

5

November, 2011
Wheaton & Kennerly Advertising — Portland, Oregon

Not that Putnam Shady had any complaints about Omaha, nobody had tried to kidnap or kill him there, and he and Darren Drucker had done a lot of good work, but he was glad to be in a place with more of a leading edge vibe.

Over the past weeks, Putnam and Drucker had not only gotten the infrastructure for ShareAmerica, the populist lobbying fund, set up, Drucker had also created a Super PAC, Americans for Equity, to back progressive candidates on the federal, state and local levels.

Foremost among those candidates would be Patricia Darden Grant. Federal Election Commission regulations forbade any co-ordination between Super PACs and a candidate's campaign, not that the FEC had ever come down hard on any candidate or Super PAC even when the two appeared to be working hand in glove. Jon Stewart and Stephen Colbert made a mockery of the situation whenever the mood took them.

Putnam Shady, however, was taking no chances that the Supreme Court, now minus two conservative justices and with a new liberal balance of power, might reverse its previous ruling and junk Super PACs. Americans for Equity would steer clear of the presidential campaign entirely. Rather it would work to help the president by changing the *nature* of the Congress. If doing that drew voters to the polls who also supported the president, *quelle coïncidence!*

To make the sale to a majority of the American electorate that Congress needed to be turned inside out, upside down and shaken several times, Putnam had traveled to Portland to visit with the principals of what he considered to be the finest advertising agency anywhere.

He entered the office building on NW Fourteenth Avenue and took the elevator to the thirteenth floor where, according to advertising lore, happy accidents in creative thinking were encouraged on a daily basis. The agency principals, Dan, Shawn and Meg, who insisted that they be addressed by their first names, were waiting for Putnam as he stepped into the lobby.

Shawn stepped forward, extended a hand and said, "Mr. Shady, love your name."

Putnam shook hands and said, "I've always liked it myself. Tried to live up to it as a young man. Lately, I've moderated my behavior somewhat."

Meg asked, "Ms. Sweeney's doing?"

Putnam grinned. "You've done your homework."

He was pleased rather than annoyed that they'd checked him out.

Dan asked, "Is that a new ring you're wearing? Doesn't have a settled-in look yet."

An eye for detail was good, too, Putnam thought.

Then Shawn said, "We've never done political work before. Don't know that we're interested."

Putnam told them, "I'm not asking you to help elect any particular candidate. What I want you to do is help make democracy work for the American people again."

The three ad hotshots looked at each other.

Meg said, "That's all? Maybe the interns can find a spare moment."

Having talked his way past the lobby, Putnam was settled in

a comfortable chair at a conference table facing Shawn, Dan and Meg. He told them, "The simple truth is ninety-nine and ninety-nine one hundredths of all political advertising is slime."

"Maybe a bit more than that," Meg said.

"You don't want to overdo the decimal place thing," Putnam suggested.

Three heads bobbed in appreciation. The man was right.

Putnam continued, "The Department of Justice is about to file fraud charges against a Super PAC supporting Senator Howard Hurlbert and his new True South Party, alleging that they've substantively misrepresented the president's record and the intentions she has for a second term, should she have one."

Dan said, "You know, that bothers me. It sounds like an infringement of free speech."

"So you'd have no problem with a competitor of one of your clients lying about your client day in and day out to take away their market share?" Putnam asked. "Maybe this competitor would also malign your client's character as well. You'd be okay with that, too?"

Dan laughed. "Well, hell, if you're going to put it that way."

Putnam said, "I am. Here's the thing. The DOJ isn't kidding around. Lying in political commercials, strange as it may sound, is going to be out for the coming election. The professional liars might take their case, essentially as Dan just characterized it, to the Supreme Court. Only the Supremes have lost two of their most conservative members. You can look for decisions from our highest court to take on a whole new slant."

Shawn asked, "What's any of that got to do with us?"

Putnam explained, "The political ad hacks are going to be put out of business. Hundreds of millions of ad dollars will go looking for people who are good at doing *positive* advertising."

"Like us," Dan said.

"Like some of our top competitors," Shawn added.

Putnam told them, "You're beginning to see the light. I like your work the best, but if you're not interested …"

Meg said, "You'll take your millions elsewhere."

"I will, but I'll have a few craft brews before I leave town."

Meg asked Putnam, "What do you think was the best positive ad done for a president in the past fifty years?"

"That's a softball question," he said. "'Morning in America' for Ronald Reagan."

Shawn asked, "You know who created it?"

"Hal Riney. Wrote it and narrated it. He also did the bear in the woods ad. Didn't like that one as much."

Dan said, "For bonus points, what shop did Riney work for?"

"When he did 'Morning in America?' His own shop, Hal Riney and Partners."

Putnam did his research, too. He knew Riney was a hero to advertising creatives.

Especially the ones who worked on the West Coast where Riney had.

"Give us a minute, will you, Mr. Shady?" Shawn said.

Putnam stepped out of the conference room and looked at his watch.

Wheaton and Kennerly signed on with Americans for Equity and ShareAmerica in thirty-six seconds.

The new business partners repaired to the Bridgeport Brewing Company to sample the wares. After the second round, Putnam excused himself to call Sweetie and tell her of his triumph, and ask if was safe enough to come home for a brief visit. Celibacy had lost its charm.

Sweetie told him to hurry. She and James J. McGill were going hunting soon.

Westbound Interstate 80 — Ottawa, Illinois

Olin Anderson sat behind the wheel of the 2012 Buick Enclave in Gold Mist Metallic. Arn Crosby rode shotgun. Damon Todd had the second row of seats to himself. Their luggage was in back. They carried no firearms, no knives, no chemical sprays. No alcohol, drugs or tobacco. Not even a pack of chewing gum.

Avoiding the temptation to spit a wad out the window.

Not catch the attention of any Barney Fife, behind on his ticket-writing quota.

What they did have was a valid title to the vehicle in the name of Michael Ludwig, Anderson's current alias. Crosby was now Gerald Hobart. Todd was Thomas Gower. Each of them had a valid Virginia driver's license in his new name. Crosby had been happy to discover that his computer hacking skills, though rusty, were still effective on state software that hadn't been updated since he and Anderson had gotten locked up.

Their cover story was that they were grassroots political organizers heading to California in advance of the upcoming primary elections. Their specialty, if anyone wanted to know, was get out the vote efforts. Their party? It would depend on where they were if they got stopped. That and the color, gender and ethnicity of the cop.

It had been Anderson's idea to go with the political angle.

What with the president changing her allegiance and a new party, True South, in the hunt, everybody was already thinking ahead to the next election. Political operatives would soon be overrunning the country like termites with timber rights. Three white guys in a Buick, they'd fit right in with the crowd.

Crosby hadn't cared to debate the validity of Anderson's points.

Todd had barely paid attention. He'd just felt, after the failed attempt to capture them in Pennsylvania, it was time to relocate from Charlottesville. Head west somewhere, exact location to be determined. They'd left Fletcher Penrose unharmed, though Todd had the feeling that Crosby and Anderson would have liked to kill him.

They did leave Penrose one hundred and forty thousand dollars poorer, a trifle compared to the enhanced earnings Todd's work on the professor had brought him. They'd used forty thousand to buy the SUV and deposited the rest in a JP Morgan Chase account to cover their expenses.

As far as Todd knew, the CIA didn't put out all-points bulletins.

The FBI, yeah, they worked with state and local cops. Sometimes. But Todd felt sure this wouldn't be one of those times.

The last thing the federal government would want was to have Todd, Crosby and Anderson taken into custody and given a chance to talk to lawyers. That happened, all sorts of secrets might come out. The kind that presidents of both parties strained to keep secret.

The way Todd saw it was —

Speaking for the first time in hours, he asked his traveling companions, "What's that euphemism spy agencies use for killing people?"

Crosby and Anderson looked at each other.

Crosby said, "You mean terminate with extreme prejudice?"

"Yes, that's the one."

"That's bullshit," Anderson said.

"What?" Todd asked.

"Hollywood bullshit," Crosby explained.

"Oh." Todd sounded disappointed. "What's the real word?"

"Kill," Anderson told him.

"Mundane," Todd said.

"Gets the message across," Crosby replied.

Todd slumped in his seat.

Anderson saw him in his rear view mirror, looking despondent, and asked, "You think bloodshed comes with a soundtrack? Cheers from the people in the movie theater?"

"It's not like that," Crosby told him.

"Sorry to spoil your fun, Doc," Anderson said.

Todd told them, "I was thinking about us getting killed."

Crosby and Anderson sighed in unison. That disturbed Todd. He didn't like the idea of them teaming up against him in any fashion. Even voicing sounds of condescension.

"What?" he asked again, trying to sound calm.

Not quite making it.

"You tell him," Anderson told Crosby.

Crosby said, "You were thinking the Agency, the FBI or your

old pal McGill is going to gun us down, but it doesn't have to be that way."

"You said you'd never let yourselves be taken prisoner again," Todd responded.

"We won't. We weren't lying about that. But if we were to find a place we like and decided to settle in there, leading quiet lives, giving no sign of causing trouble for anyone, what do you think would happen?"

"You'd be found; *we'd* be found."

Anderson snorted. "Why? Because the government's get-those-assholes budget never runs out of money?"

"You're saying finding us, dealing with us is a matter of economics?" Todd asked.

Crosby said, "If we lay low and don't cause any trouble, why should people spend money trying to find us?"

"Because we *might* cause trouble," Todd said.

"That is a consideration," Anderson agreed, sounding disturbingly professorial to Todd's ear. "But is the trouble we *might* cause worth the expense of mounting a nonstop effort to find us? Wouldn't it be a better use of resources to simply be ready for us the next time we raise our heads above the underbrush?"

"Are you saying we'd be allowed to remain free as long as we don't cause any harm?" Todd asked.

"It'd be more expensive to take us in again: shelter, clothe and feed us for years," Crosby said.

Measuring everything in dollars and cents was driving Todd to distraction but before he could muster a further argument, Anderson provided a geopolitical example as a bulwark to Crosby's point.

"Look, Doc, Saddam Hussein would be on his throne in Baghdad today if he'd let the nuclear inspectors in to see whatever the hell they wanted. If he'd shut the fuck up about the U.S. on top of that, nobody in Washington ever would have paid for that war. Hell, we'd be buying oil from the bastard and he'd still be free to pile up the skulls of his own people."

"What Olin is saying in his picturesque way," Crosby said, "is it's *always* about the cost — in dollars or pride."

Having absorbed as much of the lecture on Realpolitik 101 as he could take, Todd asked, "Do you think anyone would look for us here?"

Anderson laughed. "What, in Ottawa, Illinois? I'd say we're pretty safe here."

"The next twenty or thirty years," Crosby added with his own chuckle.

"Though I might prefer to be locked up back in Virginia," Anderson said, still amused.

"Take the next exit," Todd told him.

The Oval Office

Chief of Staff Galia Mindel stood before the president's desk for the first time since she was released from the hospital. She and the president looked at each other and smiled, two survivors. Patricia Darden Grant came around her desk and embraced her old friend.

"I am so happy to see you again," she said.

Galia's voice had a slight rasp. "Now, you know how I felt when I heard you were all right."

"Both of us must still figure in some higher power's schemes."

Galia said, "Yeah, let's hope we get renewed for another term."

Patti returned to her place behind the desk.

The chief of staff took her seat opposite the president.

She said, "In the give and take of favors, I thought I was one or two up on Mr. McGill. Now, I'll have to be his handmaiden for life."

The president shook her head. "Jim's not big on household help. I've been told that whenever we leave the White House, I'll either have to learn to cook or put up with his efforts."

"I've heard he's not half-bad in the kitchen."

"He's not, and he says we can always eat out, if Congress doesn't take away my pension."

Galia smiled. Then her face became serious.

"I wouldn't be here without him, Madam President," she said.

"Jim kicks himself for getting to you later than he says he should have."

Galia shook her head. "Men."

"God love them, the good ones anyway. Well, are you ready to get to work? I'm going to shake things up again. Make your life harder, in other words."

"What are you going to do, Madam President?"

With a woman whose very presence in the Oval Office was a rebuke to history, chances were the president was not talking about half-measures.

The president reminded Galia of her idea of running with Jean Morrissey.

"I've decided she's the one I want for a running mate."

While the chief of staff was busy mulling an all-female ticket, Patti dropped the other shoe.

"Galia, our campaign is not going to do any TV advertising."

"I beg your pardon," the chief of staff said, as if she hadn't heard right.

"I'm not going to do any TV interviews either," the president added.

"What?"

"And I'm not going to participate in any televised debates."

"I'm sorry, Madam President. My pain meds must be affecting my hearing. What I think I just heard doesn't make any sense."

"You heard me just fine, Galia," the president said, "and I'll tell you why it makes perfect sense."

Indiana University — Bloomington, Indiana

Sheryl Kimbrough and her journalism class, "Cutting Through the Bull-Puckey," sat and watched the TV at the front of the classroom with rapt attention. Sir Edbert Bickford was being interviewed on WWN by his new managing editor of broadcast news, Ethan

Judd, recently hired away from the *New York Times*.

Sheryl had prepped the class by telling them, "The combination of Ethan Judd and WorldWide News is only slightly less unlikely than a three-legged horse winning the Kentucky Derby. Judd is such an old school guy he isn't registered to vote as either a Republican or a Democrat and he might punch you on the nose if you ask him about his political views."

"More people are calling themselves independents than ever before," a student said.

"Yes, they are," Sheryl agreed, "but the truth is they're moderates who tend to vote with one party far more often than the other party. Saying you're an independent is often just a way of telling a party's base voters, 'Don't take my support for granted, buster.' Being largely free of ideological preferences, however, is still relatively rare."

Another student suggested, "Some people, it seems like they agree with the last person who talked to them. That's not independent either. Just means you're too lazy to think for yourself."

"That's why you see placards with candidates' names on them set up as close to polling places at the law allows," Sheryl said. "But Ethan Judd is the genuine article. His entire reputation is built on a dedication to finding the truth, telling it clearly and fully and letting the consequences be what they may. So having him sign on with Sir Edbert Bickford, the champion of the radical right, can mean only one thing."

"*Somebody* sold out," came a voice from the back of the class.

"Exactly," Sheryl said.

She knew where she'd put her money, but kept that to herself.

Judd opened the interview by coming straight to the point, "Sir Edbert, why in the world did you hire me?"

The media mogul gave his new employee a thin smile.

"Because, Mr. Judd, I consider you to be the best at what you do."

"And what's that?"

"Getting to the guts of a story and putting the whole bloody mess on the table for everyone to see."

The look Judd gave his new boss had once been described as the last thing a rabbit sees before it becomes a raptor's lunch.

"Did you hire me, Sir Edbert, because you think I can help save you from prosecution by the Department of Justice?"

"I'm hardly a naive man, Mr. Judd, and you're not a genie. If the attorney general means to prosecute me, I'd be astounded if he changed his mind based on a hiring decision I made. On the other hand, I don't like the way the public perceives me at the moment. I'm neither Charles Foster Kane nor Joe McCarthy. I'm a principled conservative. I hired you with the expectation that I'd become a subject for clear-eyed examination by you as fast, if not faster, than any other prominent figure."

Judd pressed on. "Wouldn't any investigative reporting I do on you be tainted by the fact that I work for you?"

Sir Edbert replied, "I'm wagering that your work product will dispel any doubt that you're beholden to anyone, including me."

"You know that by hiring me, then, the whole tone and most of the content of your news operation will change?"

"That thought has occurred to me," Sir Edbert said, forming a smile even thinner than before.

"You're not worried about that, if the people you previously favored should take power in Washington?"

"What's the worst that could happen? If I've already been con-victed of a federal crime, they'll cut my ration of gruel by half? If I'm still at liberty but out of favor with the politicians and the public, I'll have to follow Ringo Starr's advice when he was asked what he'd do if the Beatles lost their popularity."

"And what was it Ringo said, Sir Edbert?"

"I'll just have to sit on my yacht and sulk."

This time, Judd and Sir Edbert shared smiles that were genuine.

Judd asked, "Will you support a Republican for president, as you always have?"

"I think Vice President Mather Wyman would make an excellent president. On the Democratic side, I think it's possible

Patricia Darden Grant could grow to greatness if she were to be reelected. As a British subject, of course, I'll not be allowed to vote for either of them."

"What about True South?" Judd asked. "Do you think they might come up with a worthy candidate?"

Sir Edbert shook his head. "My understanding is that True South is essentially a vanity vehicle for the ambitions of Senator Howard Hurlbert. I think the whole enterprise will pass from the scene without much notice … but the matter of notice on WWN is now yours to decide."

"Yes, it is," Judd said. "Thank you for your time and candor, Sir Edbert."

Sheryl turned off the classroom TV.

Before she had the overhead lights on, a student voice said, "That English dude is up to something."

Waiting for everyone to stop blinking as the fluorescents flickered into life, Sheryl agreed and said, "Five hundred words for our next class. *What* is Sir Edbert Bickford up to?"

She looked forward to reading each paper closely.

The responsibility of casting her electoral college vote weighed on Sheryl just then.

The Oval Office

The president asked her chief of staff, "Most people hate most political ads, you agree?"

"Yes, and everybody hates traffic jams, but people keep buying cars."

Patricia Darden Grant waved the comparison aside. "True but irrelevant. People love cars as symbols of personal freedom. People regard TV commercials as intrusions on their free time. Cars get washed and waxed. Commercials get zapped."

"Debating point to the gentlelady from Pennsylvania Avenue," Galia said.

Patti said, "Galia, if we refuse to run TV spots —"

"We'll get run over by Mather Wyman's negative TV spots."

"Do you really see that, Mather going negative?"

Galia considered the question. "Not him personally, but his people, yes."

"I don't think so. You saw how Mather handled the situation at Salvation's Path. He jumped on it. He took charge immediately. Any minion in his campaign who tried to go negative would be on the street so fast his head would spin."

Patti wasn't going to tell Galia that the vice president had shared his deepest secret with her and would fear being outed as a gay man by someone in Patti's camp — Galia — if not the president herself. That wasn't the case. Patti had told no one. Would tell no one. Mather had nothing to fear on that count.

Even if knew he was safe from exposure, Patti felt he wouldn't run a dirty campaign.

That wasn't the kind of man Mather Wyman was.

Patti's moment of reverie dissipated and she saw Galia peering at her.

Trying to read her mind. A feat Patti wasn't sure was beyond Galia.

"What about Howard Hurlbert?" the chief of staff asked.

"What about him?" the president said. "We *know* he'll take the low road. We know the Super-PACs on the right will do the same. Those TV spots will have to be countered by equivalent forces on our side of the struggle, but not by us."

"We have equivalent forces?" Galia asked.

"Not that we have foreknowledge of, but there certainly are interested persons and organizations who will want us to win. My guess is the money behind each side will be comparable, but the right should be divided between the GOP and True South. You know, going third party is the nicest thing Howard Hurlbert has ever done for me."

"The money might be about the same," Galia said, "but the right will be meaner in the way they use it."

"So we'll be smarter. Not only get more bang for the buck, but win more hearts. One thing we'll be doing, Galia, is figure out how much money we might have spent on TV spots in a given city or state and when we visit there we'll donate that amount to local charities. We'll help poor people pay their heating bills. We'll help veterans find jobs. We'll buy books for libraries."

The chief of staff brightened. She was beginning to see the possibilities.

"By doing good we'll do well. We'll get *free* TV time."

"All without calling the other guy a jerk."

"What about the other things you mentioned? No TV interviews, no TV debates."

"Every major broadcast outlet has a Web presence. We'll do webcasts with no arbitrary one-minute or two-minute time limits for responses. We'll let questions be asked and responded to fully."

Galia laughed. "Some of your brethren do like to go on at length."

The president said, "If my opponents want to bore people, let them."

"You'll let True South in on the debates?"

"I'm praying Howard won't chicken out. Having him onstage will only make Mather and me look better. One traditional medium we will use is radio."

"*Radio?*" Galia asked.

"Of course. We can't ignore that. Americans from the Greatest Generation to the Baby Boomers grew up with radio. It's familiar, it's comfortable and I have a fairly nice voice."

Galia thought, you and your henchman, both. Maybe you could work up an act.

What she said was, "There could be an echo of FDR there."

"What better way to introduce myself as a Democrat?" the president asked.

Gerrard Smith International Airport — Cayman Brac Island

Jackie Richmond flew to Cayman Brac from Montego Bay,

Jamaica on a twin engine Beech Model 99. He'd never in his life had any trouble flying in a big commercial jet; making the one hundred and fifty-three mile trip in the puddle jumper almost made him leave a puddle in his seat. The flight was bumpy throughout and there were two times when the plane dropped like a stone for hundreds of feet. Both times Jackie was just about to start screaming for … he didn't know what. God sure wasn't going to help him. Then the plane grabbed hold of the sky — he didn't have a clue how — and started flying forward again.

None of the other eight passengers aboard looked the least bit bothered.

The two Rastamen in the open cockpit were humming along to Bob Marley.

At least they weren't smoking dope. They landed the plane smooth as silk, too, but the runway didn't appear until the very last moment. Made Jackie wonder how the hell you practiced landings like that. Touch down a second too early, you were in the water. A second too late, there was water on the far side of the runway, too.

The pilot and copilot bumped fists when the plane came to a stop.

Like they knew they'd pulled off a good trick.

Jackie showed the passport he'd bought in Key West as he got off the plane. He tipped a guy five dollars to carry his suitcase to a taxi. Five minutes later, he was at a marina, eyeing his next mode of transportation, a twenty-six foot motorboat called a Whaler Outrage. Seemed a lot damn smaller that Carina Linberg's fifty-foot sailboat. But the Whaler had twin 225-horsepower outboard engines. Jackie always liked packing plenty of horsepower.

The boat also had a steering wheel.

It wasn't a car, but he was sure he could drive the thing.

Wouldn't have to worry about raising or lowering sails.

If he had to turn pirate and steal his first boat.

He hid that thought behind a smile and introduced himself to the guy he'd chartered the boat from, a black guy who maybe had some Asian in him, Cap'n Thurlow. Guy stood maybe four inches shorter than Jackie. Had wiry arms and legs that looked strong. But there wasn't much to him and one good shove from behind should send him overboard.

Not to be overlooked was the knife Thurlow wore at his waist. The blade had to be six inches long, and from the shine on it was probably sharp as a razor. After Thurlow took Jackie's suitcase and welcomed him aboard with a cold beer, Jackie asked him about the knife.

"You use that blade for your morning shave?"

Thurlow laughed. "Got me a fine electric razor for that. The knife's for cleaning fish." The captain untied the lines and said, "Sit back and relax, Mr. Richmond. We got us a fine day for being out on the sea. Get you to Grand Cayman before you know it."

The captain gave Jackie a look and said, "You know, a white man like you, I better get you some sunblock. Don't want you lookin' like a lobster when we get to George Town."

Jackie hadn't thought about that, felt he'd picked up some color in Key West, but why take chances? He walked up to the console with Thurlow, got a good look at the layout of the controls. Accepted the sunblock from the captain.

"Thanks," he said. "Looks like your controls are pretty simple."

"A Whaler's easy to operate. It's the sea that can be tricky."

"But not today."

Thurlow shook his head. "Today'll be smooth. You want another beer just give a yell."

Jackie said he would. He took a seat in the aft of the boat, rubbed the sunblock on his face and arms. Took a boonie hat out of his bag and put it on. Wearing the hat and his sunglasses, he didn't think Carina Linberg or anyone else would recognize him.

His whole plan was to sneak up on whatever the situation was in Grand Cayman.

Somebody stealing the money out of his bank account, that wasn't an accident. It was personal. Somebody was looking to hurt him. Taking his money had been a damn good start. Luring him into a trap, too, that'd be even better.

Thurlow took the Whaler away from the dock out onto the open water. The waves were so small they were barely worthy of the name. The distance to Grand Cayman was only ninety-two miles, but for someone who grew up in a place as dry as Nevada that was a lot of water to cover.

Jackie leaned back and tried to relax. He sipped his beer, not intending to drink much. Be a real downer if he got tipsy and he was the one to go over the side. But the cold beer, the hot sun and the cool breeze from the movement of the boat was a very pleasurable combination.

If he knew how to do more than dog paddle, if there weren't any goddamn fish in the ocean that liked to eat people, he might have been having a good time. Still, it was a lot better than the damn flight from Jamaica. But he heard Thurlow humming to himself just like those pilots had.

He couldn't complain about that, though. The guy was just going about his job. Willing to pop another brew anytime Jackie asked for one. Not feeling he had to make conversation to entertain his passenger.

The way Jackie had things planned, he'd find the bank that let his money get taken and stroll past it. Wearing his hat and shades. If he got the feeling anybody was watching for him he'd just walk on by.

The next step was to find Carina Linberg. Grand Cayman had to be small enough it shouldn't be hard for him to spot *Irish Grace*. He'd talk to Carina, see if he could get her to drop in at the bank and plead his case. If she said no to that, he'd ask about her doing that charter trip they talked about. Ought to be cheaper, being part of the way there already.

If she said no to that, too, he'd have to sneak aboard her boat, jump her before she could get that gun of hers pointed at him. Maybe take Thurlow's knife with him, that or something else, make her take him to Venezuela.

If she came to see he had some good points, maybe she could become his partner. They'd sell her sailboat, use the money to set up house and start a new hustle. He still liked the stealing-cars-to-order idea. If Carina wanted no part of him or his plans, well she'd be writing her own end.

Thurlow called out to him from the driver's console, "Ready for another, Mr. Richmond?"

Jackie looked around. Couldn't see anything but water. But the beer had tasted great and it helped him to relax. He said, "Why not? Just one more."

Hart Senate Office Building — Washington, D.C.

"That dirty English bastard," Senator Howard Hurlbert said, clicking off the television in his office. The senator and his chief of staff Bobby Beckley had just watched a replay of Ethan Judd's interview with Sir Edward Bickford.

As usual, the senator had misjudged the situation, Beckley thought.

If anyone was a danger to Hurlbert, it was Ethan Judd.

He could expose all the times the senator had stepped on his own wienie.

Ask the country, "You really want to make *this* guy president?"

It'd be all over but the crying. Beckley was wondering half-seriously if he knew anyone who could arrange a fatal accident for Judd without it blowing back on him. Where the hell was a master hitman with a fatal disease and a desperate family when you needed one?

He'd just have to keep thinking.

Meanwhile, he poured Parker's Heritage bourbon for the senator and himself. He took an ounce neat. The senator required three ounces of the good stuff and one of water to calm him down. Beckley told the old man that he used the water from the office toilet tanks to make drinks. That always got a laugh, but it was true. He figured anyone who would dilute fine bourbon deserved no less.

Clicking his glass against the senator's, Beckley said, "Sir Edbert will come home, believe me."

The senator was not yet ready to believe. "He as much as called me a vain old fool."

"He'll make it up to you. Right now, he's just playing a game."

"You're saying he's sucking up to the attorney general despite denying he was doing any such thing."

"Of course, he denied it. What else could he say? 'I'm taking the only shot I've got here.'"

Hurlbert smiled. "No, he couldn't very well say that."

Beckely continued, "Sir Edbert's got his nuts in a twist. He'd like to keep from losing them altogether. I don't think he's going to manage that. Once he's got nothing left to lose, he's going to come back to all his old pals with a vengeance. Until then he's got to put on a front and search for some pretty country that doesn't extradite rich people."

That idea also tickled the senator. Sir Edbert being forced into exile.

After the Limey bastard had sucked up to all the people who mattered in Washington.

Beckley saw the boss was off in fantasyland again.

He yanked him back before he got too much of the good stuff in him.

He told Hurlbert, "The White House Press Office put out a release on Burke Godfrey's death. Said he was a prime candidate for a stroke. His conditions being he was old and fat, his blood pressure and cholesterol were higher than the Rockies and his heart couldn't keep the beat to waltz time."

Hurlbert was agog, half his drink gone now.

"The White House said *that?*"

"My words, Senator. Their language was a lot drier. The release also said it was delayed until Michael Jaworsky could give Erna Godfrey the details in person."

"We couldn't blame them for that. It was the only courteous thing to do."

Beckley said, "It was an *extraordinary* thing to do for a federal prisoner doing life for murder. The administration obviously is feeling skittish about the situation. So that's the bruise on their shin we're going to kick as hard as we can."

"What do you mean?" Hurlbert asked.

His drink was almost gone now.

Beckley knew he'd have to repeat the plan several times before the senator was able to voice it in tones convincing enough that people would think it came from him.

The chief of staff told the senator, "We're going to say both Mather Wyman and Patti Grant are responsible for Reverend Godfrey's death."

"I thought a stroke killed him. You can't give someone a stroke. Can you?"

If only, Beckley thought.

"We're going to say the White House caused the stress that brought on the stroke. More than that, we're going to say that President Grant and Vice President Wyman are persecuting all fundamentalist Christians. Best of all, we're going to say they're going to take away everyone's bibles."

The very thought was enough to make Hurlbert pour another drink.

"They wouldn't *dare*," he said, holding his glass up pugnaciously.

Beckley said, "Of course, they wouldn't. The thought would never cross their minds, but that doesn't mean we can't accuse them of it."

Before touching his glass to his lips, Senator Hurlbert enjoyed a rare moment of both insight and lucidity.

He said, "What you're saying, Bobby, is I have to say all this. Say it knowing it's a lie. The Justice Department is already coming after us. If I say the things you just told me I should say, they'll be coming after *me*."

Beckley smiled. "That's how we're going to make you a *hero*, Senator. We already know how many people go crazy thinking the government is coming for their guns, when that'll never happen. Ten times that number will go nuts thinking Washington is coming for their bibles. You'll be the only presidential candidate telling the fools they're right. You'll be the only presidential candidate telling them you'll save their bibles. The White House won't have the nerve to come after you. Even if they do, even if they *lock* you up, people will tear down the jailhouse brick by brick with their bare hands and carry you off on their shoulders."

Howard Hurlbert saw that picture in his mind with megapixel clarity.

He saluted it with his drink.

Bobby Beckley marveled at how easy it was to sell bullshit to people.

Once you got them to drink toilet water.

Camp David — Catoctin Mountains, Maryland

Kenny McGill caught the football he'd been tossed and said, "You're still seeing that Putnam guy?"

Sweetie caught the return pass. "You saw him arrive with me, didn't you? You think that was just a coincidence?"

"Well, he did come to see Patti, right?"

"No, he came to talk with your dad."

"He did?"

That was what Putnam had told Sweetie, and she knew better than to question him. About political stuff anyway. Some things you simply had to take on faith. Other things ... well, once you were married, that would be privileged information.

"You think that's strange?" Sweetie asked.

She usually gave straight answers to questions from the McGill kids, but there were times she'd play the old cop trick and toss a question back at them. Thinking about that made Sweetie wonder about kids in terms of her and Putnam. She might still have some slight chance of getting pregnant, but there was no question that her best ova were behind her. The thing to do might be to see if they could adopt.

She'd have to talk with Putnam about the idea.

Kenny interrupted the mindless cycle of toss and catch with an observation.

"You're wearing a ring, Sweetie."

"I am." She caught the ball and held up her left hand. "You like it?"

Kenny stepped over and gently moved Sweetie's hand this way and that.

"It's cool. Good looking but not prissy-sissy."

Sweetie laughed. "That's good because I never saw myself as prissy-sissy."

"No, you never were. You know what I thought, though?"

"What?"

"I thought someday I was going to marry you. Not Putnam."

Sweetie put an arm around Kenny's shoulders. They started walking back to Aspen Lodge.

"Don't you think I'm just a *little* old for you?"

"What does age matter? I'm growing up and you haven't changed a bit in all the time I've known you."

Sweetie smiled. "Prunes for breakfast and regular exercise can take a girl only so far. I'm getting older and it won't be long before it starts to show. By the time you're ready to get married, I'll probably be sitting in a rocking chair on my front porch."

Kenny laughed at the idea. "That'll be the day."

"Okay, probably not. But your dad and I won't still be charging around after bad guys. We'll be … doing other things. Life moves in cycles, kiddo. Smart people roll along with them. Besides all that stuff, I thought there was a girl named Liesl who'd caught your eye."

Spots of color appeared on Kenny's cheeks.

"There is. I think she likes me, too. Now. But I don't know who she'll grow up to be. With you, I do."

Sweetie could understand how a teenager who'd been forced to confront his own mortality would appreciate some sense of certainty.

"I don't know if Liesl will be the girl for you, Kenny. I don't know if any guy your age can know that, but I can give you a clue how you can find out who's right for you."

Kenny looked up at Sweetie. "What's the clue?"

"There's no better way to find a good match than to look for someone you can't stop talking to, someone you never get tired of listening to, someone you can start a conversation with and know it's going to last as long as you're both alive."

"*Talking?*" Kenny asked. "That's it?"

"Talking and listening. Sharing good news and bad. Exulting and lamenting. Arguing and apologizing. Saying good morning and saying good night. Saying I love you at every possible opportunity."

"Well, you put it that way," Kenny said. He went up on his toes and kissed Sweetie's cheek. "I love you."

"Practice is good," Sweetie told him. "I love you, too."

They went inside Aspen Lodge.

McGill and Putnam met in the kitchen of Aspen Lodge.

Keeping things strictly informal.

Two guys sipping a beer or two.

No legal privilege of confidentiality attached to their conversation. They had to be careful about what they said. They could talk directly about ShareAmerica. That was to be a lobbying effort and there were no restrictions on talking about such things. Americans for Equity, however, was now a registered Super PAC. Coordinating strategy with the president's campaign was *verboten*.

If things went the wrong way for the president in the upcoming election and, say, a new and hostile attorney general were ever to look into the conversation between McGill and Putnam, he likely would be unable to make a case. McGill had no formal role in the president's campaign. Ergo there was no legal reason Putnam couldn't talk to him.

What, if anything, McGill learned from Putnam and passed on to his wife would be a matter protected by marital privilege.

Still, Putnam could be compelled to reveal what he'd said to McGill. From there, the whole world could reasonably infer what

McGill had passed along to his wife, the president. If that revelation occurred after the president lost the election, it would cast a pall on her legacy. If somehow it was made public that Putnam and the president had used McGill as a conduit to skirt regulations before Election Day, that might cost Patricia Darden Grant a second term.

So they had to choose their words wisely.

Putnam started with what they could talk of openly.

"ShareAmerica is up and going viral already," Putnam told McGill.

"Really? That's great. What can you tell me?"

"I can tell you that if Darren Drucker was running for president, nobody else would stand a chance, no disrespect to your wife."

McGill said, "Being a multibillionaire with the common touch is a good starting point, I'll give you that."

Putnam continued, "Anyway, I was out in Portland at a bar called the Bridgeport Brewing Company with some new friends and told them about ShareAmerica. Told them what it was all about and how Darren Drucker was involved. The next thing I know, not only did all three of my new friends sign up, so did every last person in the bar, customers and employees both. The owner of the place fronted advances on salary for employees who requested it. And then ..."

McGill knew how to play along. He asked, "And then what?"

"Everybody who had a laptop or a smart phone, which was everyone there, got in touch with their friends. One guy put up a Facebook page and PayPal account for ShareAmerica on the spot. We now have donors from all fifty states and from Americans overseas. Turn on the evening news tonight. See if we aren't the top story."

"That's wonderful," McGill said.

Following Putnam's directions, he took out his own phone and signed up for ShareAmerica.

Once that was accomplished, Putnam gave McGill a look.

Hoping it communicated they were about to move on to more sensitive matters.

McGill nodded. He understood.

"The thing about ShareAmerica that's so great is it inspires a whole approach to getting things done in the right way. You look at what you want to do, to accomplish, and it becomes the model. Work with the greatest number of people of goodwill and you'll certainly prevail."

McGill nodded his head as if he understood.

But he was still sorting out what Putnam had told him.

The greatest number of people of goodwill? Was he talking about the voters who'd see things Patti's way? That would be the most basic reading of the phrase. Maybe *too* basic. Someone sophisticated enough to set up ShareAmerica wouldn't think in such simplistic terms.

So what other people of goodwill would Patti have to work with to achieve her goals?

The answer came swiftly: Congress.

The current members had done their best to stifle presidential initiatives.

So keep the president, change the Congress. That was Putnam's recipe for success. He was telling McGill that his Super PAC was going to push candidates who would be sympathetic to Patti's ideas and, of course, voters who'd put such people in the House and Senate would vote for Patti for president, too.

What that left for Patti was to beat her two opponents, Mather Wyman and Howard Hurlbert. McGill could see that happening. Splitting the vote among three candidates for president had the potential for making things trickier, but McGill was sure Galia Mindel was already making plans for dealing with that.

If Patti could win — and McGill felt good about that — and get a cooperative Congress elected to back her up, he wouldn't feel so bad about spending another four years in the White House.

"I think you're right," he told Putnam. "The greatest number of good people will prevail."

Sweetie and Kenny, hand in hand, entered the kitchen just then.

Sweetie said, "I could have told you that."

Seeing his oldest friend again reminded McGill he still had his own obligations.

Damon Todd still at large. Locking him away again couldn't wait.

George Town Harbor — Grand Cayman

The Stealth 540 flybridge yacht glided into the harbor looking like a shark. It was white with a sharply raked bow. The shadowed space between its twin catamaran hulls was a dark smile, the kind that preceded a fatal, crunching snap of jaws. At fifty-six feet long and capable of speeds even military craft would strain to match, lesser vessels were wise to scurry from its approach.

Cayman Island Port Security, however, was always happy to see the arrival of what amounted to a boatload of money. As long as the money wasn't drug sourced or involved with terrorist activity, the island's banks were ever eager to receive new deposits. If the visitors had come to call with the simple intent of having a good time, and were able to pay the island's prices for it, well, that was the other pillar of the local economy.

In the case of either big depositors or big spenders, the welcome mat was always out.

Even when the three new arrivals who debarked from the yacht looked like they did their best work with their fists and other blunt instruments. Thugs though they may have appeared, Harry, Kurt and Wally were soft spoken with the port security official. They presented their passports, had them stamped and said they should be in Grand Cayman no more than three days.

The legal niceties observed, the newcomers to the island found a taxi and told the driver to take them once around the island.

The driver smiled and said, "Grand Cayman not all that big, but it got no circle road at all. Okay with you we go out and back?"

Three nods said that was acceptable.

Then Harry, who was the most verbal of the three, said, "Pull over a minute."

"Change your mind?" the driver asked.

"Just pull over, all right?"

The driver kept a knife with a nice sharp blade tucked into a sheath under his seat. Strictly for protection, not robbery. But with these three, they got crazy, he'd have to do a *lot* of cutting.

Deciding he could pull the keys, duck out of the taxi and out-run these guys if he had to, the driver pulled to the curb. "Okay," he said, "what now?"

"You like to make money?" Harry asked.

"Oh, yeah," the driver said, his concern easing. As long as they didn't want any funny business with him personally. "How much money you talkin'?"

"A thousand dollars."

"U.S.?"

"Yeah."

"What you want?"

"To find an old friend. His name's Jackie Richmond."

"Don't know anyone by that name."

"Here's a picture of him." Harry passed it forward.

The photo had been taken surreptitiously by a colleague in Mango Mary's, so the Bus Milbaugh imitators would know who to shoot. That hadn't worked out, but maybe the likeness would still come in handy.

"Never seen this fellow," the driver said.

"Not yet, but we hear he's around." Harry passed a hundred dollar bill to the driver. "Have copies of the picture made. Give them out to all the people you know who work for tourists."

"Somebody else find your friend, I still get somethin'?"

Harry nodded. "Five hundred."

The driver could live with that.

"Done," he said. "You want to go for that drive now?"

"Yeah. Go slow. We want to take in the scenery."

Harry was the kind of guy who always wanted to know who his business partners were. He looked at the driver's hack license posted on the dashboard. Saw the name Edward Pennyman.

Number One Observatory Circle — Washington, D.C.

Kira Fahey Yates stepped into Vice President Mather Wyman's home office and told him, "Mattie, Senator Crockett is here. Shall I show him in and excuse myself?"

The senator had come to visit the vice president at his own request. He'd called and asked if he might have a few minutes of Wyman's time. He had an idea he'd like to run past the vice president.

Wyman had agreed to have Crockett visit, but his suspicions had been raised.

Would the senator ask to be Wyman's vice president?

Wyman said, "Why don't you join us, Kira?"

Having a witness to what transpired might be helpful.

"Sit quietly off to one side, speak only if spoken to?" she asked.

"Your manners are flawless, my dear. If you have something to contribute, please do."

Kira smiled and Wyman thought, as he often did, what a lucky young man Welborn Yates was. More so than ever. It seemed to him that his niece had a special glow to her these days.

"Thank you, Mattie. I'll go get the senator."

Kira returned a minute later with Senator Crockett. The two men shook hands and took their seats on opposite sides of Wyman's desk. Kira settled into a chair to her uncle's right.

Wyman told the senator, "Mrs. Yates has joined my campaign and is a trusted advisor."

Crockett didn't miss a beat. "A pleasure to have your company, Mrs. Yates."

Smoothly done, Wyman thought. The man might be an asset as a running mate.

That, however, wasn't what Senator Crockett had in mind. "If you'll forgive my presumptuousness, Mr. Vice President, I'd like to say if you're considering me as a possible running mate, I'll thank you to take my name off the list."

The pronouncement both surprised and amused Wyman.

"Well, all right," he said. "I'll keep that in mind if I'm the GOP nominee."

Crockett grinned and waved off any doubt Wyman might have.

"Oh, no, sir. The nomination is yours. I'm quite the head counter. You have a strong majority in both houses of Congress, the national committee and the state committees. You are our one chance to beat the president, and we will work very hard for you."

"Now, if we can only get the voters to agree " Wyman said, only half kidding.

"Mr. Vice President, you're a man of integrity. Your record in office is spotless. The way you filled in for President Grant as acting president only added to your stature."

"You're sure you don't want to be vice president?" Wyman asked. "I might enjoy listening to you tell me how wonderful I am."

Crockett and Kira both laughed.

"I could bring you cold drinks and snacks, too," Crockett said, "but I think I have a better idea."

"You're going to solve some problem for me, one I might not even have noticed yet."

Crockett said, "Maybe you have, but I'll bring it up anyway. Thinking about things, studying your record as governor of Ohio and a member of the Ohio legislature, it seems to me there's very little daylight between Patricia Darden Grant's positions on big issues — the economy, when to use the military, social matters — and your position on those issues. You've certainly supported the president the way any good vice president would, but it's been easier for you because your views are so close to those of the president."

"That being the case," Wyman said, "why bother making a change?"

Crockett said, "It's something people might think. It's something the pundits will definitely write. That being the case, you need something to distinguish your candidacy. Having another mature white man as your number two wouldn't do that."

"Are you suggesting I pick a woman as my running mate?" Wyman asked.

Out of the corner of his eye, he saw Kira beam at the idea.

"Not just any woman, Mr. Vice President. I think you should pick Governor Rosalinda Fuentes of New Mexico."

Wyman sat back in his chair, rested his chin on his right hand.

"A Hispanic woman." He nodded, but then he said, "You don't think that would look too calculating?"

"Of course, it will. Until everybody looks at her record. She's in her second term as her state's chief executive; she served three terms in the legislature. Her political philosophy is incrementalist. Make the changes that are necessary, don't fix the things that aren't broken."

Kira spoke up. "She's also a striking woman."

With a twinkle in his eye, Crockett said, "I must have overlooked that."

Wyman chuckled. "Senator, you've checked out Governor Fuentes like a baseball scout."

"Once I decided I wasn't the best person for the job, I started looking around a little. Governor Fuentes is a first round draft choice. Could be a very big help with a demographic group that hasn't exactly been going our party's way."

Wyman agreed. The GOP had to stop alienating Hispanics.

That situation was made easier for him, knowing most of the party's base would be voting True South in the coming election. What was foremost in Wyman's mind, though, was another matter.

"Having disqualified yourself, Senator Crockett," he said, "do you still intend to help me?"

"Mr. Vice President, I believe you're the best person for the job. I'll do everything I can to make that happen."

Mather Wyman had been in politics far too long not to know that even sincere flattery usually had an ulterior motive.

"Might there be something I could do for you in exchange, should I become president?"

Crockett smiled, one old pro acknowledging another.

"Well, the situation on the Supreme Court is particularly interesting, isn't it? The hard right will demand replacements for Calendri and Hawkins who are at least as conservative as they were, and preferably more so, as the late chief justice was backsliding a little there at the end. The Democrats would never stand for that. They have to look at those two openings on the court as divine providence. President Grant might want to name two jurists who are more moderate than her new party might prefer or she just might choose to wait until later to decide."

Wyman said, "To see which way the political wind is blowing? If it looks like she and the Democrats will be big winners, she can nominate *exactly* whom she wants after the election."

Crockett nodded. "In the meantime, the court has a working liberal majority. So there's no pain for her there. But if she waits too long and things don't turn out the way she hopes ..."

"Then the next president, possibly me, will get to nominate two new justices."

Wyman gestured to Crockett as an example of whom he might choose.

The senator shrugged and grinned.

"You ask me," he said, "a clear-headed centrist or two is just what the court needs."

Kira was thrilled at being a backstage witness to how history might be made. She was dying to tell ... no, she couldn't tell Welborn. He was working for the president. She didn't see how some couples managed it, having long-term politically mixed marriages.

It would be all she could do to make it work for a year.

Uncle Mather and Senator Crockett stepped across the room to fix drinks for themselves; Kira declined the offer to partake. Her stomach had been feeling delicate lately, and as soon as the two men had their backs to her she adjusted her brassiere.

For some reason, her breasts had become quite sensitive.

Darn if they didn't seem to be getting bigger, too.

Pennyman's Café — Grand Cayman

All the tables had been cleared and just a handful of patrons remained, only minutes from having Willa shoo them off to their hotels or boats. They got a reprieve when Eddie Pennyman pulled his taxi to the curb out front. He beckoned to his cousin to join him as he stepped inside the front door.

His gesture hadn't been as rude as Willa had thought Welborn's snapping fingers were, but there was a sense of urgency to it. Willa hated leaving any job undone, but she let the idlers keep their seats. Her decision made, she put a good face on it by smiling at them as she went inside.

Eddie had stepped behind the bar and tapped himself a Bass Ale.

"Make yourself at home, Cousin," Willa told him.

Eddie looked around. "I checked to see if Uncle Lawford was still here."

"Daddy went home an hour ago. It's date night for him and Mum."

Eddie winced. "I don't want to know all that."

Willa laughed. "What you get, grabbing a free beer."

"What you get is this," Eddie said.

He gave Willa a copy of the photo of Jackie Richmond he'd made.

"I been passin' these out all night," he said.

Willa looked up from the photocopy. "This is the bloke my friend Welborn's looking for."

Eddie said, "I know, but that's not what I told the three maulers I drove all over the island. They offered me a thousand dollars U.S. for putting them on to this poor chump."

"Maulers?" Willa asked.

"Big as houses. Got off a yacht bigger'n your terrace. Must go close to a million, if not more. So they've got money, too."

Willa said, "Tough boys don't have money; the people who hire them do."

"They're villains however much jangle's in their pockets," Eddie said. "Wouldn't want to be this bloke. They called him Jackie Richmond."

Willa shook her head. She didn't know the name.

She told her cousin, "Wouldn't be good business to sell someone to gangsters for a thousand dollars when we can turn him into the cops for five thousand, with maybe ninety-five thousand more to come."

Eddie nodded and finished his beer.

"What I've been thinking exactly," he said. "But we haven't seen any money yet from your friend."

"He paid his taxi fare, didn't he? Left a good tip?"

"Well, yeah. I meant otherwise. So what you want to do?"

Willa joined Eddie behind the bar, picked up the phone.

"Call Welborn," she said.

GWU Hospital — Washington, D.C.

On Friday morning, November 18, 2011 McGill knelt in a pew of the hospital's chapel. Abbie was on his right, Caitie was on his left. To Abbie's right were Carolyn and Lars. The prayers being said were all silent and identical in nature.

Please, Lord, let the news be good.

One hundred days had passed since Kenny McGill had received his bone marrow transplant and that was his period of greatest risk. So far his progress had been little short of a miracle to his family, friends and Kenny himself. There was no guarantee, however that something might not go wrong in another six months or a year, but clearing the first big hurdle was a crucial psychological goal.

The day had started sunny and brisk. All concerned had wanted to take that as a good omen. None of them had dared to say so. They'd all simply filed into the hospital and sent Kenny off to his medical team with hugs and kisses.

They'd done the same for Patti. She'd be having her most extensive physical exam since the transplant procedure. Normally, this would have taken place at Walter Reed. Showing solidarity with Kenny, the president had asked her doctors to travel to GWU Hospital.

McGill had always hated kneeling when he was a child, being educated in parochial schools, going to Mass every Sunday and holy day of obligation with his classmates. His conception of God, even in the human form of Jesus, was someone a lot bigger than him.

How were you supposed to get a good look at God when you were on your knees? Lowering yourself only distorted your point of view. Anybody could look grand if you were busy groveling. He thought you should be on your feet when you were directing your thoughts to God. If the priest was sermonizing, giving you his take on things, then you could sit down.

He'd shared his opinions with every nun who'd ever taught him.

Their answer was always the same, "James, kneeling is a sign of humbling yourself before God."

To which he'd always replied, "Sister, God is God. How can we be anything but humble before him?"

Having no theologically satisfying response, the nuns would tell him that kneeling would show respect for what *they* were teaching him. Respect for the sisters was demanded at home by both Mom and Dad. His parents weren't the Almighty, but when it came to determining his quality of life they came close.

Hitting his teens and puberty in the eighth grade, McGill had one last burst of rebellion. He told a few of his classmates that if kneeling showed humility, the way to really show how humble you were would be to step out of the pew and prostrate yourself in front of everybody in church — and he was going to do that next Sunday.

Knowledge of a plan that daring could not be kept among one's peers. McGill was called into the principal's office on Friday afternoon. Sister Claudius wasn't amused by what she'd heard, but she was sweetness and light compared to the way Mom and Dad glared at him. McGill had thought he was growing up at the time, was only maybe five inches shorter than Dad, but looking at the three adults in the room he suddenly felt very small.

He was told bluntly that what he had in mind was not humility, it was mockery, and it would not be tolerated. If he wished to remain at St. Andrew's School, he would behave properly while attending Mass, and he would go to confession and ask for forgiveness for the affront to the Church he'd had in mind. He could do those things or he could transfer to a public school, immediately.

McGill was only six weeks from graduating with all the kids he'd known since kindergarten. The last thing he wanted to do was leave them now. He looked to his parents to intercede for him, but he saw they agreed with Sister C completely.

McGill said, "Okay. I'm sorry. I won't do it."

He was told Father Dunphy was waiting for him in the confessional right now.

McGill nodded and walked the short distance to the church, his resentment growing. They'd ganged up on him, Sister C and his parents. He hadn't planned to do anything that was really *bad*. He was just trying to make a point.

It occurred to him as he entered the confessional that Father Dunphy had to be in on the conspiracy against him, but the priest could never reveal a word that McGill said to him as part of his confession. If McGill didn't say anything about what he had planned to do at Mass, who would ever know?

God would know, he thought. If you believed in God, you had to accept he'd know.

With a sigh, McGill began, "Bless me, Father, for I have sinned. It has been six days since my last confession." His class went to confession every Saturday during the school year.

He started out with his lesser offenses, using profanity pretty much every day, anytime he wasn't at home or school, having impure thoughts about three different girls and … thinking about behaving like a jerk.

"Would you mind clarifying that last point, James?" Father Dunphy said.

There, see. Father D knew whose confession he was hearing. He was in on the plan.

"James?"

McGill had no choice but to own up. You lied in confession, where could you go for forgiveness? He told Father D what he'd had in mind.

He was surprised when he heard the priest laugh.

"Something funny, Father?" McGill asked.

"You were right, James. Prostration is a sign of humility. It goes back to ancient times."

"Then why am I catching —"

He was going to say hell, but he didn't think swearing during confession would be a good idea either.

"So much aggravation?" Father Dunphy suggested. "There are usually good alternatives to vulgar language, James. I hope you'll remember that."

"Yes, Father."

"As to the young ladies, your interest in them is perfectly normal. What you have to keep in mind is to frame that interest in respectful ways. If you want a young lady to think well of you, you must first think well of her. No person is ever someone simply to be used for your own purposes or pleasures. Show people the same high regard you'd wish to have them show you."

"Yes, Father. How was prostration used in ancient times?"

"Sometimes people were made to prostrate themselves before kings and emperors. Failure to do so might result in their heads being cut off. In more benign times like today, candidates for the priesthood prostrate themselves before their bishop during the sacrament of Holy Orders. In that case, prostration is not only a sign of humility but also of giving yourself completely to God. Are you thinking of becoming a priest, James?"

"No, Father. I like girls too much."

"Then perhaps kneeling is the proper sign of humility for you."

"Yes, Father. I'm sorry I was thinking of being a jerk."

"Well, you've come to the right place. I won't tell a soul."

Father D told McGill to say a good Act of Contrition and to kneel and reflect on how he wanted to live his life, what would bring it purpose and meaning, what would give him joy and fulfillment. That was a lot to think about, of course, so he should kneel only as long as it felt comfortable to him.

In the hospital chapel, McGill thought about everything that brought him joy and fulfillment, and for every person, place and thing on his list he gave thanks. He might have stayed there indefinitely if Abbie hadn't put her hand on his shoulder.

"Dad," she said.

McGill opened his eyes.

Standing in front of him were Patti and Kenny.

They were holding hands.

Patti smiled at him.

Kenny showed him an upraised thumb.

The story continues in Part 2: The Last Ballot Cast.

ABOUT THE AUTHOR

Joseph Flynn has been published both traditionally — Signet Books, Bantam Books and Variance Publishing — and through his own imprint, Stray Dog Press, Inc. Both major media reviews and reader reviews have praised his work. Booklist said, "Flynn is an excellent storyteller." The Chicago Tribune said, "Flynn [is] a master of high-octane plotting." The most repeated reader comment is: Write faster, we want more.

You can read a free excerpt of each of Joe's books by visiting: *www.josephflynn.com.*

Find out what Jim McGill will be doing next and meet other friends of McGill at *www.facebook.com/TheFriendsofJimMcGill*

CPSIA information can be obtained
at www.ICGtesting.com
Printed in the USA
LVHW050710301221
707518LV00005B/20